"LISTEN, SWEETHEART, I JUST WANT TO KNOW YOU'RE ALL RIGHT," JACOB SAID.

"You don't have to talk," he continued. "You don't have to tell me what happened. Just let me hold you. You can cry if you want, and I'll keep still while you do."

Oh, Lord, she wanted so badly for him to hold her.

Jacob wondered why he couldn't hear Rachel if he could hear the sound of his own heart beating. "Please, Rach. You're scaring me to death."

Hay crackled under him as he searched the loft on hands and knees, inch by careful inch.

Maybe she wasn't here. But if not, where? Then he heard the tiniest sound, like a newborn kitten, and moved toward it.

To hold Rachel would crumble every barrier he'd tried to keep between them for the past weeks, but he had to hold her.

He had to.

<u>BOOK YOUR PLACE ON OUR WEBSITE</u> AND MAKE THE <u>READING CONNECTION!</u>

We've created a customized website just for our very special readers, where you can get the inside scoop on everything that's going on with Zebra, Pinnacle and Kensington books.

When you come online, you'll have the exciting opportunity to:

- View covers of upcoming books
- Read sample chapters
- Learn about our future publishing schedule (listed by publication month *and author*)
- Find out when your favorite authors will be visiting a city near you
- Search for and order backlist books from our online catalog
- Check out author bios and background information
- Send e-mail to your favorite authors
- Meet the Kensington staff online
- Join us in weekly chats with authors, readers and other guests
- Get writing guidelines
- AND MUCH MORE!

**Visit our website at
http://www.zebrabooks.com**

THEE, I LOVE

Annette Blair

Zebra Books
Kensington Publishing Corp.

http://www.zebrabooks.com

ZEBRA BOOKS are published by

Kensington Publishing Corp.
850 Third Avenue
New York, NY 10022

Zebra, the Z logo and Splendor Reg. U.S. Pat. & TM Off.

First Printing: October, 1999
10 9 8 7 6 5 4 3 2 1

Printed in the United States of America

To the men in my life who helped make this book possible:

Larry Beaunoyer, who became "Keeper of the Dream"
and wouldn't let me falter.
Thanks, old man.

Bob Croteau, for miles of travel, sixties tunes, and
plot ideas thrown in for fun.
Thanks, brother, especially for this one.

Bob Blair—husband, lover, best friend—for our life together.
Thee, I love.

Chapter One

Jacob Sauder drove his buggy toward the home he'd left four years before, never intending to return. The same old dirt lanes bisected greening patchwork fields and plain Amish farms untarnished by time. But despite the landscape, time had passed. Life had changed. And unlike the panorama that quickened his heart, Jacob Sauder was tarnished.

Uncertainty had dogged his every step since his decision to return, but this sense of anticipation—this was a surprise.

Jacob stopped the buggy at the top of Hickory Hill and scanned the valley. Lancaster looked the same, yet different, trees taller maybe, grass greener surely.

Home. He was home.

But would they let him stay? He flicked the reins, setting

Caliope to a trot. The last thing he'd done before he left—at his mother's funeral, no less—was tell everyone, God and the Bishop included, to go to Hell. Then he'd walked away from Mom's open casket, and the dirt hole waiting to swallow her up, climbed into his buggy, and never looked back.

He'd tried to become English, which his people called anyone not Amish, and broke every rule he'd been taught, some as slight as wearing buttons on his coats . . . others much, much worse. And he might have gone on that way, if fate had not taken a hand.

Anticipation. Dread.

How would his father feel about his unexpected return? How would Rachel feel? Rachel, who'd filled his empty soul when his twin sister, Anna, had died, Rachel who had become, somehow, his missing half. Rachel Zook. Mudpie. His brother's wife.

How were Datt and Rach? Had they changed?

Jacob slowed when he saw the thirty or so Amish buggies outside the Yoder barn. Sunday morning. Service. His heart skipped when he turned into the drive. A good sight, these buggies. You are home, they said, and welcome.

If only he believed it.

"You are not welcome here!" came a familiar voice.

Well, his brother, Simon, had not changed, not in looks, certainly not in disposition. Jacob shook his head. "Missed you, too."

"Go back to where you belong," Simon said, approaching with an angry stride.

Jacob climbed from his buggy. "This is where I belong." It tickled him to skin Simon's knuckles, especially with such faulty sentiment.

Simon's thin lips firmed, his eyes narrowed. "You would come on Church Sunday, especially this one." He straightened his frock coat and raised his chin. "I am to be ordained Deacon this morning."

Jacob was taken aback by the news, but it explained Simon's solitude; he was waiting to make an entrance. His brother would be a stern, humorless Deacon, but some people needed that, Jacob supposed. "You must be pleased."

"I am pleased to do God's will. Unlike you." Simon walked away. "Just go," he said, and disappeared into the barn.

Very unlike me, Jacob thought as he made his way around his buggy, raised the back flap . . . and grinned. After all these weeks, he still could not get over the sight of them, his two-year-old twins, now snuggled in sleep like newborn pups. "Come, Pumpkins," he said. "Up we go." What a surprise they'd been. What a joy, despite the fact that he deserved no joy. He held them, one in each arm. He was getting good at this, he thought, considering he'd only had them a short time. Two sleepyheads, one kapped, the other hatless, nuzzled his neck.

Good. They felt good there.

When Jacob walked into the Yoder house after four silent years and carrying two small children, whispers grew, then: "Shh, shh, shh."

Suddenly, not a sound could be heard save the chafing of his new black broadfall pants rubbing one leg against the other. Rough they were, and itchy, not smooth and comfortable like the buckskins he'd worn when he'd pretended to be English.

He stopped and stood in the middle of the group, the sight familiar yet foreign. Row upon row of men sat ramrod straight on simple backless benches. In the opposite room, facing the men, sat rows of women, on similar benches, the folding doors between the two rooms open for this purpose.

The women were white-kapped, the men bearded, marking them Amish.

Jacob's own beard had been shaved daily during his sojourn into the English world, with only three weeks' growth now to show for his decision to return. This marked him a rebel. And a liar. Only married men let their beards grow.

He saw old friends, nodded at a few. Some smiled back, but not many. This should not anger or surprise him, but it did. Emma sighed in her sleep, reminding him of his plan to raise his babies here. Knowing that a bad attitude could make for a bad beginning, Jacob swallowed his urge to declare that he was not sorry he'd left.

His father was not to be seen, but Ruben Miller, fellow rebel, grinned a true welcome. Jacob grinned back.

Where should he sit? He belonged in the men's section. The babies belonged in the women's. Unheard of this, a man raising his babies alone. He would be expected to court a mother for his children soon. But how could he, when the woman he loved . . .

He saw her watching him and was jolted.

Rachel was more beautiful than he remembered, but she looked. . . .

She buried her anger—he saw the effort it took—and came to him. "They're yours?" she asked.

Drinking in the sight of her, he could only nod.

"Their mother?" she asked.

Gave them life with her last breath, he thought, but he shook his head, his remorse too great for words.

"What are their names?"

Jacob swallowed his yearning, and his regret, and found his voice. "Emma and Aaron."

Rachel opened her arms. "I'll take them."

"I can't ask you—"

"Oh, please," she said, her maple-syrup eyes wide, pleading, revealing a different kind of anguish.

And Jacob knew within the deepest part of himself that Rachel longed to hold his babies with an ache as acute as his own in past years to hold her.

He'd almost forgotten this ability they shared—to feel each other's emotions, as if each lived inside the other. It had happened often to them as children, less as they grew older.

But this, just now, had been powerful. Except that she should be holding her own babies. "Thank you," he said. "Sit first. It's tricky standing."

They held everyone's attention, he knew . . . the prodigal and the woman who'd tossed him away, passing babies back and forth, her marriage to his brother a loud shout between them.

Jacob sat in the back of the men's section. Everyone opened the *Ausband* and turned to the hymn named. As always, the *Vorsinger* began the chant. The High German song soothed him, blended voices the only music. The words and chant had been passed from one generation to the next. The same song sounded different in other settlements. Better here.

With an ordination, service would be longer than the usual three hours, but he'd already missed the vote for Deaconate candidates. Simon, by the grace of God— according to Amish belief, not Jacob's—had obviously been the candidate to choose the bible with the slip of paper naming him Deacon. And from what Simon said, the ordination and laying-on of hands was yet to come.

When it began, Simon was in his element, eyes downcast, brought high in his humility for all to see.

During the ceremony, Jacob could not keep from watching Rachel, his babies asleep in her arms, her slim fingers gentling them. He closed his eyes and imagined the lips that touched Emma's tiny forehead touching his.

He remembered how Rachel's hair, now hidden by her white heart-shaped kapp, would look and feel set free as it grazed his cheek. She had hair the color of blackberry wine, with unruly curls all over her head. And if he were to wrap sections of the silky softness along one of his fingers, he could make the ringlets into long curls that hung down her back like a veil of evening mist after a new moon. And it smelled like honey straight from the hive. Honey with that extra scent of musk it had on a summer afternoon, the sun high in the sky, and you had to fight the swarm to win your prize.

He had removed her kapp on just such a day, let down that beautiful hair, and kissed her for the first time.

Back then, he thought she would always be his.

But she belonged to Simon now. Still, Jacob could not keep from imagining that musky scent . . . until the words of the new Deacon's sermon stung him.

"A cankerous apple left in the barrel will rot those around it! It must be plucked, discarded so as not to spoil the rest." Simon looked straight at him, the bad apple, and all but pointed an accusing finger as he urged all to thrust him from their midst.

Jacob almost laughed. It would take more than a vengeful sermon to scare him away. He'd lived English; nothing could frighten him now.

When he'd looked for Miriam, three years after leaving her, and found his motherless babies instead, he'd considered the best place to raise them and thought this might be it. Now, with Rachel holding them, he was damned near certain of it. But already he knew it was going to be much harder to watch her and Simon together than he had imagined.

Nevertheless, he was staying . . . unless he got tossed out.

Simon must have read his resolve, for the Deacon rocked on his heels, clasped his hands behind his back, and turned from such a rotten-apple brother as Jacob to gaze at the men about him.

"Who do you think has the most important role in the Amish Church?" Simon asked with great interest. "Is it the Preacher? The Deacon? Is it the Bishop?" He paused to build expectation, searched the men's faces.

Simon raised an arm to signal the power in his words. "I will tell you who," he shouted. "It is the women with babies on their laps who have the most important role in our church."

Jacob sat straighter. Swift and bright, understanding came. Rachel had no babies on her lap, because she was barren. And Simon was up to his old tricks. His sanctimonious judgment, dispensed now through sermon, would emerge as God's words. Coating it with pretty sentiment, the new Deacon had just shamed his wife before the entire church district.

"Lift not the sword," they'd been taught from birth. Not that the English lived it, and neither had he. But he was Amish again, for good or ill . . . and he wanted more than ever to plant his fist in his brother's face.

Good beginning.

Jacob sighed. This was not going to be easy.

Then he saw the tic in Simon's cheek, the color reddening his neck, signs of discomposure, most likely anger. And Jacob's heart lightened, for Simon was gaping at Rachel, two tiny two-year-olds to her heart, looking for all the world like an angel, her attention not on him but on the babies in her lap.

Jacob suppressed his chuckle and grinned. She probably hadn't heard a word her husband said.

With a struggle, likely visible only to his rotten-apple brother, Simon composed himself and turned his sermon toward repentance and the like . . . until a child's wail split the air, and the Deacon's voice was silenced once more.

Everyone craned their necks to see whose child dared interrupt. But Jacob knew. Emma was awake.

Simon glared at Rachel.

Jacob stood to go to her, knowing how difficult it could be to maneuver two heavy babies.

She implored him with her eyes as he came from the back.

I'm coming, Mudpie, he said with his look.

Hurry, she begged with hers.

Aaron, awakened by his sister's screams, scrambled to the floor, allowing Rachel to carry Emma to the kitchen, shushing her and kissing her tears.

The crowd tittered, and a few men chuckled, as Aaron stood in the middle of the room looking up at Simon, the uncle he did not know, and pulled on his trouser leg. "Pee-pee," his boy said.

"Ach," Jacob said as he scooped his son into his arms. "First time he asks to go. I have waited for this day."

A round of hearty laughter followed them outside. "Good boy, Aaron," Jacob said, rolling his eyes. And then he began to laugh.

Once he and Aaron were back, Jacob saw Rachel return, Emma nibbling the outer edge of a cookie in that way of hers, round and round, till the treat got so small, she would likely drop it and cry again. Jacob only hoped Simon would be finished sermonizing by then.

It was a good thing Aaron hadn't noticed his sister's cookie, or there would be hell to pay with all the noise he would make requesting one of his own.

He should have separated the twins right away, Jacob supposed. Aaron had all the parts required for sitting in the men's section, after all. But Amish women always kept the children during service, boys and girls.

Well, he would be the exception from now on. It suited Jacob's rebellious streak well enough for satisfaction, but little enough so as not to cause an uproar.

Before the Bishop's sermon, they broke for babies to be fed and necessities tended. Men went out to smoke. In North Dakota, the Amish Church banned the use of tobacco. In Illinois, smoking was banned only during service.

Funny how they could all be Amish, but have different rules.

Simon made directly for Rachel. Jacob did too. He wanted to see how Simon dealt with his children. Jacob sat Aaron beside Emma on a wooden settle while his brother stood silently by. They watched Rachel play with the twins.

"Where's Datt?" Jacob asked.

Simon glared. "If you had stayed, you would know."

Jacob resisted the invitation to bicker. "Where is he?"

"He visits Atlee Sunday mornings. Sometimes he brings him to service. If Atlee's feeling poorly, Datt comes late." Simon almost smiled. "You know Atlee."

Jacob chuckled. "Lord, he must be a hundred and ten by now."

"A hundred and three," Simon said.

When Rachel borrowed diapers and allowed herself to be shown how to fold and fit one to Emma, Simon's mood darkened visibly.

Jacob knew then that he was right. Rachel—with so much love she could fill all 120 acres of Datt's farm and still have more to give—was childless. Yet she laughed at her slipshod diapering, and when she did, Simon placed his hands behind his back, that tic going at a furious pace.

Jacob declined the loan of a diaper for his son, saying, "Aaron is a big boy now."

"Big girl," Emma said, to get her share of attention, and Jacob fancied he could hear Simon's teeth gnashing.

Jacob lifted Aaron, straightened his tiny frock coat, a miniature of every man's, and turned to his brother. "Have you met my children, Simon?"

"What need? They are English."

"They are Amish, like their father," Jacob said softly.

The sound of whispers grew, then hushed. People returned to their seats. Rachel's father, the Bishop, was waiting to begin the last sermon of the day.

A half hour into it, Jacob looked up as if summoned, and saw his father walk in. So white his beard had gone, so many new wrinkles etched his beloved face. It was difficult for Jacob to keep from rushing forth to greet him after so long. And when their gazes locked, Datt's eyes filled.

Bishop Zook saw the exchange. He looked from father to son and stopped speaking. Other than the sound of Jacob's own heart, silence held. No one so much as shuffled a foot or cleared a throat. Even the little ones seemed to sense the moment.

When Jacob raised his chin and looked into the Bishop's eyes, they were cold, piercing. On this man's whim, he and his children would be welcomed or banished.

"You are back, Jacob Sauder," the Bishop said.

"For my children," Jacob wanted to explain, "not for me," but he dared not. "I am back, Bishop Zook."

The Bishop rocked on his heels, his face stern. "You . . . ah . . . consigned us all to . . . warmer climates, when last we met."

Jacob's collar got tight. He resisted an urge to wipe his palms on his pants.

The Bishop indicated those in attendance. "None of us went."

Jacob didn't think he should smile. He didn't think the Bishop had a sense of humor.

Their highest spiritual leader looked him over as if he were a fly in his pudding, then nodded thoughtfully. "You either, I am surprised to see."

But the Bishop was wrong; Jacob had been to Hell.

Bishop Zook examined the congregation at large for a full minute, then turned back to the rotten-apple, fly-in-the-pudding prodigal and regarded him so long, Jacob began to understand the word *eternity*.

Then the Bishop nodded, as if he was listening to a voice only he could hear. "Jacob Sauder," he said like a judge passing sentence. "In the name of God, welcome home."

Jacob expelled the breath choking him and swallowed, but not fast enough to stifle his sob.

From the women came a sniffle or two. From the men, throat-clearing, coughs, a grunt.

Datt's tears streamed into his beard.

The Bishop raised his hands for quiet. "Let our fellowship meal today be one of great rejoicing, for Jacob Sauder has returned to us."

Jacob caught Simon's stunned, but swiftly banked, expression. They stared at each other. This should have been *his* day. The Bishop should have invited rejoicing over his ordination. But Jacob's return had overshadowed his glory.

An ordination was a once-in-a-lifetime event, one experienced by a select few. An event Jacob was certain defined, for Simon, his status as chosen by God. And it was shelved to make way for the return of a worthless sinner.

Even to the sinner, this did not seem fair.

As people made their way toward the fellowship meal, Jacob embraced his father. "Ah, Datt." He stepped back and cleared his throat. "You have grandbabies," he said as Rach approached. "Emma, Aaron, here is your *Grossdaudy.*"

Levi laughed as he took one in each arm. Emma called him *Daudy,* and when he kissed her forehead, she pushed his beard aside and scratched her face.

Jacob smiled at Rachel. "Thanks, Mudpie, for watching them."

Simon bristled. "My wife's name is Rachel!"

Jacob raised a brow to make light of Simon's ire and remove the sting of it for Datt and Rachel. "To me, she will always be Mudpie. Ever since she made me *schnitz* pies of mud." Jacob examined her face—a little more lined, a lot more dear. "Remember? Three years old you were, I think. I had just lost Anna, and I was lonely. I had never seen you before, but when I asked your name, you replied, 'Mudpie,' while offering one of your creations. They didn't taste so good, Rach."

Her look softened. "I didn't think a smart five-year-old would be so foolish as to taste one, Jacob."

"I did it to make you smile," he said, wishing he understood why she'd turned from him. "Such was always my desire." He yanked one of her kapp ribbons to prove it.

The sadness in her maple-syrup eyes lightened. "Welcome home, Jacob."

And Jacob felt his stone heart crack.

Simon, the new Deacon, the son who'd stayed to work the farm and care for their father, left the Yoder house alone.

Jacob slapped his father's back. "Let's go congratulate Simon."

On the way home from service, Rachel saw a yellow warbler sitting atop a thorn-apple bush. Usually, she cherished such beauty. Usually, Gadfly's proud, head-up gait caused a rocking motion that soothed her, but just now it only added to her unease.

She'd been furious when she saw Jacob, as furious as she was elated. Damn him. And damn her own heart for betraying her. Elated, indeed.

Why, oh, why, had he left her? And why now had he returned?

Yes, damn Jacob. And damn Simon too. As angry as she was with Jacob—as she had a right to be—as much as she wanted to berate him for his unexplained departure, she would never have done so publicly. Urging the district to shun Jacob was cruel, even for Simon.

But it would not go well for her if she said so.

Rachel took a deep breath and opened her senses to the morning mist over fresh-turned fields, the canopy of new-leafed maples, and the earthy scent of horse and leather. But she would not be calmed, for the silence of the bitter man beside her taunted her. "How *could* you condemn your brother before everyone?"

Simon's narrow-eyed gaze caught Rachel like a fly on flypaper. Dismay froze her, her heart quickening under his scrutiny . . . until she realized he would not show anger toward her today, not with any outward display. Because the people who would come to welcome Jacob home would see, and Simon could not bear that. Words he would use, but words of the mouth did not hurt, not as words of the heart did, and between her and her husband there had been no words of the heart for some time.

"Jacob deserves shunning," he said finally. "He married English."

"His marrying English would be wrong only if he had been baptized Amish, Simon, you know that. Besides, it's the Bishop who should decide his fate."

"I'll be Bishop one day."

"You cannot know you will become Bishop. My father is young yet." Later, Simon would punish her for speaking her mind like this, but she was too upset to care right now. She raised her chin. "You sound as if you have pride in your calling to the Church."

Fury burned in her husband's look. Pride was a serious sin. "Mind your tongue, woman. I am a plain and humble man . . . plainer and humbler than most. 'Tis not proud to know God's will."

"Perhaps it is His will, then, that we have no children."

"How dare you! 'Tis His plan that we bring forth children. And your punishment, your fault, His making you barren. 'Twill continue until you repent . . . you with your brazen hair and—"

"I cannot change my hair, Simon. And it's covered decently by my prayer kapp. No one sees it but you, as is a husband's right. I am sorry the sight repels you." Sometimes Simon could make her feel as if she was shrinking where she sat, and if she wasn't, she probably should, to save the world from the sight of her.

" 'Tis not just your hair repels me, and you know it."

"I am the way God made me," Rachel said, smaller still.

"With your frivolous play, it's a wonder the Elders let you teach their children. Such laughter we hear coming from the schoolhouse. I do not approve. There are others, I think, who do not wish to offend me by taking your position away. If you would give me children, you could leave teaching and save the church leaders the embarrassment of replacing you."

"If you would visit the school, Simon, I'm certain I would remember not to laugh." Rachel bit her lip in regret for her rash words, but Simon was too intent on his driving to notice her slip.

He tugged Gadfly's reins and skirted a rut. "And that newspaper. Your pride in it will destroy your soul."

Rachel sighed. After she'd published her first newspaper and seen the good she could do, it had given her purpose. Her people needed her newspaper. Even if they were too stubborn to set foot in the English doctor's office or call him to their homes, they read his column. Little Jake Hertzer would have choked to death if not for Doctor Sam's advice in the *Amish Chalkboard*. That should be proof enough.

So if satisfaction was akin to pride, then yes, she felt it. She would not give up the *Amish Chalkboard*. No, nor her plan to purchase Old Atlee Eicher's printing press, though, heaven help her, Simon did not know about that.

As for being barren, her heart cried at not having little ones. But her barrenness, her newspaper, her teaching, these were old arguments, ones she could not bear to have today. Not when her heart and mind were so filled with Jacob's return.

"We are coming to the farm," Simon said. "We will speak of this later, in private."

"I know," Rachel said.

Chapter Two

Jacob had returned.

Rachel was glad. Simon was not. But Simon was rarely glad about anything. And because of that, happiness for Rachel was fleeting.

But now, as she rocked Emma and Aaron to sleep, their little faces warm against her neck, she was happier than she'd been since Jacob left.

Jacob was home. And he'd brought his babies.

Emma was tiny, dark-haired, and weighed no more than a thistle. Aaron, also dark-haired, was larger and heavier. When he'd awakened during service, Rachel had seen his smiling eyes and had had an urge to offer him a mudpie. Both children had their father's dimples.

Jacob and Simon resembled each other in looks too, but not in manner. Hair, dark and curling, eyes the color of an overcast sky labeled them Sauders. Jacob's features were chiseled and square, Simon's less sharp. Her lanky husband stood taller by an inch, but Jacob had a broader, sturdier build, hard-muscled and whipcord strong.

Jacob smiled often. Simon did not.

Rachel sighed over the fact, and gazed about the room she'd prepared. The cribs were ready and waiting. Jacob's bed she'd spread with his mom's memory quilt, a welcome-home burst of color in blues, purples, maroons, and blacks.

Jacob's mother, Hannah, after her parents' deaths, had cut their clothes into squares to make that quilt. Hannah said she'd touch the squares as she drifted to sleep nights. The twill reminded her of her mom bent over a washtub, the soft rayon sateen, of Sundays and her mom climbing into the buggy in anticipation of fellowship and prayer. The plain blue weave was from her father's shirts, the black serge, his broadfalls, making Hannah see him behind a plow and six Belgian horses.

Hannah's mother had made Hannah good memories.

Hannah had made Simon and Jacob good memories.

Now Rachel hoped she would have the opportunity to make good memories for Emma and Aaron. She would enjoy them while she could, whatever time brought. Except, she never wanted to let them go. She kissed Emma's bare head and rested her cheek on Aaron's. Then she saw Jacob in the doorway, and her heart trembled.

He stopped at the foot of the bed and ran his hand over the quilt. And despite her anger, Rachel's heart opened to him. "I miss her too," she said. "She would be so happy you're raising your babies here. How she would love them."

Jacob was not surprised to hear Rachel echo his thoughts so well, not after he had read her that way at service.

He stopped before her, to devour the sight of her sitting there holding his sleeping children, wishing he understood the emotion she was hiding. He did not know, for the life of him, why she might be angry with him, when it was she who had—

"I couldn't put them down," she said, her blackberry curls escaping the sides of her kapp. And without thought, Jacob bent on one knee to tuck the curls in. Though the touch nearly seared him, he memorized the silk of her with his fingertips and wished—oh, how he wished—that she hadn't turned from him, that they had married as they'd planned and the twins were theirs, that she would slip beneath Mom's quilt with him and—

"A pretty picture." Simon's words brought Jacob up, certain, from his brother's look, that Simon knew what he'd been thinking.

Jacob took Emma and Aaron from Rachel then, and put them in their cribs. He couldn't watch as she followed her husband to their room.

And they had been arguing ever since.

Trying to ignore their angry voices, Jacob now rubbed the back of his neck. Lord, if he had returned only to bring Rachel grief, what would he do?

Buy a farm of his own and move out of here, that was what he'd do. But not so far that his babies couldn't have Rachel's love or Datt's. Not that far.

He and Datt had made a fuss over Simon's ordination after service. But Simon had resented the tardiness of it almost as much as he'd resented Jacob's ill-timed return.

After that, for the rest of the day, Simon had tensed every time Rachel touched his children, and, Lord, she couldn't get enough of them.

When Jacob could stand the angry sounds no more, he went down to the porch to get away, knowing his babies would not wake until dawn.

Leaning on the rail, he took in the smells of a farm in spring. Hay. Animals. Dirt. Manure.

For a time, he'd thought a woman's cheap perfume, cheaper whisky—even a city jail—smelled better than this. But not now. Not anymore.

* * *

"Mein Gott, Rachel," Simon said. "You shamed me before the entire church district with your attention to Jacob."

It was the little ones she'd attended, not their father. She was still angry with their father. "My arms, Simon, they ache for little ones. I could not help—"

"You can never help any of it. Your siren's curls, your strumpet's body, your barrenness, your newspaper." He grasped her shoulders. "Mind me. Stop it, Rachel, before the Elders call you on it. You would not want to be under the ban. I could not eat with you, speak to you, or take you to my bed."

Lord forgive her, to be shunned sounded like a blessing. "I should think that would suit you, Simon, since those things distress you so."

Simon shook her for her impudence, his fingers biting into her shoulder hard enough to bruise. Sometimes she feared he would snap another bone.

"Jacob's return has given you courage," Simon said. "Just don't forget which of us you are married to."

She wasn't likely to forget, even if she wanted to.

He yanked her kapp off, then her apron. When he fumbled with the placket of his trousers to prepare himself, Rachel wanted to weep. She did not inspire him to readiness, he accused. Her overripe body, her wantonness, unmanned and repulsed him. But there must be children.

And so Simon tried for children until Rachel accepted misery as the norm, and punishment became a blessing after the trying.

But sometimes, like now, the look in his eyes frightened her. "You will bear me a child and stop this nonsense," he ordered, which might make her laugh if she didn't feel so much like crying.

He tossed her down so hard, the ropes under the mattress squealed a protest and she banged her cheek against the headboard.

A new bruise there would be to explain now.

When he shoved up her gown, he scratched the tender skin on her inner thigh with the edge of his nail. Rachel could feel the burn, knew she bled, but she didn't care. It would give her something to concentrate on.

When Simon finished, she was made to kneel on the floor to pray for God to grant his seed to quicken within her, unworthy vessel that she was. But when his snores filled the room, Rachel crept downstairs.

At the kitchen table, she lowered herself into a chair, soaped a cloth, and began to lave the cut. Then she lowered her head and allowed her tears to fall, for if she held them in, her sadness would be cast upon the schoolchildren. Crying, she'd learned, healed her.

From the porch, Jacob saw Rachel in her white nightdress, lit by moonlight, her curls flowing to her waist, her tears falling nearly as far. And again, he was jolted.

"Ah, Rach," he said as he came in and placed his hand on her shoulder. "These tears of yours, it is my heart they are hurting."

She reached up to cover his hand, but she did not raise her head.

Silence.

Another bond they shared, this ability to be silent together.

Jacob went around to kneel before her and lift her chin to examine her face. A bruise was forming high on one cheek. "Oh, Rach," he said, laying his head in her lap.

She stroked his hair. "You look different, but good, with

your man's beard. And your hair, it still curls more than you like, I think. Is this a bit of gray, I see?"

"Ach." Normally, he would smile at her teasing, but not tonight. "Simon hurts everyone he touches," Jacob said.

"Only because they do not love him enough," Rachel said.

And Jacob did not bother to answer, because they both knew it was so. After a minute, he moved her hand with the washcloth to examine her cut.

"It was an accident," she said.

He tried to read her expression then, but she bit her lip and turned from his scrutiny. He took the soapy cloth from her hand and washed the scratch himself, his slow strokes soothing, mesmerizing.

Rachel tried to stay his hand.

"Let me. Please," he whispered, and she said nothing, but he put the wet cloth down anyway, and took up the dry one to dab at the cut. Then he bent to kiss the torn flesh.

She touched his shoulder. "No, Jacob."

"I know," he said.

After applying salve, he pulled her nightgown down to cover her legs, then dried her eyes, making her wince when he touched the side of her face. "Did he do this with the flat of his hand?"

"I hit the headboard."

"All by yourself? Remember, it is a sin to lie."

It is a sin to pit brother against brother, Rachel thought.

"No hand helped you, then?" he asked at her silence. "Why, Rach? Why did you decide to marry him? Why did you have him tell me when Mom had just died?"

"When she died? No. That's not right. It was later we decided. Much later. Simon said you'd been unhappy and—"

"I wasn't unhappy. It was . . . God took Mom, like he'd

taken Anna. And you wanted Simon. It was . . . all of it. I was angry. At Simon. At you. At God, even.''

"No. You left me. I didn't leave you.''

"Because Simon said you wanted to marry him." Alarm laced Jacob's voice. "You've been married four years, right?''

"Nearly three," Rachel said, and they both knew, then, what Simon had done. "After you left, I was confused, lonely," she said. "Simon understood. After a while, I . . . cared for him. Your Datt was sad, Jacob. Simon said if we married . . ." Her voice cracked. "Grandbabies would make your Datt happy again, Simon said.''

"I could kill him," Jacob said.

"Vengeance is not our way.''

It had been his way for some time. "I will let him live, then." He sighed. "Though I do not deserve Emma and Aaron, I would not have them if I had not left.''

"You do deserve them. You are a good man, Jacob Sauder.''

"I am not. Believe me.''

"I prayed for a long time you would come home.''

"I couldn't stay and watch you give Simon the love I thought should be mine.''

"And now? You can watch us together now?''

Jacob noticed that she omitted the word love. "I can do anything for Emma and Aaron.''

The anguish he'd seen in her eyes at service was back, and to Jacob's surprise, she punched his arm. Hard. "How could you!" she asked with more fury than he thought her capable. "How could you believe I didn't love you?''

"I didn't feel lovable, Rach. Do you want to hit me again? Go ahead. I deserve it.''

She folded her arms, as if to protect herself. From him?

"I'm sorry, Mudpie. Forgive me. Please.''

She looked out the window. "Someday. Maybe.''

"What about turning the other cheek?"

"It isn't going to be easy to forgive you or Simon."

"I understand," Jacob said. "I'm not good at cheek-turning either. And if I see Simon hurt you, I *will* kill him."

Rachel smoothed his brow, and because he liked her touch too much, he caught her hand to stop its movement. Then he kissed it because he could not stop himself. "I'm going to speak to him about how he treats you."

"No, Jacob! He treats me fine. Really." Her eyes sparkled suspiciously in the moonlight. "Simon and I will be married for the rest of our lives. You must respect that. We both must."

The candle's flame wavered in the breeze from the door and a water droplet hit the zinc-lined sink with a ping.

"I'm glad you brought your babies home," she said.

Jacob felt strangely uplifted by her welcome of his children. "When I saw them in your arms at service," he said, "I knew they belonged there."

"They make me feel worthy."

At the desolation in Rachel's voice, Jacob put his head in her lap again, wrapping his arms around her, clutching her gown in his fists at her back.

Rachel brushed the hair from his temple in slow, silken strokes, soothing him to his soul. "I have to go back upstairs."

"In a minute," he said.

But they stayed like that for a long time, until Rachel moved to stand. "We have to forget this happened, Jacob."

"I know, Rach."

Chapter Three

His first morning home, Jacob missed milking.

Datt would forgive. Simon would not.

Jacob wasn't leaning toward forgiveness either, but with the transgressions he'd committed, he was the last to judge ... Simon or any other man. Still, he would not let Simon hurt Rachel.

As he pulled a suspender over his shoulder, he heard her laughing downstairs, and he could just imagine his children's antics. Usually, before his eyes opened, they were calling, "Pa-pop," but this morning, their cribs had been empty.

He looked out his window and shook his head. Up close, he could see that the farm was run-down. Well, he owed his Datt a few years of hard work. He could help turn it around; he even had money to put into it. But going downstairs, he wondered who would watch Aaron and Emma while he did. He shrugged. Datt probably knew of a widow who needed work.

Jacob stepped into the apple-scented kitchen to find Rachel with two sticky-faced monkeys on her lap, each holding a mangled piece of buttered cinnamon bread. Even with a purple bruise high on her cheek, she was beautiful.

"Morning, Mudpie."

"Pie," his children chorused.

"They can say my name, Jacob." Her kapp sat askew, Aaron's cinnamon fingerprints on one side, Emma sucking the kapp's ribbon on the other. And more curls than usual escaped the headpiece to frame her face.

Her self-mocking grin belonged to the little girl offering a mudpie. Her eyes held the same sparkle. "I guess I don't do this so good."

"You know you're really lost," he said, "when they shove that mushy stuff into your mouth and you think it tastes good because it comes from them."

"Ya. I know."

Like old times, they laughed together. He reached for a child. She pulled them close. "Don't you dare."

They cuddled against her, loving it. Jacob gave up. "That your mama's strudel on the stove? You make it good as her?"

"Ya, but how about some ham loaf and potatoes first?"

"Don't eat such breakfasts anymore 'cause I can't cook and tend this pair. How'd you do it?"

"I didn't yet. I need to heat yesterday's supper."

"All right. You choose. Feed, wash, and dress these two, or cook breakfast for Simon and Datt."

"And if I choose the babies? As if I wouldn't."

"Then I'll cook."

"Oh, ya? Can I watch?"

"See if you can and tend them. I took the easy job."

Rachel put the twins in a washtub on the sideboard, getting wetter than they did. Emma's giggles made Jacob and Rachel laugh as hard as she did, which was how Simon and his father found them.

Simon's scowl could curdle milk, and Datt's smile could for certain sweeten it.

Distracted, Aaron fell into the water and came up screaming.

Rachel almost cried too. Jacob almost burned breakfast.

Datt laughed, took Aaron into his arms in a thick, warm towel, and sat him on his lap. For a big man, Datt could sure be gentle. Jacob wondered, not for the first time, where Simon got his disposition. So taken with wondering, he barely saw Aaron pick up Datt's red-beet egg. Jacob couldn't move the pan off the fire fast enough to stop him from taking a bite. It wasn't that he couldn't eat such things, but he usually didn't like half of it. Then Aaron's face scrunched up and . . .

"Arrgh!" Simon jumped up, chewed egg all over his face.

Jacob stepped between his brother and his son, skidded on the hard-boiled mess, and knocked Simon off his feet. Simon knocked the door open as he fell, his head hitting the porch floor with a thud.

Levi's belly laugh met Simon's farm-yard cussing. Aaron clapped. Of the girls, Jacob couldn't tell who looked more shocked, Rachel or Emma. Rachel's eyes widened, and she laughed like the butchering season when she was eight, when he'd pinned a pig's tail to the seat of the Preacher's coat before sermon. Jacob couldn't remember who was madder that day, his Datt at him for the doing, or Rach's pop at her for the laughing. But he could still remember her pop's face as he tried to get that pig's tail off his coat.

Simon was none too happy with either of them, on that day or this one. He washed his face at the sink and slammed the towel on the counter. That too tickled Aaron. Levi cleared his throat and gave Aaron a piece of potato bread.

Rachel, her shoulders still shaking, went back to toweling Emma's curls.

"Did you hurt yourself, Simon?" Datt asked.

"What happened to quiet breakfasts, I'd like to know," Simon mumbled into his coffee.

A suspicious squeak came from the corner, and Jacob didn't think it was Emma. He served Simon his breakfast.

"You should be farming, not doing women's work," Simon said.

Datt laid a hand on Simon's arm. "Son, these babies got no mama; Jacob has to be both. He's just giving Rachel a turn at the fun, right, Jacob?"

"It is fun," Rachel said.

"Because you have no children of your own," Simon accused.

His reproach renewed Jacob's ire. "Simon, before I left home, you said Rachel had agreed to marry you."

Simon took another bite. "As good as."

"No!" Rachel said, surprising everyone, herself included, Jacob thought.

Simon watched her for a minute before he spoke. "It didn't take you long to find someone to marry, Jacob."

Jacob opened his mouth to deny it, but he stopped himself in time and regarded his father. "I forgive Simon. Rachel is his wife and I respect that."

His father nodded, but after a quiet moment he said, "Forgiveness is good between brothers. Interference is not."

Simon had manipulated their lives, and they knew it, everyone except perhaps Simon.

Emma opened her arms and when Jacob took her, he knew he wouldn't have her or Aaron if not for Simon's interference. Rachel, he saw, realized the same thing.

"God works in mysterious ways," his Datt said.

Jacob touched Simon's arm. "You ever show my children

the kind of anger I've seen from you . . ." He glanced at Rachel. "You hurt my children, I will hurt you."

"Jacob," his father chided.

Simon nodded once. "I am not easy with children, but I would not hurt them."

Jacob took a relieved breath. "Emma, Aaron, meet your uncle Simon."

To their surprise, Aaron reached over and patted Simon's grim face with a tiny hand. "Unk," he said.

"Rachel, your kapp is filthy," Simon snapped.

"Always a kind word," Jacob muttered as he took his children upstairs, wondering why Datt had not noticed Rachel's bruise.

"When you're done playing nursemaid, we could use some help around the farm," Simon yelled loud enough for him to hear. "Rachel is back to school tomorrow, so she can't raise your English brats."

"Mein Gott, Simon," Levi shouted. "Enough!"

Rachel was glad to hear the reprimand, but when Simon stood and slammed his napkin on the table, she jumped.

"Enough you say, Datt. Well, I say enough too. I was ordained yesterday. Do you rejoice with me? No, you rejoice in your long-lost son's return instead. I stayed behind, tended the farm, kept a roof over your head, cared for you when you were missing Mom—and missing Jacob too, if truth be told.

"I have remained by your side through many a hardship, but do you rejoice in my staying? No. Well, I say enough too. Let him take over this farm, that favorite son of yours, let him slave from dawn till midnight clearing forty more acres like I did, sit up with sick cows, fight the blight and the drought. Then he'll understand what I've done here. And so will you. But in Jacob's hard work, unlike in mine, you will see prayer."

Her angry husband took his straw hat from a peg by the

door and slapped it against his thigh. "What I want to know, Datt, is . . . Ach, never mind. I am going to market for nails. Shed roof needs fixing."

The door shut with a thud. Simon spoke to Shep, their collie, just outside. And Rachel wondered how he could be gentle with animals, but not with people. She touched her father-in-law's shoulder. "He doesn't mean that, Levi."

"He does. And he's right. I have failed that boy."

"We all have."

"Not you, *Leibchen*. You endure and forgive, and I know it. Already, I fear Jacob knows it. Only Simon, I am ashamed to say, does not." He squeezed her hand. "Enjoy those babies. They need a heart like yours. Jacob is good with them, his love shows in each task he performs for them, but he is only a man. They need your soft touch. Only, Rachel, Jacob is in need too. And you . . . it cannot be. You understand?"

"Yes, Levi," she said. "I do. We both do."

"Goot. Now I go fill the manure spreader." He inhaled deeply and patted his barrel chest. "A robust herald of spring I will spread o'er the land."

While Jacob helped Levi fertilize the cornfield, Rachel took Aaron and Emma to pick violets in the woods, then to chase butterflies by the brook. When they got tired, she spread Great Gramma Esther's friendship quilt in the shade of a budding apple tree and lay down beside them.

Jacob missed his children and went looking for them. It was the first time since he'd had them that they'd been apart so long.

He found them asleep beside Rachel on an old quilt.

Emma had discarded her tiny white kapp—as usual—and lay curled around Aaron, her thumb in her mouth. Aaron was snuggled against Rachel, his hand on her breast.

Jacob was almost jealous.

He'd tried hard to forget Rachel. He went first to North

Dakota, where the government was giving away land to attract homesteaders, and got 160 acres. He survived a tornado that destroyed his home, snows that nearly froze him to death, and a million grasshoppers that came and ate his corn. The hoppers were so thick, train wheels kept slipping, and railroad workers had to throw sand down for traction.

Jacob gave up farming and went to the city. In Chicago he met Miriam working in a saloon. He stayed with her for a few weeks, decided he wanted something different, and went to Detroit. Then, one city after another, one job, one woman after another.

But he never did forget Rachel.

He corresponded with Miriam for a few months, then nothing. When he went back to look her up, he found an old woman in her house, raising her twins. His twins. Miriam had died giving them life, and he hadn't even known they existed.

Jacob decided then that he was about as English as he could get. The woman willingly handed over the twins, along with the letter Miriam had left him.

He'd taken one look at Aaron and Emma and fallen in love, a love the depths of which he hadn't known possible . . . he just hadn't known what to do with them. Amish was the only way he knew to raise children, but he fought that for a while, knowing it would be hell seeing Rachel with Simon.

And it was hell, but not in the way he'd expected.

He'd decided last night that he would watch over Rachel. What he witnessed, like the shaming, he could deal with. What he did not, like Rachel's bruise, worried the hell out of him.

Rachel Zook, of all people, deserved to be happy. She needed to laugh more.

Good idea.

Jacob plucked some grass and tossed it at her.

Rachel wiggled her nose, swatted air, and slept on. But Emma woke, gave him her lopsided grin, and toddled over to fall in his lap. She planted drooly-wet kisses all over his face, making him laugh, but the two on the blanket slept on.

He tossed more grass.

Aaron cuddled closer to Rachel and she pulled him in. Emma giggled, her eyes filled with mischief as she plucked grass, roots, dirt, and all, and went to drop it on them, but she tripped, landing with one foot on Aaron's belly and both hands in Rachel's face.

Aaron yelped. Rachel's kapp fell off, and her laugh floated up like a family of bobolinks gliding above the pasture. She lifted Emma and raised her high, making her giggle. Emma drooled like crazy, making Rachel laugh the more.

"There's plenty more where that came from," Jacob warned.

Rachel made to get up.

"Stay," he said. "Play with them. It's good for them." It's wonderful to see."

"Me too, Pie," Aaron said.

Rachel lay back down and raised him high, getting a belly laugh. "Jacob! He laughs like you."

Emma clamored to be tossed again. "Ah, sweetheart," Rachel said. "I can't wiggle you both. Come and play, Jacob."

He lay on the blanket beside her, raised his daughter, and the twins got shaken in unison, giggling, screaming.

Shep came running over, his bark adding to the din.

Jacob was caught by the happiness in Rachel's eyes. "Your eyes are as beautiful as ever," he said.

"I'll be the judge of that," Simon snapped.

Rachel scrambled to stand before her husband.

"Rachel, your kapp," he shouted. "You shame me with such a display before my brother. And you shame me doubly when I come home to find Datt trying to cook his own dinner."

Jacob picked up his frightened children. "You shame yourself with your treatment of your wife."

Rachel, shocked at Jacob's words, tucked her hair in her kapp and followed him, afraid he would pack up his children and leave. "You should not have," she whispered, taking Emma.

As they walked in silence, Aaron leaned over and grabbed Simon's nose, squeezing hard enough to make his eyes water. Jacob wrenched the small hand free. "Be nice to Unk," he said, though Rachel thought from Jacob's look that he might laugh.

As one, they climbed the porch steps, and stopped. Levi sat at the kitchen table while a dozen women, at least, offered him food.

"Is that Priscilla Gorilla serving Datt schnitz 'n knepp?" Jacob asked. "Looks like she sits kind of broad now."

Rachel hid her smile. "Don't be disrespectful, Jacob."

"I meant no disrespect, Rach. Gorillas are God's creatures too."

"Priscilla's a lovely woman."

"And looking for a husband," Simon said almost agreeably. "All of them are. It appears your need for a wife, and a mother for these two, is bringing out the best of them."

"These are the best? I mean, there are more?"

Simon frowned at Jacob's banter. "Come." Simon shoved him inside. "It might not be so bad having you home after all, little brother." Her husband gave a bark of something that might be termed laughter, Rachel thought, if it hadn't the devil's own edge to it. "Smells wonderful good," he said.

Jacob recognized Rachel's sister, Esther, right away, but

in her condition, he knew she wasn't a Zook any longer. "Looks like you finally got Daniel to the corner table, Esther," he said. "How is old Daniel?"

Esther's smile vanished, and Jacob realized she must be among the women seeking husbands. "Oh, Es. Not Daniel." Her eyes filled and Jacob pulled her into his arms, placing his cheek against her kapp, holding her like that until she stepped away.

No one moved, until a woman with morning-sky eyes stepped forward. "Hello, Chacob."

"Fannie Funeral Pie," Jacob said to lighten the mood, and Fannie swatted him.

"Chacob Sauder! Don't you go calling me that already. Years it takes to make everyone forget that name you giff me with. I make raisin pie good and you know it."

"The best I ever ate. Can I have some?"

"Oh, no," Rachel said. "Dessert after dinner."

As Jacob remembered often happened, Rachel got her way.

"Did your wife make you a quilt, Chacob?" Priscilla asked as they ate.

Jacob shook his head. "No, Pris."

"We'll have a quilting bee, then," she said. "To make quilts for you and the twins. A 'Tumbling Block' for Aaron. He looks like he tumbles a lot. And a 'Rose of Sharon' for Emma."

Jacob nodded. "A 'Lone Star' for me."

"If we're lucky, you won't be alone long," Simon muttered.

Jacob couldn't stop himself from regarding Esther. Her child would need a father and his children needed a mother. Except that—

"Hannah made your recipe for *Kartoffel Kloesse,* Rachel," Fannie said. "She got it from the newspaper chust last week. She remembered Chacob liking your potato croquettes."

"They printed one of your recipes in the newspaper, Rachel?" Jacob said, not a little impressed.

Esther laughed. "Printed her recipe? It's her newspaper. Rachel publishes the *Amish Chalkboard*. It's the only German newspaper around. We love it."

"Good Lord," Jacob said.

"My sentiments exactly," Simon muttered.

"That's wonderful," Jacob added.

Simon slammed his fork on the table. "I might have known."

Emma and Aaron ran ahead of Jacob through a field carpeted with Quaker ladies, the four-petaled bluets making the meadow appear frost-covered in places. *"Kum,"* Jacob said when they started chasing a chipmunk. "We go to the *schulhaus."*

"Pie!" Emma said, tugging his hand. *"Kum, Kinder!"*

Rachel was teaching them Pennsylvania Dutch. "Ya," he said. "Mudpie teaches lots of *kinder.*"

But it was not the schoolchildren that Jacob was eager to see.

For the past two weeks, he had tried to stay as much apart from Rachel as one could when living in the same house. Some conversations, however, could not be avoided, like, "Pass the slaw," or, "Why does Aaron have a pea stuck up his nose?"

But they were not strangers, he and Rach. She had always been his best friend. That relationship, he could claim. That she owned half his heart, he could not claim. This he accepted.

He'd kept himself apart because of the turmoil he thought his presence caused between her and Simon. But

Datt said they acted no differently since his return than before.

Jacob had known at service that first morning that Rachel would be perfect to care for his children, but he had pushed the idea aside, especially after Simon's words about her rearing his English brats.

Jacob had gone so far as to speak with several possible choices for a wife. The best of them, Jenny Moyer, had come yesterday. But when she tried to speak with Emma, his daughter had opened the corner jelly cupboard's lower door and stood behind it, kapp showing above, shoes below, and refused to answer.

Aaron, his pout fierce, had slapped Jenny's hand aside when she pinched his cheek.

Jacob was prepared to punish them later, until he realized they were upset because they understood what was happening. When they heard him and Jenny talking about her caring for them, Emma said, "No," and Aaron militantly added, "Want Pie!"

Fortunately, Jenny Moyer thought he was hungry.

It was to Rach his children went as if a mother's cord stretched between them, as if she had given them life. And in a way she had. Most fathers would not be pleased, however, when his angels became devils, playing tricks to get a laugh, running, screaming like hoodlums to get Rachel running behind. And Lord, how they laughed.

They were driving him crazy.

He couldn't thank Rachel enough.

Jacob's heart accelerated when he saw the Riverbend School, the same one-room schoolhouse all of them had attended.

Bright red geraniums decorated each open window, while drawings of butterflies and bees on the higher panes hovered above the blooms.

A funny screeching sound came from inside; then they

heard children laughing. Jacob took his children's hands
to hurry them along. When they entered, all heads turned
toward the back of the room, half hatless, the others in
white heart-shaped kapps. All faces were sweet and dear,
but the surprised face in the front of the room was the
sweetest and loveliest.

Rachel wore great paper ears, bigger than her head, and
a paper tube covering her nose reached nearly to the floor.
A smile transformed her features. "I am an elephant," she
said, and screeched again.

The children laughed and threw peanuts at her.

Jacob smiled. "When do they know to throw the nuts?"

She hunched and screeched. The peanuts came. "When
the elephant calls for them," she said.

"Ah, I see. Will you eat them all?" He stood in the back,
she in the front. Her students craned their necks back to
front, and back again, as they conversed.

Rachel laughed and removed her ears and trunk. Emma
and Aaron ran to her. She bent and caught them, kissed
each presented rosebud mouth, and lifted them together,
a knack she'd mastered quickly. "Children. This is Emma
and Aaron Sauder, and there is Jacob, their father."

"Hello, Jacob," they chorused.

"Pick up the peanuts," Rachel said. "You may have them
for recess. Hannah and Sarah Troyer, you will sweep. Then
outside."

Everyone rose talking. Unshelled peanuts got retrieved
from the floor, unthrown ones collected from desks. When
the girls finished sweeping, they came to Rachel. "May
we take the little ones outside with us? We'll watch them
good."

"You'll watch them well. You may take them, if they
want to go."

No worry there. Emma and Aaron skipped happily along,

soon surrounded by enough *kinder* to keep them content for some time.

"We can talk outside while I mind them," Rachel said.

She sat on a bench near the door, and he sat on the edge of the step to face her. "You like teaching, Mudpie?"

"Yes, Jacob. I do."

"You're a good teacher. I can see that. Do you think you will always teach?"

"Since a girl usually teaches until she is married or begins her family, I always expected to quit." Rachel hesitated and stood. "Come, show the boys how to play good corner ball."

Jacob complied and went to play ball.

After a short game, he returned, hat in hand, wiping the perspiration from his brow with his sleeve, his blue shirt wet under his suspenders. "You look sad," he said.

"No one has ever visited me here before."

"Our visit saddens you?"

Rachel smiled. "When I first married Simon, I thought. . . ." She shrugged. "Enos got you out. He will be pleased."

"I know." Jacob respected her need to speak of other things.

"You used to be quicker at dodging the ball," she said.

At this, his smile came easily. "Still am."

Rachel laughed and lifted the bell to ring it.

Jacob stayed her hand. "May we walk you home?"

"Of course," she said. "But first German lessons, and the children will copy the rest of my newspaper from the chalkboard."

"They're hand-printed, your papers?"

"Yes, but my students have to read and understand what's written on the board, before they can copy it."

"They must be smart."

Rachel's care for her pupils showed in her smile. "I'd

like them to be smarter, and they could be if they worked harder."

That made her sound like a very good teacher, and it made him worry she would not want to leave to care for his monkeys.

"From the money I make selling my papers, I'm saving for a printing press, so I can print them weekly and get them to more people. For now, I pay a penny for each copied, and sell each for three. A few students stay late and copy extras to sell to neighbors."

Jacob chuckled. "Some of them will be rich someday."

Rachel nodded. "Rich in the knowledge that responsibility and hard work are of value. Rich enough to make sufficient profit on their crops to feed their families, and to read their bibles and Martyr's Mirrors in the language of their ancestors."

Jacob resisted an overwhelming urge to lean over and kiss her. "Limitless wealth," he said, the catch in his voice reflecting his need.

As if sensing danger, Rachel rang the bell.

She *was* a good teacher; Jacob saw how good that afternoon.

They ended the schoolday with an old German folk song, and before long, not a child could be found save Aaron and Emma, still singing their version of the song.

"Erasing my chalkboard, Jacob?" Rachel said. "I'm impressed."

"Does it make me teacher's pet?"

"No, I reserve that honor for my pets in the back of the room who are emptying the trash bin all over the floor."

"Ach, you two." Jacob hastened to stop the disaster. Rachel laughed at the exasperation on his face, and the innocent surprise on his children's, as he stood over them explaining his scold. Then he made them return every scrap to the trash bin. How lucky they were to have such a good and gentle father, Rachel thought.

Not long after, spring thrummed about them as they crossed Coffman's meadow. The early June weather was middle-of-the-summer hot. Even the insects slowed their pace, and a lazy, crickety drone filled the air.

"A swarm of bees in May is worth a load of hay," Jacob recited, swinging Emma's hand. "A swarm of bees in June is worth a silver spoon." He lifted her in the air. "A swarm of bees in July is not worth a fly." He set her down fast, and her giggles made Rachel laugh too.

"Me too," Aaron said, and his father sang the rhyme again.

Jacob was no longer the young boy who'd walked her home from school so many years ago, Rachel thought, the boy who'd given her orphaned mouse babies to tend. He was a man now, with a man's wide shoulders and a man's beard.

He was a father. He'd had a wife.

Grief rushed in, catching Rachel unaware. She'd always thought *she* would be his wife. How tender and loving a husband he must have been.

Emma stopped Rachel in mid-step with a tug on her skirt. "Shoes?" she asked, raising her foot.

"Of course, sweetheart," Rachel said, grateful for the distraction. She sat in the grass to remove hers and the children's shoes; then she put them in her teacher's bag and stood to take the children's hands. "There, now, doesn't that feel better?" She wiggled her toes in the warm, sweet earth and looked at Jacob. "Why don't you take yours off?"

He tried to look stern. "You're as bad as they are."

"Bet I can change your mind," she called, running with the children into the creek. "Bet you can't catch us."

At the dare, his children began to scream and run faster.

Jacob chuckled as he sat to remove his shoes and roll up his pants. The more they ran, the more he wanted to catch them. All of them. He stepped into the creek and howled. "Ach, this is cold!"

Rachel's laughter trailed back, its song bringing such sweet memories, he could fall to his knees in gratitude for the simple moment. When he set off after them, he laughed louder than all of them.

He caught up quickly and lifted Emma, twirling her in the air. "Gotcha!" He kissed her cheek before putting her down; then he did the same with Aaron. Then the children insisted he catch Rachel. So he twirled her faster and longer, her laughter speeding his heart. And at his children's urging, he was not allowed not to kiss her.

Had the sun ever seemed so bright, the air so heavy?

As Jacob brought his face toward Rachel's, the honey scent of her called him closer. Her breathing slowed. His heart quickened.

For sanity's sake, he could not touch his lips to hers . . . neither could he resist a nip of a kiss against the shell of her ear peeking from her kapp.

Silk. Flowers.

Rachel's breath caught and she grasped his shoulders as if to keep herself from falling.

He wanted to touch her with his lips again so badly, his insides clenched with need.

His hands stayed at her waist.

They stood forever like that, just looking into each other's eyes. Hers were big, and round, and dark . . . like warm maple syrup. And Jacob wondered if he looked as shocked as she.

Such a tiny kiss, such a large feeling—in his heart, in his mind . . . in his body.

He dropped his hands from her waist, as if the warmth of her seared him. And he clenched his fists, whether to hold onto her warmth or to keep himself from touching her again, he wasn't certain.

She moved her hands from his shoulders, but could not seem to release his gaze. A need so deep it was solemn engulfed him.

Tiny hands tugged on his trousers, patted his knee.

Jacob stepped back and swung both children into his arms, closed his eyes, and let out his breath.

When he looked at Rachel again, the tension between them had eased and he was grateful. "Let's dry them off."

Wet to the skin, the babies got stripped and wrapped, Aaron in Jacob's shirt, Emma in Rachel's apron.

Each with a warm, sleepy child, Jacob and Rachel rested against the trunk of a blossoming cherry tree, letting the insects' song lull them.

Jacob cleared his throat. He needed to say this, needed to say it right. He closed his eyes, took a breath. "I talked to Jenny Moyer yesterday about caring for the twins. She'd be fine, I guess."

He beseeched her with his look. "But I want you, Mud-pie. My babies want you." He shook his head. "Maybe I'm not saying this right. We, the three of us, want you to leave your job at the school to care for them." He shrugged. "Whatever you get paid, I'll pay you double, 'cause they're double trouble, you know."

Having Emma and Aaron to raise had been her dream since Jacob returned, and Rachel was almost afraid to believe it. She cupped Emma's head against her shoulder, and closed her eyes. "Lord, but I want to. I love them so much."

Jacob seemed confused by her hesitation. "Simon has wanted me to quit since our marriage," she explained, "but I couldn't, because my life would have been so empty without . . . children in it. If I agree to leave for you—"

"It wouldn't be for me. It would be for Aaron and Emma.

Simon will understand, and he'll be glad to have you earning more."

Simon *should* understand, she thought, but with Simon, who knew?

"Look at them. When they're sleeping like this, how can you deny them?"

"I couldn't deny them if they ran around the best room covered in mud with piglets at their heels." Imagining the scene made her giggle.

"Give them a chance," Jacob said. "They'll try it. What do you say, Mudpie? Will you care for my babies?"

Oh, God. Oh, God. She'd never wanted anything more . . . except maybe early in her marriage when she'd wanted very badly for her husband to like her even a little. She couldn't say no. She couldn't bear the thought of Aaron and Emma running to another woman for kisses as they had with her at the schoolhouse. "Of course I'll give up teaching, Jacob. For these two, I'd give up just about anything." She reached over and squeezed his hand, and despite herself, tears came to her eyes. "Thank you. Nobody could love them more, besides you."

"I know that." Jacob pressed her knuckles to his cheek for a minute before he released her hand. With the gesture, her tears threatened, but she blinked them back. The night he'd returned, when he'd shown her the first tenderness she'd known in years, she'd lain awake long after, letting her tears fall silently. Tears of joy at his return. Tears of regret for her life.

But her life was her life and she must make the best of it she could. She would have his babies. And she had her newspaper. "My newspaper, Jacob! Without the schoolchildren to copy it, how will I print it? I don't have enough money to buy Atlee's press yet—oh, that's a secret, Jacob. Don't tell. Please."

Jacob grimaced. "Simon doesn't like the newspaper much, does he?"

Mild words. "Not at all." She thought for a minute. "Maybe some of my students will still want to earn a few cents. Or I could make copies when these two nap—"

"Hah! I hope you don't expect them to nap at the same time, or for long." He kissed the top of Aaron's head. "Or at all, some days."

"Last Sunday, I tried to keep them awake so I could play with them," Rachel confessed sheepishly. "But they fell asleep anyway."

"Ya, well, if you *want* them to stay awake, then that's different. Better find another way. Just in case. Are you talking about buying that old Gutenberg that Atlee's great-grandfather brought to America about a hundred years ago? Ruben and I were fascinated by it when we were boys. It needs parts for certain, but it might work. It's a simple enough machine, and it served our ancestors well."

"That's what Atlee says."

"But will he sell it? He never lets go of anything. I think he's still got the first tooth he ever lost."

Rachel laughed. "He was pretty sick a while back. I brewed sassafras tea from *Grossmutter's* recipe and made him Rivel soup. Then I went every day to make certain he ate. When he got better he said he owed me. I said, 'Sell me the press,' and he agreed."

"He should have *given* it to you."

"Jacob, this is Atlee Eicher we're talking about."

"Ach, right. How much?"

"Twenty-five dollars. I don't have near enough from my paper, and Simon won't spend a dime from my teaching money on it. I don't think there's anything he wants more than for me to give up the paper." Except maybe children, she thought.

"How much do you make teaching?" Jacob asked.

"One hundred dollars a year."

"I'll pay you two hundred, double like I said, and I'll buy Atlee's press and keep something back each month toward its cost. I'll charge you what I pay Atlee plus whatever it costs to fix. That way you'll know you earned it fair and Simon won't think I'm giving you something I shouldn't."

Jacob's generosity should not surprise her, but she had to swallow before she could speak. "I get the best deal."

"No, I do," he said. "I get the best woman to care for my babies, and they love her plenty."

Rachel smiled, more pleased by the compliment than she supposed she should be. "I'll walk to Abe's later and give him my resignation. The school board can find somebody else to teach the last week before summer break. But Jacob, Atlee said he'd sell me the press, not you. And you know how he can be."

"I can handle Atlee."

Rachel grinned. "This is a *good* plan, Jacob."

"If it makes you happy, it certainly is. I'll talk to Ruben about helping me move and fix it. Bet Atlee's got some hopping good cider left. After a jug, he'll sell me the press, don't worry."

Rachel pinched him.

"Ouch! What was that for?"

"Don't come home singing that song about the woman on the dock and the sailor who—"

"Rachel Zook, mind your tongue!"

"I only heard you sing it once. Fifteen years old you were, I think, and drunk from somebody's cider."

Jacob chuckled. "Ah, yes. And bold from so much cider, I kissed you for the first time." He drank her in just then and knew he would love her forever. "Wish I'd never stopped."

Birds chirped. Bees hummed. Leaves rustled.

"You're going to have to find yourself a wife soon."

Jacob wondered how long he could put it off. "Will you help me?"

"Me? Sure. But why?"

"I guess nobody knows what kind of woman I want for a wife better than you do, Rach."

"Why do I?"

"We're too far from the creek for you to be fishing, Rach."

Chapter Four

Rachel remained silent while Jacob told Simon at supper that he'd asked her to quit teaching to care for the twins. "Emma and Aaron love her. They need her. She's been so good for them."

But Simon sat, silent as her, until a lima bean Aaron tossed stuck in his beard. Then he growled.

Aaron opened his arms. "Unk?"

Simon sighed and lifted him—holding him at arm's length, as if trying to identify the object he held—then he frowned and placed him in Jacob's lap. "You take him. Rachel, I want to talk to you."

Rachel's heart raced as she followed her husband to their bedroom. He was not happy.

He rounded on her the minute the door was closed. "You would give up teaching for Jacob, when you would not for me?"

Rachel winced, despite the fact that this was the reaction she expected. "I gave my resignation to Abe Stoltzfus for the school board this afternoon. I *want* to care for those babies, Simon. I want to teach Emma things every little Amish girl should know. I want to show Aaron how to—"

Simon grasped her arms. "And your newspaper? You will give up that foolish paper? For Jacob?"

He hadn't listened, much less understood. "No, not the newspaper."

"How can you not?"

"Atlee Eicher has a printing press. Jacob is willing to fix it so I can print the newspaper here. That way, I can publish it weekly, instead of monthly, and get it to more people. I want to send it to other districts and invite them to send articles."

Simon's fingers bit into her arms. "A printing press cannot be managed by a woman."

"Jacob will help me."

He tossed her like a rag doll. "Of course, Jacob. But we have no money for a printing press, so it is out of the question." His statement pleased him and he smiled, looking down at her on the floor.

Rachel rose, aware she was treading deep water. "The press is part of the price Jacob will pay me to care for the children."

Simon's bark of laughter surprised her. "Your love for those children has a price, I see."

"Jacob is replacing my teaching salary, so you will have nothing to quibble about."

Simon jabbed her shoulder with his finger. Hard. "Did you speak of my quibbling, you and Jacob?" His next jab forced her to step back. "Did you?" He jabbed again. She stepped back again. And again. And when the back of her knees hit the bed, Simon pushed on her shoulders to make her sit. "Have you been discussing our marriage with my brother?" he asked, face close, voice soft.

"That would be a sad discussion, Simon."

He growled and whipped off her kapp, then tore at her dress, pins scattering.

Rachel tried to get away from him; then she cried out when something stung her.

Simon was holding a pin, resolve, and maybe satisfaction, in his eyes, as if, as if . . .

He'd pricked her on purpose, but Rachel had no time to ponder it before he grabbed a hank of her hair. "You are not happy in our marriage, Rachel?"

"As happy as you are."

By her hair, he pulled her close. "We will be married for the rest of our lives," he whispered into her ear.

"God help us both."

He raised his hand to strike. Lowered it.

Had she spoken aloud? Rachel released her breath when he turned away, but like a cat, he turned back. "Let Esther take care of the twins. Jacob favors her. Let her begin to know her children."

"Jacob and Esther have not even talked privately—"

"Which cannot be said for Jacob and you!"

Rachel inched toward the headboard. "Do you think Esther should move in here? I could move home. You would like me out of your sight. Then you would not be repelled by me."

Simon's rigid stance frightened and emboldened her at one and the same time. "Esther can conceive a child," she said. "Perhaps you would like to have her in your bed, instead of me. Perhaps she could make you man enough to want her."

Her shock at those words was no less than Simon's. His look—detached, feral—made her scoot off the opposite side of the bed, and for the thousandth time over the past three years, she wondered why she'd married him.

Any affection she'd ever had for him, he'd crushed, ruthlessly, day by day . . . beginning on their wedding night.

Suddenly, he smiled his devil's smile and examined her with great interest. "Look at yourself, strumpet. With your sloppy breasts hanging from your dress and those harlot's curls falling down your back. Has Jacob seen you like this? Is he man enough to want you? Has he had his turn with you? Even before we married?"

Something in Rachel snapped, and the years of fear stretching before her were more than she could bear. "I will tell you this, Simon Sauder, no *man* has ever had me."

Like a jackrabbit, he leapt.

She tried to run, but he caught her by her hair, wrapping it around his wrist, bringing her closer. And closer. Then he shoved her against the wall. Pain made her eyes water.

"Is Jacob the reason you have avoided our marriage bed these last weeks?"

"I have stayed up late to make Emma dresses." Her mouth was pressed so hard against the wall, her foolish excuse was distorted. "And Aaron needs—"

"Real women care for their children and still give themselves to their husbands," he said so softly, so calmly, Rachel shivered.

She tried to lessen the pressure of his hold on her hair by reaching up to pull it from his grip, but it was no use, and pain blurred her vision. "Sewing for children is difficult," she added, wondering why she bothered. "And when I come to bed, you're already asleep."

"As is your plan!"

"Yes, God help me! I did it to avoid the agony of your touch."

"Because of Jacob!"

"Because of you!"

He pulled a work-knife from his pocket and shoved her on the bed, never releasing her hair. "Look at these curls," he sneered. "They cannot be tamed any more than you. But the Bible says, a woman must submit to her husband in all things. Here, now, we will begin anew," he said, dancing that knife's blade in her face.

Prickles invaded Rachel's limbs, black dots her vision, and she had to concentrate on every breath to keep from succumbing to the darkness threatening to swallow her.

"I will tame something of you I can," Simon said, as if from a distance. "Then you will follow willingly enough." And before the scream left her lips, he slashed. Once. Twice. Three quick times.

Rachel struggled for breath and consciousness. Then she was staring, dazed, at swirled clusters of her hair marring their beautiful wedding quilt. But she didn't understand why.

Simon looked . . . victorious, and she did understand. Those severed curls proclaimed his mastery.

But to Rachel, they represented her marriage. No hope now for growth or change. Lifeless. Slain.

Severed. Her hair. His hold. Their marriage.

Simon had just destroyed every thread of hope she'd foolishly held for their marriage. And oddly enough, with the knowledge, energy infused her.

She jumped from the bed and dashed to the door, but Simon caught her arm and wrenched it behind her. Pain shot through it and her shoulder burned. Simon jammed her against the door, his face close. "A woman must submit to her husband, or be punished. You forced me to punish you, Rachel."

He let go of her arm to release the placket on his trousers, and red colored Rachel's vision. "No!" She slammed her knee between his legs. "Never again!"

With an oath, Simon fell grasping himself.

With trembling hands, Rachel closed her torn dress, and as he had done to her, she took the knife and danced it before his eyes. "Do they hurt, Simon?" she asked, not recognizing her hard voice. "I could cut them off."

When the color left Simon's face, Rachel's bravado faltered, but she held her stance. "If you ever touch me
again, I will reveal everything you have done to me since
the day of our marriage. I never wanted to shame our
families, but give me one excuse, Deacon Sauder, and I
will be silent no longer." Rachel smiled, surprised she still
could. "And you will be Deacon no longer."

Hate she saw in his eyes, fierce and deep, but she no
longer cared, and she stepped over him as if he were cow
dung.

She took up her small mirror to see how she looked,
and gasped at the red-eyed scarecrow with chunks of hair
sticking out in odd places. She swallowed hard, knowing
she needed to be strong, and tried to think of a place to
hide.

Wherever she went, she couldn't go looking like this.
But she couldn't get her hair under her kapp without
braids, and she couldn't take the time to braid it. So she
tossed the kapp aside, put on her big black winter bonnet,
and holding her dress together, she climbed out her bedroom window.

Jacob dared not leave, not even to see Ruben about
helping with Atlee's press. Instead, he worried. After he
told Simon that Rachel had quit teaching to care for the
twins, Simon had become agitated. And when he took
Rachel upstairs to "talk," Jacob knew he couldn't leave.

Hell, he could hardly sit still.

He tried to read Rachel's newspaper, but couldn't concentrate. Every sound had him ready to bolt. He almost
ran upstairs a dozen times, with no more provocation than
a heavy tread. He paced. Distracted. Tense.

Again, he tried to relax, and succeeded for all of a minute. Then a thumping, grating sound propelled him from

his chair, his heart quickening as he imagined Simon toss-
ing Rachel out a window.

His imagination was getting the best of him. He decided
to check on the twins.

At the *daudyhaus*, Datt was trying to teach them to make
cracker pudding . . . well, to crush the crackers, anyway.

They were fine. Happy. All three of them. So Jacob
headed up the stairs wishing he'd realized how angry
Simon would be about Rach keeping the babies.

She'd tried to tell him. He should have listened.

At the top, a panic not to be dismissed accompanied
the eerie silence. "Rachel!" he shouted.

Nothing.

He took a breath, ran his hand through his hair.
"Rachel?" he called more calmly.

A moan, a whimper came from inside.

"Rachel?" He tried the door. Locked. Lord if he charged
in and they were . . . He threw his hands in the air. Games
he played, now of all times. But something was wrong. Very
wrong.

Jacob lay his forehead against the door. "Rachel, if you
don't want me to break down this door, you'd better tell
me so. Right now."

Silence.

Terror lending him strength, Jacob hit the door, shoulder first. Hinges groaned, wood splintered. Good thing
Datt and the babies were next door.

Jacob battered the door and himself again.

The door gave and he sailed inside, the bed halting
his journey. And the sight froze his blood. Clusters of
blackberry curls scarred the rose-on-white quilt.

Harsh reality meets blushing innocence.

Simon lay on the floor, hands between his legs.

Jacob judged him. Found him guilty. "Rachel do that
to you?"

Simon nodded, the movement bringing a groan.

"Good. Where is she?"

Simon said nothing.

Jacob knelt, his heart pounding with rage. And fear. "Rachel could not swat a fly without regret," he said. "Desperation, only, would cause her to hurt a human being, even so lowly a one as you."

Grasping Simon's shirt, Jacob raised the man. "Tell me where she is, or so help me, I'll . . . tell me."

"The window," Simon said, his face green.

"Sick to your stomach?" Jacob asked.

When Simon nodded, Jacob smiled, then brought his fist back and punched him in the belly. "There," he said over Simon's groans. "Like *you* do. No bruise to show." He hit him again. "That was for the bruises that *did* show. Don't come after her. You hear me? You go looking for Rachel, I come looking for you." He let go of Simon's shirt and Simon's head hit the floor.

Jacob made his way to his father's, taking deep breaths and rubbing his fist.

When he got there Datt and his children were still cracker-crushing. Lots of cracker-crushing going on in this house tonight, Jacob thought, and he smiled. "Datt, can you put the babies to bed? Rachel's gone to Esther's for a while and I need to see Ruben Miller about the printing press."

"Sure. My grandbabies be good for *Grossdaudy.*"

Aaron tugged Datt's beard. "Good for *Daudy.*"

Emma showed Jacob the bowl. "Cwacker puddin."

He kissed each small head. "Night, chickens."

"Night, Pa-pop."

"Don't wait up, all right?" he told his father. "I'll get Rach on my way back."

"Too old to be waiting up for my children. But I'll sleep in your bed so I can hear them. Use mine tonight."

"Thanks, Datt. Night."

Jacob went outside, but kept himself from running in case his father could see. He checked the ground below Simon's window, measured the distance from porch to porch, and looked for crushed grass or flowers. He found Simon's knife and his heart trembled.

The barn door stood open.

It was her sixth birthday and Rachel could hardly wait to get to school, because Jacob said he would have a surprise for her today.

Spring lambs frolicked in the meadow as she passed. Full of "spit and vinegar," Pop would say. Rachel didn't think vinegar tasted so good, and she hoped it was their own spit the lambs swallowed.

She arrived at school the same time as Teacher; Jacob too, and Teacher was surprised to see him so early. "Why, Jacob Sauder. You used to be behind before. Here, help me count these books. You too, Rachel."

Rachel rolled her eyes. They wouldn't have a chance to talk till lunch now. And waiting would be hard.

The day began same as always. "All rise now and sing," Teacher said. "Ever glorious and free, Pennsylvania, hail to thee."

When Jacob's class, third grade, got up to spell, Jacob kept getting called to attention. Rachel stopped doing letters in her copybook.

Jacob pulled his hand from his pocket and looked at something he held. And Teacher laid down her book and raised her ruler. "Jacob Sauder, you come here."

Simon Sauder snickered.

"Gimme what you got in that pocket," Teacher demanded.

Jacob stepped back and shook his head.

Teacher opened her hand. "Gimme."

"Ach, but Teacher, you won't like it."

"You got no choice, Jacob Sauder. Put what you got in that pocket in my hand, or your Datt will know why."

"Ach, but Teacher, you don't want it. Really you don't."

"I want what you're playin' with."

Rachel thought Jacob was brave.

"All right, but you'll be sorry," Jacob said.

"Never you mind." Teacher extended her hand. "Give." And Jacob carefully drew forth his treasure and placed it there.

Teacher's shriek brought shrieks from the children. She shook her hand as if it burned. And mouse babies hit the floor.

"Why'd you do that?" Jacob yelled. "You hurt them."

"Pick 'em up," Teacher yelled. "And throw 'em away outside."

Rachel wanted to cry.

Jacob went out, and returned looking sad, and he got kept inside after lunch.

After school, Rachel followed him out behind the school. She watched him bend down, push aside some dirt, and remove his handkerchief, which he unfolded.

"How come they're bald?" Rachel asked from over Jacob's shoulder.

They examined the wiggling pink things together.

" 'Cause they just come from inside their mother."

"Did you take them away from her?"

"She was dead. I heard 'em crying is how I found 'em."

"Poor things. Are they my surprise?"

Jacob nodded. "Most girls wouldn't like 'em, but you're different."

Rachel cupped her hands, glad she was different for

Jacob. "Let me hold 'em. I want to see why Teacher screamed."

Jacob placed the mice there.

"Ach, I'm not surprised she jumped like that. They feel skittery . . . but sort of nice. Maybe." Their eyes were swollen and shut. Ugly. But they were dear. "Where'd you find 'em?"

"Lapp's wheat field, yesterday. Since they're orphans, I thought you could be their mother."

Simon ran over just then and slammed into his brother, just for fun. "What *you* got the rats for?" he asked her.

"I'm going to take care of them. For Jacob."

With a laugh, Simon scooped them from her hand and tossed them into the field. "Let the snakes have 'em for supper."

"Simon Sauder, you mean thing!" Rachel began to cry.

And right there, Jacob beat the tar out of Simon for the first time.

That was a long time ago, Rachel thought, shivering and huddling deeper into herself, wishing she'd remembered three years ago what a mean-spirited child Simon had been. Oh, Jacob, I need you, she cried silently.

"Mudpie, it's me. Where are you?" he called, as if he'd heard her.

But Rachel stiffened and stopped breathing, afraid he'd hear and see her.

Jacob allowed his eyes to adjust to the darkness of the loft while at the same time he hoped Rachel would adjust to his presence, perhaps even welcome it.

"Listen, sweetheart, I just want to know you're all right," Jacob said. "You don't have to talk. You don't have to tell me what happened. Just let me hold you. You can cry if you want, and I'll keep still while you do."

Oh, Lord, she wanted so badly for him to hold her.

Jacob wondered why he couldn't hear Rachel if he could

hear the sound of his own heart beating. "Please, Rach. You're scaring me to death."

Hay crackled under him as he searched the loft on hands and knees, inch by careful inch.

Maybe she wasn't here. But if not, where? Then he heard the tiniest sound, like a newborn kitten, and moved toward it.

To hold Rachel would crumble every barrier he'd tried to keep between them for the past weeks, but he had to hold her.

He had to.

A mound more substantial than hay hampered his progress, and his fear increased. That Rachel had buried herself caused him such pain, his throat tightened and he gasped aloud. It was all he could do not to tear at the hay and drag her into his arms. "Rach," he said. "Let me hold you."

He began to remove pieces of loose straw. Suppose she feared being touched as a result of her experience . . .

Jacob realized his mistake. If she feared being touched, she wouldn't want to be held. "Rach, I won't touch you if you don't want me to. I'll . . . sit with you . . . but I need to know if you're hurt . . . if you need tending."

Lord, if she bled to death while he hesitated . . . but if she was hurt, he could cause worse harm. A fear of hesitating, and a greater one of rushing forth, stopped him.

"Don't," came her voice, weak and tiny.

And if such a word coming upon the heels of his silence did not urge him on, what would?

Jacob calmed. He took a breath. Rachel was well. Well enough to speak and sound enough to ask for help, whether she realized she was doing it or not. He placed his shaking hand upon the hay covering her, gathered strength from her presence, offered the same.

Time ticked by at the pace of a garden snail climbing

64 *Annette Blair*

uphill and Rachel, buried in hay, did not stir, neither did she speak.

Jacob's patience had never been so hard won.

"I don't want you to see me like this," came the quivering plea. And his patience fled.

Panic came like lightning. *"Mein Gott,* Rachel, let me tend you!"

Chapter Five

Jacob's eyes adjusted to the darkness in the loft. As children they'd shared secrets here. Innocent, happy secrets. And now Rachel was hurt, in spirit at least . . . at worst . . .

Jacob's vision blurred and he swallowed. "Mudpie. You have to tell me. Are you cut or bleeding?" He was working very hard to stay calm.

"I don't think so."

Pain shot through Jacob, leaving him weak. "You don't *think!* Ah, Rach. I need to know."

"Oh, Jacob."

Taking that as resignation, he pulled the hay away before she could change her mind or set him straight. But as soon as she was exposed, she curled into a tighter ball. "H . . . hold me," she pleaded. "But don't look."

Jacob didn't need any more encouragement than that. He lay behind her and curled around her, gentling her with whispered words as he would a skittish colt. He ran his hand along Rachel's side, her arm. She would not put weight on an injury, so he was reasonably certain the side she lay on was fine. When he got to her shoulder, she winced. "Is it broken, do you think?"

She shook her head. "Sore."

He touched her face, slick with tears. When he attempted to smooth the hair from her brow, she grabbed his wrist to still it. In response to her unspoken request, he stopped. Satisfied for the moment that she was not badly hurt, physically at least, Jacob sighed with relief and laid his cheek against her neck.

Sliding his hand all the way down her arm, he found her fist clenched against her heart and laced his fingers with hers. "Now I'll be still and hold you for however long you want," he said, his eyes closing with relief, his mind easy for the first time since she had followed Simon upstairs.

She was squeezing his hand very, very tight, and her breathing calmed somewhat, but before long her tears began, and grew, until her body shook with sobs.

Jacob soothed her in German. "Your pain is mine. I am taking it into my soul to relieve you of its burden. Give it to me, Rachel. Share it. I will remove it if I can."

After a time, she calmed, except for an occasional hiccup.

He offered her his handkerchief.

She shook her head, denying her need.

"Like those babies," Jacob said. "They never want to wipe their dripping noses either. Use my *schnoopduff*, Mudpie, and wipe your nose. Please."

"*Schnoopduff* is silly. Even in Penn Dutch it sounds so."

"Well, use the silly thing, then."

Her moment of humor was gone; she shook her head.

"Worse than those babies," he said, kneeling over her, and as he did for them, he wiped her nose and made her blow. "If you want, you can roll toward me and wipe your nose on my shirt. I won't care."

Surprisingly, she complied, keeping her face hidden all the while. Then he held her in his arms the way he wanted, with her face tucked under his chin. "Does it hurt to rest on that shoulder?"

"Some."

"Turn over then and I'll get on your other side, so you can be comfortable and still use my shirt for a *schnoopduff*."

She turned over and wiggled backward to make room for him. "Just don't look at me."

"I already saw your dripping nose."

"That was the pretty part."

"I think every part of you is pretty."

Unannounced, her sobs came in great waves, heaving like the crests he'd seen on Lake Michigan in a thunderstorm.

It took a long time to calm her.

"What has Simon said to make you think you're not one of the most beautiful women in our district? Or should I ask what he has done? And before you answer, know that I've been in your room and seen your hair on the bed. Were you bald, I'd still think you beautiful. Now answer my question."

"Where are the babies?"

"Some answer. They're crushing every cracker in the *daudyhaus* and Datt's looking on as if the mess is the most brilliant thing he's ever seen. He's going to put them down for the night. I told him you'd gone to Esther's and I'd pick you up on my way from Ruben's. I told Simon if he went looking for you I'd give him what you gave him. Double. Any other questions?"

"Ya. You lied to your Datt, Jacob?"

"You want he should see what I saw in your room?"

Rachel shook her head.

If only he could get her to talk more.

"You lied to protect me, Jacob?"

"I'd do just about anything for you, Mudpie. You should know that by now."

"But you left me."

Her words sliced like a knife. He only wished his pain could atone for his leaving, for his being so foolish as to doubt her love. He would have saved so much suffering if he had stayed, and yet . . . he had his children.

"I wanted to die tonight," she said.

"If you had," he said in renewed panic, "you would take my heart with you. And Aaron's and Emma's, and Esther's, and your mother's and father's. So many hearts you would take, Mudpie. I'm glad you changed your mind. You did, didn't you?"

"Just hold me."

He held her tight and tried not to give into the raw fear her words provoked.

After a time, she slept.

Barn sounds quieted.

Datt and the babies would be asleep by now, Jacob thought. Must be near nine. And if justice were served, Simon would still be writhing on the floor.

Yet despite the circumstances, Jacob savored the feel of Rachel's breath upon his neck, the knowledge she was safe in his arms.

Judging from the stiffness of his body, Jacob thought he must have slept for some time.

Then his senses came alive.

Rachel lay in his arms, her hand against his heart, her knees against his thighs. He cursed himself once more for leaving her four years before . . . which gave Simon the opportunity to humiliate and bruise her, body, heart, and soul. Simon's cutting her hair was nothing in comparison to the rest, yet it seemed to signify a great deal more.

How could anyone mar such beauty? He slipped Rachel's heavy bonnet from her head. As he examined a newly cropped area with a gentle touch, his love rushed forth, shocking even him with its intensity. She sighed and snuggled closer, and he closed his eyes and savored the moment. Reveling in her trust, he kissed her forehead.

"Jacob?"

"Yes, Mudpie. You all right?"

"I knew it must be you. After you left, only *Grossmutter* ever held me."

He kissed a tear as it trickled down her cheek. "Want to talk about it?"

"About Grandmother?"

"Ach, Rachel, even now you joke. Simon. Want to talk about Simon? And what happened tonight?"

"No." She raised her mouth, inviting his kiss.

The rhythm of his heart made Jacob light-headed, as if within him beat the wings of a hundred birds making their swift way south. And their flapping echoed in his head as he slanted his lips over hers. He was drowning and she was air. He was parched and she was water.

But when pleasure clouded judgment, Jacob broke the kiss.

"It's all right," Rachel said on a sob. "I know what I am. You don't have to."

"Ach, Rach," he said. "If only you knew." Then he really kissed her, the touch of their lips sparking fire and memory, as if they'd kissed a thousand times before. Except it had only happened twice—young they were, and testing new ground.

But this . . . this was a homecoming.

Mouth to mouth. Heart to heart.

A reunion of souls.

Pleasure surged again for Jacob, fast and shocking,

pounding in his temples, everywhere, and he began to pull away.

"No," she cried. "Oh, Jacob, hold me. Please. Don't let me go."

"Oh, Lord," he said. "As if I could. As if I could."

He kissed her then with the longing of years, the desperation of a man finding a love perceived forever lost.

After a while, he pulled back to look into her eyes.

"No," she said. "Don't look at me. Just hold me. Closer, I need to be. I'm afraid, Jacob. Don't let go."

"I never will," he said, somehow certain at this moment that he could find a way to keep such an impossible promise.

Rachel tried to adjust her position, so he eased his hold. "Am I hurting you?"

"I need to get closer," she said, moving as if she wanted to climb inside him.

Jacob chuckled. "I don't think we can get any closer." He joked to lighten the mood and calm his body. Her torn dress revealed breasts soft and white, nipples rose-kissed and swollen.

And Jacob realized it was too late, there would be no calming for him. He ignored his reaction, however, to hold her. She was his Mudpie, and she needed him.

God help him, he needed her as much.

Within the safety of his embrace, and unaware of Jacob's utter, mind-stopping shock, Rachel slipped from her dress and reached for him once more.

He closed his arms around her, but he could not seem to get enough air. Or enough Rachel.

The flare of her hips under his hand beckoned. He could not help explore. And when he did, the air in the loft became thinner; he became harder. "Rachel." He used his most serious voice to bring her to reality, yet even to him, it sounded more like a plea to continue than an appeal to stop.

She rubbed her cheek against his, her parted lips brushing his ear. She combed her fingers through his beard and, God help him, he found it more sexually arousing than anything he had ever experienced.

"They feel nice, your whiskers against my skin."

"All whiskers feel the same, Rach."

"Never have I felt any in such a pleasant way, Jacob."

Oh, Lord, he thought, and what did that mean? Was there no intimacy between her and Simon?

"Your clothes," he said. "You should put them—"

"They smell of him, Jacob. And what happened was so . . ." She hid her face and her tears fell on his neck, scorching him as they trailed into nothingness. And when the air kissed where they had passed, he discerned their trail and knew he'd been branded.

After a while, she looked at him. "Simon and I . . . we . . . tried for children, but he could not bear to look at me, or hold me. He never kissed me. Not once. The sight of me displeased him. No, it was worse than that, I disgusted him. He found it difficult to . . . I am too ugly for him to . . . want me."

Jacob was shaken by the fact that Simon had never "made love" to Rachel in the truest sense of the words. "Simon is a fool," he said, humbled because she trusted him enough to reveal that part of her marriage.

He rocked her. "You are beautiful, Rachel Zook Sauder. Your hair," he said as he nuzzled its silken depths, "whatever its length, is the most glorious I have ever beheld. And who could not melt at such a smile as yours, with your tip-tilted nose scrunched up and your maple-syrup eyes twinkling."

"I must look very silly when I smile then."

"Beautiful, just like the rest of you."

"I don't need compliments, Jacob. I would not believe them, anyway." She tucked her face back into his neck. "Besides, it's not so much my face that's the problem."

"What then?"

Slowly she pulled away from him, crossed her arms over her breasts, and curled into the same kind of ball the twins tended to adopt in sleep.

Jacob knew he could not ignore this new plea, not if he wanted her healed. Layers of hurt to peel away. Where to begin?

He placed his finger under her chin and raised her face. "Rachel, look at me."

After a stubborn moment, she complied.

"Good," he said. "Here before me I see a pleasing, womanly form, not plump, but not too thin either. God has graced you with some height, but not too much." He let go of her chin and ran his hand down one of her legs. "You have shapely legs, as lovely as I have ever imagined them. And I have imagined them often."

He was pleased when Rachel's eyes widened.

Jacob lifted her foot. "No shoes?"

"They fell off."

He nodded, and began to remove her stockings. Warm, silky flesh he skimmed as he slipped them off. He took a breath and returned to his purpose. He lifted her foot, wiggled a toe, and smiled. "Your feet are not bigger than mine, which would be just too big to believe, but they hold you up well and convey you about with ease."

He kissed her fingers. "Your fingers are long and shapely, not big-knuckled and rough like Priscilla Gorilla's."

A smile raised one side of her mouth.

"Ach, finally," he said. "Your hips flare just right. Perhaps you noticed me testing that theory with my hand a short while ago?"

"Jacob!"

"I won't lie to you, Rachel. I never would. I liked doing it. And I like how you look. You are a desirable woman, and perfectly normal, except for perhaps one thing."

Rachel crossed her arms more tightly over her breasts and her breathing became ragged. Jacob uncrossed them and placed them at her sides. "Except for your breasts," he said.

She closed her eyes, and a tear slid down her cheek.

"No, love." He rocked her. "Oh, no. Don't cry. They're beautiful breasts. They make me ache with longing just to gaze at them."

"No," she said into his chest. "They're too big."

He pulled away to look very seriously at her. "Breasts can never be too big, Rach."

He could see she doubted his words. "See how they fill my hands?"

She inhaled sharply, weakening his control. He should stop. "I want to feel them against my bare chest," he said, surprised he spoke aloud.

Without hesitation, she unbuttoned his suspenders, then his shirt, and he could no more stop her than he could a railroad train under full steam. Not only did he not stop her, he helped her. "I want to feel all of you against all of me," he said.

After he removed his trousers, she came back into his arms. Oh, God. He had waited for this moment his whole life. "Are you close enough, love?" he asked. "Are you all right?" He kissed her forehead.

Skin against skin, they lay, her breasts crushed gloriously against him, her foot sliding along his leg.

"They *are* sloppy and ugly."

He smiled. "Rachel Zook, you have the most delightful breasts I have ever seen."

She pulled back. "How many have you seen?"

"A few."

She hid her face in his neck. "I would wish you only ever saw mine. Then if you said they were beautiful, I would know you believed it."

He kissed his way to her nipples. When he could wait no longer, he closed his mouth around one. In adoring the beauty of her, he would reveal it to her.

Slowly, ever so slowly, she loosened her hold, allowing him to kiss, to taste. When he made to draw away, she held him there and moved her legs to accommodate the length of him.

Again, he gloried in her trust. A fragile blown-glass treasure was his Mudpie. In the wrong hands, she had come close to shattering. But he would love her into wholeness again.

"I didn't know," she said breathlessly. "Your touch, it's doing strange things inside me, Jacob."

"Inside me too, Mudpie."

"I want to be closer, please."

Jacob brought one of her legs over his so they fit together nearly as well as two pieces of a puzzle.

Rachel realized, in a distant part of her mind, that she was in a place far away from her anguish, and that only Jacob could bring her there.

When the evidence of his desire came within intimate contact with her own, she rejoiced. And because this was Jacob, her Jacob, Rachel dared explore the texture of him.

Never had she known such intimacy or contentment, never the soul-deep warmth of being cherished. "Thank you for wanting me, Jacob," she said, sliding her hand tentatively along his length, awed and not a little curious. "You do want me, don't you?"

He shuddered, then stilled her hand. "You've pretty much had this effect on me since I was thirteen."

"I have?"

"You can't doubt my words, Rach. There is proof at hand."

That brought a giggle, a chuckle, and a long, slow kiss.

He showed her how to pleasure him, and her ability to do so excited her. And he pleasured her, bringing her to heights she had never known existed. Such places along her skin never tingled so. Such ribbons of pleasure never unfurled within her.

Her body was no longer ugly, but beautiful. Nothing mattered more than Jacob's desire for her. Hers for him.

"Ich liebe dich," he whispered close to her ear as he loved her neck with kisses.

Rachel sobbed, joy catching her unaware. "I love you too. God help me, I never stopped."

Passion, pleasure . . . love . . . deepened their need, gave it an urgency shocking in its force. Yet no fear nipped at her, no panic nor urge to run overcame her. Rachel floated within a cocoon of pleasure. Protected. Cherished. No place would she choose to be, but here, now. With Jacob.

When in the midst of their pleasure-laden journey, Jacob slipped inside her, contentment swelled and happiness engulfed her. She was complete.

And they became one. The notion filled her, carried her toward skies blue and sunny, where good reigned.

And happiness.

And joy.

Heaven welcomed them with open arms.

And they knew peace.

Fast upon the wings of morning, earth beckoned.

Milking time was little more than an hour away. Already the cows were making their discomfort known.

Rachel watched Jacob dress. Jacob. Hers undeniably

now, if only in her heart, because more than ever before, his taste, his texture, his very essence were a part of her.

She could not seem to stop her tears. She needed to have him hold her for about fifty more years before she might have enough. And even then . . .

But they both knew, though they did not discuss it, they could never be together in this way again.

She understood.

She grieved.

She could not hide from him that she was crying. After he fastened his suspenders, he pulled her into his arms and put his chin on her head for a few silent moments.

He stepped back so he could see her face. "The Elders would see what we have done as wrong."

"Yes," she said, looking into the loving depths of his eyes. Did he consider it such, deep in his heart?

"But God forgive me, I cannot accept such a notion, nor am I sorry," he said.

"Nor I," Rachel said, her eyes closed, her head spinning with relief.

"Rachel."

She opened her eyes.

"Did you feel the need to confess it, I would understand," he said, unable to hide his worry.

"We would both be shunned if either of us confessed," she said. "And if we were, Aaron and Emma could not be raised here with Datt. It would be like putting them under the ban too. Because of them, we cannot."

Jacob released his breath, raised her hand to his lips, and kissed her fingertips. "Thank you. Raising them with Datt, with you, is my greatest wish for them."

"I know." She threw herself into his arms, rejoiced at his rough hold upon her, his lips on hers, his tongue plunging into the depths of her mouth.

Not deep enough, not nearly enough time, nothing for

them was enough. This kiss became a last grasp at heaven, and because of it, her joy was dimmed.

Wantonness, a need for Jacob so strong she nearly gasped, rushed in and seized Rachel. Simon was right about her.

Poor Simon. He would never understand that hand in hand with love, abandon could be the most beautiful gift two people could give each other. It could even wash away ugliness and fear. This she knew for fact.

"If you need my help with Simon," Jacob said, as if reading her thoughts, "I will defy the Church Elders until hell freezes over to help you. True, those babies need their family and the community to thrive, but they need you more. Don't take any chances with him, Rach. Promise me you won't let him hurt you again. The next time, it could be worse."

"There will not be a next time, Jacob. Simon understands that the details of our marriage would not fare well laid bare for everyone in the district to examine."

Jacob nodded, his eyes bright. He cleared his throat. "I should never have left you. For that I will never forgive myself."

"But you have Aaron and Emma. You would not have them if you had stayed."

"And what have you but a husband who abuses you at every turn?"

"I have your little monkeys to raise, do not forget. They are worth having."

"As you are."

Jacob spoke with so much love, she could float with the pleasure of it. "Since I am barren, had we married, we would not have them. Unbelievable as it may seem, perhaps our separation, everything, has all been part of a greater plan."

"Even last night?"

Rachel bit her lip. She could not deny her worry over what they did, but as she looked into Jacob's eyes, she could not help the love within her. "We will leave it to our Maker to judge us, shall we?"

Jacob nodded. "Since He can see into our hearts, we will hope for mercy."

Chapter Six

A rooster crowed.

Cows heavy with milk shifted and lowed.

His mind far from his task, Jacob milked.

If his heart could be read, he thought, he would be damned. Perhaps almost from the first, he'd known in some tiny, distant part of his brain, though he was certain Rachel had not, the most likely conclusion to their night together.

A sparrow with a broken wing she had been, and he, her self-appointed healer.

She had believed herself ugly, within and without. And his need to reveal her beauty to her was strong, stronger than his sense. He soothed and comforted, and brought her from the depths of hell to the light of joy in the only way he knew. She needed and he gave. She begged and he answered. And in the answering, joy became his too.

For one quick second, when there was less than a fragment of a moment to stop, the depth of his sin had been revealed to him with a mountain-brook clarity. But for good or ill, it vanished in the silk of her skin and the opium of her scent.

And to Hell with him it would be.

But not Rach. Not Mudpie.

Jacob raised his face from the warmth of the cow's side and gazed far beyond the chaff-dusted barn rafters above him. "It is all on my list of accounts," he said to the One who watched. "Not hers. You know this as well as I."

Simon stepped into the barn. "You talk to yourself, brother."

Jacob's heart accelerated, his anger surging forth in the instant. "Do not call me brother. It sickens me. I was praying for the next bolt of lightning to strike you dead, preferably this very minute."

"Not a Christian thought."

"I believe a Christian's actions count as well as his thoughts. I will look to my transgressions. You look to yours."

Simon sat by the next cow to be milked and took up the task. "Thank you for starting the milk—"

"There will be no polite conversation, if you do not mind. Nor even if you do. You will listen instead. Move your things into another bedroom and leave Rachel's."

"You dare—"

"I will dare more if you challenge me on this," Jacob said. "Challenge me. Please. My knuckles itch to connect with bone. Bloodthirsty I am this morning, with no one to throttle save you."

Simon frowned as he milked, but he said nothing.

To Jacob, hard streams of milk echoing in hollow buckets was a restful, earth-renewing hymn. But this morning— Rachel's tormentor beside him, and his own torment within him—his soul refused to be soothed by the sound.

Today of all days, the peace he craved was not to be.

Mother tabby and her kittens scurrying in investigation interrupted his regret, their mews for nourishment calling simple pleasures to mind. Jacob smiled despite himself, and aimed a squirt toward the five tail-straight felines.

Such easy happiness. Lucky creatures.

He watched pink tongues lap the rich morning treat, and envied the simplicity of life for such as they. Would that he could understand the whys of the Creator's plan for mankind. But he was supposed to accept, whether he understood or not.

Faith, it was called.

Jacob sighed. "As I said, you will change bedrooms."

"Everyone will know."

"No regret do you offer for your actions? No sorrow? Fear not, Deacon Sauder." He spoke the title as if a curse. "No one who matters will know."

"Datt—"

"Will understand, if explanation there must be. Better him than the whole church district. It's your choice."

Minutes ticked by, marked by the lowing of cows and the cackle of hens in the distance.

Simon stared straight ahead, mouth taut.

"Today," Jacob said. "Now, while Rachel is preparing breakfast. I will finish milking."

Simon stood, knocked over his stool, gazed at it with disgust, and kicked it before striding away.

Chickens squawked. Bovine laments rose in timbre. Barn cats scattered.

Jacob eyed the cow whose face was turned toward him, eyes begging him to finish, please. He shook his head. "You would think I'd feel some satisfaction in getting him away from her . . . instead, I could weep for what might have been."

* * *

Rachel cooked breakfast while Emma and Aaron, in side-by-side high chairs, played quietly with the spoons and spools she'd given them.

The scent of apples and cinnamon, sizzling pork and fried potatoes gave the kitchen a warm, inviting quality. The sun streaming through the window cast squares of light on the wood floor worn smooth by generations of Sauders, bringing a comfortable sense of peace and destiny.

Rachel knew she had much that needed forgiving, though she could not be sorry that for a single beat of time, in all the time in the universe, she had experienced the exultation of physical communion with Jacob.

This morning, for the first time since her marriage, she felt whole and undamaged, though she lamented deeply that her marriage itself was the cost. And yet, had Simon not begun its destruction from the first?

No. She would not place blame, not on him or herself. *She* had chosen to marry him. Though it was a wrong choice, she had already paid the price, and a lifetime of self-reproach would serve no purpose. And she had chosen, if only at the very back of her mind, to make love with Jacob.

It was done and it could not be undone. And it had been beautiful. And special.

Jacob had proved her worthy of love, worthy of life, and from this moment on, she would make wiser choices than she had made in the past.

Rachel scooped oatmeal and applesauce into the twins' bowls to cool. Then she took the ham and the potato patties off the fire before she put the *fassnachts* in hot grease to fry.

As often in the past as Simon had said she'd seduced

him—though she hadn't understood how—she knew now that he was wrong, because last night she had gotten as close to seduction as she ever thought she could.

When Jacob had found her, she had curled deep within herself in a dark, cold place, terribly, terribly alone and frightened. She had looked to him to raise her from that chasm, had known that in some obscure way, only he could. And in his joyous, humble welcome of her, just as she was, her worth was revealed to her. He did not shun her, nor turn from her in disgust; he opened his arms and his heart . . . and she stepped eagerly in. He wanted her and showed her he did. He made love to her, in the purest, truest sense of the word.

He proved Simon's degradations false.

How blessed to discover one was not so worthless and unlovable as one believed. Oh, she did not need to be seen as beautiful, but she did need to be treated with dignity and respect.

Last night, Jacob had taught her that that was not too much to expect.

Rachel supposed she had known quite early in her marriage that she did not truly love Simon, though she'd denied it for a long time, and tried very hard—as recently as last night—to make her marriage work. But from this day forth, though she and Simon would remain married, she was released from the fear of his judgment and abuse.

Awed by the thought, Rachel gave the twins their oatmeal and ruffled each curly head as they dug in. She loved them as much as she loved their father, and she was grateful for the love they gave back to her. Though her caring for his children was the only life she and Jacob would ever have together, she would be forever grateful.

Emma tugged her sleeve, and bending to see what she wanted, Rachel got a sticky kiss on her chin. Yes, grateful.

When she went to put the *fassnachts* in a plate and sprinkle sugar on them, Aaron threw oatmeal at Emma, and faster than Rachel could stop her, Emma retaliated, hitting him square between the eyes with a sticky glob.

Aaron howled and Emma laughed so much, she could hardly catch her breath. Rachel laughed too. Like a bird set free from its cage, she felt as if she could soar. She laughed so hard, she wiped tears from her eyes . . . until Simon stepped into the kitchen.

Rachel stopped laughing. Fear froze her. Then, perhaps for the first time ever, she looked her husband straight in the eye . . . and saw that he was only a man, imperfect and flawed, just like her. And she remembered to breathe.

The look on his face was different today, less pompous . . . uncertain. He no longer held her captive with the thin veneer of perfection he'd sported like a bright feather in an English lady's hat. He knew that because she'd seen him at his weakest—and she didn't mean when she'd kneed him—he had lost his hold on her.

Her experience at his hands had reversed their positions.

She need never cower before him again. And as if her fears floated up and off her shoulders, Rachel straightened her stance. "Where is Levi?"

"Talking to Zeke Bieler down by the limekiln."

She nodded. "Good. You will move your things into the bedroom on the far side of Jacob."

"I can bring you before—"

"No! No, you can't." Rachel held the back of Emma's chair in a tight grip to keep her inner trembling from showing on the outside, but Simon's shock at her bravado was a balm more healing than Grandmother's. He looked for all the world as if he had sucked the juice from a summer apple, small, hard, and green. Wishing he had the bellyache to go with it, she chuckled, surprising him further. "Your threats are empty," she said. "I'd have plenty to say myself."

Oblivious, spoons forgotten, the twins ate from each other's bowls, communicating in gibberish.

Simon sat and began to eat in the same heedless manner. "I have already moved my things," he said. "I have no desire to be with a wanton."

As ever, the contradiction baffled Rachel. "You never succumbed to any lure of mine," she said.

Malignant hatred filled his look. "You seduced me into sin and betrayal. May you be consumed by the flames of Hell for it!"

Of any statement Simon might have made, none could have stunned her more. Often enough, he had implied that because of her barrenness, their coupling—the disturbing episodes were nothing more—was little better than fornication . . . sin. But who had she caused him to betray?

Levi walked into the lengthening silence and looked from one of them to the other with a worried frown. Even the children, oatmeal fingers in mouths, seemed to be waiting, wide-eyed, for something to happen. They didn't understand the tension, but for the life of her, Rachel did not know how to break it.

"Simon?" Levi questioned when the silence became so taut, it was ready to snap. "You went up early last night. Feeling all right?"

"Ya, Datt."

"And Rachel, did you have a good time at Esther's? Your mama is good?"

Simon's disdainful sneer said he expected her betrayal . . . so she would embrace the wickedness he claimed of her.

With sudden insight, Rachel realized that the wickedness of others made Simon feel righteous. Deacon Simon Sauder needed others to fall, so he could rise.

Rachel was foolishly astonished, and she would bet that

in his mind someone "unworthy," like her, made him feel more worthy.

As worthless as he believed her to be, as he'd convinced her she was, she must have been very good for his self-confidence. She bristled. "Well, no more," she said, surprising everyone further, especially Simon. "Thank you, Levi. Yes, Mama felt better last evening," she said, grateful Esther had stopped by with the news earlier and pleased to vex Simon.

Clearly bewildered, Levi turned to the children. "And how are my pumpkins?"

Aaron banged his spoon on the table and laughed in response, lightening the mood.

Favoring her sore shoulder, Rachel lifted Emma to bring her to the sink for a wash. "I swear, Jacob did not teach them the proper use of a spoon," she said.

"They'd rather use their spoons to make noise," Jacob said, coming into the kitchen, and Rachel's heart quickened as he stepped right up to her, bold as you please, and took Emma from her arms. "Your shoulder," he whispered. And Rachel experienced a mixture of fear and longing that with a look or a touch, he would declare their love.

As his big hand covered Emma's tiny white kapp to hold his daughter's cheek against his, he looked straight into her eyes. "Beautiful morning," he said.

Rachel nodded and moved to the corner jelly cupboard, presenting her back to the room at large, to keep from baring her soul with the love in her eyes.

Jacob sat Emma on the sideboard to wash her face. "You smell good, like applesauce," he said, then carried her over to Aaron. "How's my rascal?"

"Good boy," Aaron said, presenting his porridge-covered face, which Jacob kissed. "You *taste* like applesauce," Jacob said.

Aaron's chuckle blended with Levi's belly laugh.

"Any *fassnachts* this morning, Mudpie?" Jacob asked. "I've a craving for something sweet."

"Her name is Rachel!" Simon shouted, and only Levi was surprised.

Jacob sat with Emma on his lap. "The English call *fassnachts* 'doughnuts,' you know. Funny name, when they don't look or taste like nuts, don't you think, Simon?"

"I think it'd be nice to eat a quiet breakfast once in a while!"

Aaron furrowed his brow. "Unk?"

"Your uncle's a bear today," Jacob said.

"Unkabear," Aaron said.

"Good name, Unkabear." Jacob laughed.

Simon ignored the merriment and stood. "Come, Jacob. Timothy hay and mixed clover to cut today."

"I won't work with you, Simon."

Jacob's words resounded in the sudden silence.

Rachel watched for Levi's reaction as Simon stood and left the house. "Are you and Ruben going to see if you can move the press today, Jacob?" she asked in one breath, to give him a chance to cool his ire and keep his anger from his father.

Jacob sighed for his mistake and shook his head, asking Rachel's pardon with his shrug. Running his hand through his hair, he went to the door and put on his straw hat. "First I see Ruben. Then we make a deal with Atlee. Then we bring you your printing press. See you tonight."

"No sailor's songs when you come home," Rachel called after him.

Jacob waved away her concern. "Ya, ya, ya," he said, smiling all the way to the barn. No one could entertain him like Rachel. Well, sometimes Ruben could.

Ruben Miller, his friend nearly as long as Rach, had

made him smile often over the years, and Jacob was looking forward to seeing him again.

Maybe Ruben could turn his mind from Rachel.

After last night, he needed her more than ever. He ached just to touch her cheek or squeeze her hand. But he could not, and the sooner he tamed such impulses, the better for them both.

As he rounded the last bend in Crooked Road, Ruben's farm came into sight, and what a dilapidated sight it was. According to Levi, Ruben wasn't doing too well after losing not only his first, but his second wife too, in childbirth. And it didn't take more than a quick look at his farm to see it.

The barn door hung aslant and a wooden sap bucket on its side kept it from closing all the way. As Jacob pulled the market buggy to a stop and threw Caliope's reins over the hitching post, a scrawny chicken flew over the bucket to join his skinny friends in the yard.

When Jacob noticed how bad the house's loose boards and windblown shingles looked up close, he almost got back in the buggy. He wasn't certain he could handle Ruben's misery right now; his own was too fresh. Still, he pressed on.

A tattered *schnitzelbank* basket hung from a low hook on the front porch rail. A family of horned larks nesting inside gazed up at him with questioning, yellow-browed eyes. "Morning. Guess nobody bothers you much," he said to them.

Climbing the porch steps, he had to jump a broken one, and almost landed on his knees.

It took plenty of knocking to hear a grumbling "Coming, damn it" from inside . . . upstairs, maybe.

Ruben opened the door, hooked a suspender over his shoulder, scratched his thick, brown beard, and yawned widely. Then he looked at his visitor. "Jake Sauder, you mangy, old wolfhound." He barked a laugh.

"We could stand side by side and let somebody else judge who has the mange here," Jacob said as he stepped into the kitchen.

Ruben looked at himself, perhaps for the first time in some while, because he seemed surprised, and nodded at what he saw. "Ach. Mangy. Ya. Coffee?"

"You just get up?"

"Early for me."

"You don't keep up your Datt's farm?"

"Why bother? Farming don't call to me these days."

Jacob gazed about the ramshackle kitchen. "Neither does cleaning."

Ruben looked around too. "That neither."

"What does?"

"Ach. A little bit of this, a little of that. I dig a well, shingle a roof. Somebody needs it done, I do it. When I run out of food, I do some more."

Jacob hurt for his friend. "Where's that coffee?"

Ruben shrugged. "I'm waiting for you to make it."

Jacob shook his head, feeling selfish for his misery when Ruben seemed so much worse off. Behind a greasy stew pot, he located a dented coffeepot, then removed the lid and looked inside. "Ach. You ever clean this thing?"

"Hardly ever."

"You need a wife—"

"Jacob—"

The discord was interrupted by a blackbird stepping through a hole in the window to peck at some corn dried to the sideboard.

"I'm sorry, Ruben," Jacob said, still shocked by what he'd said. "I've got a streak of stupid a mile wide."

"All right, Jake. Here it is. You're back. We're friends. We'll spend some time together maybe. I'll say this once and we're done. I married. Two times. I got a baby on each wife. They both died trying to give me those boys. I got two dead wives, two dead sons. You got one dead wife, but two children. You're ahead. Don't think I'm gonna listen to you moan about losing Rachel. There's no sympathy in here." Ruben slapped his burly chest hard. "Empty. Your brother got Rachel. You're still better off than me. Hell, everybody's better off than me. Now give me some coffee and tell me what's on your mind."

After a good ten minutes of silence, Jacob slammed Ruben's cup of coffee down in front of him. Taking a long hot sip of his own, he eyed his rugged, downtrodden friend over the rim. "Guess I forgot you were such a self-centered, self-pitying, sorry excuse of a—"

Ruben smiled. "Missed you too."

Jacob smiled too. "Want to share some hard cider with old Atlee Eicher and talk him into selling his decrepit printing press?"

"You mean decrepit Atlee Eicher."

Jacob smirked. "Ya."

Ruben raised a brow. "Why?"

"So Rachel can use it to publish the *Amish Chalkboard.*"

"That'll tug on old Simon's chest hair good."

Jacob smiled so wide, a chuckle fell out, and before he knew it, he and Ruben were laughing so hard, they frightened Caliope as they climbed into the buggy.

"This horse smells," Jacob said, taking up the reins.

"That's me," Ruben said. And they laughed some more.

"Gonna help me fix up the press after we buy it?"

"Sure. Rachel gonna feed me while we're fixing it?"

"Sure. I'll even throw in some cash and a bar of soap."

Ruben nodded. "Deal."

* * *

Atlee Eicher had been the oldest member of the church district for sixteen years. As far back as Jacob could remember, he'd kept a nickel cigar clamped between his teeth. Jacob was pretty sure he clutched one there when he slept too.

Atlee's great-great-grandfather, an early Anabaptist, had died for his faith back in Switzerland. Atlee's great-grandfather knew the inside of a cave for worship as a young boy, hiding from those who wanted to persecute the followers of Jacob Ammann for their beliefs. That same printing press printed the notices telling the Amish in what secret place the next worship would be.

Atlee grew up knowing want, hunger, and sacrifice. He'd heard, over and over again, the story of his martyred relative's faith, his sacrifice, his torture. He'd tasted fear and determination from the mouths of those who knew it, and death-defying faith from those who practiced it. Sailing across the ocean as a young boy, Atlee lost his mother and little sister.

As a result of all this, Atlee came across as hardened, shrewd, and stubborn. True to character, like all German settlers, Atlee held a well-deserved reputation as diligent and hardworking, and he could pinch a penny harder than any man Jacob had ever known, English or Amish.

Atlee Eicher was also a man you would want beside you in battle. Because Atlee was loyal. And he fought for what he believed in with single-minded determination.

Only one thing about Atlee worried Jacob. He was a pack rat. He did have the first tooth he'd ever lost. Jacob had seen it. And that press was a piece of his family's history.

Jacob only hoped the old man remembered how good Rach was to him last winter. That would matter when it came right down to Great-Great-Grandpa Eicher's Gutenberg printing press. It would matter plenty.

Atlee's house was wide open . . . and empty.

"No wonder no woman ever married him. This place is a dump," Ruben said.

"Ya, well, then you're safe from the women too."

"Good. That's how I want it." Ruben went into Atlee's best room and stopped at the bottom of the enclosed stairway. "Hey, Atlee? You hiding up there?"

"No need to hide already, little Ruben."

Ruben spun around. "God A'mighty, Atlee!" He slapped his hat against his leg. "Scared the spit out of me again. Damn you."

Sitting in a corner chair, Atlee cackled around his cigar. "You always make so." His eyes narrowed. "That little Jake?"

"That's us," Jacob said. "Little Jake and Little Ruben, except we're bigger now. Got any cider left? We're plenty thirsty."

"Ach, the apples. A good harvest it giffs. Plenty cider. Behind the flour bin, back-door cupboard already."

"Same place for eighty years," Jacob said.

"How you know, you young pup? Been around no more'n thirty yourself, ain't? The day you were born, you 'n Annie-belle, I remember good. I never saw such tiny babes kicking." He cupped his huge, work-hardened hands side by side. "Held you here, each. Chust fit. God's own miracles. Annie doing fine?"

Jacob swallowed. Twenty-five years later, and he wished to God he could say yes.

"Atlee forgets things these days," Ruben whispered as he took down the jug. "Remembers ninety years ago one minute; forgets yesterday the next."

"That should help."

"Not much."

"Look at this," Jacob said, holding up a cigar box.

Ruben read the spidery writing on the cover. "String

too short to use." He shook his head. "Damn, he does save everything."

Jacob handed a cup of cider to their flinty-eyed host. "Beard's all white now, Atlee. Reach your ankles yet?"

"Chust about. You lookin for somethin, ain't?"

"Ya," Jacob answered. "You remember Rachel? Rachel Zook?"

"Your Rachel? Mudpie?"

His Rachel. Jacob looked at Ruben, unable to form a reply.

Ruben put a hand on the old man's shoulder. "Ya, Atlee, Jacob's Rachel. She made you some good medicine last winter, you remember? Made you better."

"Ya." The old man's beard did touch the floor when he leaned forward in his chair. "She want my old Gutenberg, ain't?"

This is too easy, Jacob thought, looking into Atlee's wide, eager eyes. "Brought the market wagon," Jacob said, worried the man's age-sharpened gaze might see into his cursed soul. "We came to get the press and bring it to her."

"*Goot, goot. Kum,* ve get." He rose and began a slow, shuffling trek out the door. "Two hundred dollars, ya?"

Jacob stopped dead in his tracks. "Chicken shit!"

"Jacob Sauder, mind your cussin'." Atlee slapped his knee with a cackle. "I got you good, ain't? Twenty-five, I say, and twenty-five is plenty good. It's besser to be rich in heaven, ain't? *Kum,* ve get, then more cider."

Rachel heard their off-key singing before Caliope pulled the market wagon into the yard. Shaking her head, she went outside.

She hid her smile as the exact words they sang took

form. "My mother-in-law's a cadaver, she lets the noodles burn, she turns the pancakes with a pitchfork—"

They stopped when they saw her, and she nearly laughed at their guilty faces. They looked at each other, shrugged, and began to sing "Bringing in the Sheaves."

When Caliope stopped, Jacob threw her the reins. "Hey, Mudpie. Got your press."

"A mother-in-law song first, then a Mennonite one you sing, Jacob? You couldn't do better?"

"Ach, Rach." He smiled sheepishly. "I couldn't remember the sailor one."

"Good. Atlee give you any trouble?"

"Just cider." Ruben grinned and lifted her in the air to turn her in circles. "Hey, Mudpie. Got something good to eat?"

"You smell like the inside of a barn, Ruben Miller."

"Why, thank you, Rachel. I thought I smelled worse than that."

"You do," Jacob said. "She's just being polite."

Simon stood by the barn door wiping his hands on a rag, his usual grimace in place.

Ruben rubbed his hands together. "Hey, Jake. Let's get to pulling those three or four chest hairs. This is the most fun I've had in years."

Rachel looked to Jacob for an explanation.

"You don't want to know. Can the rascal stay for supper?"

"Sure. Quit at four and send him home with the buggy to take a bath and change his clothes. Esther's coming for supper too."

Jacob put his hand on her arm. "Ach, not for me, Rach."

"For *supper,*" she said.

They looked at each other, and Rachel knew if Jacob married, it would break her heart. But he wasn't hers, and she'd best remember it.

"Good mothering, Rachel," Simon said, indicating the house with a nod. "Looks like those normal two-year-olds learned something new today. Without your help."

Everyone turned to look, and Jacob laughed.

Emma and Aaron stood on the porch, naked as sheep after shearing. "Pa-pop, Pa-pop," they called, jumping up and down.

"Ach, you two," Jacob said. "Where are their clothes?" he asked Rachel.

"In their beds? They were napping ten minutes ago."

"Two new things today," Jacob said as he scooped them up and brought them toward Ruben. "To climb from their cribs and to remove their clothes. Smart babies I got. Ruben, here is my Emma and my Aaron."

For a minute Rachel thought Ruben would cry. Then he squared his shoulders and gave them a big smile. "Pleased to meet you," he said. "Can you say, Ruuu-ben?"

"Boob," Emma said, raising her arms to him.

That tormented look passed over his face again, but more quickly this time. He took Emma into his arms and hugged her.

Emma sniffed daintily, then leaned back looking at him uncertainly. She crinkled her nose.

Ruben's laughter erupted full force.

Having Jacob home might bring Ruben back to the living. Or it might finish him off. Either way, Rachel thought, it would be better for Ruben than being neither one nor the other.

"Why do my children have red fingertips?" Jacob asked. Aaron opened his mouth and showed his father his tongue. "Ah, yes," Jacob said. "And red tongues too?"

"Churries!" Aaron said.

Rachel smiled. "We went cherry picking this morning. With those two, it was one for the bucket, two for the mouth. A pit or two, I think, they swallowed, before they got the hang of spitting them out. But when they understood the way of it, the spitting they did best of all.''

"Smart, didn't I say so?"

Rachel took the naked monkeys into the house to reclothe them. Ruben and Jacob went to unload the press.

Jacob and Ruben, sweating and grunting, lowered the Gutenberg from the back of the market buggy into the far corner of the barn's lower level near the window.

Simon watched.

"We could have used your help," Jacob said as he wiped his brow with his sleeve.

"Not for this will I raise one finger. Everything to do with that newspaper is against the law of God."

Jacob leaned on the press and folded his arms. "I know I'm going to hate the answer, but how?"

"Women are meant to raise children and serve their husbands' needs, not to break the laws of nature by doing men's work."

"So if Rachel were a man, printing a newspaper would not be against God's laws?"

"The entire concept is an abomination. If God meant us to . . . to—"

"Read . . . He would have given us eyes and minds?" Jacob said.

"Explaining to you is a waste of time. You cannot leave the dratted machine there. That is where I repair the buggies."

"But you can repair them where they sit. You don't need this spot."

"I do. The light is better here."

"It is better for Rachel's printing too."

"If I have anything to do with it, there will not be any printing."

"Why does this not surprise me?" Jacob asked. "All right. Ruben, let's put the machine back on the wagon

and move it to the corner where the thresher is. We'll put
the thresher here and when Simon needs to repair a buggy,
once or twice a year, he can move the thresher outside for
a time."

"I do not want the thresher outside. It will rot."

"I wish to hell you would rot, you sorry excuse for a—"

"Levi," Ruben shouted toward the upper floor where
they could see him through a ladder door repairing a
flailer. "This is your barn. Where can we put Rachel's
printing press?"

Levi muttered a string of sharp, though unintelligible,
words.

"What did you say?" Ruben called, brow furrowed.

Levi came down the ladder. "I said, 'Damn you, Ruben
Miller.' " He raised his eyes to the heavens, seeking
patience. "For bringing my attention to my children's bick-
ering."

"Datt—"

"Mein Gott, Simon, shut up! A decision I have made and
you need to hear it, the both of you," he said, encom-
passing all three in his disgruntled look. "Ruben, you ask
whose barn is this? Well, I have an answer. Jacob is home
and as youngest, the farm is his by rights. But Simon has
worked it four years without Jacob's help. Without Simon's
hard work, the farm would be worthless."

Jacob saw his Datt's look narrow and land on Ruben.
"Like your farm is, Ruben, and my friend, Zeb Miller, your
poor Datt, weeping for looking down at it."

Ruben closed his mouth tight, a look of patient respect
for Levi on his face, as he waited for the end of the reprimand.

Three chastised children, they stood, Jacob thought,
resisting the urge to smile at Ruben because he had been
included in the scold.

"And when you meet him at the pearly gates," Levi went

on, "you bet Zeb will be harder on you than I am. But this farm. This is my right to decide. Though the farm is rightfully Jacob's—"

"Datt, I—"

Levi raised his hand. "One more word, Simon, and I will thrash you."

Simon stepped back and shut his mouth.

Jacob and Ruben chuckled, and got a hand raised to them. They shut up too.

"I cannot take the farm from Simon," Levi said. "So here is what we will do. We have the main house in the middle, and my house, the *daudyhaus,* on the left. We will put another small house on the right, a *kinderhaus,* for Simon and Rachel, and leave the big house for Jacob, Emma, and Aaron. This way, the farm will be split equally between my two sons." He narrowed his eyes and examined their faces in turn.

Jacob remembered the look. He was eight years old and had switched the fowl eggs. Geese, chickens, and ducks squawked at strange hatchlings, and Datt was going to kill him.

"You will share the responsibility equally," Levi continued. "Cost, income, work, the keeping of the ledgers. But until I get Nate McKinley to write up the papers, this farm is still mine. You leave the press there, Ruben, it is the best place."

Jacob couldn't believe that his father aimed that sorrowful look at him. Why was it that Datt was always most disappointed in him?

Levi shook his head. "From you, I expect more."

Jacob mentally threw his hands in the air. Thirty years old, and his father could still read his mind. It was humiliating.

Finally, Datt turned that look on Simon. "You approve of this or you find another farm."

Simon nodded once.

"You and Jacob will share everything. Equally."

"Everything?" Simon asked.

"Everything," Datt repeated, then gave one last scowl before he walked away.

Simon watched their father go, then turned and examined his brother's face.

"What?" Jacob asked.

"Datt wants us to share everything. Equally."

Simon turned to Ruben. "You know, Ruben, I think Rachel will like such an arrangement."

Chapter Seven

Rachel removed a cherry pie from her oven, freeing a scent like almond paste to mingle with the spicy ones of sausage, onion, and pickled beets. "Smells good enough to tempt a fasting Quaker," she said.

Esther put her hand on her big belly and smiled. "Then I must be a fasting Quaker, because I'm starved."

"You've been starved for months, Es. That baby is going to be so big, he'll come out walking."

They were still chuckling when the kitchen door opened.

"Welcome, Ruben," Rachel said. "You look nice."

"Clean, you mean, Mudpie."

"Esther, you remember Ruben."

"Hello, Ruben," Esther said. "You're thinner."

"Hello, Es. You're not."

Esther's smile faltered. "I'm sorry about . . . all of them."

"I'm sorry you're going to die."

"Ruben!" Rachel nearly dropped the beets. "What a terrible thing to say!"

ruben looked as if he'd swallowed a pickle whole. "i can't believe I said that. Esther, I'm sorry. It's just that since I lost Alma, then Violet, in childbed, well, it's just . . . your chances aren't good, you know."

Rachel wasn't certain who was paler, Esther or Ruben. "Don't be stupid, Ruben," she said. "If all women died in childbed, none of us would be here talking about it."

"You're right, Mudpie." Ruben took Es's hand. "Let's start again. I'm sorry about Daniel, Esther."

"Thank you, Ruben. I miss him, just like you miss Alma and Violet."

Ruben grimaced. "It's hard having two dead wives, you know. If I miss them both, I think there's something wrong with me for wanting them both back . . . when I could never have had them both at the same time anyway. But if I think of one and get to really missing her, I suddenly feel guilty for not missing the other one."

Esther shook her head. "You're in a bad way, Ruben. That's for certain."

He nodded. "If we were luckier, you and I, I would have died instead of Daniel, before ever knowing I had killed another wife and baby."

"Oh, Ruben," she said softly, and placed her hand on his arm. "It wasn't your fault they died."

Jacob came in carrying the twins, followed by Simon, one cut, purple eye swollen shut.

"It is not our way!" Levi shouted behind them.

Judging by Levi's words, and Simon's face, it looked as if Jacob had given Simon what-for. Knowing Jacob, Jacob had good reason. Knowing Simon, Jacob had good reason.

Ruben touched Esther's cheek. "Don't cry, Es."

Simon stopped dead. "Ruben, don't go making eyes at Esther. She's Jacob's."

"Simon!" three voices shouted.

Jacob turned to his father. "You can doubt I had cause?"

"Turn the other cheek," Levi said.

"Wasn't my cheek took the blow, Datt," Jacob said, lifting Aaron.

Levi shook his head in resignation.

"Unkabear, boo-boo ouch?" Aaron said, leaning over and poking his finger in Simon's black eye.

Simon shouted and lurched back.

Jacob retrieved Aaron's finger. "Don't, Aaron. It hurts Unkabear for you to touch his boo-boo."

"As if you care," Simon muttered.

Aaron began to cry, and the two brothers faced each other, a lifetime of anger and disappointment between them.

Aaron raised his arms to his uncle, but Simon did not move.

"Don't be a jackass, Simon," Ruben said. "Take the boy."

"He is sorry he hurt you," Rachel said, trying not smile at Ruben's comment.

Simon grunted and took Aaron on his lap.

Ruben winked at Emma and opened his arms, inviting her into them, and Emma crinkled her nose, preparing for the smell. With a chuckle, he took her from her chair. "Got to show her I can smell good."

His words eased the tension, and for that Rachel was grateful. "When do you think my press will be ready to print?" she dared ask.

Ruben shook his head. "Broken armature." He gave Emma a piece of bread and butter. "Two gap-toothed gears, no letter box, but most all the lead letters."

Appetite gone, Rachel placed her fork on the table. "Most?"

"Don't write anything with an E," Ruben quipped.

Rachel's moan got her a sympathetic, if sticky, pat from Emma. At least *she* understood.

"Split shaft," Jacob added. "Not to mention dry rot in the frame. We'll need to see a blacksmith, probably a carpenter. Three bolts and two corner braces missing too."

"But we hardly had a chance to look," Ruben said.

Rachel stood. "It's not funny. That press is important to me, to this community. Sometimes you joke too much."

"Jacob," Ruben said. "Mudpie is mad at you."

Simon smiled. "Pass the pig stomach, Datt. I'm wonderful hungry today."

Soon their need for a carpenter brought a revelation they did not expect. It turned out they already had the best they could want.

Ruben surprised all of them with his skill.

The rebuilt frame on the Gutenberg was as well crafted as any Jacob could imagine, and he was glad Ruben had regained an interest in his work and some new respect for himself.

But rebuilding the frame was the easy part.

For nearly three weeks Jacob looked for press parts, or someone who knew where to find them. During that time, he kept giving Rachel heartening reports, because he didn't want her to be discouraged. He knew he needed to tell her how bad a mess they were in, but he didn't know how to say it without making her lose hope.

She resolved his dilemma a few days later when he arrived in the barn after plowing to work on the press and found her and the twins spreading hay in the lambing pen.

"What are you doing?"

"Watch." She spread a timeworn green and purple quilt atop the hay. From a basket, she took a hickory-nut doll and a jumping jack and placed them on the blanket. Emma threw in her soft cloth ball, and one by one, Rachel lifted the twins and put them inside.

"Ach," Jacob said. "A good place for lambs." Tiny fingers closed over a horizontal slat, Aaron's mischievous smiling eyes peeking between. A giggle brought Jacob's gaze to Emma, peering through a wider gap down below.

She and Rachel wore matching dresses today . . . green, like a long-fallow field after a good April shower. A sun-kissed field you wanted to run through barefoot with your best girl.

Rachel.

"Jacob," she said, reading him and telling him with the one word that he must not. She touched his arm.

He lowered his head, closed his eyes, and put his hand over hers, need pulsing deep inside.

"I am free to help you repair the press now," she said, her voice revealing her own yearning. "What do you need first?"

You. I need you. "A miracle."

Rachel removed her hand and stepped back. "We have miracles aplenty. You have come home. And here is Atlee's press in our barn. And there—"

"Your press now."

Rachel smiled. *"My* press." She pointed to the pen. "There are two miracles who might be kind enough to fall asleep so we can work."

"I told you, don't count on that happening too much." Jacob watched his monkeys fight to keep their eyes open. He shook his head, went over, and laid them down, pulling the corner of the quilt over them and patting each bottom. "Rest for Pa-pop. I'll be right here. We'll play when you wake up."

"Play," Aaron whispered, but Emma was already asleep.

"You are a good father, Jacob Sauder. You love them and they know it."

"They are easy to love." *Like you,* he tried to say with his look.

"The press," she said. "Let's get to work."

"I don't think you can help with this, Rach."

"It's my newspaper, Jacob, and my dream for our community. I need to help with the problem. What kind of person would I be if I left it to you? It would no longer be my dream."

"I share your dream, Rachel."

"Then share the joy of making it come true. Please."

He tweaked her nose. "When you smile like that, how can I say no?"

"I'll remember that for when I want something else." She took a triple-slate, hinged like a book, from her basket. "You will examine the press and tell me what is wrong, and I will note each problem as you find it. We will discuss how it should be fixed, or who might fix it, and I will write that too. Esther said everyone is talking about your search for parts."

"Esther was here?"

"Still is. She's making dinner. Mom's sisters, Lena and Ruth-Ann, went to spend the day with Mom, so Esther is free to spend it with me."

"This happened before I came home? It is not just because you want Esther and me to . . . I hope Es doesn't expect . . . Mudpie, I don't think I can do it. Things are . . . comfortable for me, for us, this way. The children are happy."

"And you?"

"As happy as you," he said, searching her face. "If I marry, I'll have to find my own farm, because living here with you would not be fair to my wife."

"If you don't marry, nothing will change between us." Even to say it broke Rachel's heart. "I am married to Simon," she reminded them both, which brought a few moments of silent mourning.

"What about Esther for Ruben?" Rachel said, to change the mood. "She brings out his tender side."

Jacob shook his head. "He is only tender with her because he expects . . . well, you know. I think he's afraid to take another wife."

"Poor Ruben."

"Never mind poor Ruben," Ruben said as he entered the barn. "Jacob's right, Mudpie, no more wives for me. Let's see to that press now."

By the end of the morning, Rachel's note-taking had given them direction, encouraging Jacob for the first time in weeks. He had forgotten that sharing problems with Rachel made them easier.

At dinner that night, they discussed finding parts for the press.

Esther shook her head. "I am disappointed in all of you. The answer is staring you in the face."

Ruben grinned at her challenge. "Why don't you tell us this brilliant answer, Miss Smarter-than-everyone."

"Advertise in your newspaper for parts."

Simon's snort was eloquent in its disdain.

Jacob slammed his hand on the table. "Esther, you're brilliant."

Esther gave Ruben an I-told-you-so smirk. "Why, thank you, Jacob."

Like their father, the twins slammed their hands on the table, but they kept at it until Rachel gave them each a cookie.

Simon was disgusted. "If you feed them every time they act up, they will be plumper than Datt's turkeys."

Jacob winked at his hellions. "We could advertise for another old Gutenberg too."

Esther frowned. "Another press? Why?"

"Ach," Ruben said. "Not so smart after all."

Esther was suspicious. "You tell why, Ruben Miller."

"For the parts."

"Good idea I had," Esther said, smiling. And when Ruben opened his mouth in indignation, she shoved his shoulder with hers.

"It's settled, then," Jacob said. "We'll advertise."

"Why can't you make the parts?" Simon asked, but when everyone looked at him in shock, he slapped his forehead. "What am I saying?"

"Unkabear?" Aaron queried with raised arms.

Ruben lifted Aaron from his chair and plopped him into Simon's lap. "Here. God help the boy, he likes you. Be a good uncle for a while and keep your remarks to yourself."

Simon looked at Aaron as if he'd sprouted horns, sighed in resignation, and took a forkful of cherry pie. Aaron promptly robbed the fork and shoved the pie into his mouth, wiping his hand on his uncle's shirt. Simon mumbled a German prayer citing children as gifts from above, while Ruben lost his struggle with laughter.

"I cannot help repeat Simon's question," Levi said, struggling with his own laughter, Rachel thought. "Why not make the parts? You are both smart boys."

"Thanks, Levi," Ruben said. "But we cannot build a letter box if we have never seen one."

"To have small slug-type letters manufactured," Jacob added, "would cost a fortune. We cannot do it."

"Why? You are a wealthy man," Simon said. "Lots of money to throw around. Two hundred dollars a year for a nursemaid. Spend more, big, important, rich man."

Jacob counted to ten while waiting for his patience to return. "Rachel is paying for the press herself. She cannot afford such costs," he said. "I am willing to lend her the money. I have already offered. But she will not allow it."

"Hey, you are rich," Ruben said. "How did that happen?"

"I've learned firsthand that wealth is not measured in

dollars, but I have those too," Jacob said. "North Dakota gave one hundred and sixty acres to homesteaders a couple of years ago and I got my hundred and sixty. Later, I sold it to the railroad to build a stockyard, for ten times what I considered a fair price. Good thing they didn't ask what I wanted."

"I'll be," Ruben said.

Simon stood, placed Aaron in his father's lap, and silently left the kitchen.

"Another burr in his beard," Ruben muttered, getting a swat from Levi, as if he'd cussed at table.

Esther giggled.

Jacob too wanted to laugh, but Levi was scowling, from one of them to the other, sobering them fast. "This farm is struggling, you may not know," Levi said. "Jacob, you have the means to turn it around, but Simon, I think, would rather fail than take your money."

"Simon, I fear, I would allow to fail," Jacob said. "But we'll bring the farm around, Datt, so you will be proud of it again."

Ruben frowned. "The farm looks fine to me."

Levi swatted him again. *"You* would think so."

In August, a farmer's slack month, people from all over the valley, and as far away as New Holland, came to build the *kinderhaus*.

Levi's respect for Ruben's ability was apparent when he hired him to be their official builder.

Ruben examined the area, did sketches, laid out and designed everything ahead of time. He oversaw the cutting of trees on the far reaches of the farm, then he got the oak beams cut at Two-Finger Zeke's sawmill.

After morning milking, a line of buggies a mile long

made its way to the Sauder house. The frolic, as some called it, would be a day of teamwork and skill that had been practiced for generations. No event was enjoyed more in the community, none brought them as close as a frolic.

By seven, teams of men—in a combination of work and competition—began lifting the first side-wall into place.

Too many children to count played far across the yard, under the trees, quilts checkering the lawn like tulips in a garden. Old Saul Yoder's children played with Young Saul Yoder's children, nieces and nephews older than aunts and uncles. A few women became the baby-sitters for the day, freeing others to cook, clean up, or serve meals.

Aaron and Emma went off happily with Lena Stutzman to play with the *kinder*.

By noon, the outside walls, locked together with wooden pegs, stood straight and tall while the workers ate. Aaron and Emma regaled Jacob with the words they'd learned that morning. As he tried to coax them to eat, rather than toss their food, Rachel came and sat beside him. "Go back to work, Jacob. I will feed them."

"Thanks, Rach." He stood, but waited to leave till they settled down.

Simon marched up. "Jacob, you are needed for men's work, for a change."

Jacob burned, but did not move.

"All right, you two," Rachel said to his children. "What would you like to put *in* your mouth?"

"Cookies, Momly," Aaron said.

"Rachel!" Simon shouted.

"Cookies, Momly?" Luke Stutzman asked his mother.

"Aaron and Emma learned that word this morning, Deacon Sauder," Lena Stutzman said. "Rachel did not teach it to them. They must think it fits her, but don't worry, they will outgrow it."

Simon grunted. "Jacob. Let's go help those who are helping us."

Jacob followed, certain of two things. People in the district were aware of Simon's anger toward Rachel—Lena had even defended her.

And his children's new name for Rachel was sweet.

And perfect.

Ruben spent the day calling out team commands, and barely stopped to eat.

Esther was worried about him.

At mid-afternoon, she offered him a drink of cool cider.

Sweat poured down his rugged face into his dark beard as he gave her a grateful smile. *"Danke,"* he said, raising the glass in a salute before gulping it down. "Thank you." He swiped his sleeve across his mouth. "You should not be working so hard in your condition."

Esther shrugged. "What matter, if I am going to die anyway?"

Ruben grimaced. "I told you I was sorry."

"Sorry because I am going to die? Or sorry for saying it?"

He thought about it for a minute, and a sickly-sheepish expression crossed his face. "For both?"

"Ruben Miller. Did it ever occur to you that you might have frightened the daylights out of me?"

He looked surprised, and repentant. "Did I?"

"No, *dumpkoff.*"

He grinned. "My mother used to call me that!"

Esther laughed. The sparkle in Ruben's eyes told her he'd made her laugh on purpose.

"Are you well?" he asked.

"I am," she said, pleased at his sincere interest.

"You shouldn't be working so hard, you know."

"I would be no kind of sister if I did not help Rachel right now."

"You are good friends too, I see, as well as sisters."

"Ach. Ya. We tease and argue just as much now as always. But either of us would give our lives for the other. And I worry sometimes about how she has suffered . . . first with Jacob leaving, and now with him coming back."

"I do not think she suffers from his return."

"They should have been together from the beginning," Esther said, then colored at the look Ruben gave her.

"If we could change the past, we would be God," he said with bitterness.

"I'm sorry, Ruben. But your suffering and mine could not be helped. Rachel's and Jacob's could have been. Their heartache came, not of Divine intervention, but Simon's, and we both know it."

Ruben took his handkerchief and wiped the sweat from the back of his neck. "Lying to Jacob about Rachel loving him instead of Jacob, and as their mother lay dying, was unforgivable. He should be horsewhipped."

Esther nodded. "Heaven help me, sometimes I hate him for it."

"Esther Zook," her father said in his Bishop's voice as he approached. "Go and help your sister serve these weary workers their supper."

To hate another was a sin. Esther knew this. Though her father did not say it, his admonishment was clear. She turned to leave, and noticed for the first time Levi standing there stunned. Oh, Lord, he'd heard them. And he'd not understood the depth of Simon's cruelty until this moment; she could tell from his look. She grasped his hand. "I am sorry, Levi. I did not mean to hurt you."

Levi squeezed it. " 'Twas not your words did the harm."

* * *

That night, Ruben helped Simon move his bedroom furniture into the *kinderhaus*. When Rachel finished cleaning the main-house kitchen about three hours later, she began to climb the stairs toward her old bedroom.

"Liebchen," Levi called as he turned in his chair to watch her. "You go check on the little ones before you go to your house?"

Rachel came back down the stairs, thinking it was the longest walk she'd ever taken, and went to her father-in-law's rocker. She put her arms around his neck from behind and pressed her cheek to his. *"Ich liebe dich,"* she said.

"I love you too." He turned to look at her, took her hand, and brought her around to stand before him. "Sit, tell me."

Rachel pulled another rocker forward and sat facing him. She took his hands and held them on her lap staring at them—big, callused, hardworking hands. She'd seen them snap a tree limb in two, gentle a skittish colt, or a sleepy grand-baby.

She looked into his eyes, her heart breaking to know she would hurt him.

"I will continue to cook and clean house for Simon. I will do almost everything a wife would, but I cannot share his house or his bed."

His eyes filling, Levi said, "Because Jacob has come home? You love Jacob more?"

"I will not deny I have always loved Jacob, Levi. You would know it for a lie. But when I married Simon, I cared for him and I thought he cared for me."

"You thought—"

"Shh, Listen. Jacob is not the reason for my decision. Simon is. He hurts me, Levi. Ever since we married, he has hurt me, more than just with the words you and others have heard. Most bruises I have been able to hide, some you have seen. The arm I broke that winter . . . I did not fall down the stairs, Levi."

"Mein Gott." A tear trailed down his cheek. He took out a handkerchief, blew his nose. "There is more."

As much as she did not want to hurt him, she must be as honest with him as she could be, under the circumstances, and still protect the innocent who bore no fault in all this. Levi deserved no less.

"There is more. Since Jacob has been home Simon's jealousy and anger have grown. My leaving teaching to care for the twins brought him to a fury that knew no bounds. He hurt me badly the night I told him I quit teaching. I have this to remember his anger." She removed her kapp and revealed the uneven places she'd tried to hide when she put her hair up this morning.

Levi gasped and she put her kapp back on, embarrassed, not only because of the sight she'd revealed, but because of the marriage she'd revealed.

Rachel looked at her hands. That was the hardest, revealing her failed marriage.

She sighed. "I am a good deal at fault for the condition of my marriage, Levi. I do not want you to blame Simon for all of it. But he does frighten me."

The pain from her shoulder, and other bruises like it, faded. But her fear had just seemed to grow. "I am frightened of being alone with Simon. He knows this. I have slept alone in the room next to Jacob and the twins since that night. Simon moved to the other end of the hall."

Her father-in-law nodded. He did not act surprised, just sad.

"Another reason, Levi, why I cannot let Simon hurt me any longer, a secret I share with only you." She placed her hand on her abdomen. "Here is another grand-baby of yours growing under my heart."

A sob escaped Levi as he stood. He hated showing his emotions, so he must be hurting badly to allow her to witness such a display. Helping her to her feet, he took her into his arms and held her until he got himself under control. "Such sorrow, such joy, all at once, is too much for an old man."

Sorrow and joy together. Yes. The same for her. She rejoiced at this new life, and yet it was a bittersweet rejoicing, for all of that. Because the man she loved would not be the man sharing this new life with her, not in the way she wished.

Levi lifted her chin. "You take care of this babe, *Liebchen*, and Jacob will watch over the both of you. Ya?"

"He will."

Levi stepped back. "It's sad."

"Surely not because there will be a new baby?"

"Because it's not the baby's papa who will be looking after the both of you."

Rachel squeezed his hand. What could she say to that?

Chapter Eight

Harvest.

On every farm in the valley, brawny six-mule teams plodded belly-deep through vibrant fields of green.

Up close, row upon row of erect cornstalks pointed to heaven, thick full ears topped with tufts of silk, jutting out on all sides.

Hands frail with age, or small and eager, toiled together. Work became play . . . and prayer. Using the same time-worn implements their grandfathers used, they gained in fellowship what they lost in speed.

Rachel's printing press sat as if dormant. At harvest, living must come first. Life.

And a new life was growing inside her. Rachel looked toward her child's father, uncle, and grandfather, working in the field in the distance. Family. Would her child be dark or fair, boy or girl . . . Rachel didn't care. She cared that this precious soul, this gift she thought never to receive, would be here soon and would be loved.

Family. Heritage. Tradition.

Levi drove the team pulling the wagon, matching Simon's and Jacob's pace as they picked corn, threw it in the wagon bed, then cut the stalks and moved on.

Levi would stop, get down, collect and bind the stalks, then drive forward for Jacob and Simon to pick from a new section. They worked with precise speed and cooperation, missing only a few ears now and again. And that was when Rachel's and the twins' jobs began.

Rachel carried two wooden buckets, while Aaron and Emma searched through the blunted stalks. When they located an ear, they'd shriek as if they found a treasure.

They were the treasures, waiting to be complimented when each ear was displayed for her approval before it was summarily dropped into a bucket. Their joy was one of adventure and discovery.

In a silent communication only the twins seemed to understand, each adopted a bucket and filled only his or her own, but checked regularly to make certain the other didn't have a larger hoard.

As the afternoon progressed, Rachel's love grew with each squeal. Aaron, with Jacob's quirks and smiles, and the same love of nature, would someday rescue orphaned mouse babies, birds, or squirrels too. Emma, with her ready kisses and dainty ways, made Rachel want to protect her forever.

They held her heart in their pudgy little hands, these, her first, her oldest children.

What would they think of the new baby? Aaron would act the big brother and protector. Emma would shower the babe with hugs and kisses.

When they deposited their next treasures, Rachel bestowed a couple of hugs and kisses of her own.

Jacob, hat in hand, wiping his brow with his sleeve, came walking toward them. Even at a distance, his smile called to her, and her urge to run into his arms took determination to overcome.

But Rachel's steps quickened nonetheless, as did Jacob's, and only Emma's shriek halted them. With the fields cut, they would have been seen from the barn had they embraced as she wished to do, as, she believed, he wished also.

Disappointment and relief showed in his look. "A near thing," he said.

She nodded, wanting his arms about her.

As if sensing her need, he took her hand. "Come, enough work for today."

"But we've more corn to fetch."

"It will be there in the morning."

"There are more fields for morning, Jacob, and night animals will surely gather it if we do not take it now."

Jacob gazed toward the unharvested corn, shaking his head. "The rest will be left to dry on the stalks for winter fodder. If there are hungry beasts out tonight, let them have it. They need to eat too. Come, walk with me." He tugged her hand.

She couldn't deny him anything, and her look no doubt revealed it, because he raised his brow. This reading each other did not ease her need, but swelled it, until she was ready to—

Screaming stopped Rachel's thoughts.

Emma came running, Aaron giving chase, a look of unholy glee on his face, a fat, wiggling, red worm raised toward his sister.

Emma slammed, face-first, into Rachel's skirts, the blow nearly knocking her over.

Aaron got caught mid-run, and was pitched into the air by his father.

Those two boys, one tiny and not knowing better, the

other big and burly, who should know better, laughed together.

Rachel lifted Emma, still sobbing, into her arms and gave Jacob a stern look. "Is there some unwritten rule that males should all be bad-mannered? You did that to me once, you know. Remember how frightened I was?"

"Ach, Rach," Jacob said, not hiding his smile.

Aaron held the worm out like a peace offering. "Momly?"

And how could she not accept it, but Emma whimpered anew.

"Thank you, darling," Rachel said to Aaron. "Carry it to my flower garden for me, will you? It will help the winter vegetables to grow."

Aaron nodded.

"Now tell your sister you're sorry you scared her."

"Em?" he said, leaning from his father's arms and tilting his head to the side, his look contrite.

He waited in vain for Emma to turn from Rachel's neck and look at him. "Sowwy, Em."

Emma peeked at him with one eye. "Bad boy."

Aaron's trembling lips turned down at the corners. That was the worst thing anyone could say to the sensitive little boy, and his sister knew it.

"Aaron's not bad, darling," Rachel said, kissing Emma's forehead. "Just playful."

"Play?" Emma asked hopefully, smiling shyly at her brother.

Another bit of unspoken communication took place; then they scrambled to the ground together. Aaron placed the worm in his father's hand before he took Emma's and walked away, Rachel and Jacob behind them.

Jacob regarded the wiggling creature in his palm and smiled.

"Aaron's just like you," Rachel said.

"Cute as a button?"

Rachel shook her head. "Mischievous, playful. Annoying, when he doesn't realize it's time to stop joking and be serious. Like you."

"But you love him anyway, despite that, maybe even because of it?" Like me, he did not say, but he implied it and searched her face.

To answer his unspoken question would not be wise. She changed the subject. "It's been more than two weeks since we printed our request for press parts in the *Chalkboard*." She straightened Emma's kapp from behind, then for good measure, Aaron's straw hat. "And we haven't heard a thing."

Jacob failed to hide his disappointment over her nonanswer, but he rallied. "It might be another week or more before we hear anything."

"Might be never, which would be fine with me," Simon said, beside them. Neither of them had seen him coming. "You gonna talk all day, Jacob, or you gonna help with milking?"

"Hey, Rachel," Mary Bieler called from her buggy in the road. "We miss your newspaper. Hope you print another one soon."

Jacob indicated Mary to Simon with a nod and a smirk. "Mary likes it."

"Thank you, Mary," Rachel called.

"It brings happy reading to our house. See you Sunday, then."

"Ya. See you."

Jacob smiled and turned Simon's hand palm up. "Present for you," he said, placing the worm into it. "From Aaron. Let's go milk."

*   *   *

Within a week, a printer's apprentice in Boston, Massachusetts, wrote that steam and cylinder presses had replaced Gutenberg's movable-type presses in newspaper offices years before. "Fortunately," the man wrote, "there are probably broken and unused Gutenberg Presses all over the world." No help at all.

Three weeks after that, Rachel brought another letter into the barn. Ruben was adjusting the new frame, while Jacob studiously dismantled and tagged parts, from joint to peg.

"I know where there is a Gutenberg Press," she said, to get their attention.

"Ya," Jacob said. "Tell us where so we will know why you frown."

"Listen. 'Dear Mrs. Sauder. For your information, there is an old Gutenberg in the cellar of the *Times* of London. I saw it there last month. I hope this helps with your search.' " Rachel looked at Jacob. "It is written by the publisher of the *New York Times.*"

"Big help," Jacob said.

Wondering if they would ever get her press printing, Rachel shrugged. "Well, it was nice of him to write."

Weeks later, when hope was dim and the press was all but forgotten, Jacob heard Rachel calling from the house, and ran so fast, his hat flew off. "Rachel? What is it?"

"It's the printing press."

Jacob took a breath. "The children are all right?"

"Of course."

Her smile slowed his anger. He shook his head, and tugged a kapp ribbon. "You scared the daylights out of me."

"I'm sorry, Jacob." She tugged his beard.

"Ouch!"

"Pay attention. Listen. I have a letter. It's from R. Hoe & Company, Pressmakers. 'Assorted Gutenberg Press parts with three odd sets of letters, being shipped to Rachel Sauder, Editor, *Amish Chalkboard*, by train today. Pickup at Strasburg Station, on or after September 15.' "

"That's wonderful. We'll have them in four days."

"Not so wonderful. We cannot afford them."

"We need them. How much are they?"

"Too much."

"Rachel, how much?"

"One hundred seventy-two dollars. Robbery!"

Jacob whistled. "That's why they can afford this fancy letter-writing paper. They do good business. Charging for the parts is only good business, Mudpie."

"It's almost two years' pay, Jacob."

"I can afford it, Rachel. Let me do some good with my money. Will you accept me as your partner?"

"How would you be my partner?"

"When you can print so many papers you begin to make ten dollars a week, you will start giving me half."

Rachel's brows furrowed. "But I don't—"

"In time, I will make back my hundred-and-seventy-two-dollar investment and more. If you don't like being partners, after I earn my investment back double, you can buy my half for one hundred seventy-two dollars, and you will be sole owner."

"All these problems tell me publishing a newspaper is foolish, as Simon says."

"Don't lose faith now, Mudpie. You have come so far. Why don't we pick up the parts and see if we think they are worth the price? We might find we have a bargain. If we think they are worth less, we will write and offer less. If he does not accept, we can send the parts back." He tapped her nose. "But if they are worth the price, I will become your partner . . . until you can buy me out."

Rachel sighed. "All right, Jacob. I agree to that. You might be a good partner."

Jacob looked at her with longing. "I would be a very good partner to you, Mudpie."

Wanting nothing more than to step into his arms and feel them close around her, Rachel turned away and went back into the house.

When Jacob and Ruben went to pick up the Gutenberg Press parts in Strasburg, the shipment was gone.

The stationmaster knew only that an Amishman had picked it up early that morning.

"I am going to strangle him," Jacob muttered as they drove home.

"You don't know it was Simon," Ruben said.

"Of course Simon. He is no longer allowed near enough to Rachel to harm her. What other way can he hurt her?"

"I would remind you," Ruben said, "I do not actually comprehend why, strictly speaking, Rachel's husband is not allowed near her. Though there has been talk, on and off since their marriage, of Rachel's sudden capacity to hurt herself."

"And you are not a stupid man."

"Why, thank you, Jacob."

"Don't thank me. I point it out so you will not need an explanation as to why I will throttle you for not stepping forward to protect her."

"I was too busy wallowing in grief and self-pity to think of such a thing. Rachel's bruises did not seem particularly important at the time. For this, I give you permission to throttle."

Jacob gave a disgusted snort. "You have been throttled enough by fate. I forgive you."

"Thank you. And you're right. I imagine Simon could hurt Rachel best by using her printing press."

"Imagine then what he did with the parts."

"Well. He could not bring them to your farm. He could not sell them; people would recognize him. Besides, who would want Gutenberg Press parts besides us? I would probably dump them along the way."

"All right. Where?"

"You think for a while now. I'm tired."

"You're always tired, Ruben."

"Ach. I am."

Jacob shook his head. "Let me see. They might be dumped in the woods. Down a well. In an old mine. A cave. Help me here."

"All bad ideas," Ruben said. "They could be seen and found in any of those places. They should be buried."

"Or destroyed. But how?"

"Fire, flood, famine, locusts," Ruben offered.

"Since Simon is not God, he probably does not have those things ready to hand." Deep in thought, Jacob allowed Caliope to set the pace. When they approached the farm, Jacob saw Simon down by the limekiln. But it was usually his father who saw to the burning of the bones after slaughter to make the lime they spread on the fields. "How about buried and burned?" he said, nodding in Simon's direction. And throwing the reins at Ruben, Jacob jumped from the moving wagon.

Despite Simon's protests, Jacob grabbed the huge fire rake and began pulling the burning contents from the pit upward and to the ground around it. He stomped out most of the fire and extracted every metal piece he saw, separating it from bones and burning wood to cool. Some of the wood, which was not the logs used to burn the bones, could not be saved.

Since a Gutenberg Press was more wood than anything,

their loss was great. Now the one hundred seventy-two dollars would *have* to be paid.

More important than the cost was how much this would hurt Rachel. Jacob wished he did not have to tell her, but she would know when she saw the scorched parts. He sighed. "Ruben. Those small slug-type pieces must be letters, though they are so black, it's hard to tell. See them here, and here. Get them out and let them cool. Go easy or they might lose their shape at this temperature."

Letting his fury rip, Jacob whipped about and gave Simon a hard shove. "You baptize on Sunday . . ." He pushed again. "And steal and destroy on Monday?" Another shove and Simon fell so far back, he teetered at the edge of the smoldering limekiln.

Let him fall? Help him? Jacob reached out.

He released his breath when Simon was safe, angry with himself for showing mercy, but not as angry as he would have been otherwise.

Simon stepped far from the pit and got his fear—he must be furious, he revealed it—under control. "You dare—"

"The deeds I have dared would shock you. Know this, if you ever do anything . . . anything to destroy the printing press or hamper Rachel's progress again, you will wish I'd pushed you in.

"The fact is, brother, there is a fiery pit waiting for you, and you will be in it for a very long time."

Simon spat into the dirt before walking away.

His own sins mocking him, Jacob shuddered. Him, of all people, threatening Hell.

"Throw ye not the first stone," Ruben said.

Jacob slapped his friend on the back. "Ach, I was just thinking the same thing. Let's clean up this mess and bring it to Rachel."

When Ruben showed her the charred letter box, Rachel

held back her tears because he'd made fun of her for being a waterspout the day before.

How could it be so difficult for her to forgive Simon for such a small sin when hers was so great?

So she forgave him, and decided Levi did not need to know.

Simon's actions delayed their progress, but it did not stop it. Parts not badly damaged could be used as patterns for new ones, which was more than they had before. Charred parts gave them approximate widths and shapes, lengths and turns. Half-burned pieces in their hands were better than whole ones they could not imagine.

Over the following weeks, Ruben showed incredible ability designing, turning, and finishing the wooden parts and putting the puzzle together.

Some of the letters had melted beyond recognition in the limekiln. Some were lost. Others, to their amazement, Atlee fixed.

A blacksmith by trade, until his retirement thirty years before, Atlee sat patiently before his make-do forge, an old iron firepot that Ruben and Jacob set up for him.

Rachel watched the first day, amazed at his skill. He held each tiny letter over the fire with his smallest fire tongs— huge compared to the letters, but they worked. He used the tools, he told her, that were for making links for chains—cross-peen hammer, file, chisel, punch, and cleaver—he named them all.

Atlee reshaped each letter with painstaking care until it slid into the letter box Ruben built. If one didn't fit, he began again.

Five long days he labored.

When he told Jacob he was finished, Rachel went to pick the letters up herself. She brought him a pumpkin pie, some chowchow, and enough jars of preserves and vegetables to last him the winter.

"Chust like old times," he said as he presented the skillfully repaired letters. "For you, Mudpie, I do goot chob, ain't? Sweat like pig, already. Hot work. Not too old, ain't?" He kissed her cheek and embraced her with the strength of a much younger man. "Sweet Mudpie." He touched her cheek. "As pretty you are outside, the same in your heart."

Rachel cried.

Two weeks later, after long days of repairing, refitting, and modifying, Rachel's press produced its first printed page.

Jacob handed Rachel the page with a flourish.

Ruben grinned like a schoolboy playing hooky, a look they'd seen often over the years.

Levi accepted the first page with honor. "Ruben," he said. "Build a frame so we can put this on the best-room wall."

At supper that night, they celebrated to such a degree that Simon left the house in a rage and did not return before they went to bed.

The next morning at breakfast, he stood watching them until they stopped talking to look at him. "Rachel," he said. "You are to be brought before the Elders at Eli Mast's Sunday morning for going against the *Ordnung* by printing a newspaper."

Jacob jumped from his chair. "You bastard!"

"*Mein Gott,* Simon," Levi said. "Will this never end?"

"It will, Datt. Sunday morning."

Chapter Nine

Gadfly hauled the buggy up Beachy Hill with a brisk, lurching gait. At the very top, about a quarter mile from the Mast farm, Rachel tightened her hold on the cracked reins and stopped.

Despite the Distlefink calendar on her best-room wall proclaiming the month as October, warmth already claimed the Indian summer morning.

When she and Jacob were growing up, they would walk home from service sharing secrets on Sunday mornings just like this. But they were no longer young, and Jacob no longer walked beside her.

Simon now stood beside her . . . at least he was supposed to. Hard to believe her own husband had brought her to this.

When Simon said she would be brought before the Elders at the Mast farm, Rachel had expected her appreciation for its beauty to be dimmed. But she was wrong.

Nestled in the valley before her, the sprawling farm

fronted Beachy Hill, the highest of Lancaster's hills, where stalwart silver pines arrowed toward heaven.

Its beauty soothed her, like a balm to her soul. And the warm morning breeze became a kiss of peace.

More ready than she thought she could be, Rachel snapped the reins and moved on.

Jacob had wanted to drive her this morning, but she could not let him. That his presence would mean everything was the reason why. The strength of their bond was fearsome, and she dared not let it be seen. Especially not now.

Ten minutes later, as she stepped into Mary Mast's best room, the thrum of voices stopped. No surprise there.

A chair waited for her in the center of the front. Serious business this, if she was not made to use a backless bench like the rest, but to sit apart. Separated, but not shunned . . . yet.

Of Levi and Jacob there was no sign, but Ruben and Atlee sat on the first bench in the men's section.

Rachel sat and faced them, Atlee's twinkle and Ruben's wink encouraging her.

Esther took her hand and squeezed as she walked by. But her mother's sadness brought remorse.

Perhaps wanting to print a newspaper was selfish. It hurt those she loved. Mom was already so sick, and her father, as Bishop, was being called upon to judge his own child. Even Levi hurt today because of her.

Simon, Rachel supposed, experienced a turmoil of sorts himself. He had spoken no word to her this morning, nor did he look at her now. She should not be surprised.

Her father stood, but unlike Simon, he smiled at her. And in the mist before her eyes, Rachel saw herself as a six-year-old about to read the Nativity in High German before the entire church district. With that same smile, he'd said, "I love you. Nothing you do will disappoint me.

My arms will be waiting when you are finished, no matter what."

No matter what.

Catching the exchange between her and her father, Simon shot her a disgusted look. As her father's smile brought memories, so did Simon's look. It had once been enough to turn her into the same quivering six-year-old. But for some reason, at this moment, it strengthened her.

Now Simon rose, looked about him, and allowed his importance to settle in every mind.

"Rachel Zook," he began, "has brought shame upon herself, her family, even upon this district, with her blatant disregard for our laws."

By naming her Zook, rather than Sauder, he was, in effect, repudiating her. Now if anyone learned she did not share his house, it would be seen as his decision. The community would think a humble man like Simon would be disgraced by her "sin," except that only a proud man like Simon would call her on such a thing.

How odd she should see him so clearly now. How sad that it was too late.

"I shall read," Simon said, "Rule Number Six of our *Ordnung*. 'No brother or sister shall introduce or begin anything in the congregation, not already there, without the counsel of the congregation.' " Shoulders back, stance righteous, Simon radiated pride. "I charge that Rachel Zook failed to follow this rule."

Ruben jumped up. "Rachel Sauder discussed her newspaper with me lots of times. I gave her my counsel. You too, Atlee, right?"

"Ya, I giff Mudpie my counsel last winter."

"Levi? Esther? She talked to you about how she wanted to publish her newspaper. Didn't she?"

They all nodded. Esther smiled.

Ruben turned back to Simon and waved a hand in dismissal. "We are the congregation. We gave Rachel our counsel. She followed the rule." He sat down and crossed his arms. "Next problem."

Red-faced, Simon shuffled his papers. "Her pride in her newspaper is evident," he shouted, his voice quivering with fury. "She has used the schoolchildren to advance her newspaper and herself!"

He looked around, calmed, and shook his head in deep sorrow. "She used your children. Used them to copy her newspaper, when she should have been teaching them. She profited from those of you who purchased that paper, when you could little afford it. Rachel Zook should be made to cease her vile pursuit. It is God's decree that we give back to the land, replenish and nourish the earth. This does not mean print a newspaper."

Rachel watched Jacob rise from the back row and march into the kitchen. When she saw him pace across the doorway, she knew he'd needed to release his anger or blacken Simon's other eye. She smiled inwardly, imagining the scene.

Ruben stood and theatrically cleared his throat. "Rachel Sauder," he said, looking directly at Simon, "prints a newspaper called the *Amish Chalkboard.*"

Jacob came to the kitchen door when Ruben began to speak, and Rachel gathered even more strength from that.

"If this is a sin," Ruben said, brows raised, "I will have to be punished also, as I read the thing from beginning to end." He leaned forward as if to confide a secret. "Sometimes twice."

Leave it to Ruben to make people laugh, even now, Rachel thought.

Ruben grasped his suspenders, his stance arrogant. "I feel no need to address the charge of pride," he said. "If Rachel Sauder is proud, then I am the greatest farmer ever lived."

All-out laughter ensued.

Now Ruben shook his head. "But the charge that Rachel uses your children." He rocked on his heels, shaking his head sadly. "Instead of teaching them?" he asked in disbelief. "This is a serious charge." He scanned the crowd and pointed to a barrel-chested farmer whose eight burly sons sat beside him. "Abe Stoltzfus. Tell me how little Perry did with his High German his first few years in school."

Abe stood, turning his black Sunday hat round and round in his hands. "Not so good."

"And Perry will finish school this year, ya?"

Abe nodded. "Ya."

Perry was her most enterprising student. He copied several papers each month, earning more than the rest of her students.

"So there will be no reading of the Martyr's Mirror nor the Bible in High German to him for his whole life now, right?" Ruben asked.

"Ach. No," Abe said. "Perry reads High German goot now. Plenty goot. Only Rachel Sauder could ever teach that *dumpkoff* anything."

Rachel saw Jacob catch Simon's eye and grin.

"So Rachel did teach Perry something," Ruben said, "despite his copying of the newspaper in her class."

"She made certain they could read and understand every German word, or they would not be allowed to copy the paper and earn their pennies. My Perry got to reading his German *goot* then. Rachel Sauder was the best teacher Perry ever had. . . ." Abe reddened and looked toward the women. "Sorry to the other teachers," he said with a nod of respect. "But it's so."

"Thank you, Abe," Ruben said. "Those of you whose children had Rachel in school, stand up if they did *not* learn good German."

Everyone looked around, but no one stood.

"If you think Rachel was a good teacher, stand."

Most everyone did.

"Raise your hand if your children learned better High German than ever."

Most of them smiled at her and raised their hands. She could barely see them through a mist of tears. She might just kiss Ruben later.

"You may sit," Ruben said. "No, wait. Anybody think the money you pay for the *Amish Chalkboard* is too much?"

"I would pay more," one man yelled.

Many more shushed him, and Rachel laughed outright. No one was more frugal than an Amishman.

Ruben eyed the Elders' table. "I believe we have answered these foolish accusations."

Simon stood. "There are more."

Ruben threw his hands in the air. "Of course more." He sat.

Simon began to pace. He stopped and held his frock coat open, his hands at his waist. A particularly proud stance, Rachel thought. He'd best take care, or others would see it too.

"One of the greatest challenges the Amish have had to face here in America," Simon said, "has been happening before our eyes these past thirty years and more. This 'age of industry' as the government calls it, they say will make our lives easier. Machines to do this and machines to do that. All the work is done for us.

"Is this our way? To have our lives made easy? Is it not our way to toil, to sweat to provide for our families? Has it not been decided by us in this district, as in most Amish districts, that if we use machines to work for us, the devil will settle in as we fritter away our time in more worldly pursuits?" He looked over the men to see how they received his words. Clearly, some of them liked what he said.

"Why do we need words printed by a worldly machine, by men who would pull us into a life fraught with temptation, one devoid of family values? It is a sin, I say, to use such a machine. Iniquity to use a machine which is the devil's plaything, merely to bring useless words to us."

The disgruntled murmurs filling the room saddened Rachel.

"But!" Simon shouted. "If you say the newspaper has helped teach our children the language of their ancestors, and if you like to read such a paper, then make it the job of whoever the schoolteacher is to publish it." The smile he gave her was victorious, enough to stop her self-pity.

Jacob surged forward, but Levi's arm shot out to stop him. They exchanged words, with Levi's chest puffed out like a bantam rooster, Jacob's stance hostile; then Jacob nodded and stood still.

Ruben stood again and raised his arms for quiet. "With respect to our good Bishop and his Preachers, I believe the Deacon's mouth has run over with the devil's own garbage."

Several serious coughs resulted from the statement.

"Sit down, Ruben!" came a command none of them dared disobey.

Atlee Eicher stood. His bent frame had lost height over the years; his beard, white as new-fallen snow, was the longest she had ever seen. Though no longer tall or straight, the wisdom in his eyes, as he scanned the crowd— his gaze pausing on her, narrowing on Simon—could not be denied.

And peace filled her.

"A sin you say, Deacon Sauder?" Atlee shouted as if he'd been insulted. "A sin to print words with my great-great-grandfather's Gutenberg already? In which secret place our martyred people would pray did that press print, and where to be baptized and marry. That same press for the printing you speak of?''

Simon did not answer.

"Well, is it?"

"I speak of any machine which allows—"

Atlee slammed his hand on the table in front of Simon so hard that Simon flinched. "Ya! That press *allowed* the stories of our ancestors' deaths at the hands of their killers to be told. And the devil's work it is, you say, to print? Ach. Like to print our bibles the devil worked? Here, my bible I have brought.'' He opened it and shoved it under Simon's nose so fast, Simon jumped as if a snake struck.

"See, Deacon Sauder!" Atlee cackled. "See your bible with the words of the sinful printing done." He raised the open bible in the air and turned about, revealing the holy words to all; then he kissed a page before closing the book and placing it reverently on the table. He lifted a copy of their Martyr's Mirror, a book twice as thick, long, and wide as the bible, and opened it. "See the printing by the devil's machine. The same, ain't?" he asked Simon. "And here. Here is our *Ausbund,* our hymn book, this devil's printed book with the sacred stories of our martyrs to sing." He scanned the faces of the men, then the women. "No sin there is here either, I say. Say any of you? No."

Atlee turned back to Simon. "This paper of the news, Rachel's *Amish Chalkboard,* makes besser use of Great-Great-Grandfather Zeke's press since the Old World. In the New World, it makes new way to use."

Atlee looked at the women. "It makes good," he said, his voice hoarse. He wiped his eyes and smiled. "I praise God I lived so long to see it. A paper of the news for our people in High German is worthy. Only good I read in Rachel's *Chalkboard.*"

He looked at the Bishop. "Ezra Zook!"

The Bishop smiled.

Atlee turned back to the congregation. "So old I am, I don't call Bishop a man who spat up on my best broadfalls." He put his hand on his chest. "Though in this old heart there is great respect.

"Ezra. In a few years, six, maybe seven, I might be too old to come to worship, ain't? And I might want to read your too-long sermons."

No one smiled more than Bishop Zook.

No one frowned more than Deacon Sauder.

"Enough of this foolishness," Atlee said to Simon. "A press is for printing. If in our hearts we listen for the word of God, His we will hear. If it is the word of the devil we seek, this we will find."

He turned to the women. "Pris. You teaching now?"

"Yes, Atlee."

"Better than you cooking, I guess. Can you do Rachel's job, printing a paper at school like she did?"

"Me?" she squeaked. "No!"

Atlee turned back to Simon. "Your best argument, you give us now. I smell *schnitz* pie. You don't talk fast, I go eat." He inclined his head toward the men. "They will follow."

Their oldest citizen shuffled away, cackling for all he was worth, as if he'd made a great joke. Before he sat, he enlivened the entertainment by stepping up to Rachel and kissing her forehead.

Rachel closed her eyes and whispered her thanks.

Jacob hadn't expected to have such a good time today. He figured he'd have to visit Atlee more often. He could learn a lot, and Emma and Aaron would probably make him feel like a young man of eighty again.

Lord, that tic in Simon's cheek was a sight to behold. Jacob didn't think it had ever gone so fast. "He's gonna blow, Datt," he said under his breath, and his father scowled back.

"A woman's place is in her home!" Simon shouted, launching himself from his seat at the Elders' table.

Hands clenched, mouth rigid, face ruddy, he looked around as if he were surprised to find himself here. Then he took a deep breath and faced the men. "A woman's role is to plant her garden, clean her house, and care for her animals. She makes food and does what she must to run a good Amish house. I charge that Rachel Zook does not perform the duties of a wife!"

"Simon!" Levi shouted.

Jacob was ready to "raise his sword," Amish or not. As one, he and his father stepped forward.

Rachel jumped up. "Your charges, Deacon Sauder, have a foundation built on sand."

Jacob and his father stopped.

"You publish your newspaper instead of tending the garden," Simon accused.

Rachel chuckled. "I canned *twenty-two* quarts of peas, *eighteen* of beans, *thirty* of pickles, *forty-three* of tomatoes. From that untended garden I gathered also squash and pumpkins, celery and rhubarb." She looked toward the back of the room. "Did you ever tend that garden, Levi?"

His father smiled and shook his head. "No, *Leibchen.*"

Rachel turned back to her bastard of a husband. "And we know you didn't, Simon." She pointed at herself. "So it must have been me."

Jacob chuckled. Others watched and listened with great interest. This would be the talk of the district for some time to come, Jacob knew. Generations, maybe.

Simon shook his head. "You write your stories instead of cleaning the house."

"I clean the house good. Ask any of the women who visit. I have washed and cleaned and cooked for you and Levi since I began my newspaper. But for the damage to your pride, you have not suffered."

A collective gasp, low but no less potent, went up at her insult. Pride was an Amishman's greatest sin. Jacob chuckled, and his father swatted him.

" 'Tis not my humility anyone here questions," Simon said. " 'Tis your pride, your sins before us."

Jacob lost his smile, and his father took hold of his arm.

"Only the Deacon questions his wife," Rachel said.

Simon nodded and smiled, as if he was pleased she grasped the situation, the idiot.

Jacob had had enough. It was not Rachel who first broke her vows to honor and cherish; it was her husband, and if need be, Jacob was prepared to say so.

"You have barely performed your duties while printing this newspaper. But now the press will make more work for you, and you will not be able to continue your duties. If you had children, you would never be able to do it."

Rachel smiled. "You said the press was a sin because it made less work, now you say it will make more. I think you do not know how much work there is, either for a newspaper, or a wife."

The women laughed.

"I have Aaron and Emma to tend now," Rachel continued. "And Jacob too, even Ruben, more often than not, to clean up after, and I still do it all. You have no argument, Simon. And I think this is not the business of the whole church district. The problems of Simon and Rachel Sauder should be discussed in private."

Simon stepped too close to Rachel, as far as Jacob was concerned, and he pushed his father's restraining hand away.

By virtue of Simon's height, he loomed over Rachel, but to Jacob's relief, he made no move to touch her.

"It is the business of the entire church district," Simon pronounced distinctly, "when a member will not do her duty and bear a child." Gasps and murmurs swelled as

Simon grasped Rachel's arms. "You would not be able to care for the house and the twins, and print your foolish newspaper, if you would do your duty," he spat.

"I do my duty," Rachel said.

"I mean, if you were a real woman!" He shook her. "If you bore a child!"

Rachel shrugged from his grasp. "I carry a child!"

Chapter Ten

Deacon Simon Sauder stood as if turned to stone.

Despite the grim circumstances of her announcement, Rachel rejoiced for the child growing under her heart. And she rejoiced for such a response to her husband's accusation. "I am not a failure. You—"

Her father cupped her shoulder. *"Liebchen,* shh. The Elders will pray now." His touch, his soft words calmed her. "Their decision will be announced shortly." He smiled, and it was all Rachel could do not to throw herself into his arms and weep.

Instead, she smiled. People stood in small groups, their talk rising to fever pitch, many glancing furtively in her direction.

Her neighbors were excluding her from their talk, for the first time ever. An odd feeling this, to be singled out but standing among so many.

As one, her people judged her. But how would they

react if they knew her deepest secret? The answer was not to be contemplated.

Because of her disclosure, she must make a decision, here in the midst of them, that would affect the future of her unborn child ... perhaps his very life, if Simon ever learned the truth.

One particular, painful truth she must face right now.

The one person she could go to under any circumstances, bare her soul to, no matter its dark secrets, and still expect welcome from, was Jacob. But that gentle man with whom she craved refuge was the one person on earth she most needed to exclude from the truth, while at the same time being the one who deserved it most.

The injustice made Rachel want to scream at a God she believed, for the first time in her life, might have deserted her. And if He was not watching over the life growing within her, then she must. At any cost.

She would not lie, but she would not offer unnecessary facts either. This child was hers first. Hers to protect, to nurture, and to raise. She must do that in the best way she knew, within the protection of her place in this community ... as Rachel Sauder, Deacon Simon Sauder's wife.

Decision made, Rachel raised her chin and looked about. Atlee and Ruben were standing in the middle of a group of men, or she would go and thank them. Later she would make Atlee some sassafras tea for his rheumatism and take it to him. He'd saved her today, he and Ruben. Sometimes Ruben really surprised her.

Mom was nowhere to be seen, Esther either; she must have taken Mom home. Rachel was uncomfortable all of a sudden, and remote. But to leave, she must walk past everyone.

Well, if she must, she must.

She took a breath, rehearsed a few sorry excuses, and prepared to jostle her way through the crowd. Focusing on the outside door, she began the long trek through the Mast house. But she needn't have worried. When her neighbors saw her coming, they parted before her like the Red Sea before Moses.

The Deacon and his wife had just aired their pitiful life before the world. Were there a place for her to hide, she would go. Lately, she'd wanted to hide more and more often.

She knew she must face everyone at some point, head up, eye to eye. And she would. But not today.

Jacob met her halfway and took her arm, sheltering her and guiding her at the same time.

She was coming with him, his look said. He wasn't taking no for an answer. Denial did not come to her mind. Gratitude, relief came. Outside, he helped her into his buggy. "Let's get out of here." He slapped the reins. "Get up, Caliope."

"My wagon. Gadfly," she said, her sense of responsibility almost as strong as her dread of Simon's reproach if something should happen to them.

"Datt said he would have Simon take them."

She nodded. "Where are we going?"

Far, far away, Jacob thought. Forever. It frightened him that his need to run away with Rachel, at this moment, was stronger than his need to breathe. "Will the children be all right at Fannie's for a while if we don't go right back? I mean, will Fan mind?"

"They'll be stuffed with raisin pie," Rachel said, "but other than that, they'll be fine and she won't mind. She likes babies."

He searched her face. "You do too," he said, almost afraid of what he would see, but her eyes were vacant, unreadable, as if she'd closed that window to her soul usually open to him. "It's a good thing."

She looked at her hands. "Yes."

Jacob's disappointment cut sharper than a sickle through parched wheat. But he would not let her know how badly he needed her to look at him, to open her heart to him. Why was she shutting him out, now of all times?

He covered her trembling hands with one of his.

She grasped his fingers, hard.

He ached to ask the question burning in his brain. *Who is your child's father?*

After two years of barrenness, why would she conceive now? And yet, he knew couples who'd conceived a child after years of marriage, and then several more. This could be such a case.

Because of Simon's abuse, disturbing pictures came to his mind—of her being frightened and forced to submit. "Was he more caring of you when . . ." For the life of him, Jacob could not refer to them as making love. He looked back at the road, cleared his throat. "In bed, was he at least gentle then?"

"No."

Jacob turned so sharply, he sent the buggy into a stand of walnut trees. Pulling Caliope up short, he stopped and stared at her. "The day you married, when Simon came to you for the first time as a husband, he was loving that night at least? Tell me yes, please."

Rachel closed her eyes. "Only one man has ever taken me in love," she said, revealing a deep inner regret that nearly broke him.

Fear clawed at him, remorse hammered in his head. From where did her regret stem? Did she grieve over their night together, because his gentleness had revealed Simon's lack of it? Because she knew now what could be?

He reached for her and pulled her blessedly close. "If sorrow is your legacy from our loving, I will never forgive myself," he said into her hair.

With Jacob holding her, offering succor, Rachel could

not keep from weeping. She wept over the events of the morning, over Simon's obsession to break her. She wept in anger at herself for succumbing to his goading and baring her marked soul.

She wept for her mistake of a marriage. For herself and for Jacob . . . alone, but together. So close, yet so far apart. For their bittersweet love. For the child she carried with joy, yet with sorrow, because she could never give him the life she wished for him.

Jacob kissed her brow, kissed the tears from her eyes. He slid his hand from her face, to her neck, across her breasts, and down to her abdomen. His touch spoke more of comfort than desire, and yet, she ached.

She looked at the man she loved. *Hold this child in your hands and in your heart. Love him as I do. He will need you, so he can grow up to be a good man. Like you.* He absorbed her with his look, his pain her own, and she reveled in the oneness.

"This child beneath my hand and your heart," Jacob said. "Was he conceived in love, Rachel?" His voice broke with the question.

Her answer could change his life—many lives. Lord forgive her, she wanted to give him what he sought, no matter the consequences. But she could not, she must think of her child.

She pulled from his arms. "Take me home. No. Take me to get Aaron and Emma. I don't want them stuffed with raisin pie."

As he silently urged the horse forward, disappointment was etched on Jacob's face in sharp angles, and Rachel wanted to weep for hurting him.

He sighed. "They won't vote against your newspaper, Mudpie. Ruben and Atlee did a wonderful job of defending you."

"Which cannot be said for how I defended myself."

"Simon gained nothing by taking you before the Elders, except to bar himself from respect over his impending fatherhood. Only a self-centered man would not notice the changes in his wife's cycle or her body. He has, in all but deed, shot himself in the foot. Would that I could shoot the other."

Jacob had not been so vengeful before he left. "Did you know, without being told, that your wife was carrying?" Rachel asked, surprised at how her question seemed to affect Jacob.

"No, Mudpie. Because I never had a wife. I only found out about Emma and Aaron eight months ago, and only then by accident."

"Jacob. They are nearly three years old."

"Yes," he said with regret. "They are, and since their mother died at their birth, that makes me her killer."

Rachel was too stunned to speak.

Jacob shook his head. "For the life of me, I don't understand why God saw fit to give me Emma and Aaron. For I do not deserve such a reward."

"Are . . . are they your only children?"

"I think so. I tried to find out after I knew about them."

"How many women did you . . . did you . . . see to find out?"

"Several."

"Several is three, Jacob."

"More than several, then."

"Twenty? A hundred?"

Jacob took her hand. God help her, she needed his touch so badly, she brought it to her heart.

"Hush, love," he whispered. "Are you angry that I am such a sinner? Or that I have known, in the Biblical sense, a dozen women?"

"A dozen! You made love to a dozen women—"

"No! I have only ever made love to one. And if you do not know who she is, then I do not know you."

Rachel bowed her head and swallowed. "Thank you," she said. "I have only ever made love with you too."

"I know," he said. "But do you forgive me?"

"It is not for me to forgive, Jacob."

"There is more chance of your forgiveness, Rachel. Think about it. Please."

She nodded, but her heart was breaking. "Let's go get the children."

Caliope had stopped to munch grass, and neither of them had noticed. Jacob snapped the reins and the horse trotted on.

As they neared Fannie's house, a chill ran up Rachel's spine and it had nothing to do with Jacob's revelation. At the sound of Emma's crying, she pulled her shawl tight.

Fannie came out to the porch, Aaron clutching her skirt, Emma shrieking in her arms. Before Jacob could stop, Rachel made to jump from the buggy.

"Rachel!" he shouted.

The word conveyed such command, she sat.

"Mein Gott. Have a care for such foolishness. You could fall. 'Tis not only yourself you would injure if you did."

His words surprised her. She'd forgotten about the baby just then, and she was ashamed. "I wanted to get Emma. Her crying is . . . different."

"I know. I will drive you to the porch, and when I stop, you may get down. Safely."

"Yes, Jacob."

"Thank you for thinking of Emma before yourself. 'Twas not selfish. I know. But if you do not take proper care of yourself, I will have to see that you do. We've another babe to consider now, along with the two of them."

Jacob would love this child as much as he loved Emma and Aaron, no matter the father, which made Rachel realize that he must have been driven by deep pain to commit such transgressions.

"Whoa, Caliope. Shh. Whoa." Caliope slowed and raised his head, once, twice, before he settled to a stop.

Jacob came around to help her. "You may get down now."

"It is not your fault their mother died," Rachel said as he swung her down. "She forgives you. I do too."

Jacob nodded once and turned to hide the sheen that had come to his eyes.

Up close, the red of Emma's cheeks were as frightening as her sobs. She raised her arms to Rachel, but once in her arms, she was restless and uncomfortable. After Jacob hitched Caliope and came up the steps, she wanted Papop. No sooner did she settle with him than she wanted Momly again.

Fannie was beside-herself upset. "She has been like this all morning. Nothing I gave her helped. She vomited everything, even clover-honey water."

Rachel fought the squirming girl to press her lips to Emma's small forehead to test her temperature. "She has fever."

Jacob lifted Aaron when Rachel took Emma back again.

"Emma sick," he said in a worried tone.

"We'll make her better, son."

"Let's take her home where I can brew a tea for her," Rachel said. "You did good, Fannie."

Rachel had Emma in the buggy before Jacob left the porch.

"Thank you, Fan," Jacob said. "Emma will be fine. Better they stayed with you."

"Is Rachel all right? Will she keep her newspaper?"

"Rachel will be fine. We do not know yet about the newspaper. Right now, it is Emma we must worry about."

An hour later, Emma's fever had climbed higher, but

Emma, to Rachel's and Jacob's concern, became more quiet.

When Rachel went down to make sweetened oatmeal water and consult her Grandmother Sarah's book of remedies, her father and Simon came into the kitchen.

"Rachel, can we talk?" her father asked.

"I don't have time, Pop. Emma is sick."

Aaron came down the stairs. "Momly, Emma sick. Emma cry." He pushed his face into her skirt. Emma's crying was distressing them all.

"Rachel? You have Aaron?" Jacob called from the top of the stairs.

"Yes, Jacob."

"Can you come up here? Emma's all-over-red now, some kind of rash, I think."

Rachel took the oatmeal water off the burner, looked about the kitchen, picked up the yarrow tea she'd made earlier, then *Grossmutter's* remedy book. But Aaron was still clinging to her, so she put everything down to lift him.

Her father placed his hand on her arm. "A rash could be catching. No need for the both of them to be sick. We'll take him. You go up. Don't worry about Aaron until Emma is well. He will be fine."

Her father lifted Aaron into his arms and kissed his cheek. "Shh, little one. Come, Simon, drive me."

Rachel knew it was a measure of Aaron's distress just then that he did not seek his Unkabear's arms.

Simon gave her a searching look. "Datt has gone to visit his sister down Briar Patch Road. He won't be back for a few days. Jacob and I will have to do the chores by ourselves."

Her father swore, a rare occurrence "You will do the chores by yourself for as long as need be."

Ruddy color stained Simon's cheeks.

"Tell Jacob to tend his daughter and not to worry about

the farm," her father said. "I will send Esther tomorrow to see if you need anything."

"Thanks, Pop." She started up the stairs, but her father's call stopped her.

"I almost forgot. The Elders are praying over their decision about your newspaper. We will meet tomorrow to discuss it."

Rachel sighed. "Right now, the only thing that matters is getting Emma well."

Simon pondered his wife's words as he climbed into his buggy to bring the Bishop home. So gentle to her father. So tender to the girl. Little did she care for his anguish. He wanted a decision about the press. Now. Today. A decision calling for its destruction. It was the only way.

But none of the Elders liked the idea. They could not even come to a lesser decision among them. His father-in-law had decided to wait and pray over it. Foolish man.

Each Elder had a different idea of what should be done. Things did not look good. Preacher Swartzentruber thought Rachel should keep the press and continue to print her foolish newspaper. Preacher King thought the printing of the newspaper should be given over to a man. The Bishop, clearly torn, did not want to look as if he sided with his daughter. But to give him his due, neither did he wish to make a decision harmful to the people of his district.

Simon sighed. He would like to speak to the Preachers alone. But such a move would be seen as going against his Bishop. He must be careful if he wished to be Bishop himself one day.

Once his father-in-law and nephew were settled, Simon

flicked Gadfly's reins. At least he had made his point today.
Everyone in the district knew Rachel's failings now. Despite
the way things looked after the hearing, she would no
longer be so highly valued in the community. Soon perhaps, they would no longer wish to read her newspaper.

Now that Rachel expected a baby, she would not have
time for such foolishness as a newspaper. Simon shook his
head. A baby. He was not certain how he felt about that
now. He'd always wanted children. It was God's plan that
man bring forth children to glorify His name.

But children bothered him sometimes. Even this nephew
of his, who sat quietly on the Bishop's knee, disturbed him.
Simon didn't imagine there was much to raising a boy.
Rachel would handle most of it, as was her duty. As father,
and head of the house, he would be required to influence
and mold a son in his image.

Simon nodded. Put that way, fatherhood sounded agree-
able enough.

Perhaps Rachel would want more children. Once Jacob
had a wife to give his attention to, Rachel would be free
to return to his bed where she belonged. He would give
her more babies. Then her time would be limited, and if
something happened to the press . . .

Simon smiled. With a large family to tend, for Rachel
to hand-copy her paper would be impossible.

When the Bishop cleared his throat, Simon was almost
surprised to find him there. The man frowned. "Mrs. Zook
is having a bad day. This morning did not help."

Simon did not understand his exasperation.

"I need to get home quickly," the Bishop snapped.

With a flick of the reins, Gadfly clip-clopped toward the
Zook farm with new vigor.

Simon decided that Esther would likely care for the boy

until the girl got better and Rachel was free to tend both of them again.

At the Zook farm, Bishop Zook got out of the buggy and turned away without as much as a good-day. Simon thought he was rude; then Aaron tugged on his beard. "Wait," Simon called. "You forgot the boy."

The Bishop turned with a frown and marched back. "That boy is your nephew. His name is Aaron. Take care of him until his sister is better. Your skill as a husband leaves much to be desired; see if you can learn to be a father before it is too late."

"My skill . . ." Simon stopped, speechless.

"As your Bishop, Deacon Sauder, I remind you we are told to 'Preach the gospel always, and if necessary, use words.' Your actions and words in the past, and especially today, have brought forth pain and bitterness—neither the intent of the gospel. See if you can do better with the task before you. Remember, what you do today, you sleep with tonight."

Simon sat, stunned for the second time that day. He looked at his nephew. "The least he could have done was invite us to the noon meal."

The boy looked back wide-eyed. His nephew. His. Smiling. Not alarming at all. Aaron.

Aaron climbed into his lap and took the reins from his hand. "Unkabear?"

Simon put his arm around the boy and pulled him close.

Aaron hugged him hard.

Simon did not know what to make of it. No one that he could remember had ever embraced him before.

Uncomfortable, Simon pulled away.

Aaron's smile, his hands on the reins, said he anticipated learning buggy driving. How long, Simon wondered, since anyone had looked at him with trust?

How long before this one turned on him too? He shrugged. No matter. It would happen. Eventually.

What was different about this child, this small person, that he should want this uncle's company, when most people seemed to dislike him?

Simon frowned, for there was no answer to be had. "What am I going to do with you?"

"Play?"

"I don't play."

Aaron giggled. "Yup!" He flicked the reins to get Gadfly going.

And go Gadfly did.

Emma lay unmoving in her crib.

"Where's Aaron," Jacob asked, looking up from his perusal of Emma's tummy with a similar concerned look over his son's absence.

"Safe," Rachel replied, hanging Emma's dress and apron over the hook on the wall near her cape and bonnet. "Pop took him home. He said not to worry about Aaron or the farm."

"Look at her, Mudpie, red as a beet and hot as a bake oven. So helpless. I don't know which is worse, when she's quiet like this or when she's screaming." He stroked Emma's brow. "Does it hurt anywhere, Pumpkin? Tell Papop."

Emma looked pitifully up at him.

Rachel handed Jacob the tea. "See if you can get her to sip this. I'll go strain the oatmeal. Sweet oatmeal water is good for measles and such."

"You think that's what this is?"

Rachel sighed. "I wish I knew." She bent over the crib railing to kiss Emma's cheek. "How do you feel, sweetheart?"

"Momly?" Emma whimpered.

"Drink for Pa-pop, will you? I'll be right back."

The tear that slipped down the small parched cheek was like a knife to Rachel's heart.

Jacob looked up, his face a mask of fear.

"What is it?" Rachel asked.

"I just remembered that Anna was like this, before . . . before . . ."

Rachel lowered herself to the chair, her legs shaking too much to hold her.

Jacob stared at her for a minute, his eyes wide with terror. Then he took Emma from her crib and held her as if he would never let her go.

"Tell me everything you remember, Jacob."

"I have only a five-year-old's memories."

"Tell me anyway."

He nodded, almost relieved, and closed his eyes, patting Emma's back. "Anna cried for long stretches, then she'd get so quiet. All the adults, even me . . . we waited and watched her, especially when she was quiet, for something to happen."

Jacob opened his eyes, shaking his head. "It went on for hours. She had a rash like this one, though it seemed redder to me. I remember Mom wringing her hands and saying Anna was hotter. That didn't make sense to me, because it was January, you know."

Rachel nodded. "What else?"

Tears ran down his face. He kissed Emma's forehead. "Get better for Pa-pop, will you?" he said. "Oh, Rach," he sobbed. "Two years I didn't know them and now . . ."

He rocked Emma in his arms while he walked. "Anna had . . . fits. I don't know. Her whole body started jerking and Mom screamed something awful. I was so scared, I ran out to the barn and hid in the loft. I stayed three, maybe four hours, hardly feeling the cold. Then Datt came to tell me. . . ." Jacob swallowed. "God took Emma. . . ." He gasped. "I mean Anna!" He sobbed again, hugging Emma.

"I remember Datt's exact words," he said after a long silence. " 'Jacob,' he said, "God has taken our Anna home to heaven.' "

Soul-deep fear traced Jacob's features. Rachel stood and put her arms around him.

"Maybe girl twins in this family are not . . . as strong," Jacob said. "Maybe . . ."

Rachel stepped away, her mind working again. "No more warm tea," she said, feeling a surge of hope. "Anna convulsed from the high fever, so we have to cool her down. *Grossmutter* wrote about it in her remedy book. People used to laugh at her, but she thought cooling a fevered body would bring down the fever. She was a smart woman, Jacob, Grandmother Sarah. I want to try cooling Emma. What do you—"

"Anything, Rach. I'll try anything. Make Emma better. Please."

Jacob's trust frightened her. Lord, please help me live up to such confidence, Rachel prayed. "Bring the copper tub up here, Jacob, and fill it with cool water." He searched her face for a minute, but he set off to comply.

They gave Emma cool oatmeal water, instead of warm. Over the next few hours, they sponged her with cool water, then wrapped her in blankets against the chill. Still the fever kept rising.

Toward evening, Emma's eyes began to roll and her body to spasm, so they put her in the tub until her body calmed and she breathed more easily. They kept her there until she shuddered with cold; then they took her out and wrapped her in towels.

Rachel took her to the rocker before the fire.

Jacob knelt before them. "Which is best, do you think? The warmth from the fire, or the cold water?"

"I don't know. I just don't know."

Jacob put his lips to Emma's forehead. "She's cooler. Let's keep her like this for now. If she starts to . . . shake . . . again, we'll put her back in the water. She stopped shaking when we did it, Rach. It worked."

His face changed as he seemed to look inward at what must be a grim sight. "I remember hearing during Anna's funeral that when the spasms finally stopped, she was gone. But Emma is still with us."

"She'll be all right, Jacob."

Hope shone from his eyes. "Promise, Mudpie." He examined her face for long moments, and his hope seemed to fade. "You think this is God's judgment on us?"

Rachel had wondered herself if this was their punishment, and yet . . . "For what sin of your parents do you think God took Anna?"

Jacob lay his head on her knees, Emma's hand in his. "Thank you," he said.

Rachel put her lips to Emma's forehead, her hand on Jacob's shoulder, and she prayed.

Four more times before midnight, the convulsions wracked Emma. Four more times, they put her in the tub of cool water.

Sometimes Jacob thought the night would never end. Then, fearing what morning might bring, he prayed it never would.

Emma roused around one. After making her thirst known, she drank every drop of oatmeal water. Rachel had to slow her down, she was so greedy. Jacob chuckled at her chubby little fingers grasping the cup when Rachel would take it from her. He thought he'd never seen such a beautiful sight. Her rash was worse, but her fever was lower.

She received the drink so well, Rachel warmed the oatmeal and fed her some. Her hunger gave them further reason to hope.

But before long, she vomited everything in her stomach, over herself and both of them. Rachel washed and changed her and put her in her crib.

"Clean and sweet-smelling again," Jacob pronounced as he kissed his daughter's fingers. "And the fever down a bit too."

Rachel examined her dress, then Jacob's pants. "At least one of us is sweet-smelling."

"Go wash up and get into your nightgown. Try to sleep. I'll call you if I need you, I promise."

Rachel nodded and left.

Twenty minutes later she came to stand beside him near the crib. "How is she?"

"Better." He put one arm around Rachel's shoulder and brought her close until their foreheads touched. "Thank you."

"Wasn't me who did it."

"Already thanked Him, and considering we haven't spoken in a while, He must have been surprised. Thought you agreed to sleep."

"As if I could."

Rachel's beauty was as open and natural as her love. An age-softened, tawny wool robe covered her white cotton nightgown, a rebellious ruffle peeking out at the neck. He touched it. "You add that since you moved from Simon's room?"

Her eyes sparkled. "Ya."

He shook his head. "Daring."

She nodded. Kapp off, her curls hung down her back

like rich burgundy velvet. Simon's cruel work, hidden by the thickness of the rest, showed hardly at all now. Still, scars from that night remained in both of them.

Annoyed, Emma murmured Aaron's name in her sleep.

Jacob looked at Rachel and smiled. "Ach," he said, touching Emma's forehead once more. "She is better."

"Ya, if she's ready to bean him, like normal."

Rachel's presence in his bedroom, all warm and ready for sleep, was like a dream. He slid his hands over her abdomen. "Go and get some sleep. There's another babe needs tending here. I want you both healthy."

She shook her head. "I can't leave. Don't ask me to."

He lifted her in his arms, making her gasp in surprise, and carried her to his bed. He threw back the quilt and placed her dead center, facing both cribs. "Can you see her?"

"Ya," she said, not turning around, but he could hear the smile in her voice.

"Good. Stay there then, and watch her."

He sat in the rocker for about an hour, his gaze moving from one of his girls to the other. Funny, he thought, how love could both fill and break your heart.

When they both slept deeply, Jacob slid into bed behind Rachel and put his arm around her.

She turned to him. "Jacob?"

He savored the moment. In her sleep-filled daze, he was the one she expected to find holding her, into whose embrace she turned willingly. "I just want to hold you and our child for a bit," he said.

She stiffened. "No, Jacob."

"No? Well, if you don't need to be held, I think our child does."

"I did not say it was ours."

"No, you did not. But I wish you would."

"Even if I do not know?"

Her words cut him. "Do you not? I suppose it is possible. He came to you nightly, then, even up to the night before he . . . hurt you last."

"I've a need to hit you for saying that, yet I do not know why it should be so."

"Neither do I. Well?"

"This child is my child, Jacob. And I am married to Simon, therefore Simon is my child's father."

"This is not what I wish to hear, Mudpie."

"I'm sorry."

He felt her tears as they slipped from her cheek onto his shirt, and tightened his hold. "No, I'm sorry. Though it might break me, I promise I will never ask you again. I also promise that I will always be here for you and this baby. I love you both. Never forget it."

"There is your answer, Jacob."

"What?"

"You will love this baby, no matter the father. I thought about that this afternoon in the buggy, when you worried about me, for the baby's sake—"

"For your sake."

She held tighter. "Do you think the same could be said of Simon? That he will love this baby, no matter the father?"

"Oh, Lord," Jacob whispered. "Heaven help us."

Rachel closed her eyes. "All of us." After a minute, she pulled away from him. "We should not be like this, in each other's arms. No matter how peaceful and wonderful it feels after our frightful day."

"Your baby needs to be held, Rach. Be quiet and let me hold you both. Sleep. Too soon it will be morning and the world will intrude. Emma could wake at any time, though she is cooler and sleeping well. If you can't sleep, just close your eyes for a bit. I'll keep vigil."

Rachel sighed and calmed. "I won't be able to sleep. But I'll close my eyes just to shut you up."

The last thing she remembered was his chuckle.

The next was her father calling her name.

Rachel opened her eyes.

Her father stood at the foot of Jacob's bed, a frown on his face. "Judgment has been passed, Daughter."

Chapter Eleven

Caught.

Rachel sat up, heart pounding, warmth infusing her.

Caught. In bed with Jacob.

Then she saw him. Jacob. Asleep in the rocker, Emma in his arms.

Her senses returned; she remembered to breathe.

Still, this did not look good, her sleeping in the bed of a man not her husband.

Jacob yawned, opened his eyes, and saw her father. "Bishop Zook." He stood, put Emma down, and ran his hand through his hair. "Rachel refused to leave Emma's side last night," he explained. "For the sake of her own babe, I made her lie down and rest."

Her father nodded. Rachel could not read him, but of approval there seemed no sign. This was, perhaps, one instance where he could not give her his look that said, "Nothing you ever do will disappoint me." And for such a loss, Rachel grieved.

She rose, glad she was still wearing her robe, and stood awkwardly, facing the tall, commanding man who had given her life.

When he opened his arms, she stepped joyfully in, his big heart beating under her ear. This reminded her of every childhood fear he'd calmed. How she wished he were not Bishop, so she could confide in him now, without ruining all their lives.

He squeezed once and loosened his hold. "About the newspaper—"

"Bishop Zook? Where is Aaron?" Jacob asked. "I thought he was with you."

"I did not keep him last night. Simon did."

"Simon!"

"Not Simon," Rachel said.

"Stay with Emma," Jacob said as he left the room.

Rachel shook her head, rather than answer the question in her father's eyes. If Simon frightened Aaron the way he'd frightened her . . . "Oh, Pop. How could you?"

Emma roused when Rachel touched her forehead. Rachel lifted and hugged her. Then she took her downstairs, her pop behind her. In the kitchen, she could tell by the sun that it was early yet. At least eight, if the Elders' meeting had already taken place. "Pop, didn't Simon vote with the Elders? Wasn't Aaron with him?"

"They did not want him voting."

Rachel entered Simon's house from the kitchen. "He won't like that. When was the last time you saw him and Aaron?"

"Yesterday noon."

Rachel shook her head as she climbed the stairs to the bedrooms. "I thought you were taking him, Pop."

"I would have if I knew how upset you would be."

Simon's room was empty, the bed made, everything neat. "I didn't want you to worry about the boy," he said, "so

I let you think I was taking him. But Simon needs to learn—"

"You don't know what you did, Pop. Aaron might have been frightened."

Her father scowled.

Back in the main house, in the middle of the best room, her father put his hands on her shoulders to turn her around, and she tried to hide her fear when she looked up at him.

"You're frightened, both you and Jacob. You can tell your pop why, Rachel. You know you can tell me anything."

But she couldn't. There were times when having a Bishop for a father didn't help, and this was one of them. She shook her head as she stepped from his hold and went outside. "You don't know Simon, that's all."

He followed her to the barn. "I am beginning to learn more than I want to. And it's not making me happy." In the barn all was peaceful. The milked cows had been led to pasture. There was plenty of fodder. Everything tended as usual.

Emma pointed out the window. "Aaron," she said.

Near the open doorway of the tobacco shed, across the sweeping back yard, Simon examined a tobacco plant to test its moisture. Aaron, hale and hearty, hid beneath a leaf bigger than him. He kept peeking out to get Simon's attention, and Rachel sighed with relief.

Jacob strode toward them, but they didn't see him coming.

She and her father followed at a distance.

Jacob stopped when Simon "found" Aaron by catching him up in his arms and throwing him into the air with a bark of laughter.

Rachel stopped too. "I never heard Simon laugh before."

Her father threw her a look with as much shock as

disgust. "Why did you marry him, then?" he snapped, but
he did not break stride for an answer. He passed Jacob
and made for Simon.

Jacob stayed where he was.

When Simon turned at the sound of her father's
approach and saw all of them, his habitual scowl returned.
Aaron got put down with a firm move, indicating their
game's end, and he began to cry. Spotting his father, he
ran.

Rachel could only imagine Simon's mortification at
being caught laughing and playing when he chided her
for it so often.

A heated discussion between Simon and her father took
place, and though Rachel could not hear, their postures
and scowls held her in place.

When Ezra Zook faced his son-in-law, he shook with an
anger that had been simmering for years, but had come
near to boiling since yesterday. He took a minute to pray
for composure before he began. "I am happy to see the
boy is all right," Ezra said. "After I spoke to your father
this morning, I needed to make certain."

Simon straightened in affronted dignity. "Of course he
is all right. Why would he not be? Was you who gave him
into my keeping."

"More fool me. But I did not truly know you until today,
though I should have. When you shamed your wife for
her barrenness before the entire congregation, I tried to
believe your higher goal was your mission in the Church,
and I held my tongue.

"When I learned some weeks back of your deceit in
separating Rachel and Jacob before your marriage, no
matter that I grieved for my daughter, I hoped your union
was part of God's plan.

"But when you brought her before everyone for so foolish a reason as publishing a newspaper . . . When your true purpose was to humiliate her once again . . . Bah, what is the use? I will be plain.

"As I reflect on these things, on you, 'Deacon' Sauder, I am disquieted. I have watched you cover self-interest with piety, shroud condemnation in sermon. I even saw a feigned, deceitful regard for the community. For those reasons, I do not quibble to tell you, for the sake of our brothers and sisters, I am uneasy with your membership in the Church, never mind with your performance as Deacon."

Simon's lips tightened and his stance stiffened.

"As Deacon, your admonitions at service are often harsh, though sometimes that is necessary. You spend less time than I would wish looking after our needy members, but I understand the needs of a farm. However, the role you perform best, and with great relish, is the finding of transgressors. But the one you have found most often—and pursued doggedly—is your own wife.

"My daughter is no transgressor!"

Ezra knew his words mattered less because of his status as father-in-law than Bishop, which made him angrier. "Yesterday, when I gave Aaron into your care, I did not worry for his physical well-being. That sin I did not expect of you . . . not until I listened to your father this morning tell me, with great sadness, of my daughter's bruises and her fear of you."

Shock whitened Simon's features to such a degree that Ezra thought the man might lose consciousness. But as Rachel's father and as Bishop, he needed to go on. This business was too serious to sugarcoat.

"Because of what you did to Rachel, and how you hurt your father in the process, were I a man given to rage, I would. . . . But it is not our way. Instead—may I be granted such grace—I must forgive you. But I will not, I cannot, until I see that Rachel does.

"You will change your ways. You will show your wife, and all of us, that you honor and respect her. I will know if she forgives you, because she will be happy again. And I can tell when my Rachel is happy, so there will be no fooling me on this. And I pray this will happen before the child is born.

"The sins you commit against Rachel, you commit against your Maker. If you cannot care for one of His daughters, you cannot care for any of His children, especially not their souls. Change your ways, Deacon Sauder. If you do not, I will bring you before the district for excommunication. Since I do not see you right now as a good man, much less a fit husband—or Church Deacon—you will not preach again until I say so."

"Everyone will know."

"Everyone knows how you treat your wife. What is the difference? One lowers you in their respect as much as the other."

"All the Elders must decide such a thing. Not just you."

Ezra laughed. "You wish me to bring this before them? I can tell you, there would be no chance for you. They are not pleased with you. They are angry and embarrassed you forced them and their families to witness your personal rage against your wife. And now they are compelled to make a decision none wished or needed to make. Not one feels it is his right. Mildly put, they are not kindly disposed toward you right now."

Ezra let his words settle. "Well? Shall we put it to them?"

"No."

"No. Good. We'll put it to them instead if you do *not* change your ways, shall we?"

Simon nodded.

If he could turn any more purple, he might expire,

the Bishop thought, and begged forgiveness for wishing it would happen. "It is time for you to begin," he said before he left.

As he came away, Rachel could see her father was struggling with his anger, but Simon passed silently by him and reached Jacob first.

Rachel stepped up to them as Simon approached.

Jacob hugged Aaron protectively. "What did you do to him?" he asked.

Simon sighed and clenched his fists, his jaw rigid. "I did nothing."

"Where have you been since yesterday morning?"

"I went—"

"Have you kept Aaron with you since then?"

"Of course I have!"

"Tell me what you did then."

"Why?"

"I want to know what my boy did and saw, and experienced. Tell me now or I'll—"

Aaron opened his arms to Simon. "Unkabear?"

Rachel was glad, though Simon shook his head, that he took Aaron anyway, because the call had been a plea. And when Aaron closed his arms around Simon's neck, Simon allowed it!

Her husband's actions in the past half hour had almost made Rachel dizzy.

"We went to market down Cattail Crossing," Simon said.

Aaron giggled. "Yup!"

"Oh, yes. I forgot. Aaron learned to drive the buggy."

"Honest to heaven, Simon, if something had happened to—"

"Do not be stupid, Jacob. We drove so slow, you could have shoed the horse as we went. He sat on my lap the whole time and I held him good."

"After that?" her father prodded. "Did you feed the boy the noon meal, and then supper?"

"Breakfast this morning even." Simon's tone was sarcastic, and Rachel had to swallow an urge to giggle.

"Where?" Jacob asked.

Simon sighed again. "We ate the noon meal with Sarah Yoder, up Applebutter Hill. Her Abram is sick; I went to visit him. After we milked the cows here, we ate supper with Joel Schrock and Gerta. Oh. Aaron has a lamb."

"Pokey!" Aaron scrambled down from Simon's arms and ran to Rachel, then stopped to look at Emma and smiled. "Emma not sick." He took Rachel's hand and tugged. "Come see Pokey, Momly."

They fetched and brought the lamb to show Jacob.

Black with a white face, Pokey had a tender caretaker in Aaron, who cherished him almost as much as he cherished the uncle who'd purchased him.

Jacob would have none of the emotion. "Where did Aaron sleep last night?"

"Where did *you* sleep last night?" Simon countered.

Jacob and Simon stepped toward each other.

Rachel's father practically growled, which stopped them in their tracks, and surprised the daylights out of her.

Simon sighed. "He slept in my bed. We only went to the outhouse four times. Six if you count before bed and when we got up this morning."

Rachel could not help laugh at what Aaron had put Simon through. "He never wakes up during the night."

"In a strange bed, without Emma nearby, would make the difference," Jacob said. "Thank you for taking care of Aaron, Simon. I will pay you for the lamb."

Simon scowled as only he could do. "The lamb is a gift. No repayment is necessary. The girl is better?"

"The girl is Emma!" her father shouted, this rare fit of anger so unusual for him.

"And Emma needs a bit of breakfast and to go back to sleep," Rachel said to bring a measure of calm to the conversation. "There is still her rash to watch. And we need to keep Aaron away from her. I worry it is catching, and last night was frightening. I do not want Aaron sick as well."

Jacob looked at Simon as if he were seeing him for the first time. "We will keep him with us . . . while we check and sort the tobacco leaves?"

Simon nodded. "Tobacco's ready."

This first sign of peace between the brothers was tenuous at best, but a beginning. Rachel sighed with relief. Could Jacob and Simon toil peacefully side by side? Could they share the same house, love the same children?

Rachel examined the periwinkle sky. *Help them. Help us all.*

Down the lane came Ruben's buggy. "Hello!" he called, Esther sitting beside him.

When they stopped, Ruben helped Es down and held her arm as she lumbered toward them. Lord, she'd gotten big with that child the past couple of weeks. "Heard the news about the *Chalkboard*," Ruben said.

Jacob and Simon looked as if they questioned the statement as much as Rachel did, but Rachel was afraid to ask.

Her father sighed. "I didn't have a chance to—"

Ruben tapped Emma's nose. "Hello, baby girl. No crinkle-nose for me today?"

Rachel moved some of Emma's dark curls behind her ear. "This baby girl isn't feeling too well."

Ruben kissed Emma's cheek. "Get better, so you can tease me about my stink." He straightened. "Jacob! Congratulations. The Elders decided publishing a newspaper was a man's job, and you're the one they picked."

"What? It's my newspaper, Jacob Sauder. You can't have it."

Jacob shook his head, his look patient. "It is your weariness and worry makes you react so, Mudpie. We are partners, remember? And the *Chalkboard* belongs to the community."

Rachel nodded, her anger dissolved in the face of his sense. "I did not mean to sound selfish. You're right. I am tired."

As a fancy carriage came barreling into the yard, the geese set up a terrible ruckus, mated pairs flying in every direction. "Bishop Zook," the English doctor called. "Your wife has taken a bad turn. You'd best come."

If ever there was a time Jacob wanted to hold Rachel, it was now.

Bishop Zook came from his wife's sickroom and approached his daughters. They rose, along with twenty or so friends who'd come in the past few hours to offer support.

"Your mama is home with the Lord," he said. "He is merciful."

Ruben stepped up to Esther, her self-appointed rock, and she turned into his embrace.

Jacob fisted his hands and willed his feet not to move as Simon went to Rachel. He was pleased that Simon had thought of Rachel first for once. He was. Past time he was there for her, but, oh, how Jacob ached to be the one she leaned on.

Simon seated Rachel, spoke to her for a minute, then brought her a glass of lemonade. After a bit, he came to Jacob. "Come and help me with Zook's milking."

Everyone would take over the Bishop's chores until after his wife's funeral. That Simon was the first to offer made Jacob as confused as he was about everything else these days. Instead of being glad Simon did what he should, Jacob worried over his sudden change.

Rachel and Esther lovingly washed and dressed their mother for her laying-out. They combed her hair and placed her kapp on her head for the last time.

Fannie went to the Sauder house to care for Aaron and Emma. Rachel sat up for the next two nights beside her mother's coffin with Esther and their father. Simon did not stray from her side, except to do chores, his and the Bishop's. Jacob and Levi helped with both.

Aaron and Emma cried for Momly. Jacob spent as much time with them as he could, because they missed Rachel, but after they slept at night, he left them with Levi and returned to the Zook house to keep vigil by Mary Zook's bier, thinking about his own mother.

How protective Mom had always been of him and Anna. He remembered Simon's look—he was three when they were born—when Mom would scream at him for going near them, as if he meant them harm. Sometimes she called them God's special children . . . because He'd saved them when they'd been born too soon, Jacob knew.

He wondered if Simon knew.

What would Mom say about this mess he'd gotten him and Rachel into? Jacob wondered. She would not approve of what happened between them. She would not think him so special now.

He could imagine her telling him to move on with his life, so Rachel and Simon could have theirs. Marriage was sacred and forever to Mom. She would say they needed him gone so they could make their marriage better.

She would be right.

Jacob looked at his brother kneeling in prayer by Mrs. Zook's casket. He seemed determined to change. This death had made a difference in him.

Jacob shook his head. No, that was not right. Simon

had changed before this. His care of Aaron was the first noticeable change. His care of Rachel now, in her sorrow, was another. Would there be more? Would Rachel come to accept Simon again as a wife should? If so, Jacob wondered, would he have the grace to step aside and allow it?

The morning of the funeral, freezing rain lashed the half-mile procession of buggies as they plodded toward the Mud Creek bridge. When they crossed, the bridge's roof gave them respite from ice pinging on buggy roofs, but the echo of their passage was ominous.

Jacob saw the carving on the beam as he passed. "Where will you spend eternity? Heaven or Hell?" To him, the answer was clear . . . unless something changed. Could he redeem himself, and Rachel too, by living his life so as to allow her and Simon to live theirs? He sighed. The question plagued him these days, but the answer, he feared, would not come anytime soon.

The hearse, a one-horse spring wagon, seat pushed forward, carried Mary Zook in a canvas-covered walnut casket to the *Graabhof*, the Amish district cemetery.

As one of the men, including Ruben, who carried the casket to and from the hearse, Jacob stood by the side of the grave. They viewed Mrs. Zook—her husband's black umbrella keeping the rain from her face—one last time before the top half of the hinged coffin covered her for eternity.

Rachel's weeping called to him. Simon whispered to her, held his arm about her, kissed her forehead in comfort. And Jacob's heart clenched. Could he set her free? Could he not?

Each Preacher had spoken at Zook's house before leaving for the cemetery. Simon had waxed particularly eloquent. He'd even said he would not make the sermon long that the weather must be unpleasant for the horses standing in the freezing rain.

Simon surprised Jacob more every day.

The Bishop closed and kissed the coffin, then opened his bible. "Here on earth, discover what you are, what your existence is, and how swiftly flees your span of life from time to eternity. For after you are gone, your deeds will speak louder than when you lived."

With the other pallbearers, Jacob lifted the coffin by a set of straps as supporting crosspieces were removed, then lowered it to its final resting place. Ruben placed boards over the casket, and each pallbearer lifted a shovel and began to fill the grave.

The sound of weeping grew.

Soil hit the wood with mournful thumps, turning swiftly to cold mud. With the grave half filled, they halted for the Bishop to read a last prayer. The men removed their hats, icy stings on their heads and faces going unheeded as they prayed. Then the task of covering the grave was finished, the dirt mounded.

As one, all turned to leave the cemetery for the Zook house and the fellowship meal. On this cold November day, hot coffee and warm raisin pie would be welcomed.

Ruben placed his shovel into the back of the hearse and took Esther's arm as her father accepted condolences from friends.

Esther stumbled, cried out, and grabbed her stomach. "Oh, no. My baby."

Jacob caught her other arm.

Ruben passed out.

"Rachel," Jacob called. "Esther is in labor."

As Rachel ran to Esther, she thought of the saying in Fannie's kitchen. "God will give me nothing today that He and I cannot face together." She put her arm around Es wondering why God thought they could handle this on the heels of their mother's death. A minute ago, she'd doubted her own ability to take another step, much less hold someone up.

Perseverance, it was called.

Forcing herself not to seek out Jacob, she looked at Simon. "Let's take her to our house. Then everyone can go to Pop's as planned."

Simon nodded and supported Es. He was trying. Rachel would too.

An hour later, after searching for a doctor as Ruben had loudly demanded, Jacob came to Rachel's bedroom, where Esther lay in labor and Rachel watched over her.

"The doctor's in New Holland," Jacob told Ruben, who was pacing outside the door.

"Well, find another one!" Ruben shouted.

"She doesn't need a doctor, she has Rachel," Jacob said, coming into the room.

Always, everybody has Rachel, she thought. And who does Rachel have?

She has Simon, she silently answered. But if he was the same Simon as before, he would only turn on her once she was his again.

Jacob she could count on . . . though not according to the vows she'd taken with Simon.

Rachel almost sobbed. Lord, she was too sad and too tired, and too worried about Es, to think about that right now. But she hated how it ate at her.

Jacob offered his hand in support, and Rachel took it. "I don't know what to do," she admitted.

He squeezed her hand. "You can do it."

Emma cried in Esther's arms. Esther crooned to her, stopped to pant, then settled Emma by her side. Fannie, who'd stayed with the twins during the funeral, had gone to help with the fellowship meal at Pop's.

Rachel touched Emma's forehead. "She doesn't feel too good."

Esther's smile became a grimace. "Neither do I."

Rachel took Esther's hand. "For what good I will be, I'm here for you. Promise you'll stay with me when it's my turn."

"Nothing could keep me away."

Jacob stood so close, it was all Rachel could do not to step into his arms and ask him to take this burden from her.

When Esther and Emma seemed settled and drowsy, Rachel stepped from the room, Jacob behind her. "I'll get some cabbage juice," she said. "Maybe it will help settle her stomach. I don't know what else to do."

Ruben followed too, the two men acting like lost puppies.

"You don't know what to do about who?" Ruben asked. "Emma or Esther?"

"Ya," Jacob said. "Whose stomach are you trying to settle? Emma's or Esther's?"

In the middle of the kitchen, Rachel looked from one anxious face to the other. Why did they think she had all the answers? She didn't know anything about children's illnesses or delivering babies. Pregnancy and childbirth had always been a great mystery to her, so unattainable, she thought her problems would all be solved if she could only have a baby of her own.

Now she would. But no problems were solved because of it. More were added.

Delighted and grateful—oh, so very grateful—as she was over her approaching motherhood, as much as she loved this child, her world was more in turmoil than ever.

And they wanted her to solve these frightening problems? Rachel looked through the kitchen window, but she could see nothing save rain sliding down in sheets. Out of control. Like her life.

She began to cry.

By the looks on their faces, she didn't know who she shocked more, Jacob or Ruben. Their astonishment made her laugh.

Frightened by Rachel's changing moods, Jacob took her into his arms. "Go get Emma, will you, Ruben? And bring her downstairs. See if there's anything Es needs while you're at it."

Ruben looked as if he'd been asked to step into the mouth of Hell.

"Just do it," Jacob said. "I can't believe you're afraid of a birth."

Ruben made for the stairs. "A death, you mean."

"If Esther dies, it will be my fault, Jacob," Rachel said. "I don't know how to deliver a baby."

Simon came in, with Aaron by the hand, and stopped short when he saw her in Jacob's arms. She disengaged herself, and Jacob stepped back, waiting for Simon to say something.

But Simon's face showed more sadness than anger, another indication he was changing.

Rachel lifted Aaron. "Give Momly a hug, will you, darling. I'm sad today."

"Don't cry, Momly," Aaron said, patting her back, her kapp, her ear, trying hard to console her. "Momly sad," he said, searching for help from either his uncle or his father.

Simon's look had hardened, and Rachel wasn't certain if it was her in Jacob's arms or Aaron calling her Momly that did it. Could be either, or both.

Jacob turned to go back upstairs, and Rachel missed his presence before he was out of sight.

Simon, his face a mask of caring, came to her. "Are you

crying for your mother?'' he asked. "She's in a better place now, and suffering no longer."

Rachel wondered if she would ever get over being startled when he acted like this. Attempting not to show discomfort when he drew near, she tried to respond openly as he approached. Glad Aaron was between them, she put a hand on Simon's shoulder, touching him, yet holding him at bay. "I haven't been able to think about Mom since this morning." She looked away when she thought she'd cry, saw Jacob watching, then looked at the floor.

For years, she'd refused to let Simon see her cry. But this was different. She turned back to him. "I'm worried Esther will die because I don't know what to do for her."

"I'll pray she doesn't die. But remember, Rachel, it is not in your hands, but God's. Do not raise yourself in importance to such a degree that you think you have dominion over life and death. To do so would be prideful."

Rachel sighed inwardly, almost relieved he was the old Simon still.

Simon hesitated before placing his arm around her. Then Aaron put his arm around Simon's neck pulling him in. They must make quite a family picture, Rachel thought, forcing herself not to pull from his embrace.

"I'll worry about you too when your time comes," Simon said.

"You will?"

He kissed her forehead for the second time that day. "Of course."

Rachel was as skittish over this kiss as she had been at the cemetery. Simon's sudden and unnatural concern bothered her in ways she could not name.

Jacob's step startled them both. "I'll take Aaron to Datt's and keep him there. Simon, you stay with Rachel."

Prickles ran down Rachel's back; heat invaded her limbs. She couldn't do it. Not without Jacob. "No!"

Simon's eyes narrowed. She touched his sleeve. "I need Jacob's help, Simon." She turned to Jacob. "You helped when the twins were born, didn't you, Jacob?"

Jacob wondered what was happening here. He had told her that he wasn't at the twins' birth, but the look in her eyes was desperate, pleading. Was she frightened of Simon even now? "I can—"

"Then I need you here. You've got more experience delivering babies than I do." She turned to Simon. "Please, will you take Aaron to your house and watch him?"

"It's supposed to be our house, you know."

Jacob's fists ached to connect with Simon's jaw for those words.

"I'll take him," Simon said with a sigh, and squeezed her shoulder. "Don't worry. Esther will be fine."

Jacob watched Simon close the door to his house, and sighed with relief.

Ruben came down the stairs like a jackrabbit before a hound, Emma in his arms. "There's blood."

When Rachel swayed, Jacob took her arm, and she leaned into him taking deep breaths. "Dammit, Ruben. You're frightening Rachel."

Ruben shook his head. "Sorry, Mudpie. But I'm not going back. I'm leaving. There's no reason for me to be here."

"There is," Jacob said. "A good one. And you're holding her in your arms."

Ruben took a deep breath himself.

"Aaron can't be with Emma," Jacob said. "So he won't catch whatever she's got. I need to help with Esther and I need you to take Emma to Datt's and keep her there. Aaron is with Simon."

"There's cabbage water in the jar by the stove," Rachel said. "If she drinks that, see if you can get her to eat some cornmeal mush or stewed crackers."

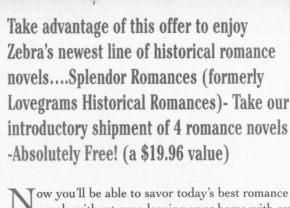

Take advantage of this offer to enjoy Zebra's newest line of historical romance novels....Splendor Romances (formerly Lovegrams Historical Romances)- Take our introductory shipment of 4 romance novels -Absolutely Free! (a $19.96 value)

Now you'll be able to savor today's best romance novels without even leaving your home with our convenient and inexpensive home subscription service. Here's what you get for joining:

- 4 BRAND NEW bestselling Splendor Romances delivered to your doorstep every month
- 20% off every title (or almost $4.00 off) with your home subscription
- A FREE monthly newsletter, *Zebra/Pinnacle Romance News* filled with author interviews, member benefits, book previews and more!
- No risks or obligations...you're free to cancel whenever you wish...no questions asked

To get started with your own home subscription, simply complete and return the card provided. You'll receive your FREE introductory shipment of 4 Splendor Romances and then you'll begin to receive monthly shipments of new Zebra Splendor titles. Each shipment will be yours to examine for 10 days and then if you decide to keep the books, you'll pay the preferred home subscriber's price of just $4.00 per title plus $1.50 shipping and handling. That's $16 for all 4 books plus $1.50 for home delivery! And if you want us to stop sending books, just say the word...it's that simple.

Check out our website at www.kensingtonbooks.com.

4 FREE books are waiting for you!
Just mail in the certificate below!

If the certificate is missing below, write to:
Splendor Romances, Zebra Home Subscription Service, Inc
P.O. Box 5214, Clifton, New Jersey 07015-5214
or call TOLL-FREE 1-888-345-BOOK

FREE BOOK CERTIFICATE

Yes! Please send me 4 Splendor Romances (formerly Zebra Lovegram Historical Romances), ABSOLUTELY FREE! After my introductory shipment, I will be able to preview 4 new Splendor Romances each month FREE for 10 days. Then if I decide to keep them, I will pay the money-saving preferred publisher's price of just $4.00 each... a total of $16.00 plus $1.50 shipping and handling. That's 20% off the regular publisher's price plus $1.50 for shipping and handling. I may return any shipment within 10 days and owe nothing, and I may cancel my subscription at any time. The 4 FREE books will be mine to keep in any case.

Name _____

Address _____ Apt. _____

City _____ State _____ Zip _____

Telephone ( ) _____

Signature _____
(If under 18, parent or guardian must sign.)

Terms and prices subject to change. Orders subject to acceptance by Zebra Home Subscription Service, Inc. .
Zebra Home Subscription Service, Inc. reserves the right to reject or cancel any subscription.

SP1010

SPLENDOR ROMANCES
ZEBRA HOME SUBSCRIPTION SERVICE, INC.
120 BRIGHTON ROAD
P.O. BOX 5214
CLIFTON, NEW JERSEY 07015-5214

AFFIX
STAMP
HERE

"Do I look like a nursemaid?" Ruben groused.

Rachel kissed his cheek. "Thank you for taking care of her. Esther will be fine."

That haunted look returned to Ruben's eyes, but he carried Emma toward the *daudyhaus,* nonetheless, a jar of cabbage water in his shaking hand. The last thing they heard was Emma calling him Boob.

Jacob climbed the stairs beside Rachel, unable to forget the sight of her and Simon embracing. He still didn't trust his brother. But he should try, especially now since Simon had given him reason. He'd been good with Aaron, and just now he'd been better with Rachel.

But how long would it last?

Jacob was worried that his jealousy was coloring his thinking. Should he go away and leave them be, or stay to protect Rachel?

He could howl in frustration.

But somebody else was howling right now. Esther. And he needed to set his mind to delivering this baby.

Rachel touched his arm. "I'm sorry I got you into this Jacob. I . . . I couldn't do it without you."

His frustration evaporated in the face of her need. "As it happened, a girl where Miriam worked went into labor and no one would help, so . . . since I'd delivered calves—"

"Why wouldn't anyone help her?"

"Because she was a dance hall girl, Mudpie, like Miriam."

"Was the baby all right?"

"He was noisy and healthy."

"Oh, Jacob, I'm glad they had you." Her face lit up. "I'm glad I have you. You *have* delivered a baby!"

"Come," Jacob said. "Let's go help Es."

He sent Rach to make pads out of newspaper to put under Esther. He needed a pan for the afterbirth. Some string. She needed direction, someone to take over. And part of him needed her away for a bit, so he could overcome

the part of him that wanted to snatch her up and never
let her go.

Esther's labor progressed at the speed of sap dripping
from a maple tree. She called her dead husband's name
over and over, as if Daniel might hear and come for her.
His name became her litany as her pains came close and
strong.

Still no baby.

After two hours, she called Daniel less often.

Jacob shook his head, checking the baby's progress.
"Rachel, you stand here and see if you can see the head
when it comes." *If you're up there, Daniel, we could use
some help here,* Jacob thought as they changed places.

"I'm afraid, Jacob," Rachel said.

He gave them both courage by taking her into his arms
for a minute. "You up to this? It's not too much in your
condition?"

"I need to help, so Es will be all right. I'll watch, like
you said. What are you going to do?"

"I'm going to feel her stomach to see if I can tell if the
baby's bottom-first. I might need to turn it." *As if he knew
how.* "You all right, Es?"

Her pasty-white face glistening with perspiration, eyes
closed, she didn't answer. He dabbed at the moisture, put
a wet towel on her forehead. "You with me, Es?"

She turned her head away. She was giving up. As Jacob
ran his hand along her stomach, it hardened, rose, held,
then lowered.

Esther's moan was weak, her cry for Daniel weaker still.

Panic filled Rachel's wide eyes. "Is it turned?"

He shook his head. "I wish to God I could tell." The
realization that this was how Miriam had died hit Jacob
hard. Had she called his name the way Es was doing? Until
she'd died?

Jacob held back the sob trying to take over his entire being.

Miriam was lost to him, he reminded himself. Esther was not. And by God, he'd do better by Es. By God he would.

Filled with determination, Jacob placed his hands flat against the top of Esther's belly. When the next contraction came, he pushed.

"Daniel!" Esther screamed.

Rachel's smile dazzled. "I see the head! I see it . . . no, it's gone." Worry replaced happiness.

"That's good. Let's see if the baby can take over from here." Jacob knelt by Esther and took her hand, kissed it. "Es, can you hear me? It's me, Daniel." He saw Rachel's shock, ignored it.

Esther opened her eyes and turned her head as if it was almost too heavy. "You trying to spook me, Jacob?"

He let out his breath. "No, but I would have been spooked if you'd believed me. I would have pretended, though, to get this baby born. Daniel's with you. He's watching and waiting. Don't give up, Es. He left you a great gift. Just like Miriam did me."

"I'm gonna be . . ." A contraction took her, and Esther flowed with it, better than she had been. That was what she needed to keep doing, going with it, instead of away from it. She needed to care about life.

"Did you see the head that time, Mudpie?" he asked.

Rachel nodded with relief. "For a minute."

"Good. We're closer."

"I'm gonna be like you," Esther finished. "All alone to raise a child, with no one to share the joy, or the worry. Isn't it lonely at times, Jacob . . ." She went with another contraction.

"Push, Es."

"I can't, Jacob. I'm tired. Too tired. If God cared, he'd take us both to be with Daniel. It's what I want."

"Dammit, Esther!" Jacob shouted. "Push. For Daniel! For me."

Esther reacted as if she'd been slapped, but when the next contraction came, she pushed with every bit of strength she could gather. And she screamed just as hard.

Rachel screamed too as the new life slipped into her hands. She cried and laughed, holding up a bloody, bawling scrap of humanity. "It's a boy, Es."

"Daniel Jacob," Esther said. "Because you made me do it, Jacob. I needed to do it for Daniel, like you said. For you too."

Rachel placed little Daniel Jacob in Esther's arms, the cowl of birth still on him.

Esther touched her son's cheek as he looked at her with wide, dark eyes. "He's beautiful. I don't know how I'll raise him alone, but I'll manage." Esther smiled. "Guess I have to."

Jacob nodded, clearing his throat of emotion. "Let me have him so Rachel can tie and cut the cord."

Rachel squeaked. "Me? I can't cut into this fleshy thing." She touched the cord and pulled back. "It's alive."

"It won't hurt him."

"Don't make me, Jacob. I need you to do it."

She shouldn't depend on him like this all the time. This was how she had always looked to him for support, for answers . . . for love. She had Simon to look to now . . . for everything.

Esther had no one. And she needed a father for her son.

He needed a mother for his children and a wife for himself.

He could do now for Esther what he could not for Miriam.

He could atone.

And wouldn't it be best, especially for Rachel and Simon, and the baby—for so many of them—if he started fresh?

Jacob tied the string around the cord, then cut above it.

Rachel and Simon needed to make their marriage work. And he needed to let them.

He traded places with Rachel so he could take Esther's hand and prepare her for discomfort. He told Rachel how to deliver the afterbirth, and saw the surprised look on her face when it slid into the pan she held. "I'll bury it later," he said.

Ruben came rushing into the room, his back to the bed. "Couldn't one of you come and tell me what was happening? I was going out of my mind down there!"

"Where's Emma?" Jacob asked.

Ruben did not turn toward him or the bed. "Levi's got her." Ruben looked at the pan of afterbirth and turned white. He grabbed the bureau to keep himself from keeling over, but he almost lost the fight when he looked at the bloody baby Rachel was washing. "Esther?" he asked, voice atremble.

"Esther's fine, Ruben," Rachel said.

A few minutes passed before Ruben could look at Esther. "I'm glad you didn't die, Es."

"I wanted to."

Ruben sat by the bed. "I know how that feels."

"But Esther's strong, Ruben, like all the Zook women. Special. And she's worried about raising this baby alone. I think. . . ." Jacob looked from Esther to Rachel and thought his heart might break.

Both women questioned him with their looks.

He cleared his throat. Dear God, let me do the right thing. He sat on Esther's bed and took her hand. "I'm glad you didn't die too, Es. Feel better about being alive now?"

She nodded. "With such a beautiful baby, how could I not?"

"You did good," Jacob said. "Daniel's grinning down right now. Your mama too."

Silent tears slid down Esther's face. She really was special. Beautiful too, in a different way from Rachel, and different again from Miriam. "Daniel and your mama wouldn't want you to raise Daniel Jacob alone," Jacob said, surprising her. "How about if you don't have to?"

Rachel's look nearly stole his resolve. She knew. She understood what he planned, and he couldn't tell if she approved or not.

By the shock on Ruben's face, he knew too.

Esther, it seemed, was the only one who did not. He kissed her hand. "How about if we raise him together, Es?"

Esther shook her head in confusion. "What?"

"You, me, Aaron, Emma, and Daniel. A family. Marry me, Esther."

For a few silent beats, Jacob thought she might say no. Almost wished she would.

"All right, Jacob. I'll marry you."

Chapter Twelve

The Gutenberg by lamplight cast a bestial shadow across the barn floor. Six kerosene lamps placed on barrels, two atop a scarred old desk, yellowed the paper under Rachel's hand to the color of parchment.

A new editorial for tomorrow's issue of the *Amish Chalkboard* was finished.

Midnight. A new day. A new beginning.

Esther and little Daniel slept peacefully after the ordeal of labor and birth. Emma was spending the night with Levi, Aaron with his Unkabear in the *kinderhaus*.

Unkabear.

Rachel shook her head, wondering again at the surprising difference in her husband. After the hearing over her newspaper, he'd changed. How could that be, considering his cutting, hateful words to her there?

Unkabear.

Could Aaron's innocent, unconditional love have wrought such a difference in his once-hard-edged uncle? If so, it couldn't be just a day and a half of Aaron's company that made the difference. No, it had taken longer than that. Aaron had been breaking down Simon's defenses bit by bit since his very first day here.

But if Simon had returned Aaron's regard before yesterday, no one had seen it . . . yet Rachel couldn't help think Simon had wanted to return it. Perhaps he'd been afraid, or he hadn't known how. More than likely, he had fought the urge. Knowing Simon, she realized he would have seen it as weak.

However it had come about, Simon was suddenly and surprisingly the same man who'd comforted her four years before. As she'd sat beside her mother's coffin, Simon next to her, his quiet support had reminded her why she'd married him.

But support was not love. His caring had been false four years before. It could be false now. Before they wed, to win her, he'd been pleasant and caring. He'd supported her through losing Jacob. All to win her. But for the life of her, she couldn't understand why he wanted her. He disliked her in every way. She didn't think he loved her, not even at the beginning, not even with a love as weak and brief as hers had been for him.

The answer to why he married her had to come down to the one fact that had colored Simon's entire life; he wanted what belonged to Jacob.

So why pretend now? She no longer belonged to Jacob. Simon no longer needed to win her. They were already married and would be for the rest of their lives.

Why would he pretend now?

The question plagued her.

Perhaps there was no pretense. Perhaps Simon cared for her at last.

The new question was, could she find it in her heart to care for him again? After everything they'd been through, would it be possible for them to make their marriage work? Couples with a good marriage were the best parents. And for this baby . . . She placed her hand on the child's haven. For this child, she was willing to do anything, even become a wife to Simon again. Her babe would need a good home. A family to love.

Though family without Jacob seemed no family at all, Rachel knew she must be strong.

She might see if Simon had truly changed by the way he reacted when he learned that Jacob had asked Esther to marry him. If Simon knew he no longer needed to win her from Jacob—because Jacob had Esther now—he might revert to his hurtful ways, as he had when she was his upon their marriage. But if he continued to be caring and thoughtful, knowing Jacob no longer posed a threat, perhaps they could repair their differences.

If so, she would work it out with him, her mind said.

But she loved Jacob, her heart cried.

It didn't matter now. As surely as she belonged to Simon, Jacob belonged to Esther. He'd left Es tonight when it was time to wash her after her son's birth. And he'd sat in the dark kitchen when Rachel came down and passed through, but he hadn't spoken, and neither had she. What could be spoken between them not already said anyway? Especially now?

How could she say she was happy for him, when her heart cried at the final proof they would never be together. Two marriages now there would be between them. They would live separate lives in separate places. Her father would welcome Jacob and Esther to his farm with open arms. She would remain here with Simon.

Rachel's eyes filled. Aaron and Emma would be her sister's to raise, which Esther would do admirably. But right now, Rachel's heart bled at the thought of them not being hers to guide into adulthood. That she would see them often, probably daily, was the only thing keeping her from utter despair.

Would they call Es Momly?

She covered her child with a possessive hand. "Mine you will always be," she whispered. "Come what may. No one will ever take you from me."

Was the cost of her night with Jacob being exacted in painful fragments? She'd lost Mom. . . . No. Rachel shook her head in denial. Mom had been ill for years. An end to her suffering was a blessing, not a punishment.

And her newspaper had *not* been taken away.

Jacob was right. Of all the men the Elders might have placed as publisher, he would respect her wishes. He was already her partner, a fate Simon had sealed by destroying those parts. But she would not anguish over that again. She already forgave him.

Jacob was right about something else. No matter who oversaw its printing, her paper was for the community.

As right as Jacob had been about that, Simon had been wrong about something else. Barrenness was not her punishment for her pride in her newspaper. She carried a child. A miracle she'd thought never to have.

No, she was not being punished. She must be grateful for this miracle of life and stop feeling as if Jacob and the twins were being taken from her, because they were never hers in the first place.

If there was a forfeit due for her sin, it had not been exacted yet. She would continue to hope for mercy.

Rachel looked at the work before her. When she'd conceived the idea for the *Amish Chalkboard*, she'd decided there would be a different kind of death notice. Her column called "Legacies," other newspapers called "Obituaries." At a person's passing, Rachel told his or her story. She spoke of how the world was left better for him or her having been here, intending that people rejoice for the life lived and remember the person who'd passed with smiles as a result of Rachel's words.

It was sad, though, she thought, going over what she'd written, that the first "Legacy" she set in type was about her mother.

Rachel slid her hands over a tray of letters carefully set, slot by tiny slot. Her second story was a joyful notice of Daniel's birth.

One story for a life fulfilled, one for a life begun.

Poor Mom, she had missed the pleasure of holding her first grandchild by days.

Without warning, a warmth replaced Rachel's sadness, and she knew in her heart that Mom was happy, that she rejoiced at Daniel's birth.

Then elation became awareness, and Rachel sensed a presence.

She need not look to know who stood behind her. But she turned toward the open side door anyway, where Jacob stood backlit by moonlight. Always she sensed him. Even at the funeral yesterday, she'd known every move he'd made, how he'd endured almost with pain, as had she, Simon's attention to her.

How she'd wished he was the one holding her.

She scraped her chair back and stood. To share her first printed newspaper with him would be enough. "I'm setting type for tomorrow's *Chalkboard.*"

"I had to do it." Jacob stepped forward and offered his hand.

But she dared not take it. "Because of how much you love Esther. She deserves no less."

"I do love her, but not in the same way I—"

"Shh." She put her fingers to his lips. "You'd better make her a good husband, Jacob."

"And Simon had better make you one."

Her sob threatened to choke her, and she could not

stop it from bursting forth. Then Jacob's arms held her so tight, so well, so beautifully and lovingly well, that she wanted the moment never to end.

Tears and kisses mingled until, seemingly at the same moment, they remembered they must stop. Jacob held her while she cried in his arms. "I just want you to be happy," he said over and over. "Just be happy, Mudpie."

When she calmed, he put her firmly from himself and stepped back. "I pray Simon has truly changed, and I needed to give the both of you, and that baby, a chance to be a family. If you will live a long and happy life, then so will I. Now, let's finish printing our first *Amish Chalkboard* on your very own Gutenberg."

No other word did they speak of his sacrifice. He would be good and loving to Esther, Rachel knew.

As she would be good and loving to Simon, God grant her the strength.

They worked all night, side by side. They were of like mind when it came to the stories and their placement, and their combined efforts made the work she loved more rewarding. Often they went for long stretches in silence. A good, comfortable silence.

This they would always have between them, this printing of the newspaper together. In her heart, Rachel thanked the Elders.

The last of one hundred copies came off the press at cockcrow.

They left them near the press, on *Grossmutter*'s old desk, to be distributed later, and went to begin their day, Jacob with the milking and she with the twins.

Emma's rash was completely gone this morning, so Rachel decided to allow the twins to play together again.

She sent Levi off to help Simon and Jacob with the farm chores.

When Ruben came to the door looking for Jacob, she sent him to distribute the newspapers around the valley. Then she took the twins and went to bring Esther her breakfast. "He's still sleeping?" Rachel asked, entering Esther's room.

"Not still." Esther smiled. "Again. He has a good appetite, my Daniel Jacob."

Aaron took a disinterested look into the cradle, and found the food Rachel was setting beside Esther of worthier note.

It took a minute before Emma noticed the baby, but when she did, she giggled and hopped up in down in her excitement. Then, fast as a wink, she reached into the cradle with both hands.

Esther caught her hands in time, and gently she tugged Emma around the cradle and up onto the bed.

"Rachel," Esther said. "Get Daniel for me and we'll let Emma hold him here where I can help her."

Rachel let out her breath and chuckled. "A mother's instinct must come the minute the baby is born, because you did that good. Do you think I'll have it when mine comes?" She lifted Daniel, and took a moment to savor his warm face in her neck and stroke his tiny silken fingers. "I don't want to let him go."

Esther nodded in understanding. "Last night, when he woke up, I held him long after he finished nursing, and I prayed. I . . . asked for Daniel's blessing for me and Jacob."

"I'm certain you have it," Rachel said, handing Daniel over. She watched while Esther put the baby into Emma's arms and held both of them at the same time.

"You do that good too."

"Ya." After a minute, Esther sighed. "I don't know if this is right."

"It looks right to me."

Emma rubbed noses with Daniel, stroked his tiny fingers.

"Not them. Me and Jacob. I just don't know about us."

"But you said yes, Esther."

"I know I did. But I'm frightened. And Rach, I know how you feel about him."

Rachel sat on the bed facing her sister. "If Simon continues acting the way he has been for the past few days, I'm going to be a good wife to him. In every way."

Esther looked stunned.

"Both of us need to think of our babies," Rachel said.

Esther nodded. "We do."

"Did you deliver all the newspapers already, Ruben?" Rachel asked at noon as she placed the egg-bread and "soup balls in broth" on the table. "Some corn pie, Levi?"

"Ya. *Goot.*"

"Didn't get to the newspapers yet, Rach. Sorry. Needed to talk to Jake."

Rachel looked up from cutting Aaron's sausage. "But the papers are gone. I just came from the barn. Jacob, did you take them around?"

Jacob stood, ready to act, but looked confused about where to begin. "Not me, Mudpie. Are you certain they're gone?"

"I have my copy," Levi said. "Already read most of it. Found it on the porch, thought you left it, Rachel. *Goot* story about little Daniel Jacob."

Simon came in and sat down. Rachel tried very hard not to judge, but she was worried he'd destroyed their night's work. "Did you see the newspapers, Simon? The ones we left in the barn?"

"I did. Can I have some chowchow, Datt?"

Levi passed the bowl.

"Did you take them?" Jacob asked, not hiding his suspicion.

"Thought they were ready for people to take," Simon said, an innocent look on his face. "They were, weren't they? Ham loaf, please. Did I do something wrong?"

Jacob skirted the table and stood next to Simon until his brother finally looked up. "I've had about enough of this. We played by your rules. We have official approval of the Elders. I acted as publisher like they wanted. What did you do with them?"

"With the Elders?"

"The newspapers, dammit!"

"Dammit!" the twins echoed.

"Dammit! Dammit!" Aaron giggled.

Levi laughed, and got a stern look from Jacob.

"The newspapers are gone," Simon said. "It's too late to get them back. I can't say I'm sorry. You'll just—"

Everyone looked up when someone knocked at the kitchen door. Bishop Zook stepped inside and came right to Rachel. *"Leibchen,* the story about your mama . . . Ach." He ignored his tears and hugged her. "You make your pop very happy, Rachel. Mom too, I know."

Rachel pulled back to look at her father better. "You read my story? About Mom? Where did you get a copy of the paper?"

"Simon brought it to me this morning. Like he brought Adam Skyler's and Elam Yoder's to them."

Rachel turned to her husband, not certain she believed he'd helped, despite what her father said. "Simon, you delivered the newspapers? All of them?"

"All of them." He fished in his pants pockets and brought out some coins. "Four cents each printed, to pay for the ink, I told people. You wanted to mail some to the other Amish settlements, I know, but there are none left. You'll have to print more next time."

Rachel gripped her father's sleeve. "Simon, you delivered my newspapers?"

Simon chuckled. "You already asked me that question, Rachel. And I answered you."

"Why? You hate my newspaper."

Simon looked at her father before answering. "The Elders decided the way it should be," he said. "You followed their rules. Our people like your newspaper. I . . ." He cleared his throat. "I have much to make up for, I know. I thought if people saw me deliver them, they would know I accept the Elders' decision and also I . . . understand . . . I was wrong."

Rachel sat in the nearest chair, because for the life of her, she did not believe she had ever been more shocked by anything. Simon Sauder had humbled himself before the district, and not the kind of humility from loud proclaiming, but the deep-in-the-soul kind from quiet acts.

Simon had humbled himself for her?

Jacob shrugged in confusion, but seemed less ready to believe.

But Rachel felt she owed her husband the benefit of her trust. "Thank you, Simon."

He nodded and stood. He smiled, almost. "I spoke to Esther early this morning."

He knows about Jacob and Es, Rachel thought. *And still he is kind.*

"Bishop Zook," Simon said. "As Deacon I am the *Schtecklimann,* and as such I have the proud honor to be the go-between in the arrangements for marriage."

"A new couple wishes marriage?" her father asked. "Then they'd best settle things soon. The first Tuesday in November is only a week away and there are not many Tuesdays or Thursdays open next month without weddings. Have you secured the girl's father's permission yet?"

"Not yet."

"Well, then, it is too soon for you to come to me with the request."

"Bishop Zook. Will you come and walk outside with me for a bit?"

"I want to go see Esther and my new grandson."

"First walk with me, then you can go see Esther."

"Simon, I—"

"Please, Bishop Zook."

"Very well," her father said, a bit annoyed.

When they left, Rachel looked at Jacob. "You'd best tell your Datt. He was gone yesterday."

"Tell me what?" Levi asked. "Simon did a good thing with the newspaper, ya?"

"Ya, Datt, Simon did a good thing," Jacob said. "About the marriage Simon mentioned. Esther must have told him I asked her yesterday—"

"Jacob Sauder!" the Bishop yelled as he came storming into the kitchen.

Jacob stood. "Sir, if you have an objection, I will respect your—"

Her father hugged Jacob with great exuberance. "Objection! *Nein. Nein.* I have no objection. Levi! Jacob will be my son too."

Eyes wide, Levi looked at Rachel. "But you're married to Simon."

"Datt!" Jacob said. "It's no time for joking. The Bishop is saying he has accepted me to be Esther's husband."

"Esther's husband?" He turned to Rachel. "Is this true?"

"I'm happy for them, Levi. We all are."

Simon stood by Rachel. "Yes. We are happy for Jacob and Esther. Jacob, you and Esther must decide which Tuesday or Thursday you wish to marry next month. I will give you a list of open dates and announce your wedding day on Church Sunday two weeks prior. If you don't want to wait until the end of the month, you should choose before this Saturday. Harvest is already finished and you need to marry before winter brings new chores. Until the first or second week in December you can wait, maybe, but no later.''

When Jacob went up to visit Esther after her father left, he found Ruben sitting with her, holding little Daniel as if the boy were made of spun sugar. Jacob chuckled. ''Be careful you don't break him, Ruben.''

Ruben looked appalled.

Jacob all-out laughed.

Esther swatted him. ''Stop teasing him, Jacob, you know he's frightened silly. Ruben, pay him no mind. You can't break him.''

''Just the same, I'd rather not chance it. Here, Es, you take him.'' He kissed Esther on the forehead. ''Rest. Jake, see you in the field. Your pop's hired me to help with the winter wheat.''

Jacob nodded as he watched Ruben leave.

''Honestly, Jacob. Take pity on your friend. He's afraid of his own shadow around me and Daniel. I just got him calm enough to sit and hold the baby and you come in and ruin everything.''

Jacob frowned. ''Sorry, Es. How do you feel?''

''All right, I guess.''

''You're not sure? Should I try to find the doctor for you?''

Esther smiled, which took away the niggling uneasiness Jacob had felt since walking into the room. She would be his wife soon. Right now, he didn't even have the kind of ''need'' for her he'd had for Miriam, not to mention the kind of love he felt for Rachel, which he must deny. ''We need to set a wedding date,'' he said.

''I guess we do.''

Like a rope-line in a blizzard, he reacted to her doubt. "If you're not ready . . ." He sure in hell wasn't.

"It doesn't seem right, so soon after Mom's funeral. And with just having the baby, I'm so tired, I don't feel ready. Can we wait a few days, a week maybe, to talk about it?"

Such relief flooded Jacob, he was almost giddy with it.

A week later, when he brought the subject up again, Esther still wasn't ready. Jacob was so glad, he decided to wait until she mentioned setting a date.

He would be happier to forget about it. At least for now. Maybe next November would be better. It certainly seemed better.

Simon asked Jacob every other day what date in November he and Esther wanted, but Jacob guessed November was too soon.

Ruben visited Esther every morning before chores, sometimes after chores too.

When little Daniel was two weeks old, it was Ruben who came to get Esther and bring her to her father's house.

Jacob wondered why she'd not asked him to do it. Maybe he wasn't visiting as often as he should. But the *Chalkboard* was taking a lot of time.

When the wedding month was half over, Simon's impatience for the date to be set so he could announce it was out of proportion for the Deacon. To Jacob, his impatience seemed more in keeping with the old Simon, rather than the new.

As they milked side by side one morning in late November, Simon cleared his throat. "Tomorrow is the last Sunday I can announce your wedding to Esther. If you don't give me a date tonight, you won't be getting married for another year."

"Well, then, we don't have anything to worry about for

another year, now do we?" Jacob stood and left the milk
parlor.

The next day at service, when Jacob and Ruben sat in
the front row of the men's section, Jacob knew his course
was set for another year, and he wouldn't have to take the
step he'd dreaded since the day he'd proposed to Esther.
If God ordained marriage between them, they would marry
next year. If not, they wouldn't. That was that. Esther didn't
seem any more ready than he was right now.

Even her father had stopped asking him, so he figured
Esther must have told her pop she wasn't ready.

Jacob smiled and nodded at Esther across from him,
Daniel on her lap, then at Rachel beside her. He winked
at Emma, sitting on Rachel's lap. Datt sat with Aaron with
him in the back row, and Jacob could hear the both of
them. That boy of his was getting plenty noisy at service
these days, and Datt was shushing him to beat all.

After the break, Simon got up, as he'd done every
Church Sunday since the second week in October, to
announce the weddings to take place within the next two
weeks. He read his list: "Hannah Bieler, daughter of Joshua
and Lena Stoltz Bieler, on November the 23rd to Jacob
Stoltzfus; Mary Miller, daughter of Samuel and Anna-May
Lentz Miller, on November the 25th to Adam Schmidt;
Esther Zook Lapp, daughter of Ezra and Mary—"

"Do something," Esther mouthed.

Ruben jumped to his feet. "Esther Zook Lapp is going
to marry Ruben Miller." He jabbed his finger into his
chest. "Me." His smile grew. To Jacob, it looked a little
forced at first. Then it sort of blossomed to fit his whole
face. Ruben had made his announcement in a manner
that brought laughter.

But Jacob did not know who was more stunned, he himself, Simon, or Esther. Bishop Zook looked furious, and
Rachel smiled.

After service, when it was time for the fellowship meal, Esther bundled up little Daniel, passed them without saying a word, and continued out the door.

"Now what d'you suppose is wrong with her?" Ruben asked.

Jacob shook his head. "I expect she didn't know she was marrying you. Maybe you should have asked her first."

"Well, I didn't know either. And how could I ask her if you already did?"

Jacob nodded. "Exactly."

Ruben slapped his knee with his hat and turned to Rachel. "Mudpie?"

"You'd best go after her, Ruben."

Rachel always seemed to know what needed to be done, Ruben thought. He wasn't sure why he was chasing Esther, but he damned well knew that for the life of him, he better catch her. Boy, she was fast too. She passed the last row of carriages as he caught up to her.

He took her by the arm. "What do you think you're gonna do, walk all the way back home? It's November, you know. Too cold to keep that baby outside so long. At least wait until I get my horse hitched to my carriage and I'll take you."

"And why would I get into a carriage with you, Ruben Miller?"

"Don't know why you're so mad. You told me to do something, and I did."

"I told Jacob to do something."

"Oh. Well, I did instead. And now we're gonna get married."

"Hah! And why would I marry you?"

"Ach, Es. You know we're perfect for each other."

Her face softened. He thought for a minute she might

smile. "How are we perfect for each other, Ruben?" Her voice sounded sweeter too.

"Well, gee. Isn't that obvious? You need a husband to help you raise little Daniel. And I can get a baby on you, and you won't die."

"Ruben Miller," Esther cried. "You are a horse's hind end!"

When she shoved him, one-armed, because little Daniel took up her other arm, he knew she was really mad, because she was awfully strong all of a sudden. When the force of her shove landed him in a pile of horse shit, he knew he was right. Esther Zook Lapp was plenty damned mad.

He sat up, laughing. And stinking.

Esther was frowning and fuming. And she kicked him a good one, right in his big clunky shoe, just for good measure.

And wasn't she just the prettiest darn thing he ever saw.

Chapter Thirteen

After service, both during and after the fellowship meal, people talked about Ruben Miller's announcement.

Outside, Aaron was trying to break the ice over a puddle near his pa-pop's buggy. "How do you feel about Ruben and Es?" Rachel asked Jacob.

He lifted his mischievous son and put him in the buggy. Then he needed to take the reins from his hands so he wouldn't set Caliope to trotting. "Aaron, stop. Give Pa-pop the reins now, and go sit in the back to wait for Emma. Good." He put Emma inside. "There you go, Pumpkin." And he turned to Rachel. "Come home with us."

"I should go with Simon."

"He has to stay to meet with the Elders, Datt said. If you want to catch up to Es and Ruben, I'm your man."

Rachel accepted Jacob's hand and climbed inside. As soon as she got settled, Caliope began moving.

"You didn't answer me," she said after a while. "How do you feel about what Ruben did?"

After a quiet minute, Jacob turned to her and his smile was just about the nicest she'd ever seen. "I think it's what they both want. I'm happy for them. And, oh, Mudpie, I am happy for me. It would have been all wrong for me and Esther."

Rachel thought she was probably happier than any of them. But should it matter so much that Jacob remain free when she was not? Selfish of her, she knew, but she just could not help rejoicing that he and Esther would not marry. "You're right, and I think Esther knew it too."

"I wish she'd told me."

"I expect she did not want to hurt your feelings."

"Well, she scared me half to death. Do you think Ruben will win her?"

Rachel shook her head. "I don't know. Ruben can be pretty thick sometimes. He might not see how easy it could be."

"Ya. I think that's what I like best about him. Big and dumb and lovable. The *dumpkoff.*"

"Boob!" Emma said.

Jacob chuckled. "See, Em knows who we're talking about."

"There's Ruben's carriage," Rachel said. "In Pop's yard."

Jacob pulled the team in behind Ruben's. A minute later, they saw Esther, Daniel cradled in her arms, come from the barn.

Ruben trailed behind her. "Well, gee, Es," he said, a pleading note in his voice. "How can I be both a mule's and horse's behind? What kind of animal am I exactly?"

"Ya," Jacob said, "big and dumb."

"The kind that slithers along the ground on its belly," Esther said.

Ruben laughed, and backed her up against the closed barn door.

"I don't think they heard us when we drove in," Rachel said. "And they can't see us now. We should say something."

"Judging from the kiss Ruben's giving Esther right now, I think you're right. Should I jump from the carriage to protect her virtue?"

"Jacob Sauder, don't you dare."

"I think one of them might suffocate."

Esther pushed Ruben away with surprising strength. "You stink, Ruben Miller!"

Ruben chuckled when he regained his balance. "Your fault, Esther Zook Lapp soon-to-be-Miller. When we're married, you can help me take a bath every night."

"Jacob, Es'll die when she realizes we heard that."

"I think they're too busy kissing again to hear us if we leave."

"No, wait." Rachel scrambled from the carriage and ran over to her sister.

It looked to Jacob as if it took some doing for Rachel to get their attention. Then Esther, red-faced, looked over at the carriage. Jacob waved. Ruben, smiling widely, waved back. Esther handed Rachel little Daniel, then swatted Ruben's arm.

Rachel came back to the carriage and handed Daniel over to Jacob. Then she went around to the other side to climb in. "Give him to me," she said. When he did, she nodded. "We can go now."

Jacob watched Ruben and Esther go into the house, Ruben's hand on her arm, Es's head lowered, probably in embarrassment. Then he turned and looked at Rachel.

"I said we can go now, Jacob."

Beautiful. So beautiful, his Rachel, with a baby in her arms, it almost hurt watching her. He started Caliope going and cleared his throat. "We're taking Daniel? Es didn't mind?"

"They're going to talk."

Jacob couldn't help his bark of laughter.

Rachel hit his arm. "They're coming for supper in a couple of hours. By then Daniel will be hungry."

"And Es and Ruben will have to get married."

Rachel's face got all pink and warm-looking.

Like us, I wish, Jacob thought. It might have happened to him and Rachel years ago, having to get married, if he had not been so determined to protect her. How he wished he had not been so noble. So much sadness could have been avoided. He reached for her hand and squeezed it. "Let's pray they'll be the kind of happy we could be. Let's pray too we can be happy with what we have."

Rachel nodded. "I'm going to give Simon every chance to change. I'll be a good wife to him again when I move into the *kinderhaus.*"

"When will you?"

"When I'm certain he's the Simon I thought I married."

"I think he already is the same Simon you married, Rach."

"I pray not," Rachel said in a whisper. "The Simon I married was cruel. I want the one I thought I married. But I'm not even certain he exists." She turned and checked on Emma and Aaron. "They're asleep."

"Carriage rides always do that to them."

"I'm glad I'll still be taking care of them. I almost cried for thinking Es would be raising them."

When they got home, Rachel and the children waited for Jacob to put Caliope in her stall. While they did, Rachel noticed something on the floor and stepped closer. The black paw prints going in circles, then in all directions, made her giggle. Mama tabby and her kittens had gotten into something. "Jacob. Look at this," she said when he approached.

"What the . . . ?" Jacob tracked them directly to the Gutenberg, Rachel right behind him.

"Oh, no! What a mess. Bad kitties!" Rachel said, shooing the last one away.

The tin-lined ink barrel lay on the floor, thick, gloppy ink spilling out of it. Aaron bent right down and slapped his hand into the black muck. Fast on her brother's heels, Emma did the same.

"Ach. You two!" Jacob said, pulling them up in unison one under each arm, legs kicking. "Let's get them inside and settled. Then I'll come back and clean this up."

The way he carried them did not keep Aaron from placing a black hand print on his pa-pop's good Sunday shirt, and Rachel was entertained by Jacob's astonishment when it happened.

As if that was not enough, halfway to the house, Daniel began to cry. "You know what?" Rachel said over his screams as they stepped into the kitchen.

"What?" Jacob asked, smiling despite Daniel's screams, his wiggling monkeys, and his ruined shirt.

She shook her head. "I don't know what to do with Daniel when he cries. This is the first time I ever took care of him by myself."

"You're not alone," Jacob said, plopping the twins near the sink. "You have me to help."

"And me," Simon said, wiping his hands on a towel as he stepped inside from the summer kitchen stairs.

Rachel unwrapped her crying nephew. "Simon, you didn't stay for the Elders' meeting?"

"We decided to meet next week instead."

Upon seeing his brother, Jacob remembered his anger over the marriage announcement. "Why did you try to announce my marriage to Esther when I told you not to? And with her there?"

"To nudge a nervous bridegroom. I was trying to help."

Jacob scowled. "You would not have helped if Esther and I were not meant to marry, which we are not."

"Well, your friend made a laughingstock of himself, and me too, with his foolish announcement."

"I think they will be happy," Jacob said.

"Jacob," Rachel said. "How do I make Daniel stop crying?"

"Let me." Simon took Daniel from her and put him against his shoulder. The baby quieted instantly. "I seem to have a way with nephews, don't I, Aaron."

"Unkabear," Aaron said, raising black hands to Simon.

"What did he get into?"

"The barn cats knocked over the ink barrel and ink poured all over the floor," Rachel said.

"The barn cats did?" Simon began to laugh.

"I did not think it was funny," Jacob said.

"I did not think you would." Simon laughed the more.

Bishop Zook grudgingly accepted Ruben for Esther's husband—rather quickly, actually—when he came home early after the Elders' meeting was postponed.

Like all prospective bridegrooms, Ruben moved into his father-in-law's house right away so he could begin working the farm and help with wedding preparations.

With Ruben and Esther both widowed, less elaborate arrangements were made for their wedding, so the day approached quickly.

The night before, Ruben came to see Jacob. "He makes me work hard that man," Ruben grumbled. "When the farm chores are done we scrub floors, move furniture, polish silverware, and even crack walnuts to get ready for this big event. Two weddings I have had, and never so hard have I worked."

"Every man wants a son-in-law who is a hard worker," Jacob said. "With your reputation, you're lucky the Bishop didn't throw you out the day you announced your wedding before you even proposed."

Ruben grinned. "Esther wouldn't let him."

Jacob chuckled.

"I love Esther and Daniel. I will work hard for them."

"I know. No more fear?"

"Some. But Esther is strong and well after Daniel's birth."

"What are you doing here the night before your wedding anyway, running out on chores like the old days?"

"Ach," Ruben quipped. "No more of that for me. I have come for the turkeys we will roast for the celebration. Levi said he would put them aside for us. Esther wants me to kill them, so they can be cleaned, dressed, then roasted overnight. I think a bridegroom's worst job is cutting off the fowl heads for the bridal dinner. Who ever thought up such a foolish tradition, do you think?"

"Some bride's father, I expect. But Ruben, just think what you'll be doing tomorrow night." Jacob elbowed his friend in good fun.

Ruben grinned again, then got serious. "You are not angry at me for what I did?"

"I'm grateful to you. My reasons for asking her to marry me were good ones—to help her and my babies, and Rachel too—but not good enough to make a life on."

"Esther knew that too. We all did. I want this marriage to last the rest of my life, Jacob. It frightens me how much I want that."

"It will. And the rest of your life begins now. Let's go quiet those noisy birds."

* * *

Rachel's father waited beside Simon and the other ministers in the center of Eli and Mary Mast's best room as the congregation sang the chant based on the passage "Behold, the bridegroom cometh."

Holding hands, Ruben and Esther walked in together. Rachel and Jacob, as Ruben and Esther's attendants, walked behind them, also holding hands. The four of them sat on two benches in the center, Ruben and Jacob facing Esther and Rachel, and Ruben couldn't seem to stop his grin.

Her father had once considered Ruben the laziest good-for-nothing in the district, but Rachel didn't think anyone could have worked harder than Ruben had to prove to his soon-to-be father-in-law that he would be a good husband to Esther. Rachel knew, because her father told her—out of Ruben's hearing—that he put Ruben through such paces the likes of which four men could hardly do in a day. And Ruben did it all.

Because of that, her father thought this would be the making of Ruben and a good life for Esther.

Rachel wiped away a tear when her father placed his hand over Esther's and Ruben's clasped ones. "Do you stand in the confidence that this, our sister, is ordained to be your wedded wife?" her father asked.

Ruben looked Esther over, tilted his head, as if trying to decide, and nodded. "Yes."

Rachel closed her eyes when her father asked Esther the same question, and tried not to remember how she felt when she answered it at her own wedding. She wished she could recall believing Simon was ordained to be her husband. But with unfortunate clarity, she remembered nearly crying out in panic.

Unfortunately, she'd held her tongue.

Alarm over that which could not be changed threatening to strangle her, Rachel opened her eyes . . . and found herself looking into Jacob's anguished face.

Heartsore, she turned her gaze and her attention toward her sister.

"Do you also promise your wedded husband, before the Lord and his church, you will nevermore depart from him, but will care for and cherish him. . . ."

Never depart from him. Another hit.

Rachel could no longer run from her transgression. She had broken vows made before God. She could not look at Jacob; she could not keep from it.

His expression was bruised with deep regret.

She looked away, his pain overwhelming her, and with great will, Rachel took a calming breath and smiled for her sister as their father pronounced Esther and Ruben husband and wife.

Many, including her pop, had bright eyes, but Rachel could not allow tears, even of joy, because those banked from sorrow would intrude.

When everyone stood to leave, Rachel took another deep breath and looked about for Fannie, who sat with all three children. When she spotted her friend, she was able to smile.

Fannie's own smile was wry. Her arms were too full to stand. Emma sat beside her, holding little Daniel's hand as she probably had through the long service. Aaron sat on the floor in front of her, his arms wrapped around Fan's legs and his cheek resting against her knees.

Jacob saw them and chuckled. "Fannie is a good friend."

"She is. I should go and rescue her."

But when she made to move in that direction, Jacob took her arm and led her to a table where he poured her a lemonade.

"Rach," he whispered as she drank. "To cherish and

care for are not vows broken by you. You departed from him because you were thrown away. These sins you think you own, you do not. They are mine. And they are Simon's. Every one of them.''

"You would take on my sins, Jacob?"

"It is not a matter of taking any more than I deserve. But if you will not heed me in this, then at least remember what we've been taught. 'He who knows everything, also forgives.' '' He turned away and took a glass of lemonade to Fannie, trading the drink for Daniel, who began to set up a ruckus. And Rachel knew Jacob Sauder was a good man no matter what he had done.

The guests, including Simon and her pop, headed for the wedding breakfast at Pop's farm a half mile away. Her job, and Jacob's, as attendants, would be to get Ruben and Esther to the wedding dinner.

Esther heard Daniel, and made her smiling way through the waning crowd. "How many brides have to nurse their babies before their wedding celebration?" she asked, taking Daniel from Jacob to follow Mary Mast upstairs where she could nurse him. But Emma did not want be parted from Daniel.

"Let her come with me. I won't be long," Esther said. "He eats fast, my Daniel Jacob."

Ruben frowned and sat. "I wanted to go with them, but I couldn't with Mary there."

Jacob chuckled. "You'll have them all to yourself tonight."

"Well, that seems a long way off. I don't understand it. Esther has always been here in the valley. We went to school together. She married Daniel. I married . . . often. And now, years later, here we are married to each other. And suddenly I have this feeling I cannot bear to let her out of my sight. How did I live without her before now, I'd like to know. I tell you, Jacob, it scares me silly, this feeling I have never known before. As if my whole life I have waited for Esther."

"I understand. . . ." Rachel's voice cracked. "You are very lucky you will have each other for the rest of your lives."

Ruben took her hand. "I walked some dark miles, Mudpie. I felt as if my life had ended but I had not left the earth yet—to my frequent regret. Now, I feel as if I have everything. Remember, none of us knows what the future will bring. You need to have faith." He leaned forward and looked at Jacob. "You too."

Jacob cleared his throat and nodded halfheartedly.

When Mary Mast came downstairs, Ruben eagerly rose. "Let's go get my bride."

He got to the bedroom first, where Mary said Esther was feeding Daniel.

Emma cried "Boob!" when she saw him, and launched herself into his arms. When she crinkled her nose, Ruben chuckled and kissed it. Then he stepped further into the room and stopped, as if the sight stunned him.

Esther, in her heart-shaped white prayer kapp and her white bridal apron over a deep cornflower-blue dress, sat rocking Daniel as he nursed. She was radiant, her smile bringing out a natural, breathtaking beauty as she gazed at Ruben with love in her eyes.

"Mein Gott," Ruben said. "Look at this family I have been given." He turned back to her and Jacob, tears in his eyes. "I know I do not deserve them, but Lord, I am so grateful to have them."

Rachel stepped into the room and took Emma. "We'll bring the carriage around to the front and wait for you."

As they left, Ruben had removed his hat and was bending on one knee before Esther and his new son.

* * *

Fannie took Daniel and Emma, and Simon took Aaron, once they were all back at Zook's house. Then Ruben and Esther, Rachel and Jacob went upstairs to a spare bedroom to wait for the signal calling them down.

Rachel and Jacob left the room almost immediately to wait at the top of the stairs so Ruben and Esther would have a few minutes alone.

After a wedding, every couple waited alone for the first time in an upstairs bedroom for when they would descend together for their wedding dinner. Though it was not for very long, fifteen minutes at most, many a lasting memory was created then.

Pink cheeks and hushed whispers often accompanied a woman's smile when she spoke of her time in the "upstairs room" on her wedding day. Rachel remembered hers well.

Simon said her purple dress was prideful and she should push her indecent curls under her kapp so as not to shame him.

Yes, a first. But no first married kiss, no tentative touch, no fingertip to the cheek . . . not even a kind word. Instead, she'd had her first glimpse of the man she married, not the one feigned during courtship. And his manner had not wavered from that day . . . until the day after her hearing over her newspaper.

Did Simon care so much about what others thought that if they approved of her so openly, then he would too?

Only one thing Rachel knew for certain. Her husband had never offered to take a sin of hers to bear as his own. Nor would he. She sighed and chided herself for her selfish thoughts on such a happy day, and turned her attention to the celebration.

When she did, Jacob was beside her, at the top of the enclosed stairway, waiting patiently for her to look at him.

"If we were in that room, I would do this," he whispered, placing his lips against hers in the softest, most tender kiss she had ever experienced.

When Esther and Ruben came to stand behind her and Jacob, Esther's cheeks were rosy, and Ruben's smile wide, but no more than hers must be, Rachel thought, just as her father opened the door at the bottom of the stairs to call them down.

At their places, Ruben and Esther exclaimed over the beautiful plates, bowls, and dishes on their table, all filled with fancy desserts and treats. A wine flask held cider, matching goblets beside it. The food was to be eaten during the wedding celebration, the dishes their wedding gifts.

The *Schnutzler* carved the turkey for the *Eck,* the corner table where the bridal party sat, and saw them well served.

"Do you know," Ruben said, "we are eating five turkeys, twelve ducks, twenty chickens, forty loaves of bread, two bushels of potatoes, and two of celery. Not to mention pies and cakes."

Jacob chuckled. "And how do you know this, Ruben?"

"I was up until two this morning preparing it!"

Esther's laughter rang out, and Rachel smiled to hear her sister happy again.

"Not bad," Jacob said. "For a man who could not make coffee, or find his coffeepot, some months ago."

"Ya. I'm *goot. Nein?*"

"Nein," Esther said, patting his cheek.

Ruben's smile turned to a frown when he understood the insult. Then he raised a brow. "Tonight, I will show you, then you will know." And Esther's blush seemed to satisfy him.

It took three sittings for everyone to eat, but the bridal party remained seated throughout.

When people were finished eating, they brought out their song books, the *Lieder Sammlungen,* to take turns sere-

nading the couple. But Ruben and Esther must only listen;
it would be considered a bad omen if they sang too.

Disregarding Simon's frown, Rachel sang to her heart's
content. The songs—hymns really, though not so solemn
as at service—kept a happy, quick pace when heartily sung.

Ruben and Esther sent sweets from their table to special
friends, or to the singers. Every time Daniel let out a yell,
they sent something to Fannie.

"Do you think she's pinching the boy?" Ruben asked.
"So she can taste everything?"

After a while, the young people went to play games in
the barn. *Skip to Ma Lou, There Goes Topsy through the Window,*
and *Little Red Wagon Painted Blue* were favorites. They
allowed for hand-holding and partner-swinging, but were
not considered dancing, which was frowned upon.

After supper, the final song, the *Guter Geselle,* the "Good
Friend," was sung, and Rachel hated to see the wonderful
day end.

Emma cried for having to leave Daniel behind; then
finally, she and Aaron were sleeping soundly in the back
of the buggy.

Simon had left about two hours earlier than Rachel and
Jacob, when most of the adults had left and Fannie had
put Daniel, Emma, and Aaron to bed upstairs and gone
home too.

Most of the younger, unmarried guests stayed until midnight. As attendants, Rachel and Jacob stayed with Esther
and Ruben, who could not go to bed until their guests
left.

Ruben had grumbled, on and off, for the remaining two
hours about those thoughtless youngsters, making Esther
laugh.

Rachel did not think she had ever seen her sister laugh
so much. Daniel, her first husband, was a good man, but
quiet. Ruben was anything but.

"A good day," Rachel now said as Caliope trotted before their buggy at a slow, soothing pace, the late November night crisp, but not cold. "You're quiet, Jacob."

"Look at the stars, Mudpie. There are millions of them, and they are all ours tonight." His hand sought hers and she took it. Just for a minute, she thought. It would hurt no one if they touched for a minute.

"They're happy," she said.

"I am happy for them."

"Yes." The quiet times she and Jacob shared, like these, often the most comfortable, restful moments of her day, Rachel treasured. She was especially grateful for this time now.

"Your condition is beginning to show. You look more beautiful than ever," Jacob said.

"He is kicking."

Jacob looked at her, his eyes wide. "Now?"

Understanding his longing, probably because he'd missed this with Aaron and Emma, Rachel raised their clasped hands and flattened them over her abdomen.

When the baby moved, he smiled. "He is all arms and legs and happy energy. He has enjoyed the day too."

She stopped herself from saying more than she should, and nodded. "We are nearly home," she said.

Jacob understood Rachel's warning, and moved his hand back to the reins. He stopped the carriage by the front door so he could carry Aaron inside and help Rachel put the twins to bed. "I'll go settle Caliope now. Thank you for a lovely day."

He watched Rachel go to her room before he went out to drive the buggy to the barn. Tonight, two needs warred within him—one, to free Rachel from Simon; the other, to free her from himself.

Jacob only wished he could be certain which freedom was best.

Today he'd tried to set her free from her guilt, but without success, he suspected.

As he brushed Caliope down, Jacob worried that his need to free Rachel from a husband who did not cherish her was more selfish than anything. Simon did seem more caring lately. Jacob wanted to believe it would last. Besides, to free her from her husband, of all people, did not count among his rights.

Only one freedom was his to grant—the freedom from himself. And would that be good for Rachel?

To leave her, to take his babies away from her, from Datt, would hurt Emma and Aaron; it would hurt them all. Especially him.

Leaving her would destroy him. But he, more than anyone, did not matter.

It was Rachel who did. What would be best for her?

Jacob filled a bucket with oats and extra molasses and left Caliope to enjoy her late supper. As he picked up the lantern, he noticed slats from the lambing pen on the floor. Aaron's Pokey was missing.

A crash turned Jacob on his heel. "*Mein Gott,* do you animals have something against the press? One would think Simon had paid you to . . ."

His words hung in the air.

Oh, it could not be.

But two animals damaging the press? Different animals at different times? And at such particular times?

The first accident had followed upon the heels of Simon learning he and Esther would not marry. The second accident now, tonight, after Esther's marriage to Ruben, to someone other than himself . . . him and Rachel spending the day together so openly, so happily.

The more he thought about it, it sounded less and less like the animals, and more and more like . . . like a child's tantrum at not getting what he wanted. More like revenge. Hate.

A strong word, hate.

Did Simon's emotions run so deep then? And where was this hate of his directed? Toward the press, toward the brother his wife would have married if not for his interference, or toward Rachel herself?

Jacob held the lantern higher. Pokey had stepped into a splash of lead letters and splintered wood. The sheared, broken armature lay on the ground.

How could a little lamb cause such damage? Jacob lifted the piece, ran his hand along the turned, thick oak. Snapped clean. On purpose? Oak? Solid, hard, sturdy . . . by a lamb?

Should he tell Rachel what he found and allow her to think the animal caused it? Should he tell her his suspicions? Or allow her to come to her own conclusions?

He could be wrong. He should at least give his own brother the benefit of the doubt. Datt would be so hurt if . . . One thing for certain. His leaving at this point might not set Rachel free; it might place her in danger.

If Simon's anger ran this deep, if he transferred his ire to the press because he could no longer hurt Rachel, then she needed looking after, both her and the baby.

In a month, the most holy season of the year would be upon them. He would stay at least for Christmas and Second Christmas. It would be Emma's and Aaron's first with the family.

Jacob hoped it would not be their last.

Chapter Fourteen

Jacob was pleased Rachel intended to keep alive the Christmas traditions his mother had started.

When he saw her preparing Mom's secret-recipe fruitcake, his mother seemed close again, his anger over her death less sharp.

Jacob laughed when Rachel admitted his mother had taught her the recipe fourteen years before, when she was only eight, and still Mom had always called it a "secret" recipe. When Rachel said she would teach Emma to make it when she was eight, Jacob hoped, with all his heart, that she would have the chance.

Mom's fruitcakes—tied up in white muslin cloths like a bad case of toothache, mellowing in blue-rimmed crocks in the summer kitchen the whole month before—had always been the first sign of the season for Jacob, and this year was no exception. Most would be given to friends to symbolize the gifts of the Wise Men, but one or two would be theirs to savor.

For the past two weeks, the women had been going from house to house to make their favorite Christmas treats together, *Springerlies, Pfeffernussen Kuchen,* and Tangled Jackets.

In a little while, Fannie, Priscilla, and Esther would come to help Rachel bake, and new Christmas memories would arrive upon the wings of frosted gingerbread angels smelling of anise, nutmeg, or peppermint. Lively Pennsylvania Dutch chatter—everyone speaking at once, yet understanding everything said—would complete the tradition.

Jacob daringly suggested that Rachel make some of Mom's souse, because pig's feet jelly on toast seemed to belong to Christmas morning. After her swat over the work he was giving her, he went out to milk.

"It snows, it snows," Fannie said as she stomped her shoes on the rag rug at the kitchen door. Over one arm she carried a basket of walnuts from her pop's trees. "Ach, Rach. Wide as a barn, you are. *Mein Gott.* That's some big baby you got there."

"Just what a woman likes to hear," Rachel said. "A barn, Fannie?"

Fannie looked embarrassed, but Rachel laughed.

"*Siss am schneea,* it's snowing," Esther said as she deposited two-month-old Daniel in Rachel's arms and began to unwind the tawny wool blanket their mother had knitted twenty years before from around him. And suddenly the formless bundle with tiny blue eyes peeping out became an angel wiggling happily to be free.

Ruben stepped into the room, missed the rug entirely, and stomped his shoes on the floor to get the snow off. "*Iss kalt.* Brr," he said as he carried Daniel's cradle into the toasty kitchen and set it near the quilt where Aaron and Emma played. Then he curled his finger in a come-along way, to draw the twins from their quilt and nearer to him, and when they stood side by side looking up expectantly, he removed his hat and shook snow all over them.

Delightful shrieks turned to downright giggling as the twins tried to get the snow off before it turned to cold water and trickled down their necks.

Esther shook her head. "Two little boys I got."

But Rachel didn't think Es minded a bit. A sparkle lit her sister's eyes these days, one Rachel had never seen before, not even when Es became Daniel's bride.

Ruben walked over and kissed Es's cheek, his face ruddy with embarrassment. Then he turned to leave after doing the same with Daniel and the twins. "Back in time for supper," he said as he went out the door.

"Always in time to eat," Esther said, which started them all on stories of men and mealtimes.

With so much to cook and bake, they even used the cavernous fireplace where cooking used to be done before Levi bought his wife a fancy new coal-burning stove. Hands to her back, pushing her belly out, Rachel straightened after placing a cake in the low brick oven. Ach, poor Hannah, leaning over like this to cook all day; no wonder she was bent with age.

The four women, despite one baby and two toddlers, moved in harmony. Batter got mixed and baked. Cookies got cut and decorated, and spoons were licked by Aaron and Emma, and sometimes by Rachel, who for some reason found the taste of everything wonderful this year.

Luscious chocolate fudge poured into greased pans to cool and set made mouths water. Aaron dipped a finger in for an early taste, then got his burned finger plunged into a bowl of cold water and covered with butter.

Later, Simon came in and snatched a fresh-cut piece of fudge. Without thinking, Rachel smacked his hand with the back of a wooden spoon, and while her heart pounded with fear, he retaliated by kissing her cheek.

Her face flamed. That was the most playful thing Simon had ever done. And in front of everyone!

Maybe he really was changing.

Before he left, he grabbed her hand-slapping spoon and held it in the air out of her reach. And she laughed.

Simon made her laugh!

He snatched three more pieces of fudge then, handed one each to the twins, and popped the last into his mouth. With a wink and a tip of his hat to the ladies, he went back outside.

Most of the treats got taken downstairs to the unheated summer kitchen to cool or be stored. Everything kept better down there, and tomorrow was Christmas Eve anyway.

Priscilla arrived late, more than an hour after school should have been finished. "Down the snow flutters still," she said as she came in. Once free of her heavy shoes, outer bonnet, and cape, she went over to sit on the quilt with Aaron, took Daniel from his cradle, and sat him in her lap facing everyone. "Sorry to be so late. Those kids! I worry so. None of the words they'll remember in the pageant tomorrow. Weeks we've been practicing already."

Rachel went to pour the water from the noodles into the zinc-lined sink. "You like teaching, don't you, Pris?"

"Like nothing ever. No insult meant, but I'm glad you left, Rach." She slapped her forehead. "Oh, foolish me. I almost forgot to invite you already."

"Invite me to what?"

Priscilla looked at her as if she were daft, and Rachel wondered for a minute how she succeeded in teaching the children anything when she forgot so much. She grinned at the notion.

"To the pageant, of course. You'll come? All of you and

the twins?" Priscilla looked concerned. "It's important to the children you should come."

"Of course," Rachel said, and wondered if the new teacher was nervous about making mistakes in front of the old one.

But if Priscilla was nervous, it didn't last long. She began to clap Daniel's hands. *"Botsche, botsche, kuche. Der Baker hot gerufe."*

The twins sang the English words, "Paddy, paddy the cakes," and clapped with little Daniel.

Christmas Eve dawned crisp and finger-cold. The pageant would begin promptly at two. Everyone in the Sauder house had been invited, and Rachel was especially surprised when Levi and Simon wanted to go. When they arrived, generations of families were pulling up in a line of buggies half a mile long.

Her classroom—Priscilla's rather—looked beautiful, and a smile filled Rachel's heart.

Along one side, hooks with boys' coats and black felt hats of every size met a row of shawls and like-sized blue winter bonnets. For a minute, until her baby kicked, Rachel missed being a teacher. But placing her hand on her stomach, she knew she would not go back for anything.

Most of the visitors sat on benches placed in rows along the sides and back of the one-room school. Some sat at their children's desks, while the students were off preparing for the pageant.

Little Ruth Vost led Rachel to a chair in the front and center of the room. The twins came too; Aaron sat on the floor at her feet—Emma sat on her feet. Simon, Levi, and Jacob stood in the back.

A cord was strung across the front of the room, and a sheet of muslin, with painted hills and blue skies, was folded over it to form a curtain. In the room's side windows sat lit candles with evergreens around their bases.

When the visitors were all sitting, Priscilla turned down the lamps, the candles giving a soft glow to the overcast winter afternoon. Then she rang a bell and the room quieted.

Rachel's good impression of the new teacher grew.

Elam Lapp stepped before the curtain and began by reading the Nativity in High German. Christmas Eve as it was meant to be.

When Elam finished, Lena, Hannah, Mary-Rose, and Amanda, first-graders wearing paper angel wings, stood, three on each side of him, and sang *"Ein Kindlein zart in der Krippen."* "Away in the Manger."

After the song, Priscilla came out. "What we wish to do today is called "Cradle Rocking," from a fourteenth-century German Christmas custom I read about in a book Atlee lent me." Pris smiled and nodded, and that was when Rachel saw Atlee.

"This custom replaced Nativity plays after they were banned," Priscilla said. "A cradle with a doll or baby, to symbolize the Holy Child, would be rocked while the congregation sang and prayed." She took a breath and looked for her place on her script. How hard Pris must have worked to perfect her public speaking for this occasion. "By the sixteenth century," Pris continued, "this custom too was banned. But since our people have never allowed themselves to be stopped, it seemed right, as we celebrate Christ's birth, to honor our Amish martyrs for not giving up."

Pris blew out the candles.

One edge of the curtain was pulled back, where a single lantern revealed Daniel in his cradle. No wonder he and Priscilla were so comfortable with each other.

Behind the center of the curtain another light came on,

outlining Mary and Joseph in shadow. An unseen hand rocked the Holy Child's cradle while Daniel kicked and gurgled in glee.

Ida Lapp, Rachel thought, began to recite:

> Joseph, dearest Joseph mine,
> Help me rock my baby fine!
> What Gabriel foretold
> Is now fulfilled.
> Eia, Eia,
> The Virgin bore a child
> As the Father's wisdom willed.
> Eia, Eia.

Three Wise Men, judging by the shawls wrapped around Joseph, Jacob, and Joshua Stutz, and by their camels—children on all fours beside them—came from the opposite end of the room and began to recite:

> Out of the Orient they came a'riding,
> Three noble kings of humble heart and mild.
> They came to see the Blessed Lord of Heaven
> Descend to earth, to be a little child.
> Precious gifts of gold and myrrh and incense,
> Bringing God the gifts which God had made:
> Low the kings in homage bowing,
> At the feet of Mary laid.

Then the angels returned to the center of the room and sang:

> To Christ our Lord we raise this song,
> Hol-di-ah-di-ay.
> Chimes are ringing, angels singing,
> Hol-di-ah-di-ay.

Oh, look here! No, look there!
Angels' choirs everywhere.

Then the cast came from behind the curtain to end the
program with *"Still Nacht, Heilige Nacht."* "Silent Night."
Rachel was not sure she could hold her tears back. Nor
was she certain who made her more proud, the schoolchildren for being so good, or Priscilla herself for becoming such a good teacher.
Rachel turned around to see if everyone else was as
moved as she, and saw many teary eyes just then.
"We have a special presentation we wish to make before
we're finished," Priscilla said, and Rachel looked back to
the front. "Elam, if you would . . ."
When the boy pulled back the curtain, a beautiful white
quilt hanging on the wall behind Pris's desk was revealed.
The pupils' names were embroidered in rainbow colors,
surrounding a quilted school, flowers and trees, clouds,
hills and valleys, even horses and buggies.
Priscilla surprised Rachel by taking her hand and urging
her to stand. "Rachel, the children wish you to have this
quilt, so you will remember them and to thank you for
your patience and kindness in teaching them. Most of the
girls stitched their own names. The boys' mothers did
theirs. Family names are grouped together. We worked
evenings and took turns doing the quilting for the last two
months to finish it."
Rachel opened her arms to the pageant's players, who
had been standing by and watching, and they came to her
with hugs and kisses. Then she called the rest of the children from their desks. So many hugs, so much love, she
was sobbing fit to start a Biblical flood by the time she was
done.
Simon came to stand by her, placing his hand at her

back, looking as if he might be . . . happy. Rachel cried the more.

When her tears finally stopped, and the laughter at her weeping stopped, and Aaron was in Simon's arms, Emma in hers, Rachel was able to speak. "Thank you, all of you, for such a very special gift, sewn and pieced together with love, I know.

"Christmas is the day when the inner light is shone on everyone and the true story of the Christ Child should be told. This afternoon has been one of the most beautiful tellings I have ever seen or heard. And the inner light in this room right now is blinding."

Everyone stood and clapped; some of the women had to stop to wipe their eyes.

Priscilla hugged Rachel.

Daniel cried from the noise, and Ruben came to take him from the cradle.

The noise grew as people began to leave.

"*Glick salich Grishtaag,* a most blessed Christmas," people called as they left.

"*S'nehmlich zu dich,* the same to you."

A dusting of snow made the evening magical.

Levi had left early; he was getting old and tired, he'd told Jacob, but Rachel knew he could not deal with such emotion. So Jacob and the twins rode in the back of their buggy with her and Simon, and they sang carols all the way home.

After supper, Simon read the Nativity while they sat quietly in the best room before the fire. When the twins became sleepy, she and Jacob oversaw their leaving plates at their places at table so that in the morning they would be found filled with candy, nuts, and a toy or two.

Simon asked Rachel to stay downstairs when Jacob took the children upstairs, and Levi went to the *daudyhaus.* And when they were alone, he put his arms around her and held her close. And for the first time in years, Rachel was comfortable enough to let him.

"Rachel, it is Christmas," he said. "Come with me. Come to our house and into our bed. Let me show you I have changed."

Just then, Rachel believed him. But she'd believed before and been wrong. She wanted to make her marriage a normal one. She owed it to her husband, and to her child, to do so.

But she also owed her child protection.

She sighed and stepped back. "Simon, I am . . . uneasy. Not so much as I was. But for so long, I never knew what you would do, and it always seemed that . . . at night . . . I had more reason for fear. I do not think I am ready."

"Ach, Rachel. For Christmas. Please? There would be no more wonderful a gift."

She wavered, for a moment, then her heart began to race. "I am frightened yet." She touched his arm. "But I become less so each day. I see how different you have become. I see in your eyes kindness and understanding. I love how you care for Aaron. I know you are trying, Simon. Give me time. Please? Will you accept that if we continue in this way, after the baby is born, I will return to you and be your wife again?"

Could he? Would he? Like St. Joseph, accept a wife under such conditions? Could anyone change so much? And how dare she judge him when her sins loomed so greatly before her?

Simon sighed and kissed her forehead. "It is not the Christmas I would want, but it is a gift of sorts and I accept it. You have reason for the way you feel. I know that."

"You do?"

"Ach, Rachel. I am not a stupid man. Just foolish sometimes. Headstrong. Driven by something I cannot name and it frightens me, perhaps as much as it frightens you.

I get to blaming you, I think. Your father and I have talked. It helped me to see things more clearly.''

Rachel allowed herself to be taken into her husband's arms. He bent his head slowly to kiss her good night. A lovely, soft kiss.

She might have fallen in love with him if he'd acted like this beyond their wedding.

Upstairs, Jacob was sitting on the floor in the hall, his back against the wall, his knees bent, waiting for her. "I thought you might have gone with him," he whispered.

Rachel ignored the agony in his voice. "I told him that after the baby was born, I would return to him."

"It is best."

"Yes."

Jacob stood to face her. "A blessed Christmas, Rachel."

"You too, Jacob."

Their fingers touched, then dropped away, and as she went to her own room, Rachel wondered how her heart could be both healing and breaking at the same time.

Christmas morning Jacob came in from shoveling his way to the barn to find Rachel filling the children's plates with treats. She put a *lumba bubba,* a stuffed baby doll with prayer kapp, apron, and cape, beside Emma's plate and a stuffed, black lamb by Aaron's.

"These the ones you made, Mudpie?" Jacob picked up the lamb and examined it. "They're nice. I brought mine down earlier." He retrieved a wooden cradle to fit the size she'd told him the doll would be, and a wooden marble chase game, both from the inside bottom shelf of the jelly cupboard.

Levi came in yawning and put a tiny carved horse, brown with horsehair main, shiny harness, and plaited tail, in Aaron's plate, and a white one, just as fancy, in Emma's.

"They'll like them, Datt. Thanks," Jacob said. "Happy Christmas. Here, got you some pipe tobacco."

"Thanks, son. Where's Simon? Still milking?"

Jacob looked out the window. "He was right behind me when we finished. Here he comes. Oh, no, what is he up to?"

Simon came in, his jacket bulging in way too many places. He wore such a sincere, happy smile, the likes of which Jacob never hoped to see. Aaron deserved the credit for coaxing Simon's smile into place over the past months.

"I guess I can't put these on the table," Simon said, as the twins came running into the room.

"When did you wake up?" Jacob asked them. "I didn't hear you call Pa-pop. Look at you, no socks on your feet. It's cold in here. Come on."

"Wait," Simon said. "I feel something warm." He looked into his jacket. "Ach, what did you do?" Jacob and the twins stopped to watch.

With a groan and a wink, Simon pulled a tan pup from inside its cocoon, black-tipped tail wagging furiously, and handed it to Emma.

Her squeals were deafening.

Then a similar wiggling bundle, black with one white eye, stuck its face out for an inquisitive look. Simon knelt down before Aaron. "Take him. He's yours."

"Unkabear! A doggie!"

For a minute, the lump in Jacob's throat threatened to choke him. Simon had never in his life showed this side of himself.

Despite the burden Jacob carried, he knew Christmas had never meant so much.

"One for each of you." Simon petted Aaron's puppy and smiled at his brother. "Both of them for your part of the house, Jacob."

"Why, you—"

Simon raised his hand to stop the curse. "Not in front of the children."

Jacob couldn't believe it; his brother was joking! "All right, you two," he said to Aaron and Emma. "Upstairs for warm clothes now, before any more gifts for anybody."

Jacob placed the pups back in Simon's arms. "Find a wooden box with nice high sides for them, brother, or you'll find them in your part of the house more often than you'd like."

Simon chuckled as they walked away. Then Aaron turned and ran back. Simon bent down to see what he wanted, and got his neck hugged tight. Jacob nodded to his brother when his son returned to his side, but he could not speak for the love he'd seen for Aaron in Simon's eyes.

As his brother stood watching the children with longing, Jacob thought Simon just might take good care of Rachel and the baby after all. As should be.

This was going to be a good Christmas.

This did not bode well for a good Christmas.

Rachel looked from Simon to Jacob. Their easygoing manner with each other had lasted nearly all the way through a hearty breakfast, complete with souse for toast. It had survived puddle-making pups and Emma's bowl of hot oatmeal upside down in Simon's lap.

But the test of gift-giving was at hand.

Nothing as silly as envy over who had the better gift. That was never their way. No, this problem was older, more deep-rooted.

This rivalry had started when they were children, Rachel knew better than anyone, and it held her, almost as a prisoner, in its center. Which of them did she like best? Which would be her husband? Now, heaven help them all . . . which man had the right to present such a gift?

From the way Simon and Jacob stood staring at each other—each of them holding a wooden baby cradle to give her—Rachel knew if someone did not say something soon, words best left unsaid would once again come between them. Words that could destroy.

"Levi?" she implored.

But it was Ruben who harumphed and stomped both feet, propelling himself from his rocker to a standing position. "Like two schoolboys trying to give your lunch to a pretty girl, you act," he said. "Rachel does not have to choose which cradle she wishes to keep—no, nor the giver either—witless boys.

"She can keep both. One can stay upstairs, the other down. Then there will be no toting, like I have to do."

Ruben looked from one frowning man to the other and sighed. "Still not happy, I see." He shook his head. "And on Christmas day too. All right, I will decide. Your painted one, Simon, matches the painted secretary in the corner there. Leave it down here in the best room. Jacob, put yours in Rachel's bedroom. It's a fine match for the chest of drawers she's always favored."

Rachel admired Ruben's ability not to point out in which bedroom the chest now stood. She could tell Es was downright impressed.

Simon placed the cradle he'd repainted by the secretary. "Looks good," he said before he settled in one of the rockers.

Jacob carried the cradle he built upstairs to put in Rachel's bedroom. He knew he was acting like a horse's hind end . . . a little boy, just as Ruben said, and damn him for pointing it out.

It *was* Simon's place, as Rachel's husband, to give such

a gift, not her brother-in-law's, and as soon as Jacob grew up a bit, he would tell Simon so.

When Jacob came back down, he followed the aroma into the kitchen. Rachel was spooning cinnamon apples over the ham in the oven. He reached over to touch the curls at her nape below her kapp, then thought better of it and clasped his hands behind his back instead. "Sorry, Mudpie. I should know better."

She shut the oven door. "You should." Then she turned to him with a sigh. "But thank you for saying so. Did you say it to Simon?"

"Ach, Rach, do I have to?"

"What did Ruben call you? Witless?"

Even when she insulted him, he wanted her. He wanted to smooth his hand over the mound of her stomach to feel her child's movement visible beneath her apron. When she was bent over the stove, he'd not only wanted to touch the curls at the nape of her neck, he'd wanted to kiss her there. Lord, how he wanted.

Simon stepped into the kitchen, and turned right around to leave.

"Simon," Jacob said. "I was wrong. The cradle should have come from you. Not me."

Simon relaxed his stance and nodded. "For the most part, you have been a good brother."

No. He had not. Not lately. "I thank you for the words, but I do not deserve them," Jacob said in earnest, and was glad he had a reason to smile just then. "I hear the twins squealing. Let's go see what the pups wet now."

"Pa-pop, look," Aaron said as they came into the best room. "Unkabear, look. Momly. A barn from Boob."

"And a Pokey," Emma added, holding up a carved, black lamb for their inspection.

Levi laughed. "They will think all lambs are black."

"And a moo-cow."

"A whole farm, Ruben. You made them a farm?" Rachel asked. "It is so good. You could be a toy-maker."

"Pop would scold you for that, Rach. He likes Ruben fine as a farmer. He never had it so easy."

Ruben slapped his knee. "Never so easy."

Aaron ran to the window. "They come, they come."

"Pop must be here with Atlee," Esther said. "Don't crow so around Pop, Ruben, or you'll be working twice as hard."

His father-in-law entered the house. "Good man, your pop," Ruben said with resounding zeal.

Esther patted his cheek. "Smart man, my husband."

"You staying, Pop?" Rachel asked as she kissed her father's cheek and gave him a wrapped present, which he took with no comment. He felt that gift-giving should not have primary importance on Christmas, so he would open his gifts alone later.

"No, little one," he said. "I bring Esther's cakes to the older members of the church and say blessing for them over their dinners. I eat with you tomorrow, Second Christmas, at our house."

Rachel accepted that happily. Second Christmas was always as good as the first in her book. Better, maybe. It was downright lazy not to work two whole days in a row.

Atlee wasn't having a good day. He thought at first Emma and Aaron were Jacob and Anna when they were little; then quick as a wink, he got it straight.

Ruben shook his head when Atlee gave everybody a handkerchief. "Everybody needs a *schnoopduff* already," Atlee said.

"Ya, and they don't cost too dearly either," Ruben muttered.

Atlee laughed heartier than any of them at the words. "You betcha already."

Simon placed the plates of roast turkey and ham on the table.

Rachel wiped her hands on a towel. "*Kum esse,* come eat, everybody."

"Hard to choose what to eat, Mudpie," Ruben said. "So many good things. Ah, German noodle ring." He rubbed his hands together. "My favorite."

Esther shoved his shoulder with hers. "Everything's your favorite."

With his return shove, Ruben managed to kiss his wife's cheek. "Good pickled relish and chowchow, Rach." He smiled innocently.

"Told you he liked the sours," Esther said.

"Kissed you first. Proves I like sweets more."

"The Christmas turkey, he fattens long enough, and he eats good," Atlee said.

"In North Dakota, we didn't celebrate on December 25th, like this, we celebrated Old Christmas on January 6th instead."

"Pass the chestnut stuffing, Jacob," Simon said. "When did you have Second Christmas, then?"

"We didn't, and I missed it. Christmas is better here."

After dinner, in the cozy best room, a fire burning in the fireplace, Atlee began the carol singing. The twins sat on a quilt near the fireplace, Daniel in a cradle beside them, while they played with their new toys.

Later, Jacob took out the old sled and they all went out to get some exercise and make room for cake and pie. Esther's long cumbersome dress did not stop her from taking a slide down the hill with Ruben, who was screaming all the way. When they turned over at the bottom, Ruben kissed his wife with great fervor, then covered her face with snow.

Esther got back at him by shoving snow down his neck. He chased her around the barn.

The snow fight Jacob started went on a long time before Ruben and Esther returned.

Rachel doubted she and Simon would ever play that way. She could not look at Jacob while Ruben and Es were gone. She knew what would happen with her and Jacob in the same circumstances.

Throwing off such thoughts, she went to take Simon's arm. Come and take a fat lady for a walk. Their talk was of the day, mostly the children's excitement and the puppies. It was good to be pleasant with Simon. It was good to remember why she married him, that she had not been stupid. He had been a good man then; he seemed to be so again.

Rachel woke on Second Christmas to the twins' calls. *"Siss widder am schneea."* It was snowing again.

"Come on then," she heard Jacob tell them. "We'll hitch Caliope to the sleigh, give the lines a jingle, and across the fields we'll fly to see Uncle Boob, Aunt Es, and *Daudy* Zook."

Tucked warmly between the adults, the blowing snow tickling their faces, the twins giggled the whole way. Es's roast pork with apple dumplings "ate good" too. So did the oyster pie and pickled pears.

During the meal, Rachel's father surprised them all by inviting Simon to give the *Anfang* the next Sunday.

To give the opening sermon was a great honor for the Deacon. Simon lowered his head. "Thank you, Bishop Zook."

Again her husband's humility amazed her. Determined to show her appreciation, Rachel rose to go to him, placing her hands on his shoulders and her cheek against his. "I'm happy for you, Simon. That's a fine Christmas gift, Pop."

"It is not a gift. It has been earned."

A minute of silent communication seemed to pass between her father and her husband.

Second Christmas was good. As good as First. That afternoon, everyone went skating on Echo Pond, with a big bonfire to warm their hands. Aaron loved that best.

They built snowmen and started another snowball fight.

On the way home, snow covered the cornfields and became the only light to brighten their way. At the crest of the hill, Jacob stopped the sleigh. "Emma, Aaron, see that starry sky?" They looked up and nodded. "That's the same sky that looked down on Baby Jesus."

"Oh," they said, eyes wide, awe in their voices.

He began to sing *"Ihr Kinderlein, Commet,"* "O Come, All Ye Children," and Rachel knew this was the best Christmas ever.

Chapter Fifteen

The darkness of midnight filled Rachel's bedroom.

And her heart. And her mind.

Sleep would not come.

The January weather made it necessary to bundle up, even at night, and though she was snug and warm on the outside, she shivered with cold inside.

For months her husband had been good and kind. Loving almost. He seemed to respect her for the first time in their marriage.

He'd smiled and played at Christmas. He'd bought the twins puppies.

Rachel swallowed a sob. She had come to like her husband, to want her marriage to work. Despite everything, she had been so willing to try, to forgive everything and begin anew. She wanted almost to ask if he could forgive her. But she wondered if any husband, even one who loved his wife, could forgive the kind of sin she had committed.

But now he had begun to frighten her again, more as each day passed. Tonight most of all.

Rachel lay her palm protectively over her child to ride the crest of each life-affirming motion. A foot here she felt, an arm there. Sometimes she thought he must be tumbling head over heel, so many arms and legs did she feel kicking all at once.

If Simon realized three weeks were left before the birth, she feared for the safety of this beloved innocent kicking furiously below her hand.

The time for her to have borne the child, if it were his, had come and gone and still she carried high and proud.

Big. She was so big, she'd carried off the look of being near her time until here she was, almost two weeks beyond it. And now Simon watched. He watched her like a caged beast waiting for the cage doors to open so he might leap free . . . and devour everything in his path.

As in years past, when Simon walked into the room, Rachel's heart beat furiously. And now, even her child stopped stirring, as if sensing some slight movement might draw the wrong attention.

Lord, she was teaching an unborn child fear, and she did not know how to keep from it. If her babe did not also know joy, she would weep for him.

Would that there were less fear in store for them both.

Rachel must admit, at least to herself, that when Jacob walked into a room, her heart leapt and so too did her child, as if he sensed her happiness and joined her revelry. He danced in joy, did her baby, as his mother would like to do. And she could not help the gladness that bubbled up within her when it happened . . . when Jacob's son rejoiced in his father's presence.

Jacob. Her son's father.

Simon would be furious when he realized the child in

her womb was not of his seed . . . and worse, that he was Jacob's.

Rachel had once thought herself willing to pay any price for her night with Jacob. And now—she closed her eyes— now she held something of such value, she understood what price could be too high.

"Please, God," she whispered. "Keep this child, Your child, safe, no matter the sins of his parents."

She had reason to pray. Simon had been on edge, angry all this evening. Even Aaron's silly play had failed to bring a smile to Simon's lips, and Aaron usually managed it, even if no one else could.

After she'd put the twins down and said a quick good night to Jacob, whose eyes showed love even though his words could not, Rachel had gone downstairs to do the final stitching on the Rose of Sharon quilt for Emma.

Simon had come to sit with her. And watch her. "This child of yours is stubborn. He will be like his mother, I fear."

With only a moment's worry over the root of his comment, she had spoken. "Do not assign the child faults before you even know him, faults you will tend to punish him for all his life."

"Like I punish you for yours?"

She saw, from the narrowing of his eyes, he wanted her to argue with him. Like old times. "I only mean you should judge him for himself, not for who his mother is."

"Or who his father is?"

Her heart leapt in fear and she was certain she'd paled. Though she tried to make a quick recovery, she feared she did not fool him. "You might just like this child. He could be like Aaron."

But Simon said nothing.

"Aaron is more like Levi," she said. "More than either you or Jacob. And Emma is like Anna, Jacob says. Do you think so, Simon? Do you remember your sister, Anna, very much?''

Pain changed Simon's face then, making her think there might be some emotion in him. He showed his feelings rarely, and only, it seemed, with Aaron. And this was not mild either, it was torment ... soul-deep. Raw and bleeding.

He brought his face close to hers. "Whenever this child is born ..." He let the words linger before he continued. "Do not forget there are two other children who need your attention. Do not set those babies out in the cold to face life alone."

As had happened to him, he had not said, but she knew. Oh, she knew.

After that, and until this moment, her heart would not calm.

Whenever this child is born, he'd said. Whenever ...

If Simon's patience ran out before her child's birth, which it was likely to do, how could she keep her baby safe? *"Ich liebe dich,"* she said, smoothing her gown over her belly. "I love you."

Sleep would not come.

Unable to lie still any longer, Rachel got out of bed and went to her window to look toward the barn. Lights she saw there, spilling onto the ground's hard crust of snow, bright, then dim, from one window to the next as if someone prowled, lantern in hand.

The light stopped moving and remained in the corner window near the Gutenberg. Becoming agitated, Rachel went down to the kitchen, threw her cape over her robe and nightgown, and slipped her feet into her heavy outdoor shoes.

Moving as quickly as her ungainly self would allow, she made her way to the barn and entered through the open side door.

The cows were shifting and lowing, too much for this time of night. Even with someone moving around inside, it wasn't normal. She made her way down the row of them, and stopped when she saw empty places along the stall line.

How could two cows get loose and Simon not see them?

A loud crack turned Rachel around. Cautiously, heart racing, she moved toward the corner where her printing press sat, where the sound had originated.

From behind the buggy, Rachel could see Simon's arm, hammer in hand, bear down; she heard the same resistant, shattering sound, then a splintering. She bit her lip to stifle a shout, and grabbed a post to keep from rushing forth. She could not place her child in danger. She knew Simon's fury well. He could as easily direct those blows at her.

Slapping the cow's rump, he made it back-kick the press.

"Goot," Simon said. "Do your worst."

Rachel inched back, step by step, trembling overtaking her. Only when she was far enough away that Simon could not hear her, did she run outside and back to the house.

She shut the kitchen door and leaned against it to catch her breath. The accidents were not accidents. The cats, the lamb, they did not damage the press.

Rachel closed her eyes, took a deep breath.

Simon had only changed the face he showed. He'd smiled and laughed and pretended to care about her at the same time he'd damaged her press, mistreating it because he could not mistreat her.

In his heart, if he owned one, Simon had never changed at all.

Again she'd believed.

Again he'd betrayed.

But this time, there was some validity to his rage because of what he suspected.

How much more fury would he command, how much more harm would he do, once he was certain he had cause?

In three weeks, she would know.

Her own safety worried Rachel not at all. But her child ... "Dear God," she whispered, overwhelming fear, apprehension, alarm rising within in her.

Only one person could keep their child safe. She needed Jacob. Now. Perhaps more at this moment than at any other time in her life.

The sound of his door opening woke Jacob, and he rose on his elbows trying to make out the form in the doorway. For a minute, he feared Simon was looking to do mischief, but he realized, with Aaron nearby, it was unlikely.

Then he knew and sat up. "Rachel. Are you all right? Is it the baby?"

Emma stirred and mumbled her brother's name, then quieted.

He threw off the covers and made to get up, but Rachel placed her hand on his shoulder to calm him. "I'm all right, Jacob," she said. "It's not my time."

In her virginal gown, hair cascading down her back, she stood trembling beside his bed, and even in the middle of a cold and lonely night, Rachel was a whisper of sunshine. She had always been so for him. His dream. His life.

Always.

Jacob covered himself with the corner of the quilt, his heart still racing. He kept his arms firmly by his sides, his need to pull her down and into his bed almost frightening.

Then she wrapped her arms around her child, cradling and protecting it, and whispered, "But my baby, Jacob. My baby needs very badly to be held right now." Jacob tried to remember that what they both wanted and what was best were not one and the same.

"Please, Jacob," she pleaded. "My baby wants holding."

And Jacob lost the battle. He rose to kneel on the edge of the bed facing her, trailing a finger down her neck to the edge of her nightgown. "And this beautiful vessel nurturing such a needy baby, Rachel, does she want holding right now too?"

When Rachel nodded, he laid his head on her breast and slid his hands down the sides of her belly to meet under the child, who bid him welcome by settling in.

He felt Rachel sigh and knew that for them both, emotion sought escape. Such intimacy as this they craved like those drowning crave air. "I will always be here for you and our child, Rach."

"I did not say—"

He silenced her, his finger crossing her lips. "Shh." He began, slowly, to undo the buttons at the bodice of her gown, waiting for her to stop him. He moved close enough to feel the child push against his abdomen, and placed his palm over the movement with a chuckle. "We have awakened him, I think."

Rachel placed her hand over his, her look joyful, and nodded at the cribs by the far wall. "I fear we will awaken them."

"A tornado would not awaken them. Such sleep habits have been a blessing."

Rachel turned her smile on him, bringing a quickening to his soul, and his body.

He unfastened more buttons, and she did not stop him.

The placket on the bodice of the gown fell open, revealing the rounded top of an ivory breast. Jacob savored the sight and stroked it with exquisite leisure, wanting, more than his next breath, to make love to her.

He lifted a rich blackberry curl and brought it to his cheek, then his lips for a kiss. He inhaled its rain-fresh scent, and floated to heaven.

Placing his hands on each side of Rachel's beautiful face, her look open and filled with love, he combed his fingers back, weaving his hands through her hair until the silk filled his palms and her love filled his soul.

Her heart sought communion with his.

Her lips parted and he accepted.

He drank her contented sigh and matched it, serenity swelling to perfect happiness. This long-awaited kiss, reflecting months, years, of love and need, was erotic and spiraling.

Eternity and heaven.

Jacob's hands shook, his legs too, as he pulled away. Reaching for the skirt of her gown, he raised it slowly to allow Rachel to put finality to this extraordinary madness . . . and waited on the brink of heaven or hell.

Long moments passed. Their gazes locked, held.

"I will not be the one to stop this, Rachel," he said.

"Neither I," she said, raising her arms.

Elation made Jacob dizzy.

Rachel trembled with joy when Jacob pulled the gown over her head and tossed it to the floor. He examined her swollen body with a heated look, and held out his hand. "Come."

She placed her knee on his bed, her joy almost too sharp, and again destiny came to mind. Their first time had been for soothing and healing. This was for loving and giving pleasure, for rejoicing.

Then she was in his arms, where she was meant to be, skin to skin, her body swollen, yet beautiful to him, she had seen in his look.

"I will love you and our child until the end of my days," he promised.

And her heart skipped. "Jacob—"

"Do not mar the night by denying it," he pleaded. "In my heart, you are my wife and carrying our child, and I am going to love you until the moon seeks rest and the sun's glow pinks the horizon.''

Rachel arched into his hands as they sought remembrance of her every curve and hollow. "Yes," she whispered, allowing herself to become Jacob's wife in heart, mind, and body.

Closing her eyes, she savored each touch, as with hands and heart her body memorized his. Here was a dear sun-roughened face, a wiry-soft beard, a warm mouth, with smooth parted lips, pleasure-pulling and deep.

Jacob's Adam's apple rose as she caressed his neck, and he shuddered as she ran her hand along his torso, parting chest hairs, budding a hidden nipple.

And he whispered love words as he kissed her face, her neck, while her hand made its downward descent, testing, stroking, learning—hard and soft, sinew and bone, muscle and throbbing man.

He took suckle as she closed her hand over him and he touched her. Soft. Wet.

Thunder roared. Hot. Loud.

Lightning struck in short, fast bolts.

Rachel urged Jacob to enter her.

He was hard. Ready. But he pulled away and lay back, taking great draughts of air, his arm at his brow. "Rach, we have to stop."

"No, Jacob. I need you inside of me."

He shook his head. "The babe. You're too far along."

Minutes. A heartbeat of time in a universe of time . . . a step into eternity . . .

"Aren't you?"

Rachel closed her eyes.

Inevitability. Fate. Overwhelming. Ordained.

Rachel rolled toward Jacob and took his hand, sliding it over their child. "In the darkness of this one night," she said, "when, in our hearts and minds, we are man and wife and free to be together forever, I tell you, Jacob Sauder, that my child was conceived in love . . . with your love did you give me our child.''

Jacob buried his face in her neck, and they held each other so intimately, so close to being one as two could be, Rachel thought she might bleed if they separated.

He raised his head and looked into her eyes. "Thank you," he said, and kissed the haven of their child with reverence.

How could God see their love as sin?

Then with sudden clarity, as if God spoke to her, Rachel realized that this child was His blessing.

Then Jacob hovered above her, the moment too perfect to be earthly.

"I will love you slowly and tenderly," he said, as if she had not known it. "But you will stop me if you are uncomfortable. For I would not hurt either of you for the world." He kissed her belly again and again, chuckling as their child seemed to push wherever his kiss landed. He gazed at her, his look awestruck and reverent.

She raised her arms in welcome and sighed in contentment when Jacob slid gently inside her.

This was true loving, Rachel thought, sweet, heart-whole lovemaking, the way it was meant to be. Like the love given and shared when this child between them was conceived.

With each thrust, each soothing stroke and reverent kiss, and with each vow to cherish, Jacob told her how much he loved her.

He raised her to heights she remembered from their first loving as glorious, and realized the word did not do the tumult justice. No words ever could.

It was higher than the moon and brighter than stars.

Heaven, but better.

Afterward, when he lowered himself to her side and pulled her against him, stroking her sweat-slick body with wonder, Rachel realized their ecstasy had not been merely physical, but a communion, both emotional and spiritual, a melding of souls rising together toward a hallowed place. Blessed.

To tell Jacob now of Simon's treachery seemed misplaced. Cruel. And so Rachel did not. Instead she lifted her face for his kiss and allowed herself to glide peacefully to earth . . . and rest.

Rachel tossed upon a raging sea, gulls squawking in the distance, and wondered how the dream could seem so real when she had only ever read about such a thing.

A dear, beloved chuckle touched her ear, and the sea raged the more. She opened her eyes.

Aaron and Emma were jumping on the bed. When they saw she was awake, they pushed their way between her and Jacob offering morning kisses, calling "Pa-pop" and "Momly."

Pudgy fingers poked her eyes to be certain they stayed open.

And Rachel laughed. If God took her at this moment, she would die happy, she thought, kissing two small sleep-warm faces.

Jacob sat up and tried to remove his children to his other side. "Are you all right?" he asked her.

"Come here, scamp," he said to Aaron, who was proving more difficult to catch than his sister. "Momly is in no condition for you to be using her as a stairway." When he got Aaron settled, he gave Rachel his lopsided smile. "You've already been badly used." He ran his hand through his sleep-tousled hair, and Rachel knew this moment would be etched on her memory forever. "I never meant—"

"There was no using. Only giving, by the both of us.

Gentle and beautiful it was, with no discomfort. Only joy. I feel no discomfort, no remorse. We will have last night for the rest of our lives.''

She saw his pain at her reminder that their life was not as they'd pretended in the dark of night. "Do you see my nightgown anywhere?" she asked to change the mood.

"Me get it," Emma said, and scrambled off the bed to retrieve it, climbing quickly back up to hand it over with a proud smile.

Rachel kissed her on the nose, but she was shaken. "Thank you, love." She looked at Jacob, not bothering to hide her shock. "They understand more than I thought. What will they make of this?"

"That it is as it should be. Surely you can see that."

"If they remember in future years, when they understand more about—"

"They will be told how it has always been with us. They will know, from experience, the goodness in us, that we are not perfect, but strive to do better."

"And we will do better. We must, Jacob."

"Yes," he said sadly. "We must."

They heard a familiar creak, a footstep on the bottommost stair.

Jacob jumped from the bed.

"Aaron?" Simon called. "Are you coming with me to feed Pokey?"

"Unkabear!" Aaron said, and ran to open the bedroom door before Jacob could stop him. Then he bolted out and down the stairs.

Jacob got his pants on and picked up Emma faster than Rachel could catch her breath. Then he left and shut the door behind him, except that, after a minute, it opened on a long, mournful squeal.

Wide-eyed and heart pounding, Rachel could see Jacob

holding Emma at the top of the stairs. Simon was speaking to Aaron as they ascended.

Snatching her gown from sight, she pulled the covers over her head. Naked, frightened, Rachel was filled with shame. She should have stayed in her own room last night.

She did not deserve forgiveness.

And Jacob did not deserve to suffer the consequences of her seduction.

Jacob thought his pounding heart would escape his chest.

"You missed milking," Simon said, Aaron in his arms, from the middle of the stairs. Jacob made sure his brother could not move beyond him.

"Momly," Emma called, pointing toward the open door of his room.

Jacob curled his hand over her pointing finger and kissed it. "We're going to let Momly sleep." He looked at his brother. "So close to her time, she must need rest, if she has not arisen yet."

"Is she?" Simon raised a brow. "Close to her time?"

"I have never seen anyone bigger." The beat of Jacob's heart increased when he realized Rachel was awfully big if her time was weeks away.

Big enough for twins.

Big enough to die in childbed, like Miriam.

"I should check on her," Simon said, concern on his face. "It could be her time and she cannot rise."

Simon's swing from concern to anger and back troubled Jacob, because he could never tell which was real. "I'll check on her," he said.

"I'd like to remind you, I am her husband."

"I'd like to remind you, only one of us has ever hurt her. I will check on her."

"We will check together then," Simon said.

"Simon?" Levi called from the bottom of the stairs.

Years of discipline and respect had them both turning at their father's commanding voice.

Jacob wondered how long he'd been standing there. "Simon, bring my grand-babies down to me and we will feed them breakfast. You have forfeited your rights, and you know it. Jacob will check to see Rachel is sleeping well, and then he will be right down. Won't you, son?"

Jacob knew Simon was too embarrassed to have caught the command their father gave, that he himself should not linger in the bedroom of a woman not his wife. Ah, Datt, he thought. I do not deserve such trust. He nodded. "Right down, Datt."

After taking Emma, Simon glared. "Remember, brother. 'The Lord knows how to rescue the godly from trial, and to keep the unrighteous under punishment until the day of judgment.' "

"And you are the godly, Simon?"

"I am not the unrighteous." He turned to go.

Jacob grabbed his arm. "Let he who is without sin cast the first stone."

Simon's nostrils flared, but he remained silent. And as Jacob watched him go, another verse ran through head. "I will give to each of you as your works deserve." Then, and with some surprise; "I will put my trust in Him." And hope filled Jacob's heart for the first time since the day he'd left.

Chapter Sixteen

"Jacob! Jacob, help me!"

Jacob was pulled from a dreamless sleep by the words he'd been dreading for weeks. He leapt from his bed and ran to her room. "I'm here, Mudpie."

He heard her harsh breath as he lit her bedside lamp.

Her quilt was thrown back. Clutching her robe, she rested her head on her pillow, but her slippered feet hung off the side, as if she'd begun to rise, but then lain back down. Fear etched her features. "I think the baby is coming," she said. "But it's too soon, Jacob."

Jacob's heart raced, but he did not allow Rachel to see his fear. He nodded matter-of-factly, removed her slippers and raised her legs to the bed, then took the robe from her stiff fingers. "I'll get Esther and Hannah Bieler." He drew the quilt over her and kissed her forehead. "I'll be back in no time."

Rachel grabbed his arm. "Don't leave me. Please. You're

the only one in this house who's delivered a baby. Oh, Jacob, suppose something goes wrong."

He squeezed her hand. "Give me a minute to rouse Simon and send him for Hannah then. Once she sees you, she will know if we need to send for the English doctor, and if that's what it takes, we will get him."

"Simon will not approve."

"He will want what is best for you."

Rachel looked uncertain, but nodded finally.

"How many pains did you have? Hannah will want to know."

"Three, no four."

"How far apart?"

"The first two came close together, the third more than an hour after the second, but this one was strong, and I am so scared."

Jacob brushed his lips against hers in the lightest of kisses, one meant to convey encouragement while hiding soul-deep fear. He cupped her cheek. "Ach, Rach. I would take the pain if I could."

She turned her lips into his palm. "I know."

Jacob returned from sending Simon off in a flurry of panicked activity, and found Rachel sleeping. He sat forward in the chair, his elbows on his knees, and watched her for nearly an hour. When Esther arrived with Hannah Bieler, he motioned them from the room and followed them out. "She has been sleeping since I sent for you. Is that normal?"

Hannah smiled. "False labor, I think, but we should wake her and get her up to see if they start again, and we need to talk about what happened."

Near dawn, three hours later, a red-faced Rachel walked

into the kitchen to find Jacob, Simon, and Levi sitting at the table drinking coffee. "Did Esther and Hannah leave?"

"I took them home," Levi said.

"I guess I got more sleep than most of you did last night." She lowered her bulk into her chair. "I'm sorry," she said, staring at her hands.

Levi chuckled and leaned over to squeeze her clasped hands. "It's normal, what happened. Good practice."

She knew Jacob would feel the same, so she looked at Simon. It was always difficult for him to keep his anger and frustration from showing, but this morning, he was even worse. She might have saved his pride if she'd given birth to this child last night. A child born in February he could claim as his. Babies arrived late all the time.

An early birth might have kept peace. Still, Rachel was relieved her child could grow stronger before he came into the world.

Rachel had never given anyone an indication when her baby was due. Conception and birth were private and the women accepted her silence. "When a woman's husband came to her nightly," Anna Yoder had commented with a twinkle in her eye, "who could tell when the child was conceived?"

Simon had not questioned the child's paternity at first. He never doubted his ability to father a child. But her childless state must not have been her fault. Time was, she would have been happy to shout such knowledge, if only to keep him from badgering her with his painful charge of barrenness. But none of it mattered now.

In another three weeks, Simon would know this child could not be his. Oh, he would be furious over her adultery certainly, but inside, he would be more furious that she must realize, if she was not barren, he must be.

And she was afraid.

* * *

As spring settled on the land, the song of the bluebird drifted once again across the meadow. Cress began to grow in the run. Chickadees and sparrows built new nests.

No one loved these signs of earth's renewal more than Rachel.

With unusual eagerness, she took on the annual March cleaning of the summer kitchen, to prepare the room for another season of hard use. As she worked, she imagined a cradle placed just there, in the corner, her child napping as she mixed scrapple or tossed slaw. Shot with energy, she scrubbed the four huge iron kettles Jacob had lined up on the floor, while Aaron and Emma came behind her with dry rags to wipe the kettles dry—more or less.

Though temperatures began to creep back up toward warmer days, the nights still tended to freeze, and it was time to tap the maple trees. Rachel's grandfather had told her the story of how the first Amish settlers had learned sugaring from the Indians, and they still they did it nearly the same way.

Maple syrup was a gift from the forest, her *Grossdaudy* used to say. A gift the Amish settlers had accepted with thanks.

Two weeks ago, she and the twins had spent an afternoon gathering elderberry and alder branches, which were cut short and their soft centers pushed out—hollowed, they made perfect spouts.

Today Jacob, Levi, and Simon were collecting the first filled buckets, leaving empty ones in their places. In a little while, they would bring her the sap to boil. The Indians used to heat rocks and drop them red-hot into wooden vats of sap to make it boil, but in the Sauder house four huge iron kettles would be filled and set to boiling.

"Pa-pop! The maypou comes, Momly," Emma said as the flatbed wagon stopped outside the door.

Aaron climbed up to the window and banged on the glass. "Unkabear!"

"Ach, Rach!" Jacob said, stepping into the room, a bucket of sap in each hand. "Get up from there. I'll fire the logs once we get the kettles in place. Move now. You've done too much already."

Rachel took each twin by the hand and moved out of the way. Giving in to the heaviness of her body, she sat and took a child on each knee, her lap long since claimed by another.

Jacob and Simon lifted the heavy round-bottomed kettles one by one, and settled them into the circles cut out of the top of the low iron stove.

She used those kettles for everything. Cold, she used them to mix slaw. During butchering, she mixed meat products to fill sausage skins. Other than the bake oven outside, and the smokehouse beside it, no other household convenience was as well used. And at no other time did she enjoy their use more than at sugaring.

For two days, the scent of maple wafted through the house from potato cellar to attic beams.

Esther came Friday night to help Rachel filter, jar, and seal the syrup supply for the year, and to help prepare for their annual sugaring party.

"That batch ready?" Rachel asked.

Esther raised a spoon coated with boiled syrup tip-down over the pan. "No," she said. "It dribbles from the bottom of the spoon yet. Check the one in that kettle, Rach."

"Ouch," Rachel said, as she bent over the pan, and rubbed her back.

Esther looked concerned. "What's the matter?"

"My back is sore from leaning over these kettles." She grinned. "But my mouth is watering." Dipping her spoon in the syrup, she held it over the vat tip-down and just like magic, a thick layer of maple syrup began to fold itself from the top of the spoon, over and over as it made its way down the spoon's bowl to apron off in one huge glob. "Perfect!"

Ezra Zook watched his daughters from just outside the summer kitchen door.

Esther made for Rachel's kettle so fast, he almost chuckled. Rachel dipped the big wooden spoon into the syrup to coat it and suspend it above the kettle. Each with a small spoon at the ready, giggling as if they were six again, they waited. And as the thick, sweet mass parted from the wooden spoon, Rachel and Esther caught some of the bounty with their small spoons, amid cries of success.

Mouths pursed, they blew on their treats to cool them, and at exactly the same moment, they raised mischievous eyes to each other . . . and spooned the sweetest syrup of the season into each other's mouths.

"Mmm," they said together, rolling their eyes and dissolving into giggles.

The Bishop laughed, stepping into the room. "Twenty years I watch you two do that, and still it tickles me."

Only one part of the tradition was missing this year, they all knew. Their mother's annual scold.

Ezra blinked his eyes to clear them. "Ach! You two. A bellyache it giffs, the saltpeter," he quoted his absent wife. "I tell you always, filter first, then taste."

His daughters stepped into his arms. Sniffles he heard, so he held his own in check and kissed each forehead. "She is watching now, and she is smiling. So must we." He forced a chuckle. "Ach. I cannot hold you so close, Rach. You are getting too fat."

The girls stepped back, their smiles belying their tears, and wiped their cheeks with their hands.

Levi stepped into the room rubbing his hands together.

"*Kum,* sugar on snow and dandelion wine we have, to celebrate spring and new beginnings." He squeezed the Bishop's arm as he passed. "And we remember, with smiles, those who have gone before us. Ya?"

Bishop Zook nodded.

Levi told a story about his wife and an ornery mule who'd tried to kick her. "She was so mad, she kicked the stubborn cuss back," he said, slapping his knee. "After that, that mule loved that woman until we buried the mean thing out beyond the pasture."

"Mom? Or the mule?" Jacob asked.

After a shocked second, a smile broke on Levi's face, and he roared with laughter.

"I have a story to remember Anna," Jacob said. "You know, she was slow to talk." He eyed the company. "But that didn't matter, because I always knew what she wanted. Twins always know about each other. So I would tell Mom, 'Anna wants a drink,' and mom would give it to her. Or, 'Anna is tired, or she is hungry. . . .' Always, I knew what Anna wanted and I told whoever needed to know so they could take care of her."

"Ya, and when Anna finally spoke," Levi said, picking up the tale, "her first words were for him. She said, 'Shut up, Yacob!' "

Ruben shook his head. "But he never did."

Jacob's frown brought laughter.

With Emma leaning against his knee, Ruben showed her how to dip her finger in a cup of warm syrup and lick it off. Then he let Daniel, in his arms, lick some off the tip of his own finger.

"Ruben Miller! That baby's going to be sick," Esther scolded, her smile giving little meaning to her words.

Ruben winked at her. "This baby's just like his mother. He likes sweets. Look at him licking his lips. He wants more."

"Don't you dare!" Esther chided.

Jacob laughed at their banter as he dribbled hot maple syrup atop a pan of clean snow. "Come and get it," he called. When it cooled to a brittle candy, he handed pieces to the children first, then offered some to the adults.

Simon refused to take any.

"Go ahead, you could use some sweetening," Ruben said.

Esther told her husband to hush, and poked him for good measure as she took Daniel. Ruben grabbed her poking finger and kissed it. "Even without maple syrup, it's still sweet."

"Hush, I said."

Rachel stood and rubbed her back.

"You all right, Mudpie?" Jacob asked.

Simon snorted. "Does she look all right to you?" He stood and took her arm. "Come along, it's time for you to rest." He led her toward his section of the house. "I'll take you upstairs."

Rachel could not imagine what had gotten into Simon, but when she turned to stop him, she saw a significant look pass between him and her father.

Simon did not want her father to realize they slept apart, and she understood that. "I'm not ready to lie down, Simon. I need to walk for a bit." She disengaged herself from his hold. With her hands on the small of her back, she paced the perimeter of the room. After a while, she went into the kitchen, where Esther nursed Daniel.

"Back hurt?" Esther asked.

"Ya. Bad all right."

"How long?"

"All day, but worse now."

"Oh, Rach. Side back or middle back?"

"Middle. Why?"

"You're in labor."

"You think?"

"After your false start, Hannah said it would probably take you this way. I should have told you, but until this minute, I didn't think of it again."

"Don't tell anybody, Es. Please? Simon is trying to get me to go up to the bedroom in his house while Pop is here, and I just can't."

"I must say, I wondered when you had false labor why you were not in the *kinderhaus* with Simon."

Rachel sat at the table and stared at her hands. "It's a long story."

"You don't need to tell me. I've seen plenty enough to imagine. But you do need to lie down soon, and we should send for Hannah."

"I feel more like I need to walk right now," Rachel said. "When I feel like I need to lie down, I'll bring the twins up to bed. Then you and Ruben can leave and Pop will go too. Will Ruben bring Hannah by after he takes you home?"

"Of course he will. He's a good man, my Ruben."

Rachel squeezed her sister's shoulder when she passed by her chair in her trek around the kitchen. "I'm happy for you."

"I wish I could be happy for *you.*"

"You should be. I have many blessings. And Simon is . . . has tried to change."

Esther nodded. "Listen to those men. Too much dandelion wine, I think."

"You'll have to drive home. Oh, no. I need Ruben to drive Hannah."

"Make some coffee," Esther said as she patted little Daniel's back, and he blew a bubble while closing his heavy eyes.

"I don't think I can manage it, Es."

"Go put those babies to bed, then. I'll make sure Jacob

gets the notion to follow so he can do the work. A cup of strong coffee and Ruben'll be fine once the cold air hits him."

"Thanks, Es."

"What are sisters for? I'll come back with Hannah."

"Then don't leave."

"But how—"

"I'll tell Jacob once I'm upstairs and he'll send Simon. Pop will probably stay, but we'll say I'm too taken with labor to be moved, if he asks. Maybe he won't."

"You know Pop."

"Ya," Rachel said. "He'll ask."

When Rachel came to the best room from the kitchen, she found Emma sleeping in Ruben's arms and Aaron in his father's. Simon was nowhere to be found. Her father and Levi were playing checkers. "You all calmed down fast," she said.

"Simon told us to quiet down so the twins could sleep, then slammed out of here," Ruben said.

"Bring the twins, you two," Rachel said to Jacob and Ruben. "I need to put them to bed."

"I'll put 'em down, Rach," Jacob said. "You don't need to go climbing those stairs."

Standing behind her father, Esther rolled her eyes at Rachel. When Jacob caught the byplay he looked from one to the other. Esther made a go-along motion with her hand, giving him the idea he should be quiet and do it.

Ruben and Jacob looked at each other and shrugged. Their manner suggested that going along was better than arguing. Rachel marveled how so much could be expressed with shrugs and rolled eyes.

Each holding a sleeping three-year-old, Ruben and Jacob followed her to the stairs.

Jacob knew something was wrong as soon Rachel began

to climb with that slow, determined pace. He turned to Ruben. "Take Aaron."

Stepping up beside Rachel, he took her arm. And as if she'd been waiting to let go, she faltered. Certain no one was at the bottom of the stairs watching, Jacob lifted her into his arms and carried her to her room.

When he put her down, his arms were wet. "I think your water broke, Rach," he said, somewhat shocked. Then he saw her abdomen become high and round. When he placed his hand over it, it was hard.

Rachel moaned, and Ruben began to sweat.

"Put them to bed, Ruben," Jacob said. "Their night clothes are hanging on the peg near their cribs."

Like a man in a trance, Ruben nodded and left.

Jacob removed Rachel's kapp, then took the pins from her hair. When another pain took her so fast, he too began to sweat. This baby seemed to be coming awfully fast. He slipped the pins from her clothes very carefully and removed her apron. Then he opened her dress and prepared to free her from the sleeve.

Feeling a hand on his arm, he looked up.

"I'll do it," Esther said.

"But I—"

"I understand, I do, but it would be better if I undressed her, in case somebody—"

"Yes," Jacob said. "Of course, Es. You're right. I'll wait outside."

"Don't act like a man suffering the fires of Hell, Jacob. Everyone will see, and Simon won't understand."

Jacob nodded and went to his room. Ruben was putting Daniel in one of the cribs.

"Esther said put the twins together in one and Daniel in the other. Is that all right?"

Jacob smiled. "Lots of nights, one climbs in with the other anyway. They'll be fine."

"Will you?"

"I guess."

"Simon gone for Hannah Bieler?"

Jacob ran his hand through his hair. "I forgot the midwife. I'd best go."

"Shouldn't Simon?"

"Es said I can't stay around here like a man crazed." He sighed and ran his hand through his hair. "She's right. And if I heard Rach suffer, Ruben, you know how I would be."

Ruben slapped him on the back. "I'll come with you. Screaming won't be too good for me either. If I have to be around another birthing, it'll take me another two months to go near Es."

Jacob stopped. "You didn't go near Es for two months?"

"Shut up, Yacob!"

"But I saw you kissing her."

"Yes, and that's about all I did for a while. You need details, nosy man?"

"Jacob!" Rachel screamed.

Jacob moved to respond to her call, but Ruben grabbed his arm. "Let's get out of here."

Jacob was grateful Ruben propelled him forward because, for the life of him, he could not leave on his own.

Simon, Levi, and the Bishop stood at the bottom.

"Rachel's in labor," Ruben said. "We're going for the midwife."

"Jacob, I need you," Rachel called again, and Ruben did not know who was more upset by it, Rachel's father . . . or her husband . . . or the man whose arm muscles under his hand screamed to be let free, so he could go to her.

In Levi's eyes, there was only sadness.

* * *

Hannah Bieler was not at home and the English doctor was in Philadelphia.

It took them more than a half hour just to discover where Hannah was. After several calls on neighbors, they discovered she was at her sister's in Strasburg, nursing a sick nephew. When they got there, she said if she left, her nephew might die.

It was two more hours before they arrived back at the Sauder house.

Inside, Ruben was struck by the quiet.

Jacob, ahead of him, stopped at the threshold of the best room.

Ruben, coming up behind, gazed about, the buzzing in his head threatening to fell him.

Levi sat alone, elbows on knees, face in his hands.

"Datt?"

When Levi looked up, there was deep sorrow in his look. "You're too late."

Chapter Seventeen

A scream tore from Jacob as he raced up the stairs. At the threshold of Rachel's room, he stopped, stunned.

On her bed, Rachel lay unmoving. Beside it, Bishop Zook gave the Amish blessing for the dead. Esther was standing with her back against the wall, eyes closed, face wet with tears.

Simon rose from his kneeling position at the foot of Rachel's bed, his face hard with hate. "An eye for an eye," he said for Jacob's ears alone, before he left the room, the Bishop behind him.

Jacob dropped to his knees and placed Rachel's cool, limp hand against his cheek. "God, no," he begged. "No! Please!"

Through a haze, Jacob imagined that Rachel's fingers moved at his shout, and a palsy overtook him, salty tears wetting his lips, regret swamping, threatening to drown him.

The imagined movement came again. Longer. Stronger.

Jacob shot to his feet, bent close, and touched Rachel's cold cheek. He gazed in anguish at her perfectly serene face . . . and she opened her eyes.

Jacob's breath caught. Mighty sobs, with no beginning nor end, broke from him.

Rachel held his hand in a weak grip.

With another sob, Jacob touched his cheek to hers. "I thought that . . . that you did not . . ." He took a breath, shuddered, raised his head. "The blessing for the dead your pop was giving."

"Not for me," she said, large tears shivering down her cheeks. "For them."

Jacob spied the cradle he'd not seen in his anguish, where two tiny, bloody little girls lay. Despite the cowl of birth, they were very red. He knelt beside the daughters he would never know, lifting them, one in each hand, bringing them against his heart.

He heard a whimper so soft, it might have been a mouse, felt a ripple so slight, it might have been his imagination. But the sound came again, the merest cry, weak, thready, the movement weaker still.

"They're alive! Alive and freezing to death! What the hell's the matter with you, Esther?"

Esther rushed from the room.

Remorse stabbed Jacob, but he could not spare the time for concern. "We've got to warm them. Datt, Datt, come up here!"

His call made the babe who squealed cry in earnest. "Good," he said to Rachel, who was watching with wide, round eyes. "Crying will warm her. I haven't lost my mind," he said, answering her look. After each babe lay wrapped mummy-like in the small blankets set aside for this purpose, Jacob laid them side by side and wrapped them together in another blanket, until just their faces showed.

He pulled Rachel's blanket down and tucked the twin

girls against her. He was about to tell her to put her arms around them to warm them with her body, but he did not need to.

Her sorrow turned to joy as Rachel cradled her babies and crooned to them. As if no one else existed for her, she fussed and tucked, whispered love, kissed tiny foreheads, and prayed aloud. After some time, her pleas sent to the One who watched over them all, she looked at him. "Thank you."

And Jacob thought, "For what?" For giving her a few minutes of her children's lives? She deserved more than that. She deserved better than to be branded a sinner by her husband. Jacob closed his eyes. Rachel deserved more than to be seduced and brought down by him, the man who professed to love her.

From her, he deserved no thanks. From above, he deserved no forgiveness. He cleared his throat. "In a minute, I'll carry you down to the best room where it's warmer."

His father entered with hers, the Bishop clearly surprised she held the babies.

"Bishop Zook, go into the room two doors down, if you please, and take the bed apart. Bring it downstairs and set it up near the big fireplace."

"This is not the time for crying," he said to calm his own father. "This is the time for doing. How did you and Mom warm me and Anna when we were born? You saved two tiny babies who should have died." Jacob looked beyond the ceiling toward the heavens. "Help us save two more, Lord."

"Amen," said the Bishop from the next room.

Rachel echoed her father, and hope shown in her eyes.

"We wrapped you in raw sheep's wool and put you in a bureau drawer by the fire," Levi said. "Your mama fed you every half hour even if you only got a drop. When her milk dried up, we used a lambing bottle." His brows furrowed. "I have the bottles, but we have no sheep for wool."

Jacob shook his head and went to the top of the stairs. "Ruben!"

Ruben stepped into range at the bottom, his face ashen. "Nobody's dead, Ruben."

"I know, Es told me. But . . ."

"And nobody's going to die. I need you to go to Atlee's. Shear some of his sheep if you have to. I need their wool to wrap the babies in."

Ruben did not move.

"Dammit, now, Ruben. Es, bring up all the quilt batting you can find."

"Surely the blankets are enough," Levi said.

"They need layers to keep in their body's warmth. I learned that in North Dakota from an Australian sheep farmer I helped rescue some calves in a blizzard. Unusual man. Smart, though."

With Esther's help, he swathed the babies in quilt stuffing, individually, then side by side again, and handed them back to their waiting mother. "They're pinker than they were before, Rach. That's a good sign," Jacob said.

"Thank you for saving them."

He scoffed, embarrassed, guilt-ridden.

"Bed's all set," Bishop Zook said.

"All made up? Fire roaring? Extra blankets?"

"Fire going, bed made up. I'll get the extra blankets." He left again.

Jacob lifted Rachel, bedding and all, and saw the bloody linens she lay on. "Ach, Rach, nobody even cleaned you up." The clean blanket over her had been hiding the mess. He put her back down, took the babies, and handed them to his father. "Take them down by the fire, hold them against you, and pray. Send Esther back up."

"Esther deliver the afterbirth at least?" Jacob asked when his father left. He peeled away the blanket, then the sheet, still red with blood.

Rachel floated in a different world. She nodded in response to Jacob's question, then looked down at herself, her nightgown bunched at her waist, her body exposed, bloody. Great gasping sobs overtook her.

"Ach," Jacob said to cover his concern at the blood flowing from her. "A flood from both ends."

Her smile was not for his forced jest, but because he could look at her, soiled with blood, and show only love.

"Better for you to smile than cry," he said. "No more tears now to spoil the day such beautiful babies were born."

Esther stepped into the room just as Jacob placed padding between Rachel's legs, and Rachel marveled that her sister did not so much as blink at finding him tending her so intimately.

"Es, I'm sorry I yelled," Jacob said.

Esther nodded. "You had a right to be angry. I was not thinking straight."

"Neither me."

As they worked efficiently side by side tending her, Rachel wondered if she would ever recover from the embarrassment of being unable to tend herself.

"Let's get this gown off her," Esther said. "Then you can raise her so I can remove the soiled linen and replace it with fresh."

Lifting her in his arms, while Esther replaced the linen, Jacob took a minute to press a kiss to her forehead. Rachel closed her eyes and accepted the words he did not speak, that he loved her and their daughters. The moment brought forth the dread buried deep in her heart. "I'm frightened," she said. "That we do not deserve them and God knows it."

"Me too, Mudpie."

Esther's gaze shot to their faces, her shock turning quickly to understanding, but she revealed no judgment. "Jacob, your Datt said you and Anna were smaller. Did you know?"

"Oh, Es. Were they?" Rachel asked, her heart near bursting with hope. Smaller babies than hers had survived. Their own father, even. Had he passed his strength to his daughters?

Rachel closed her eyes to ask the impossible of the only one capable of granting it.

Jacob laid her back down. Together he and Es finished washing her; then they put her in a clean, soft nightgown.

Clean felt good.

Esther tucked the quilt around her.

Warm and clean felt better.

Jacob carried her downstairs to the big bed by the fire.

Being in Jacob's arms felt best.

When he settled her in the bed downstairs, and took his arms from around her, it was all she could do not to cry out, the pain of separation was so keen.

He took the twins from Levi and tucked them into her arms under her blanket.

Levi sniffed. "I go to my house and sleep now. Too much for an old man, all this excitement," he said gruffly.

"Night, Datt."

Upstairs, Daniel began to cry. Esther excused herself. "Middle-of-the-night feeding," she said. "Best get there before he wakes Emma and Aaron."

"Lord, yes," Jacob said. "A tornado couldn't wake them, but Daniel probably could."

Once they heard Esther moving around upstairs, Jacob sat on the bed facing Rachel and his daughters, the look in his eyes speaking of crippling fear and growing hope, of lifetime vows unspoken . . . yet no less binding.

He took them all into his arms and buried his face in her hair. "This is where the three of you belong," he said.

After a while, she felt him calm and he began to pray in German. They spoke the words together.

And peacefulness washed over her.

As if it had happened to Jacob at the same moment, he sat back and nodded, then examined the tiny faces. "Have you seen their eyes?"

"Not yet. You?"

He shook his head. Like her, he was probably thinking it might never happen.

He put his finger toward one tiny mouth, prodding it.

"What are you doing?"

"I want to see if they can suckle. If they can, they've got a fighting chance."

"But she isn't, Jacob."

He did not look away fast enough for her to miss the pain in his eyes. "Well, she's not the hungry one. Let's see if this little one . . . yes! Look at her go. Oh, oh, she's gonna cry 'cause there's nothing there for her. Your turn, Mudpie."

"How can I with them bound together?"

Jacob moved the babes about in their cocoon a bit, then angled the hungry babe toward her, while holding the other.

Rachel blushed, exposing her breast.

Jacob chuckled. "After everything, you can blush with me?"

"I blush for my stupidity. I don't even know how to nurse her."

"If we're lucky she'll show you how." He nudged the baby's mouth toward Rachel's nipple. "Come on, Squeaky. Time for breakfast."

"Ouch!"

"Guess she knows how. Smart girl."

But her nursing did not last long before she drifted to sleep. Rachel feared the baby might still be hungry. "Maybe she's not strong enough to nurse."

"She's small, she doesn't need much. Even a drop or two is good for the first time. It's all right, Rach. They're going to make it, I know it. Let's see if lazy Anna here is hungry now."

"Oh, Jacob, Anna is a good name. Let's call her that, for your sister."

"Guess that's who I was thinking of when I said it. She reminds me of Anna, the quiet one. But I think our girls are identical, Mudpie. See each dimple and single arched brow—"

"Like yours," Rachel said.

"Like mine," Jacob agreed, looking embarrassed.

"If this is Anna, then what shall we name her sister?"

"Squeaky?" Jacob joked.

"I think Anna and Squeaky sounds funny."

"How would you like it if we named our squeaky, hungry baby after your mother?"

"Mary. Pop will like that. I do too."

"Good, now let's feed our Anna."

But Anna did not suckle. After a bit, Rachel closed her gown and held the babies while Jacob kept his arms around all of them.

Ruben came back with the sheep's wool at about two A.M. With shaking hands, he helped Jacob bathe the babies for the first time at the foot of Rachel's bed where it was warm from the fire. Then they wrapped each in raw wool, a blanket, quilt stuffing, then a final blanket.

"Do you think it will help?" Ruben asked.

"The sheep's wool is warm and the lanolin will coat the babies' skin creating another barrier from the cold," Jacob said. "Saved a calf in a blizzard that way once."

"With sheep's wool?"

"With layers of clothes. Mostly mine."

Ruben came to the head of the bed and kissed Rachel's cheek, his own growing red. "Glad you're all right. Where's Es?"

"Sleeping by now, I imagine," Jacob answered. "Go on up. There are two beds. I'll stay here."

"Only need one bed, thanks."

Squeaky nursed twice more in the next two hours, Anna not at all.

When Rachel was ready to sleep from sheer exhaustion, Jacob took the babies, holding them in the rocker near the fireplace . . . and he prayed.

That Anna would not nurse broke his heart. He'd had her so short a time, yet he could not bear to lose her.

Near dawn, he heard the kitchen door open and close, and then Simon stood in the doorway, between the kitchen and the best room, looking from him to Rachel and to the babies. His brother's face wore no expression, neither did he speak. He just stood there.

Finally, he slapped his hat against his leg, turned, and went toward his house.

"He was awfully quiet," Rachel whispered.

Her words surprised Jacob. "Quiet we can live with." When he stood, Squeaky woke.

As Rachel fed one daughter, she cried for the other.

Ruben and Esther came down at dawn, Ruben carrying Emma and Aaron.

The new babies delighted them. Rachel showed off the daughters she feared would never see the summer flowers.

Would Emma and Aaron ever know Anna and Mary? Jacob wondered.

Emma and Aaron were so distressed at Momly's tears, Jacob took the new twins so Rachel could cuddle and calm the older ones, and their determination to love her into smiles seemed to lighten her heart.

Esther herded everyone into the kitchen for breakfast. From her bed in the best room, Rachel smelled maple syrup warming as she nursed her ravenous daughter. Es must be making funnel cakes.

Before long, Emma slipped into the room alone, her movements and her impish, smiling eyes saying she'd sneaked out and was pleased she got away with it. She came around to the babies, and before Rachel could get a hand free to stop her, Emma put the tip of her finger into Anna's mouth.

Looking at Emma's sweet smile, Rachel couldn't scold. But when she went to take Emma's hand away, she saw that Anna was sucking on Emma's finger.

Rachel almost cried out, but feared she'd upset everyone with the cry. "Emma, sweetheart, what did you give the baby?"

Emma held up her wet finger. "Baby like mapou."

As if it happened before her, a picture of last night flashed before Rachel's eyes—Ruben teaching Emma to dip her finger in maple syrup and suck it off. Ruben giving it to Daniel the same way.

"Go get Pa-pop, sweetheart, and bring him here. And bring some maple with you."

After Emma went into the kitchen, Rachel heard Jacob laugh. Then he came in, his look changing when he saw her tears. She shook her head, to tell him he need not worry, but her action made him pale.

"Emma," Rachel said. "Show Pa-pop how you feed the baby."

Emma put her little syrup-covered finger into Anna's mouth; Anna suckled for a minute and fell promptly back to sleep.

Jacob gasped.

Rachel blinked to clear her eyes. "Maple syrup," she said. "Anna likes maple syrup. If we can get her to take that for now, maybe she'll grow strong enough to nurse."

Jacob lifted Emma into the air making her giggle. "And my smart little Emma found the way."

"And who taught Emma to suck maple syrup off her finger?" Rachel asked.

"Boob!" everyone said.

The English doctor came to examine the babies, but to everyone's distress, he gave little hope, taking the light from Jacob's eyes. What they were doing made sense, the doctor said, and they should continue. He marveled at the way Emma had made the sick baby eat, saying she had likely extended Anna's life, but he should be called when . . . well, if either of the babies took a bad turn. "Each day they live will give them more strength to face the next one," he added before he left.

And those words gave Rachel hope and her life purpose.

Ruben and Esther moved into one of the upstairs bedrooms. Besides helping with both sets of twins, Esther cooked for their house and her father's, and cared for Daniel.

Over the next weeks, Jacob, Rachel, Esther, Ruben, even Levi gave their body heat, and their hearts, to the new twins. Daniel, Aaron, and Emma adapted easily to sharing the adults with two more little ones.

Rachel regained her strength as each day passed.

Everybody loved the babies.

Everybody except Simon.

He ate in silence, and worked the farm the same way.

But Jacob and Rachel did not have time to worry over Simon's forbidding demeanor. It took all their time and attention to care for the tiniest and neediest baby, Anna. Mary—better known as Squeaky—needed nearly as much.

Emma and Aaron needed their time and attention too. Rachel did not forget Simon's warning.

They kept the fireplace in the best room going till almost the middle of May when the English doctor declared, with patent disbelief, that the babies were out of immediate danger.

Ruben, Esther, and Daniel moved back to the Bishop's house. Ruben had been doing his farm chores there, and many of Jacob's, since the babies' birth.

Life began to return to normal.

For everyone except Simon. And Levi, who was becoming a broken man. No matter his coaxing, he could not get Simon to hold or notice "his daughters."

When Rachel and Jacob went to the *daudyhaus* to ask Levi to stay with the children while they put in a long night in the barn to print the *Chalkboard,* they found him weeping.

Jacob's pain for his father's suffering told Rachel what must be done. Once again, she hugged Levi. Once again, she began by telling him she loved him.

Then, with Jacob's nod of approval, for he knew without words what she intended, she sat facing his father and released one canker in his heart to replace it with another.

"Levi, your heart is sad. But it is sad for the wrong reasons. Simon is not ignoring his daughters."

Levi's bowed, broken stance changed. He straightened his shoulders, and raised his head until his piercing gray eyes bored into hers. He turned to Jacob to search for some nameless answer, then shook his head. "Go on. No sense do your words make, but I am listening."

Jacob put his hand on her shoulder and squeezed, asking for her silence, and Rachel nodded without turning.

"Do not be disappointed in Simon, Datt," Jacob said. "He has reason for his anger."

"There is no excuse—"

"There is, Datt. Just listen for a minute. Anna and Mary are not Simon's daughters."

Rachel watched Levi try to make sense of the puzzle, but he failed.

"Anna and Mary are mine," Jacob said. "Your grandchildren still, but not the children of Rachel's husband."

"The blame is mine," Rachel said.

"No. Never!" Jacob nearly shouted. "It is mine. When Simon hurt Rachel, I let my comfort of her go too far. She was like a fawn caught in the light of a pine torch, frightened and uncertain. She cannot be blamed for taking comfort from where and whom it came. I offered too much and knew it. She did not."

Levi stood. "I am too old for this." He led them toward Rachel's room, where each set of twins slept in a separate crib.

He lay down in Rachel's bed, his arms crossed over his chest, his knees bent, his back to them. "I watch my grandbabies," he said. "Go."

"Datt—"

"Enough, Jacob. You have said and done enough already. My love is no less for you or my grandchildren. Nor for you, Rachel. Despise the sin, not the sinner," Levi said in a ragged whisper, his shoulders beginning to shake.

Rachel stepped forward, but Jacob's hand on her arm stopped her.

The next morning, Levi was more his old self, though to Rachel's mind he seemed to have aged overnight.

Simon did not seem to notice that his father's badgering had stopped. He continued to go about his life, performing his farm chores and Deacon's duties, taking Aaron with him more often than not—but to everyone else, he spoke little, if at all.

When the twins were out of danger finally, and hearts lighter, Ruben tried to draw Simon out. He wheedled and cajoled, and even tried to get Aaron to approach him, but it did not work. Not even insults did.

After a while, Ruben gave up.

Rachel wished Simon would show some emotion.

He should be angry. He had a right to be.

If he would only give vent to the anger boiling within him, she could bear it. She deserved it. His anger frightened her, but his silence frightened her more.

The night Levi told Simon that the doctor had pronounced Anna and Mary healthy and out of danger, the hate in Simon's eyes nearly stopped Rachel's heart.

He rose and looked from her to Jacob. "I waited for you to get what you deserve. It seems that will not happen. But be warned . . . you will not go free."

The clatter of Emma's spoon hitting the floor deepened the tension.

Anna began to cry . . . and Simon smiled, as if the sound infused him with purpose.

Levi stood, a plea on his lips, but he seemed unable to speak.

Simon strode to the door and turned, his look turning Rachel to ice. "Vengeance is mine, sayeth the Lord."

Chapter Eighteen

Simon was so preoccupied as he drove the market wagon down the Pike, that he was startled when a turkey vulture swooped toward him from a rock formation at the side of the road.

With a nasty memory of that bird's habit of throwing up on uninvited guests, Simon kept a wary eye on the ugly black-winged creature circling above him.

But when two young ones, covered with white down, scurried from the rocks stamping and hissing, Simon understood that the creature was only doing what God meant it to.

Protecting its world from those who would destroy it.

As he was . . . which was why he was on his way to Philadelphia.

Three days he would be gone, little anyone cared. They could fornicate to their hearts' content, as they'd likely done all along. After all, it took more than one night to create a child. Weeks, it must have taken, from the day Jacob returned, most likely.

Just thinking about it brought a near-blinding rage, but Simon tamped it down with determination. Later. There would be a time and place for rage later. A perfect time.

Let them have their wicked satisfaction. It would not last.

Nothing ever did.

Besides, it mattered no longer. Retribution would be served.

Those babies should have died. He did not understand why they lived still. Rachel did not deserve them. She deserved pain and regret for the rest of her life. And by God, she would have it. She would. He would see to it.

A woman was called upon to bear the children of her husband's seed, not his brother's. Rachel had proved him right about her wantonness. With her sin, she had washed away his, along with the guilt that had plagued him for so long.

Simon didn't question the contradiction. Everyone knew God worked in mysterious ways.

Disguised in modest clothing and sweet smiles, Rachel was a seductress. She had been since she was young. That he had lusted after her even then should have warned him of the wickedness in her. But a young man whose body quickened at the sight of a young girl could not be expected to see danger. Especially if that girl was sweet and innocent.

Or so he thought.

Rachel was only sixteen when he happened upon her and Jacob in the woods by the stream. She was pressed against his brother so brazenly, she didn't even pull away as they tumbled to the ground together. Then Jacob practically covered her, thrusting his hips against her, kissing her, skimming his hand along her body.

Simon was so close, he could hear Rachel's little cries, Jacob's groans. Watching, listening made him throb painfully against his broadfalls until he needed to unbutton them to allow himself room. And when Jacob's hand touched Rachel's breast, Simon had stroked himself.

The feeling was nothing he had ever known or imagined, and he became lost picturing Rachel beneath him, without the clothes that formed a barrier for the two by the stream.

That night, unable to get the image from his mind, Simon had gone to the Welsh mountain village. He'd been told that a woman there would lie with a man who could pay the price.

There were several to choose from. The one he picked had hair the color of wine and breasts full enough to fill his hands, and when he reacted to her touch the way he had at the stream, he knew she was the one.

She didn't smell like spring, but if he closed his eyes, she could be Rachel. And he needed Rachel. Badly.

The hovel she took him to had a roof that pitched so far, it might upend in a good windstorm. The inside smelled musty. Something crunched under his shoes. And with the candle lit, she looked different, so Simon snuffed it with his fingers.

Then, in the dark, when she touched him—in ways that brought heat to his face even now—she was Rachel, and he was lost.

Simon remembered closing his eyes while Rachel did the things he saw her do with Jacob—and more, so much more. And the surge that flowed through him as he released his seed had been the most wondrous experience he had ever known.

Later, unimpaired by lust, Simon had looked at himself. At his surroundings. Soiled sheets. An unwashed woman, hair matted, breath liquored. And he was sick.

Self-loathing stung him. Remorse, strong and furious,

throbbed against his brow. On pleasure's heels came shame, fast and deep.

Awful, indescribable, physically painful shame. Burning like the fires of Hell.

He had committed a vile sin.

Fornication.

He had fallen . . . fallen for Rachel. But it was her sin. Her fault. Damn her to Hell.

Driving home that night, he thought about Rachel and Jacob that afternoon. They'd pulled away from each other and talked of the sin that could result if they continued, promising that one day they would be husband and wife, where no sin could intrude.

Simon knew then that what he'd done would not be wrong if Rachel were his wife. To save his soul, he must marry Rachel.

To make it happen, he had deceived Jacob at a time when his grief over their mother's illness had clouded his judgment. Guilt over that too had gnawed at Simon for years. Yes, he had succumbed to temptation, but it was Rachel's wantonness that had seduced him into deceiving Jacob.

He, a humble, pious man, had fallen prey to Rachel Zook's wiles. And received just punishment. For on their wedding night, when he'd tried to recapture the moments before he'd fallen, the incredible wonder, he couldn't forget the squalor and the stench. The sin.

He'd raged in fury and frustration, frightening Rachel with his anger, and she ran. He caught her so hard, he broke her arm, and was so shocked, he wept.

He wept before the woman who caused his fall. Rachel Zook had seduced him to sin and then unmanned him. She had castrated him with her wickedness. From that night on, he had punished Rachel with every word, every unsatisfactory thrust, until gratification became vengeance deserved and served.

The exhilaration he experienced that night never came again, but the shame did . . . and it grew.

He hated Rachel for that. More as each day passed.

And now, finally, after all these years, his guilt was gone. Rachel had proved she was the wicked one.

Fornicator.

Adulteress.

Simon smiled. Soon the district would see her for an instrument of the devil. A temptress. He had been merely human, falling prey to lust . . . a weak lust that proved false. The proof was how it had fled once she became his wife.

All those years he could barely become a man to enter her, he was being sent a message he was too foolish to heed. His seed did not quicken within her, because she was not a worthy vessel.

Jacob's seed took, because he was a sinner too.

Jacob, the beloved son, the welcomed prodigal, had returned to their midst, poisoning the very air they breathed, and fornicated with his brother's wife.

And Simon knew exactly how to punish them both. Rachel's own father had given him the means to exact retribution and destroy his demons forever—both of them.

The new babies were not a problem. They were, by law, his children. He would find someone to take them. Even such as they deserved better.

And Aaron was too good a son for Jacob.

Simon knew he would be a better father than Jacob. Levi would help him raise Aaron to be a pious Amishman. A grandfather and an uncle accepted by the Church would be better than a immoral father.

He would keep Aaron's twin sister too. He was a man capable of forgiveness. He could overlook the children's origins. Given time, he could drive the sinful tendencies of unworthy parentage from them.

First, however, would be his task to destroy Rachel and her lover. Jacob. The chosen one.

The perfect situation was his. Simon could just imagine the scene.

Time to use the gifts given him. Everyone listened to the Deacon. Especially at service.

Too bad stoning was frowned upon these days. Simon laughed as he approached the city.

For his plan to succeed, he needed to purchase a powder that could not be found in Lancaster, because of its dangerous properties.

Dynamite.

He would not purchase it around home anyway, for he could not allow a hint of his brilliant plan to be known. In Philadelphia, he would buy what he needed.

And he would blast that printing press to Hell where it belonged . . . and send Jacob and Rachel there with it.

Elation filled him as he urged the horse faster. "Yup, Gadfly."

Vengeance would be served.

Excitement grew in Rachel's breast. Tomorrow would not only be the first time she'd attended service since her girls' birth, it would be the first time some of the district would see her two miracles, though many of the women had visited already to see and exclaim over them.

Church service would be held in their barn. Jacob, Simon, and Ruben, with Aaron's and Emma's interference, were unloading the benches even now from the bench-wagon delivered yesterday.

Esther was helping her bake shoofly, apple schnitz, and half-moon pies, and a dozen loaves of bread—just enough to hold everyone until they arrived back at their own homes for supper.

Rachel was relieved that Simon had returned from Philadelphia smiling and friendly again, just like at Christmas, with renewed interest in Emma and Aaron. Even toward Mary and Anna he glanced now and again. And if she was not mistaken, Mary's toothless smile this morning, just for him, had softened him. He'd smiled and declared Mary her mother's daughter.

Life seemed to be settling into an almost comfortable, if abnormal, pattern. Rachel knew that a life of tolerance and compromise, while not every woman's dream of happiness, was more than she deserved.

After their daughters' births, Jacob and she had vowed never to stray into dangerous waters again. They too would live with compromise. It would be enough for them to share in the raising of the children. Jacob's role before the world would be father to Aaron and Emma, uncle to Mary and Anna.

If Simon could accept arrangements as they stood, then Rachel was satisfied. She grieved, though, that she had hurt her husband and her father-in-law. Even Jacob suffered for loving her. And if he ever decided to find a wife, she would be happy for him.

Buggies began arriving on Sunday morning before seven. Rachel dressed Emma and her baby girls in dresses the color of mulberries, the babies' tiny white aprons and heart-shaped kapps almost too small to believe.

Pride. That was what she felt right now, recalling Simon's preaching. Yet when she looked at her two miracles, their big sister beside them, what else could she feel?

Emma climbed onto the counter and sat by them, taking a hand of each. "Annamary come to service?"

They gurgled in delight.

Rachel chuckled at the way Emma ran the girls' names together.

"No, Emma," Rachel said. "This is Anna. And this is Mary."

Emma shook her head. "No, Momly." She pointed to Anna, saying, "Annamary," then Mary, saying, "Squeaky."

Rachel gave up. "Yes. They're coming to service. Will you sit by me and hold one of them?"

Emma nodded solemnly, understanding the depth of her responsibility.

"Which one would you like to hold?" Rachel asked.

"Annamary."

Jacob chuckled as he came up behind her. "I guess it's settled then. No use fighting it, Mudpie. One of your daughters is called Squeaky."

Simon and Aaron, in their Sunday best, were there too. "Figures you'd think that's funny," Simon said, narrowing his eyes. "Those babies deserve better than parents with no morals who give them silly names."

Lightning struck. Rachel's heart clenched. Her hands began to shake. It was the first time Simon had given voice to the girls' parentage, and the loathing with which he spoke was enough to fell her. That he did so on Church Sunday, their neighbors waiting in their barn, brought dread. Suddenly, his high spirits seemed ominous.

He took Mary and offered Rachel his arm. "Come."

Rachel wanted to refuse. Panic, icy and deadening, filled her. She wanted to snatch Mary back. Instead, she picked up Anna and looked to Jacob for guidance.

Go, he indicated silently, taking his children's hands to lead the way.

Best not feed Simon's odd turn, Rachel thought. Probably smart to go along for now. Everything would be all right. He wanted people to see him carrying one of the babies, and that was a good sign. But she shook inside and out, screaming for help that would not come, as she entered the barn beside her husband.

Rachel reminded herself that appearances mattered to Simon. That was all this was, a proper show. What their marriage had always been, a show for the benefit of others.

Still, after his words in the kitchen, a desperate need to turn and run clutched her center.

Everyone smiled as they entered. Condemned criminals about to be sentenced.

Rachel raised her chin and stepped forward.

Alarms were going off in Jacob's head, so loud it was a wonder no one else heard. Before all of them, Simon was claiming Anna and Mary as his own, which should make him happy, and yet . . .

Perspiration trickled down his temple, his heartbeat as rapid as his trembling, and he squeezed Aaron's and Emma's hands to calm himself by reassuring them. But he couldn't shake the notion that they were all sliding toward destruction, and he didn't know how to slow their descent, or bring them to a safe stop.

As he was leaving Emma with Rachel, he heard Simon whisper, "Don't worry, Rachel, I will take good care of your babies."

Jacob grabbed his arm. "What the hell does that mean?" Though he'd whispered too, he spoke too loud.

"Go and sit down," Simon whispered sternly. "You are making a spectacle of us."

It was true. Jacob took a deep breath. No good would be served by reacting before there was anything to react to. "In a minute," he said.

Simon nodded and left.

Emma was all smiles as her sister—God, he should not think of them that way—as Anna wiggled in her arms. "Emma big girl," she said. "Emma hold Annamary."

"You certainly are a big girl." He kissed the top of her kapp. "Take good care of Anna."

"Annamary," she corrected.

Jacob took Aaron to the men's section, hauling him onto his lap and hugging him in the bargain. He did not take his gaze from his family across the room—yes, his—as if by watching them he could keep them safe.

But the decline they were rushing down seemed to be getting steeper.

When the hymns began, Jacob calmed somewhat. Giving up to the prayer of song, he pushed fear aside and opened himself to hope.

The *Anfang* was short for an introductory sermon, and it failed to bring any measure of peace.

When Simon read a chapter from the Bible, the assembly stood. Then he stepped into the center of them, and everyone sat to hear his words.

Fairly shot with inspiration, Simon waxed profound, his sermon more humbly delivered than Jacob could have imagined possible. If he did not know better, he would see before him a man who would never abuse his wife, a pure, honest servant of the people, generous and giving.

Jacob knew enough not to judge. But in truth, the man before him was one Simon had never portrayed before.

That notion took root, and the idea that several men lived within the one filled Jacob with a new and greater dread.

Though he had not really listened to Simon's words, everyone seemed moved by them. In the rows of women across from him, eyes were moist. If he did not know Rachel so well, he would think she too was overcome with the spirit.

But he did know her, and her panic sat so near the surface, if Simon moved too fast, she might scream.

Jacob tried to catch her eye, to calm her with his look.

"Simon is only a man," he wanted to say. "A weak, not-so-humble man. Flawed, like us."

Whispers began and grew, and Jacob gave credence to the murmurs. What was everyone talking about? Why were they standing in the middle of service? Where were they going?

Simon threw open the double doors at the side of the barn and the congregation followed him toward the pasture, like lambs to the slaughter. Lord, he wished he hadn't thought of that.

Like some holy prophet, Simon led them, God help them all.

Simon held up his hands. "Stay. Wait," he shouted, stopping them in the middle of a new-sown field. "Here, under heaven's canopy, in this simple place of worship, listen with a righteous heart and heed God's judgment."

Judgment? God's?

Jacob pushed his way to the front of the crowd where Simon could see him. And when Simon approached, Jacob thought he had his attention, but he passed him by and entered the whispering throng.

With a hand to her back, Simon propelled Rachel forward, her arms filled with Anna and Mary, Emma holding her skirt. And Jacob grasped Aaron's hand tighter to keep himself from beating his brother bloody for touching his own wife.

Rachel faltered and stopped, as if she'd gone as far as she could, as if her legs would carry her not a step further.

Simon's furious whisper brought a pink to her cheeks, and she nodded and continued her journey, stopping at his side.

Simon "placed" Rachel just so beside him, Jacob pondering murder the whole while. Then Simon took Mary from Rachel, and placed her in Jacob's arms, standing back as if to admire the scene. "Perfect, don't you think?"

Simon asked, before striding away from the crowd and deeper into the field. He stopped by a sheet-covered object Jacob hadn't noticed before, taller than he was and three times as wide.

One of Aaron's small, shaking hands sought his, and Jacob grasped Mary one-armed to accommodate the silent plea. Emma wound an arm around his knee, though she still grasped Rachel's skirt with the other.

Jacob wasn't certain if he was happy or sad that his children were smart enough to be frightened.

How could he put a stop to this?

How, without destroying the people he loved?

"Where's your pop?" he asked Rachel in a whisper. "I can't believe he's letting this happen."

"Bishops' Conference in York. He won't be home until tomorrow," she said. "Simon was so pleased Pop put him in charge."

"Which is why he is doing this, whatever it is." "Let's just go in the house. Maybe everyone will follow us."

Jacob shook his head. "If we walk, he will be furious. At least he's calm right now and his thinking is not muddled by rage."

"But it is," Rachel said.

Oh, Lord, and she was right.

Discontent rose behind them.

Simon raised his arms.

The restlessness stopped, but silence held like a bowstring about to snap.

Simon began sermonizing about the virgins lighting the bridegroom's way with the lamps; then he went on to the wedding miracle of changing water to wine. With his entire sermon revolving around the sanctity of marriage, Simon was eloquent.

Then he began an old tune. "Who do you think has the most important role in the Amish Church?"

He asked all the right questions. Who? Who? And who? He spoke slowly, stretched the parody from its original form. Jacob wanted to shout for him to finish.

Finish, please, he thought.

"It is not the Preacher, the Deacon, or the Bishop," Simon said. "None of them!" he shouted now. "It is the woman with babies in her arms who has the greatest role in our church. For in Amish life, the family is central. To be a mother is a high and holy calling." He indicated Rachel with a sweep of his hand. "Observe my wife, Rachel Zook Sauder, babe in arms, a mother at last."

At Simon's evil grin, a powerless rage filled Jacob, and he turned to the crowd. "It's me," he said. "It's my fault." But few heard or understood.

"Adultery!" Simon shouted, and even from a distance, Jacob could see the cords in his neck tighten. That word the congregation understood. And it was too late.

Ignoring the shocked silence, Simon narrowed his gaze on them. "The father of my wife's babies stands—not your humble Deacon before you, but the man beside her. I give you Jacob and Rachel Sauder, shameful in God's eyes, the lowliest of sinners. Adulterers."

Startled cries, bold exclamations of denial, hushed cries of "no, no" and "can't be," trickled to silence.

Levi came and took the babies from him and Rachel. "Come, *Leibchen,*" he said to Rach. "He is sick and angry, our Simon. Come along now."

But they hadn't moved before Simon whipped the sheet from the large object in the center of the field, exposing the printing press.

"What is he doing?" Jacob said.

"He's gone," Ruben said, lifting Emma into his arms, his frown fierce.

One by one, members of the congregation began to turn away.

Simon lit a pine torch and teased the hay-covered mound below the press. "Behold the wrath of God!" he shouted.

Hay ignited. Flames grew.

Aaron laughed.

Simon noticed people leaving and rushed forward. "No, wait! Come back. Watch. Witness God's fury." He pulled at men's arms. Turned women around. Some remained, anger, fear, sadness etched their faces. Others shrugged him off and kept going.

Furious, Simon lunged toward Rachel. Jacob let go of Aaron's hand to intercept him. And they scuffled like schoolboys, except that Jacob couldn't shake the notion that this was a matter of life and death.

"Aaron!" Ruben shouted.

Breathing hard, they stopped, and saw Aaron running toward the fire. "No!" Simon shouted. And Jacob ran.

But Simon grabbed his arm . . . stopped him.

"Let me go," Jacob shouted. "I thought you loved him." Then Simon's fist cracked his jaw.

The world spun.

Jacob tasted grass.

Simon screamed Aaron's name.

Slowed to a dreamlike pace, impossible to speed, Jacob got on all fours. In a tilting world, he saw Ruben carrying Rachel, kicking and screaming, to the house. Datt and Esther carried the girls.

He took a breath. Rose. The world tipped again. But he stood straight . . . and saw Simon scoop Aaron in his arms mid-run, continuing beyond the fire and away from it.

The earth rumbled. Moved.

Jacob swayed. He fell to his knees.

Screams. Shouts.

A force raised the press. It hovered. Splintered.

Flames burst.

Jacob's cry was lost in a second explosion.

Debris rained like hail.

The spiral shaft of the Gutenberg flew in a perfect arc.

Simon pushed Aaron's face against his chest and presented his back as a target.

The shaft struck Simon's head.

He fell and rolled, holding Aaron the whole while.

When Jacob reached them, Simon was gone.

And Jacob freed his terrified, sobbing son from beneath the man who loved him more than life.

Chapter Nineteen

Refusing all offers of help, Jacob carried his brother's body back to the house, Aaron walking somberly beside him holding his jacket. How young his boy was, yet how mature he seemed, suddenly, as he respected the solemnity of their journey, though he did not understand it.

When Jacob placed Simon on his bed in the *kinderhaus,* their father insisted he be the one to wash and dress his oldest son for the last time. "He is with Mom now," Datt said, which, Jacob realized, was his father's salvation in the face of this disaster.

Some of the men put out the small fires that had resulted; others were cleaning up the wreckage. Two men and one woman had been injured by flying debris. No children, thank God.

The Elders remained after the frightening service to keep vigil and pray.

Ruben and Esther took Emma home with them, but Aaron would not be removed from Jacob's side.

By evening, after the wooden casket was delivered, Simon's body was displayed in the best room. He looked unscarred, natural, merely asleep, the deadly wound on the back of his head invisible to any who gazed upon him.

Jacob prayed Simon had finally found peace, and if he had, it was likely for the first time.

Frightened even more by this aspect of Simon's death, Aaron stationed himself by the coffin and refused to move from it, so Jacob pulled up a chair, sat, and took his son on his lap.

Silence held for a long while, then: "Unkabear?"

When Simon did not respond, Aaron turned his face into Jacob's coat.

Rachel agreed to lie down, the babies beside her, at around midnight. She'd been frightfully quiet since service. Jacob wished she would cry or rage . . . something.

Aaron slept finally, and Jacob held him as he kept vigil, worrying about the ramifications of the ghastly tragedy.

Rachel would be judged.

Aaron's and Datt's hearts were broken.

It was all his fault, Jacob knew. His foolish flight four years before had fueled the problem, but not as much as his return. His love for Rachel too.

His great fear was that he might, somehow, have put a stop to the anger between them years ago.

God forgive him if it was so.

Jacob sighed. There was no going back.

An uncertain future hovered just beyond dawn.

Still holding Aaron, Jacob knelt before his brother's bier.

Simon had paid for his vengeance with his life. Had he known the cost in advance, would he have sought retribution?

Jacob did not ponder the question long. He expected Simon would have deemed vengeance necessary at any cost. But a life was too high a price for any reason, except perhaps to save another . . . as Simon had ultimately done.

So Jacob would not dwell on Simon's vengeance, but on Aaron's life as the gift Simon left him. And he would be grateful. He pulled his son close and wept silently for the brother he'd never really known.

Rachel was glad when Squeaky woke hungry. Feeding her would occupy some of the long, dark hours of the night. Jacob had ordered her to sleep . . . as if she could.

When her daughter suckled with contentment, relief shot through Rachel. They were safe. Her children were safe. She'd experienced bone-deep fear during service over Simon's frenetic actions, frightened that somehow her babies would be snatched away, but they were safe.

She should not feel anything akin to relief, she knew.

Simon was dead.

She had, in turns, feared and hated him today. . . . *Sorry, Lord, I know it's a sin to hate.* She had feared him almost to the point of wishing him dead.

Oh, God. And when she'd been told he was dead, for one tiny portion of one tiny second, relief had made her giddy. Then as swiftly, remorse had shattered her relief.

What was the matter with her? She had cared about Simon once. He was her husband.

Her husband had died today.

She should feel more. But sorrow was lost to shock.

Would she ever forget the sight of Aaron running toward the flames? Jacob bloody and hitting the ground?

Damn Ruben for carrying her away when she should have been going after Aaron. Thank God he was safe.

Rachel shifted Squeaky to her other breast, hoping Anna slept a while longer so there would be milk for her too. She fluffed the curly down on her little girl's head, as awed by the miracle now as she'd been when she'd realized she'd conceived . . . in love, not sin, as Simon accused. He was wrong about that.

But how would the Elders see their love? The members of the Church?

She and Jacob had a lot to face. And they would . . . together. Beginning with Simon's funeral.

Her husband's funeral.

Her husband was dead.

Rachel thought of the man who'd snatched fudge while holding her slapping spoon in the air, who'd presented puddle-making pups at Christmas, who'd thrown the little boy he loved in the air with a laugh. The same man who'd died to save the life of that very boy.

And she wept.

Jacob drove his buggy toward the cemetery, Aaron silent beside him, his little hand resting on his father's leg. Aaron could not seem to give up contact, as if he was uncertain of everyone and everything. With good reason. Jacob put his arm around shoulders too small to carry such burdens, and brought his son close. The look on Aaron's face was so needy, Jacob pulled him on his lap and gave him the reins.

Aaron looked up with a question on his face.

"Teach me what Unkabear taught you," Jacob said.

Aaron's smile was wistful as he flicked the reins. "Yup," he said.

For three nights, he had cried for his Unkabear, and nothing would soothe him but to sleep tucked against his father's side. Truth to tell, Jacob had needed him as much.

Jacob hoped, more than anything, that Simon was happy in the next life, for he had never been in this one. At least now he had Mom's full attention.

It near broke his heart this morning to see Rachel in the buggy beside Levi, when she should be in his buggy with him.

"A man's widow cannot drive with her lover to her husband's funeral!" the Bishop had snapped when he questioned the decision, draining the color from Rachel's face, and the heart from him for her pain.

When the Bishop arrived home the day after Simon's death, and was told the gruesome story, he'd aged before their eyes.

He blamed himself . . . almost as much as he blamed Jacob.

The funeral procession wound down Buttermilk Lane, along Maple Street, and up Crooked Hill. Deacons and Preachers from other districts came to pay final respects to a fellow Elder.

Though no one would ever speak of it again, Simon's mental instability the day of his final sermon would never be forgotten. Neither would anyone forget his revelation.

But Simon had not caused their problems. He had not committed adultery. Even Rachel could not be faulted for that. As Jacob drove into the cemetery, he promised himself that he would make the Elders understand and accept that it was his fault, all his. He would by God.

Beside the open grave, by Simon's open casket, people offered condolences to Levi and Bishop Zook. But they were "politely" shunning Rachel and him.

Oh, no one openly avoided them, but they would if the Bishop called for the *Meidung*, the shunning. And how could he not?

If he and Rachel confessed and offered apology for their actions, they might be forgiven. But Jacob fought the notion. To apologize would be tantamount to denying their love. And he could never do that.

Their future and their children's would be settled at

their separate hearings in two weeks. Anna and Mary would be four months old that day. Despite everything, there was something to celebrate. Still, waiting would be difficult.

At the end of the service, Jacob was not invited to throw dirt onto his brother's casket as he should be, but he stepped forward anyway, Aaron's hand in his. "Simon loved Aaron," he said to everyone, yet to no one. "And Aaron loved him. For that reason, I wish my son to have the honor denied me."

When no one spoke, Jacob whispered in Aaron's ear and handed him a clod of dirt. Aaron looked at it a minute and threw it on the casket. "Good-bye, Unkabear," his boy said. "I love you." Then he buried his face in his father's coat and cried.

Jacob vowed then and there that he would allow no one to tarnish Aaron's memory of his uncle. Simon's nature would be buried here with him.

Rachel was nervous. After the funeral supper, when everyone left, her father stayed, asking her, Jacob, and Levi to sit down.

The scent of cinnamon buns did not soothe, sitting untouched as they did in the center of the table, as if the occasion did not warrant their sweetness.

"I want to know everything," her father demanded of Jacob in his hardest Bishop's voice. "About how you came to be the father of Rachel's babies."

In her nervousness, her father's words not being what she expected, Rachel giggled, and her father slammed his hand on the table so hard, a cinnamon bun rolled off the stack and landed icing-down on the table.

Everyone looked at it, but no one moved to touch it.

"*Mein Gott,* Rachel, but when you marry, whatever kind your marriage, good or bad," he shouted, his voice louder with each word, "you keep yourself only unto your husband!"

Jacob was hard put not to yell himself, but he had no right to tell Rachel's father to stop bullying the woman he loved. No right at all.

Levi intervened, giving Jacob a chance to calm down, and told what he knew of the night Simon hurt Rachel for the last time. His Datt told of Rachel's bruises over the years, and he cried in shame for saying nothing.

Datt, of all people, blamed himself for everything.

Jacob remembered his first morning home, wondering why Datt had not mentioned Rachel's bruise. Now he understood that Datt had not wanted to see the truth. If he had, something extreme would have been called for, and it would have broken his heart to hurt Simon. Datt had blamed himself for Simon's problems as far back as Jacob could remember.

His father told of Rachel's broken arm, and how he only recently learned Simon caused it.

"He broke your arm?" the Bishop asked. "Didn't that happen on your wedding night?"

Rachel lifted a cup of coffee to her lips with shaking hands and nodded.

The Bishop paled. "How?"

She put the cup down and ran her finger along the rim, back and forth. "His anger always made him grab hard and move fast." She looked up at them. "I ran to get away. But when he caught me by the arm, he shook me so hard, we heard the crack, and he let me go. That's when I felt the pain. The shape of my arm surprised us both, as if it had no bones in it.

"Simon was so sorry, he cried," she said. "I believed and forgave him, and I never told anyone. He never hurt me so badly again . . . not my body anyway. But sometimes I think maybe he hurt something deep inside even more."

Rachel placed her hand over her father's, and did not begin to speak again until he looked into her tear-filled eyes. "I think, when there is not a cut or a bruise to see, it is difficult to believe you are being hurt," she said. "And when you do begin to realize it, you think it must be your fault, so it is easier to forgive, or to pretend it is not happening. Sometimes I felt foolish to let it go on, yet I did not know how to stop it."

"Rachel," her father said, covering her hand with his. "You must tell me all of it."

Rachel took a deep breath and stood. "Stand up, Pop, and I will show you how his anger would begin, before there would be worse to come."

The Bishop stood.

Using the belittling words Rachel said Simon used, she backed her father across the room poking her finger into his shoulder over and over again as she spoke to him, until she backed him flat against the wall.

The Bishop was clearly insulted, but whether it was because Simon had done it to Rachel, or because Rachel was doing it to him now, was unclear.

Jacob understood, seeing it, how Simon could make her feel less worthy each day, and as she continued to demonstrate, he wanted to shout for her to stop.

When she stopped to describe Simon's disgust over the shape of her body, Jacob fought even harder to keep himself from going to her.

"Tell me the rest," her father said.

Rachel's eyes were bleak. "Then he would push me down on the bed and . . . you don't want to know what happened after that."

"Rachel, I need to know."

Rachel stared far into the past and began to speak in a very detached way.

And there they were, three strong men, glancing at and

away from each other, because she shocked and embarrassed them with her words.

"Bishop Zook," Jacob said. "If we cannot bear to hear it, imagine how she felt going through it."

And he scowled at that raw truth, especially, Jacob thought, because it came from him.

Rachel's explanation faltered. "Simon said it was my fault he could not . . . could not seem to . . . reach a state where . . . that is—"

Jacob stood so fast, his chair hit the floor. "Enough! I don't care how high you are in the Church. I don't care if you are her father. I would not care if you were God. I would say the same. Enough. No more." Then he pulled Rachel from her chair and into his arms. "Never will you be made to speak these things again," he whispered against her hair. "I promise."

Her father rose as swiftly. "You cannot make such a promise. If she told these things, she might be forgiven, which cannot be said for you, you selfish—"

"Selfish? You ask your daughter to repeat these things before her neighbors so you will not be called the father of a sinner, and you call me selfish!"

"Jacob!" his father shouted.

But Jacob ignored his father's warning. "Can't you see how she has suffered before her own relatives in the telling?"

Jacob did not let Rachel go even when the Bishop stepped menacingly toward him. "You are not her relative, Jacob Sauder. And if I have my way, you never will be."

And that, Jacob thought, was because he was right. Guilt was a hard thing. He should know.

"I am Rachel's husband in all but fact. And I will tell you this. I am proud of our love."

The Bishop's shoulders fell and he shook his head. "With that attitude, you will never be forgiven."

"So be it," Jacob said, shaken by the Bishop's words, despite the fact that he had already acknowledged the fact in his heart.

Levi touched his friend's arm. "Ezra, my son may be a sinner, as are we all, and he is rude to his Bishop for certain, but he loves your Rachel. There are many sins for which to fault him, but fault him not for his need to keep her from hurt."

"Keep her from hurt! He has caused it."

Jacob stepped away from Rachel. "I love her in every way a man loves a woman. And I will never deny it."

"Then you will never be forgiven."

Her father examined her face, and Rachel saw the sadness in his eyes. "And you?" he asked her. "Will you be able to say you are sorry for your sin?"

"I will forever regret that I am as responsible as his own tortured soul for Simon's death. He had been angry with me since the day we married, Pop, and this time his anger was justified." She touched her father's arm and let her hand fall away. "I'm more sorry for what I've done to you."

She turned to Jacob and placed her hands on either side of his face. "I will never deny loving you. Nor the love that brought our babies into the world." In an unspoken act of unity, they joined hands and turned to face her father together.

He shook his head and looked at Levi. "It will not be an Amish world our grandbabies will know."

"I do not want to leave my Amish world!" Rachel cried out, as if she'd been wounded. "It would be like dying."

Those words nearly felled Jacob. His hand to her back, he urged her into her chair, wondering which of them was trembling more. When she drank the glass of water he brought her and nodded that she felt better, Jacob looked straight at the Bishop, allowing him alone to read the anger he was trying to hide from Rachel. "You would ban your own daughter? Even if I say I sinned, not her?"

"I will not be her father when she is brought before me, I will be the Church leader. And it is part her sin to bear; it took the two of you, unless you forced—"

"He did not!" Rachel said, face white. "And believe me, I know the difference."

Bishop Zook raised his hands in a gesture of defeat and mumbled a German prayer for mercy, but Jacob wasn't sure for which of them he sought it. With an offhand peck on his daughter's cheek, and a nod to Levi, the defeated man left.

The Bishop came to the Sauder house daily after that, to sit with Rachel and to play with Anna and Mary. But to him the Bishop did not speak, and Jacob understood.

The night before the hearing, Rachel wept in her father's arms before he left. And after he was gone, she watched out the window until well after his buggy had disappeared from sight.

Jacob's heart broke for what he had brought her to, his guilt like a canker inside him.

"That will be the last time he ever holds me," Rachel said, still watching the horizon. "After tomorrow, if he comes to see the girls, he will not look at me, nor take meals with me." She swallowed audibly. "I will not be allowed near his deathbed to hold his hand and send him to Mom." She turned from the window, her eyes full. "To my own father, I will be as one dead."

Jacob stood a distance away, only his rigid control keeping him from going to her.

"Being banned must be like having your soul leave your body," she said, almost too softly for him to hear, "but still, you are unable to die."

And that broke him. Jacob swept her into his arms and carried her to a rocker in the best room where he held her on his lap, soothing her with kisses and whispered words to her ear, not caring who might come upon them. "I will be sorry my whole life that I have brought you to this," he said.

Rachel sat back. " 'Twas not you alone. Even Pop knows that."

" 'Twas my doubting our love; my leaving started it."

"And my marrying Simon."

"He could appear so sincere. That's why we both believed him four years ago, and again at Christmas. He seemed a good brother and a good husband, until our girls were born."

Rachel smiled. "They are miracles, despite—"

Jacob touched her lips. "They were conceived in love . . . a strong and abiding love. Never forget it."

Rachel bit her lip and nodded. "You rescued me when I needed saving."

"And made love to you when it was not my right."

"And gave me Anna and Mary. I am not sorry."

"Neither I." He kissed her and she welcomed him. "Rachel, let me hold you through this night. It will be so long, endless, for not knowing what tomorrow will bring."

Jacob knew that this would be their last night together, even if Rachel did not, that holding each other would have to satisfy them both for the rest of their lives.

She stood and took his hand, her love humbling him.

At the door to her room, he removed her kapp and freed her hair into his hands before she went inside to change and wait for him.

Rachel's need for Jacob made her heart race. She wanted his arms around her, his body next to hers in her bed . . . and not just for tonight.

As far back as she could remember, Jacob had been

there for her. At four, when she skinned her knee climbing where they shouldn't, Jacob tended it. At six, when she drew a silly picture, Jacob admired it. At ten, when she baked a cake with salt instead of sugar, Jacob ate it. And at sixteen, when she wanted her first kiss, Jacob gave it.

Jacob, her husband, married or not.

Knowing they would face the most difficult time of their lives together held her panic away. Together they would be shunned, or together they would be forgiven—please, let them be forgiven. But no matter what was in store for them, together they would remain . . . forevermore.

Jacob came in wearing a nightshirt and Rachel giggled. "I have never seen you in your nightshirt before. You still have skinny legs and knobby knees, Jacob." And she had never loved him so much.

"And your nightgown hides too much," he returned with a wink.

Suddenly shy, they stood facing each other from either side of her bed. Whatever happened tomorrow, Rachel knew they would marry. Tonight was a beginning, not an end, and in each other's arms, they would wait for dawn and the beginning of the rest of their lives.

From either side of the bed, they slipped under her quilt to meet in the center.

Nothing felt so good as the length of Jacob against her, his beard against her face, his heart under her hand.

"I could hold you like this forever," he whispered. "Your very presence fills my soul with peace."

But before long, Rachel wanted more than to be held, and she smiled and sighed when, as if reading her thoughts, Jacob began to learn her, his hands skimming her body in so familiar, yet so unique, a way, soothing every crest and hollow.

Rachel wanted to do the same, and more. But not here

with four babies sleeping nearby—Emma and Aaron had moved in with her to be near Anna and Mary.

Throwing off the covers, Rachel rose and came around to Jacob's side, offering her hand. "Come."

Jacob followed her to his room, a quiet haven with no babies to disturb. He watched her light the lamp and shut the door. "I want to make love," she said. "I want to feel you against and within me and I want to hear your love words and speak or shout my own if I wish."

Jacob groaned and pulled her into his arms, opening his mouth over hers like a man starved. This kissing with the mouth open was new to her, but wanting to learn, Rachel eagerly followed his lead.

And learn she did.

She learned of hard muscle against warm, wet lips and of shuddering pleasure. She learned to make her love cry with wanting, while at the same time he begged her to stop. She learned to make him feel more than he said he could—and for far longer—until he threatened to explode, and then she let him rest and made him ready again.

She acquired a taste for his flesh against her tongue.

And she let him do the same for her.

He described what he would do to her before he did it, and Rachel did not know which aroused more, words or touch.

She did know that together the two could be explosive.

Jacob Sauder became the master of her body, and Rachel Sauder gloried in his mastery. When she thought she could climb no higher, feel no more whole, no more a part of him, he showed her she could.

Together they soared beyond the cares of the world, where only two people who loved with their souls could go.

Their night passed in a blaze of passion so intense, they

fell into a sated sleep, only to be awakened by loud demands for midnight feedings.

Jacob chuckled when he entered Rachel's room behind her, because Aaron and Emma sat in the babies' crib, each four-year-old holding and bouncing a four-month-old.

"Annamary hungry," Emma said.

Aaron nodded. "Squeaky too. Me too."

Jacob took the older two downstairs for a glass of milk while Rachel nursed the girls. When their children slept again, Jacob and Rachel stood by the cribs watching them.

"What will become of them?" Rachel whispered.

"They will be so loved, they will grow up happy."

"Love is no assurance of happiness."

"It can never hurt."

They lay in her bed like two spoons, watching their sleeping children until slumber took them too.

But morning and stark reality slipped upon them unaware, and it was only the memory of their night together that held Rachel beyond fear and anguish . . . but not far enough beyond it.

When they finished breakfast, Esther came to watch the children while Rachel and Jacob went to meeting. "I will never stop speaking to you," Es said airily as she poured herself a glass of milk.

"Then Pop will have to excommunicate you too."

Esther lowered the glass and tilted her head. "What would happen, Rachel, do you think, if everyone decided they would not shun you and we all kept speaking to you? Then Pop would have to ban everyone, and no one would have anyone to talk to. Some families would need fifteen tables so no one would eat at the same table with anyone else!"

Rachel's smile came despite her fear. "Leave it to you, Es."

"If that happened . . ." Esther grinned. "Pop would

have to remove everyone's ban, yours too, and everything would be back to normal."

Rachel shook her head. "Have you told Pop your theory?"

"I'm saving it for later, after I know what happens. Like in a war? They save the big guns for when they have no other choice?"

"What do you know of war, Esther Zook?"

"I have been reading Ruben's heathen books."

"What heathen books?"

Esther's eyes widened, and she lowered her voice to a whisper of conspiracy. "History books."

Rachel kissed her sister's cheek and hugged her. "I think living with Ruben is beginning to pickle your brain."

Es finished her milk and smiled softly. "It's probably little Ruben here," she said, patting her flat stomach.

Rachel went for a bigger hug. "Oh, Es. Does Ruben know?"

Eyes wide with warning, Esther shook her head. "Lord, no. I don't want to scare him too soon."

"I'm so happy for you, Es." But sadness enveloped Rachel and her smile faltered. "I want to hold this baby in my arms, Es. I don't want to be the aunt he will grow up never knowing because she isn't spoken of."

"You won't be, Rach. We won't let that happen. No matter what."

As Levi drove Rachel to meeting, it was Esther's "no matter what" that frightened Rachel most. "It's foolish, Levi, that Jacob has to go in a separate buggy. What do people think we can do in a buggy on the way to meeting already?"

"Hush, *Leibchen*. Talk like that will not go well for you."

She sighed. "I know, Levi."

When they got to meeting, Annie Yoder silently led Rachel to an upstairs bedroom and shut her inside like a naughty child. For hours, she paced, not knowing what transpired, or how Jacob fared.

Minute by slow minute, Rachel died a little more.

Jacob looked for Rachel as Saul Yoder led him in. She wasn't there and panic almost overtook him. Had she already had her turn and left? Or did she wait still in one of the rooms upstairs?

He needed to know. Then he caught Ruben's eye. He'd told him this morning how much he wanted to be first.

Ruben pointed at him and held up one finger. Jacob sighed in relief and Ruben smiled, nodding.

Jacob had what he wanted. They would hear him first. Now he could make a difference. He knew he could.

As Jacob expected, the Bishop's obvious anger toward him infused many who watched. He understood the Bishop more than he might imagine, at least he hoped he did. A father first was Ezra Zook.

If Anna, Mary, or Emma—Lord and if they were ever in this position, would he even be there?

What would become of them?

The Bishop stood. "Jacob Sauder, did you lead another into adultery with full knowledge of your sin, while knowing yourself to be the only one capable of right thinking in an emotional situation?"

He wouldn't miss any beehives with that slingshot, Jacob thought. "I did. Exactly as you said. Let the sin be mine."

If he could make them understand he deserved all the blame, it would go easier for Rachel later. He'd already lived apart and survived, but he knew living under the ban, apart from her family, her community, would destroy Rachel in slow measure.

"Jacob Sauder do you know any reason why you should not be banned from this congregation?"

"None. I was aware of the danger, but continued. I sinned with full knowledge of my actions."

"Are you sorry you led another into adultery?"

"I am sorry my actions resulted in my brother's needless death, and in Rachel being called here today."

"Did you feel any compulsion to . . . protect or defend Rachel, which might have given you occasion for the sin to be committed?"

Jacob had not expected the Bishop to offer him an opportunity to shift some of the blame to Simon, but he would not take it. He could never destroy Aaron's respect and love for his Unkabear. "I felt no such compulsion."

"Have you any other sorrow?"

"I am more sorry than you will ever know that my actions have hurt Rachel and put her in jeopardy of losing the support of her community. I love Rachel Sauder. I always have and I always will. Am I sorry I love her? No. Am I sorry that because of our love, we have two daughters? No, I am not. But I tell you, Bishop Zook, and all of you, Rachel was like a wounded fawn when I set out to comfort her. 'Twas I who betrayed her trust.

"You forced her?"

"Trust from the heart needs no force."

"What would be your wish were you granted one?"

"My greatest wish would be that forgiveness be granted Rachel and me, that we be allowed to marry and remain here as a part of this community."

"You expect to be rewarded for your sin?"

"No."

"If you expect no reward, give me your next choice."

Jacob looked sharply at the Bishop, understanding his offer. "I ask that Rachel Sauder be forgiven and allowed to live in harmony and union with all."

The Bishop gave no indication by word nor action, not even by the blink of an eye, that a bargain between them had been struck. "Jacob Sauder, for your sin you are excommunicated from this congregation. Go out from among us for all time."

It was a blow. He'd seen it coming, and still it was a blow. His limbs shook. His soul cried.

Holding his head high, Jacob walked from among his people for the last time.

As he climbed into his buggy, he knew that if the Bishop did not keep his end of their silent pact, he would lose all respect for the man. If he kept it, however, it would be good to know that a father's love can even soften a stern Bishop's heart.

"Yup, Caliope. Take me home," Jacob told the fidgety horse, his voice cracking. Home. Did he have one still? Could he be so selfish?

Jacob took the long route, thinking about what Rachel might be suffering right now, and considered returning to rescue her like some knight of old. But when the idea sounded good, he knew he would be of no use to her. Keeping from turning back toward Sam Yoder's farm, he laughed harshly at himself.

What should he do now?

If Rachel were not forgiven, his decision would be easier, though Rach's pain would be so much worse. They would face life together in the English world, because they would be banned together. And their babies would go with them.

But the English world would kill Rachel. He knew it as well as he knew her. Like losing your soul, but not being able to die, she'd said.

If the Bishop did as Jacob hoped, he would see his daughter forgiven.

If Rachel were forgiven while he was banned, no hope existed for them. None. Their lives must follow different courses, and the best thing for Rachel—God help him in this—would be for him to leave her.

If he stayed he would be playing Satan. He would tempt her to break the ban with every word she wished to speak to him, and with every word she would know he wished to speak to her.

He would become the snake in the Garden of Eden with every look he gave her, because he could never keep the want from his eyes. And even if he succeeded, Rachel would not believe it, for she knew him soul-deep.

Jacob pulled over to the side of the road by Mill Creek. Down into the valley the creek's ribbon of water meandered to and fro as if in a slow, plodding journey. Along with Caliope's snuffling and sidestepping, Jacob heard the raspy, buzzing music of grasshoppers. The hotter the days, the louder they played.

Hell must be hotter than today.

And if he stayed, he'd bring Rachel there with him.

And Datt. It would about kill his Datt to have him in the same house and not be able to take anything from his hand, nor sit at table with him. In silence they would live and in silence they would work. There were good silences and painful ones.

These would be so painful.

If Rachel and his Datt shunned him, what would Aaron and Emma think, and later Anna and Mary? What would they learn? That their father is no good?

And when they grew up, his four babies? What would they be forced to? Even if he stayed and raised them Amish while keeping himself from fellowship, there would come a day when they would have to choose their own course. Should they become Amish adults—which is what he would wish for them with every beat of his heart—once baptized, they would be made to shun him.

It was not cruel. It was just their way.

How could he put his children through that?

Better they should forget him.

A cottontail hopped by, a mother followed by three little ones. She stopped, raised her head, and perked her ears. Then she swiftly led her family to safety, scooting between a Juneberry and a hickory.

Ach, a smart one, that mother rabbit. Scurry from the dangerous creature. A beast to be avoided, run from, and shunned. Ya, smart she was.

And smart his family would be to avoid him too. But they would not, if he stayed.

So he must go.

But his babies needed a mother's love. They needed Rachel.

Aaron and Emma needed the Amish home and family he'd brought them to. He had been right to bring them here.

Anna and Mary needed their mother. With them, there was no question. They would stay with Rachel.

Even though Rachel was not, strictly speaking, Aaron and Emma's mother, none of them cared about such a thing. Their hearts were entwined.

Where would his children best be raised? he should ask himself. Among the English, where the language was foreign, the dress odd? In a world where material value mattered more than the value of God and family? Where almost everything mattered more than their eternal souls?

Jacob laughed, his own voice mocking him. Almost English, so rude and callous he sounded. Well, he'd best get used to it.

But his babies did not belong in that world.

He knew where they belonged. They thrived under Rachel's care like new butterflies, wings spread, colors vibrant. It was Rachel who'd brought them from their cocoons, who'd taught them to laugh and make mischief, and to speak Pennsylvania Dutch.

Rachel Zook taught his quiet babies how to play and

sing. And now they loved and needed her. They belonged with her.

And he did not.

The older ones would forget him. That would be better than tearing out their hearts later. The little ones would not remember him, which was best.

And as soon as he figured out how to tear his soul from his body, he would begin.

Jacob urged Caliope on, startling a family of bobwhites. Like them, he must take flight.

When it was her turn, Rachel began the overlong walk into meeting, shatteringly aware that everyone watched. The air began to hum, silence speaking louder than words or foot-shuffles, and the gravity of the situation hit Rachel like an ax blade in the center of her back.

She faltered when her knees nearly buckled.

The culmination of Simon's disapproval was about to take place . . . without him . . . and for a heartbreaking moment, Rachel mourned her husband's death. She'd never meant to hurt him. Oh, she'd never loved him— feared him more than anything—but she'd never wished him harm.

This, her darkest moment, was his moment of triumph— and she was strangely sorry he was not here to glory in it.

This trek into service while everyone watched altered Rachel's view of her neighbors. The blur of unmoving, white kapps on one side and bearded, sober-faced men on the other made a different impression on her than it usually did.

Today their looks were forbidding, grim, all minds set upon punishment. Of a sudden, these were a people to fear rather than embrace. A welling of emotion akin to the panic she experienced at her mother's passing—as if she vainly willed time to turn back—filled her.

Rachel swallowed rather than allow the cry hell-bent upon release.

Neighbors and friends did not become enemies overnight, she reminded herself. But they might as well be, were she to be excommunicated this morning, for not a one of them would smile upon her again.

She knelt as told to do, seeing for the first time, just before she bowed her head, two dear smiling faces, friends' faces. Ruben and Atlee. But she knew, when she closed her eyes for her father's blessing, that on this occasion of her chastisement, they could not help her as they had on the last. Her consolation was their smiles. They had not given up on her, despite everything.

Would they do so when this day's work was done?

Rachel shuddered, cold within and without.

When the blessing and the prayer for divine guidance ended, she prepared herself for the onslaught of questions that would be directed toward her in her father's sternest Bishop's voice. Now would be the most perfect time under heaven for his look that said, "nothing you ever do would disappoint me," but Rachel knew she had leapt beyond ever receiving it again.

Quiet reigned too long. She opened her eyes, raised her head, and questioned her father with her look.

But his look held no answer.

Whispers began and grew, and she turned to see Levi coming toward her.

Her father must have known beforehand, before service even, that Levi planned something, because, without doubt, he'd waited.

Levi knelt beside her, reached for her hand, then thought better of it and lowered his to his side. "I wish to make a confession," he said to the room at large. "Before these proceedings go any further." Sorrow seeming to age him, he looked about and took a deep breath.

Rachel wanted to put her arms around her father-in-law, to comfort him, but she held herself in check.

"A man in his life has choices," he said. "And I made choices that have brought us to this pass. I saw many times, and refused to believe even more times, when my conscience questioned me, that my son, Simon Sauder, hurt his wife in ways for which he should have been ashamed, both as a husband and as a man of God."

No one in the congregation seemed surprised. And why they should be, Rachel did not know, especially after Simon had dynamited the press before their eyes?

"It took a better man than me," Levi said. "It took my son Jacob to acknowledge the terrible facts and put a stop to Simon's abuse of Rachel. Had I done so long before now—and I had such power, you must all know—I believe none of this would have happened."

Levi gazed about examining the face of each neighbor, his own begging an open heart. "We, all of us, have just heard Jacob speak," Levi continued. "Of Simon's abuse, he refused to tell. But Jacob going to Rachel's defense put them in a position that led to their downfall. I am going against Jacob's particular wishes in saying this now, because he would have no memory taint Aaron's love for the uncle who saved his life.

"I have chosen to reveal the treachery of one son, and the sacrifice of the other, to save a woman who should be held blameless. Rachel Zook Sauder. On all of us now rests the responsibility to see that this will never be spoken of again." Levi turned to the Bishop and bowed his head. "For the broken bones, cuts, and bruises I did not question; for the humiliating words Simon spoke and I let pass, I beg forgiveness of you, Bishop Zook, and of this congregation.

Rachel would not have sought aid elsewhere if she could
have come to me for it. Let the sin be mine to bear."

The Bishop cleared his throat.

Rachel looked up to see tears in her father's eyes. "Levi,
your Bishop is as guilty as you in this." He turned to his
people. "Before we proceed, together with Levi Sauder,
I, Ezra Zook, beg the forgiveness of all." He looked at her.
"Especially yours, Rachel."

She nodded, humbled, embarrassed. Those faces about
her, both men and women, no longer held such fearful
looks, but ones of compassion and understanding. They
were nodding. No one seemed disinclined to forgive. She
sighed, relieved Levi and her father would not be hurt by
her weakness like Simon.

"We are forgiven, Levi," her father said. "Go and be
one among us."

Levi had let everyone know of her abuse without her
having to tell the sad details. But she worried about what
Jacob would say to his father for going against his wishes in
this. Would their people respect Levi's request for secrecy
about Simon's treachery? Or would his good intentions
eventually tarnish Aaron's memory of his uncle?

She hoped Jacob could forgive his father as he forgave
his brother.

When Levi sat, her father faced her again.

Rachel's heart began to pound, her head to throb. She
clasped her fingers together to still their shaking. The
scent of warm schnitz pies waiting for their fellowship meal
became an oasis of comfort in a desert of uncertainty.

Memories of Pop's gentleness flooded her mind.

Her first monthly. After service, everyone rose for the
fellowship meal, and still she sat, afraid everyone would
know. Then Pop came and sat beside her. He put his arm
around her and pulled her close. "It is natural," he said,

and kissed her forehead. "A gift from God. But woman or no, you will always be my little girl."

Rachel looked into her father's eyes now, in what seemed an altogether different world, wondering if he still thought of her as his little girl. And for a wink in time, that crinkle of skin beside his eye gave his inner smile away, and she knew he did.

Hope it was called.

"Rachel Sauder, did your husband hurt and abuse you?"

"Yes."

"Why did you marry him?"

"He did not hurt me until after we married. I did not know him capable. I married Simon because I had come to care for him. I chose to marry him."

"You know marriage is forever, good or bad."

"I know."

"Have you anything for which to ask forgiveness?"

"I beg forgiveness for the pain I caused my husband, and I ask that we pray Simon will find peace, finally, in heaven."

Her father called for that prayer, and Rachel breathed easier for the pause, a respite she'd unwittingly invited, yet appreciated all the same. It gave her time to reflect on the possibility of forgiveness, but her reflection gave her no peace. Her father could be so much more pointed in his questioning than he had been, and it was not over yet.

Rachel swallowed her apprehension.

He turned back to her when the prayer for Simon ended. "And did you keep yourself only unto your husband, as the marriage ceremony calls for?"

The directness she had wanted came with a vengeance. She sighed. "No, I did not."

Her father's face seemed carved from stone at her answer, as if he expected a different one. "Are you sorry for that sin, Rachel Sauder, and are you ready to ask the Lord's forgiveness?"

She faced the people of her community chin raised. "I have my girls, Jacob's daughters, and I am grateful for the gift of them." Her next words would bring her destruction, she knew. Still, she could not be silent. "For the gentle love that brought them into the world I am not sorry."

She waited for her father's condemning words.

Silence held. Remained. Stretched.

"Rachel." Her father spoke her name softly, startling her nonetheless.

He put his hand on her shoulder. "Rachel, had you borne your husband children, would you be able to say they had been conceived in love and gentleness?"

She could not mask her surprise at the question, and she thought very carefully of her father's words before she answered. "In . . ." She cleared her throat. "In no aspect of my marriage did I experience gentleness from my husband in . . . in that respect. Because of that, in time, the caring I felt for him withered and died. Had there been children of our union, they would have been loved, but they would not have been conceived in love."

Her father indicated she should kneel. He placed his hands on her head. She tried uselessly to read some sign from him, but with gentle prodding, he urged her to lower her head. "Our God is an all-forgiving Father," he intoned in his song-prayer voice. "Go forth, my daughter, and sin no more."

What?

Forgiveness?

Then she saw Ruben's and Atlee's smiles, and she knew she was forgiven. But how did it happen?

Because of Levi?

Because of her father?

He gave her his hand to rise and led her to a bench,

but she did not sit. Instead, she turned to leave, not daring to look back at the disapproval she knew she would see on his face.

She needed to find Jacob. Had he been heard yet? Would his turn come now? She ran outside to look for his buggy. Gone.

She turned back to get Levi, changed her mind, and ran toward the barn for Gadfly.

An arm caught hers. She screamed.

"Hush, Mudpie."

"Ruben, you scared me. Where's Jacob? Has he been heard? His buggy is gone."

"He has left. Come, I'll take you to him."

After Ruben prepared his buggy, she climbed inside. They rode a good distance in silence. She never knew Ruben to be so quiet. "Tell me what happened."

"Well your father started—"

"Jacob?"

"Well—"

"Banned or not?"

"Banned."

"No!" she cried, beating on Ruben's arm, her sobs overcoming her. "You were supposed to say 'not'!"

For a while Ruben let her hit him, then one-handed, he stopped her wild flailing and pulled her close. "Shh, Mudpie. You will do him no good like this. And those babies, all of them will be wild if they see you. Blow your nose."

She sniffed. "You sound like Jacob."

"Then you must never know enough to wipe your nose."

"What are we going to do, Ruben?"

"That, you two will have to decide."

"I can't think. I can't think about it. I just want him to hold me."

"I'm not good enough, huh?"

"You are a good friend to us."

"Better than you know. Living with my new bride in somebody else's house all those months. Nosy four-year-olds, no privacy."

Rachel accepted his handkerchief. "Don't even try to tell me you couldn't go near your wife. I know better."

"Esther tells those things? Or did she tell you about the new baby coming?"

"You know?"

"I'm not stupid, Rachel. A man knows about his wife."

"You're smiling. You're not afraid this time, Ruben?"

"I am. But I have some kind of new faith. Probably comes from watching you and Jacob take on your problems. With help from above, you'll handle this one too."

"I'm not sure He's on our side anymore," Rachel said.

"He's always on your side, Mudpie. Shame on you for forgetting it."

She squeezed his arm. "We're here."

He stopped the wagon. "So go already."

She flew into the kitchen and stopped at the look on Jacob's face. Stone-hard and just as cold. "You're forgiven?" he asked.

She nodded.

"Your father's a better man than I thought."

"Jacob, I need you to hold me."

He shook his head. "I cannot just hold you and you know it, especially after all this. There won't be any marrying for us now. Another baby of mine and your father will ban you without a hearing. I am worried about last night as it is. What was I thinking?" He shoved his hand through his hair as he turned to look out the window, his back rigid.

His stance frightened her. "Just hold me. For a minute. Nothing more."

"No."

Rachel sat, beginning to feel as if dead winter blew about

her, no fires burning within. Ice in the middle of July.
"What are we going to do?"

"You're a wonderful mother, Rach. Emma, Aaron, Mary,
and Anna, they're lucky children. Growing up here with
you, with Datt—it's everything I want for them. You'll do
a good job."

"What are you saying?"

"You will keep them. I will leave. It's the only way."

Chapter Twenty

Jacob stared out at the gray afternoon.

Rivulets of water from the sudden shower ran down the windowpane with seemingly no beginning or end.

He felt like that rain, falling aimlessly, no direction. Just falling. He shuddered, whether from the dampness, or the turn life had taken, it was difficult to say.

Yesterday morning, the Bishop's decision had been made. Yesterday afternoon, he'd moved into the *kinderhaus*. Alone.

Now he understood the isolation Simon must have known here, and wondered if it might have contributed to the complicated lengths to which he went to exact revenge. Long quiet hours of brooding had surely gone into the unholy production he'd staged.

But Simon had been lonely his whole life.

Jacob wondered if he could have done something to change that, and wished to hell he had tried.

Now, like Simon, he was in exile.

Without family, Amish or otherwise.

Without Rachel.

Without his children.

He'd kissed his babies, all of them, when he arrived home after service, wondering how many more times he would do so before he must leave them.

How long would they look for him before they would forget he existed?

Would they ever forget?

On the one hand, he wished, for their sakes, they might forget; on the other, he prayed they never would.

They had come full circle, he and Simon. When they were young and Jacob had Rachel, Simon wanted her. Then Jacob had come home with his children, only to discover how much Simon wanted children.

Rachel belonged to Simon then, and he had taken her away—though he might not have been able to do so had Simon cherished her.

Now the circle was closed. Neither of them would have her.

Simon's ultimate revenge.

No. Jacob shook his head in denial. No, he could not blame Simon for the turn his life had taken. His sins were his own and he knew it. And they had hurt the woman he loved.

Rachel had suffered at her husband's hands, and she did not deserve to have that suffering, or the result of her rescue, known.

Rachel deserved goodness. She worked hard and offered her toil as prayer. She loved her fellow man. She loved her children . . . his children. She would make them a good mother.

Jacob pressed his powerless fist against the glass that separated him from the world, a world where the sun now peeked through the clouds after a good rain.

A symbol of hope.

But not today.

Jacob pressed hard, wishing the glass would break and cut him, make him bleed. He deserved to bleed.

His chest ached, as if his children were already hundreds of miles away.

They might as well be.

Aaron and Emma were probably snuggled together in their crib for their nap, the babies taking turns at Rachel's breast.

"I love you all," he said, wishing they could hear him. Then he shouted it. "I love you!"

Wanting to say it, to show it, was the reason he needed to leave. It was difficult enough to stop complicating Rachel's life, without the added temptation of having her in the next room. Lord, he'd already given into loving her there, not once, but twice.

Jacob gazed beyond dwindling rain clouds and brightening skies. "How much do You forgive before you stop?" he asked.

He and Rachel should never have allowed themselves to love in such a free and unencumbered way the night before the hearing.

What had he been thinking?

The truth, that's what. Deep in his heart he knew that night was their last. He knew they would not be rewarded for their sin with forgiveness and a future together.

Life did not always work out the way you wanted it to.

Hardly ever.

Mostly, it seemed, it worked out the worst way it could.

Rachel had not yet reached that sorry realization, and Jacob worried that this would be too brutal a lesson for her. When she realized later, after he left, that they would never be together again, never see or speak to each other even, she would be more than a sparrow with a broken wing. She would be broken in ways that could never be mended, into pieces that would never fit together in quite the same way again.

But he knew his Mudpie. She would pull herself together and make a life for their children—the best life they could have—an Amish one, with his father and hers, with their Aunt Esther and Uncle Boob to look after them.

Jacob punched the wall by the window, cracking the plaster—and maybe a couple of fingers, he thought, as pain shot through his hand. Well, good. Such pain was no more than he deserved.

He needed to be punished. He needed to leave.

What other choice did he have? If he stayed . . .

Ah, if he stayed, he would claim her, love her, hold her, and never let her go . . . and in the claiming, he would destroy her, tear her from the life she loved, from her Amish family and community, from Esther and Ruben and their children. From her father and his.

Rachel could not survive in the English world. Too brutal it would be for her. Neither could she survive in an Amish one as an outcast. She loved her joyful, unchanging Amish world. She said so herself. It would be like losing your soul, except you could not seem to die.

Her words haunted him.

And his babies. If he left them with Rachel, they would grow, in heart, body, and soul, surrounded by the love of their big Amish family, grandfathers, aunts, uncles, cousins, just as he wanted for them.

They would be so loved.

And if he told himself often enough that he was doing the right thing, maybe he would come to believe it.

An anguish so keen shot through him, it nearly broke him. He started to flee the lonely, haunted room, cried out, and slammed the door instead, shutting himself away where he belonged.

Falling to his knees by the bed, Jacob brought the corner of the quilt to his face to muffle his sobs. He cried for the brother he lost. For his Datt, who'd lost both sons at once. Then he cried for himself and Rachel and their children, for the life they would never have.

And still Jacob sat on the floor. His children.

Emma. Aaron. Bright beacons guiding him, saving him, giving him a reason to go on. A reason to look forward to each new day. A reason to come home.

Home to Rachel. Mudpie. Momly.

She'd welcomed them the way a sunflower welcomes the sun. She'd needed healing too, and together they'd begun the process.

If not for Simon . . .

If not for Simon, would their lives be as they wished? Who knew? Sometimes, like now, the master plan, which he must accept without question, seemed difficult to comprehend, impossible to accept. Especially if one could not imagine what it might be.

Jacob wiped his eyes and rested his back against the side of the bed. Head back, eyes closed, he prayed for the strength to leave them.

Two little faces came to mind, tiny, dimple-faced girls whose new smiles filled him with the knowledge God could be merciful. He'd prayed for them at their birth, willing to do anything to keep them alive.

He tried to pray again, recited words he'd heard and said hundreds of times. Prayer, he thought, a quick and easy remedy for every hurt. Like a bandage or a sling, a short prayer could always be counted upon to bring hope for recovery.

Except, from this, there would be no recovery.

Jacob sighed, halted his foolish, wandering mind, and attempted to pray in earnest.

As he recited the most familiar of prayers, the words

"Thy will be done" stopped him. Suddenly they meant something. He repeated them again, louder. Could he accept the meaning of those words with his whole heart? Did he have the strength to place this impossible situation in the Creator's hands and accept, unconditionally, the will ordained for him?

Jacob went to the window to look out at the valley he loved. A light breeze rippled fields of ripe wheat in never-ending waves. The Bontranger children, their exuberance tamped down inside during the shower, now danced around the family dog and her playful pups in the hollow.

With his eyes, he followed the slope of the land upward, past the horizon and into a sky slashed pink-through-blue. Sky-blue-pink, Mom used to call it. He wondered if she would consider putting in a good word for him right now.

He sighed again. Up to him now. Too late for Mom to fix.

"If this is Your will, Lord, so be it," he said. "And if You have other plans for a wretched soul like me, show me the way. It frightens the hell out of me, Your will, but I'm listening."

Rachel roamed the empty, lonely rooms.

Night had come for the third time since the hearing.

The children slept peacefully.

She had cried off and on for the better part of two days. Jacob would not unlatch the door between the main house and the *kinderhaus,* no matter how much she called, begged, and pounded.

He'd let Atlee in after the hearing and she'd been so hurt.

She'd seen nothing of Jacob since he'd told her of his decision to leave her with the children. Her distress had seemed a mountain she could never hope to scale, and so she'd sat at its base and cried for lack of recourse. Even to calm the children, she could barely stop. Anna and Mary were so agitated by her state, they fretted and nursed for short, unsatisfactory lengths of time. They cried too much too. She needed to get hold of herself or starve her children.

Though Aaron and Emma did not understand why she cried, they missed their father. Emma kept asking for Papop. Aaron said nothing. At nap times, she had to lie down with them, her arms over them, before they would give in to the rest they needed.

If only Jacob would explain this foolish need of his to desert her and his children, for desertion it would plainly be if he did not stay.

Desertion. Again. By Jacob.

The pain of his leaving four years before had nearly destroyed her. She did not think she could bear it again. And his children. Oh, God, his children.

True, if he stayed, she could not talk to him because of the ban, though she would never shun him inside the house where no one would see them. Levi would not care if she spoke to Jacob, even if *he* could not. Neither would Esther or Ruben. Of course if her father took it into his mind to enter their door unannounced, which he sometimes did, and she and Jacob were caught conversing, or even if he happened to be taking something from her hand, or she from his . . . Well, perhaps they could not converse, strictly speaking. But they would at least be together, in a way. But to be together and not touch. Not love . . .

If he stayed, though it would be difficult for them, Aaron and Emma would at least grow up with a father. Except, if they chose the Amish way as adults . . .

Jacob would never make his children face such a decision.

Rachel slapped her skirt as she paced. It could not be impossible. It could not.

Their babies should know their father. Already Anna and Mary smiled when he spoke to them. How could they not, when half their lives he'd spent cuddling them before the fire? He'd surely given them life in more than the usual way. If he had not shouted the house down at their birth . . .

Rachel heard a noise. Stopped pacing.

Past midnight, and someone besides her prowled?

An outside door closed. Levi would never stir so late.

She took her light cape from the door, put it on, and threw the hood over her head. Despite the warm night, a light drizzle fell. She followed the crunch of hurried steps. The children's windows were open, and she would hear them if she did not venture too far from the house.

Her heart hurried even if her steps dared not. That same defiant heart clamored to run.

It was Jacob.

He stopped, hands in pockets, beside the greening field that bore the scar of an explosion in its center. He looked at the sky, searched the vast expanse. Praying for guidance, she expected. For answers. Answers they both knew would not come.

She stepped close behind. Taken with his thoughts, he did not hear her. She touched his arm.

He spun about.

"If we talked," she said, holding the arm he would pull from her grasp did she let him, "perhaps we could find some of the answers you seek."

She felt his muscles under her hand tense. "You should not be speaking to me."

She shrugged her hood away, pulled off her kapp, and shook her hair free. "As if I could keep from it."

"Which is why I must go."

"That is not a good enough reason."

"How about this, then, for reason?" He caught her in a rough, possessive embrace, claiming her lips with a force she answered with as much frustration and desire as he had.

Warm rain bathed them. Rain and tears. Alive she was in his arms. Alive and wanting to live to another day, something she would not wish should he leave. "I won't let you go," she said between kisses. "I won't."

Jacob combed his fingers through her hair. "There is no letting. I am leaving. Shush, now. No more words. Kisses only."

Rachel yielded. There in the rain, every kiss bore soul-deep yearning, as if each were their last.

One would soon enough be.

"Not to be Amish would be a choice for us," she said above the clamoring of her heart. "We could be English; we would be fine, our little family."

Jacob pulled back and despite the hopelessness in his eyes, he laughed, the sound harsh. "Not to have arms and legs would be the same as being English for you, Rachel. Alone I could survive, but dragging you into the outside world with me would kill us both." He wiped her cheeks with his thumbs as if he could erase the rain that continued to fall. "We would never be certain what tomorrow would bring."

"Whatever it did, we would face it together. Anything together, Jacob. For the rest of our lives, whatever tomorrow brought, together would be better than alone."

"And if we wandered the earth and never belonged anywhere, you would not be sorry?"

"Together, where we go does not matter."

He stepped back and let his arms fall by his side. "You are wrong. And someday you will thank me, if only in your heart, for setting you free. I will be leaving on Monday."

He turned and walked away, the slump of his shoulders speaking of burdens too heavy to bear.

Stubborn, stubborn fool. "You deserted me once, Jacob Sauder. This time, I will not forgive you!" she shouted to his retreating back.

Monday morning.

An hour till dawn.

Jacob shoved the last of his clothes into the cloth bag before him on the bed. He had not spoken to Rachel again after that night in the rain.

He'd gone into the main house after that, upstairs. She'd followed him. He'd stood at his children's cribs, for hours it seemed, before he'd turned to leave. He preferred thinking it was rain dripping down her face when he closed her bedroom door for the last time . . . her on the inside, him on the outside.

He'd touched the door with the palm of his hand. "Better you should hate me," he'd whispered, "than be cast into Hell beside me."

More than a year ago, he'd returned home to stay a lifetime, but as often happened in this world, his intention—to raise Aaron and Emma among his family—had been thwarted. They would be here, but he would not be raising them. Rachel's purpose, to print her newspaper and help her community, had been destroyed in the same ghastly sweep.

Yes, Simon had had his revenge.

But he'd left them a precious, incredible gift. Aaron.

He and Rachel were blessed with the lives of their children. Yet they could never give them the greatest gift, to be raised in a family whole. For their father would be gone.

But they would always have their mother.

For the rest of his life, Jacob would remember the beauty of Rachel's soul. His children would grow up knowing such beauty, learning it at her knee. With her, they would have the best life he could give them.

Before cockcrow he would be gone. There would be no last-minute good-byes, no last-ditch effort at making him change his mind. He could imagine her plan to be in the barn come dawn with her arguments.

He lifted his carpetbag from the bed and left without looking back. He went quietly down the stairs and outside.

He'd packed his buggy last night. He did not need much. Without lighting a lamp, and as quietly as he could, he backed Caliope into her place between the traces to hitch her up. Before long, his eyes adjusted to the dark and he had no trouble finishing his task.

He opened both barn doors wide and then climbed onto the plank seat. He did not flick the reins. He could not seem to raise his arms; they were too heavy. His chest ached with heaviness also, as if some great beast sat there, keeping him from moving.

Rivulets—not rain—ran down his face, and he let them go. Better he should mourn here in the dark than out there in the harsh light of day.

Today would be more cruel than most, he knew—a first of many such days.

As he wiped his eyes with the sleeve of his jacket, a strangled sob caught him, and he was angry at himself for releasing the sound. He cleared his throat and raised the reins.

"Don't cry, Pa-pop," a tiny voice said as a small hand patted his back.

Jacob whipped around in his seat. "Emma? What?" And

then he saw, only too clearly, all he carried. "Rachel Zook Sauder, get out of this carriage right now!"

"No. I'm coming."

"No. You're not. You've not even packed what you need, for heaven's sakes."

"Everything I value is here." She held Anna over her shoulder. Squeaky slept belly-down inside a wooden cracker box, her little bum in the air. Aaron slept on a quilt. Had his son grown taller in the last week?

Jacob could feel Emma's arm tighten around his neck, as if she would never let him go. He bowed his head and gathered the strength he needed to thrust them from him and rip out his heart in the process. "Get out," he said. "Now."

Before she looked up at him, Rachel placed Anna beside Squeaky and tucked the blankets around them. "I will not. Not of my own accord."

"Then I will help." Jacob got down from the buggy and lifted the box with his baby girls in it. Without allowing the animal-like howl building within to escape, he set the precious cargo gently on the old desk in the corner. He placed a hand on each little back, felt the rise and fall of their breaths, stroked a pink ear, a dark curl.

So keen was his pain, he almost wished he could die of it.

He took a breath, firmed his resolve, and turned to lift Aaron, still sleeping, from the back. The feel of his boy in his arms stabbed deeper.

Hell, it was called.

Rachel's quiet tears were more heart-wrenching than Emma's sobs. He lifted each down, thrusting away arms he wanted around him badly enough to die for.

As Rachel tried, and failed, to soothe Emma, Jacob climbed into his buggy and slapped the reins so hard, the horse bolted.

He did not look back.

Emma's cries consumed him, even when he could hear them no longer.

The moon's smile mocked him as it faded.

And Jacob wept.

Chapter Twenty-one

Rachel watched Jacob's buggy disappear from sight. She couldn't let him go. She wouldn't. She scooped Emma into her arms and raced for the house. In her haste, she tripped on the step, recovered herself, and continued forward. She threw the kitchen door wide. "Levi!" she screamed. "Levi, I need you!"

The kitchen was dark, silent as a graveyard.

Finally she heard Levi's tread. Hurried, panicked. He came running from the *daudyhaus,* true fear whitening his face. *"Leibchen. Vat's iss?"*

"Jacob's gone. He's gone, Levi. I'm going after him—"

"How? You cannot—"

"Over the rise and down to the Pike." She stopped to pant, shushed Emma, kissed her cheek. "Go to the barn, Levi. Aaron and the girls are sleeping. Here." She tried to hand Emma over, but Emma screamed and kicked, crying, "Pa-pop," with every breath. "I'll take her," Rachel said, relief over Emma's presence filling her. "Go, watch the others."

Levi nodded.

Out of the house and around back toward the rise, Rachel ran, faster than she ever thought she could. She crossed two fields carrying Emma sobbing all the while; it was difficult running with the extra weight.

Fast as she ran, Rachel feared she was going too slow.

When she topped the first rise, she saw Jacob's buggy pass, knew she would miss him. She looked around, remembered the shortcut through Manny Smitt's cow pasture. A messy trek it would be. She took it.

Running through it, she covered desperately needed distance on her journey. When she got to the top of Windy Hill, she watched Jacob's buggy approach the last point at which she could catch him. *Oh, no. Oh, no.*

"Jacob! Jacob," she screamed. "Oh, Lord, please let me catch him. Please."

She pointed toward Jacob's buggy. "See Pa-pop? I'm going for him." She kissed Emma's forehead and sat her in the grass. "Wait here."

Rachel knew from the near sound of Emma's sobs that she didn't wait, but ran right behind, and it gave her a measure of relief to have her near.

So much depended on her reaching Jacob, Rachel almost dropped from the weight of the burden.

The stitch in her side was fierce.

She thought her lungs would burst. She needed to run faster. She could see Caliope plodding forward, slow, but too fast.

Too fast.

She was going to miss him.

Her soul was leaving with her love and she couldn't seem to do anything to stop him.

* * *

At Cornfield Corners, Jacob had turned right and right again, doubling around to get to the Philadelphia-Lancaster Pike.

His heart was at the farm where Emma's last, shrill "Pa-pop!" echoed in his head.

"It's best for them. It's best," he cried aloud. "This is best!

"I can do this. I can." He shook his head, wiped his face with his sleeve. "I can't. Oh, God, I can't."

Tears blinding him, Jacob stopped the buggy and looked toward the One who watched. "I can't!" he screamed. "Please don't make me."

Then he saw them, Rachel and Emma, dawn stirring behind them, running down the hill and toward him.

If he hadn't stopped, he would have missed them.

Oh, God. Oh, God.

Rachel's kapp flew off, her hair came undone. Emma's kapp was already gone. He didn't know how she managed to keep up with Rachel. But she did.

He jumped from the buggy. Emma cried as she ran, her sobs worse, coming faster than when he'd left.

"Jacob," Rachel called. "Don't go. Jacob!"

Dawn's blessing seemed to shower them with light.

His heart expanded and his smile came.

He ran, caught them in his arms, fell to the ground with them.

Breathless.

All of them.

Emma's sobs controlled her. She could barely breathe for crying. He lifted her, held her tight. "I love you. I won't leave you. I won't. Shh, my little one, shh. Pa-Pop's here. He's got you."

Rachel's hair shimmered free, sweat dotted her brow,

tears reddened her eyes, rolled down her chin. Cow dung clung to the hem of her dress, covered her shoes. She'd never looked more beautiful. He kissed her wet face, her mouth. Shaking still, gasping for breath, she kissed him back.

They both cried.

"I can't. I can't leave you. God help me, I can't." He sat back, took her shoulders in his hands, gazed into her eyes. "Forgive me, Rachel. Forgive me, please. For leaving you before. And for now. Can you? Ever?"

"It's done." She looked at the morning sky. "If He can forgive us so much, we can forgive each other so little."

They kissed again.

Catching breaths, holding on, the three of them sat in a heap in the middle of Windy Hill, dew-kissed meadow grass swaying about them.

Beautiful.

The world was beautiful just then.

They were together.

Emma's sobs quieted. She clung to his neck.

"You will take us." Rachel said.

"Either that or cut out my heart."

"As mine. Let's get the rest of our children. Levi is with them."

"Ach, Rach, I didn't want to say good-bye to Datt again."

When they pulled into the yard, Levi went silently back to the house. Aaron and the babies were still asleep where he'd left them.

They re-packed the buggy and trailer. All the while, Jacob accused himself of being selfish, of putting his needs before his family, but he kept packing.

Jacob lashed the cribs to the trailer. "I'm relieved, but sorry, I won't have to say good-bye to Datt again."

"He's in the window," Rachel said. "Wave."

Jacob waved after he got Rachel and the children settled, but he didn't look.

Even as he sat, reins in hand, Rachel beside him, Emma clutching his jacket, he doubted the wisdom of taking them. He understood his heartfelt need, and theirs, but hated tearing Rachel from a place and home she loved.

"You may as well get going," Rachel said. "We are ready. We said all our good-byes days ago."

Jacob sighed heavily. "Ach, Mudpie, but you love this place so."

"Ach, Jacob. You foolish man. 'Tis thee I love."

Emotion overwhelming him, Jacob sat silently for long moments, Rachel's words filling his head, his heart. Thee I love. *"Ich liebe dich,"* he said.

Rachel touched his face. "I love you too. More than any place or way of life. Your children love you the same."

"Ach, Rach, what are we going to? What kind of life will we be giving them? I don't even know. It can be ugly for Plain folks out there in the English world."

"We could become Quakers."

Silence rather than smiles came. It was difficult to make jokes in such circumstances.

"You said good-bye to your father?"

Rachel nodded. "Don't be surprised if he is waiting with a shotgun when we pass. Though I think his angry bluster the other night covered more sadness than anything."

Jacob nodded, understanding. "Esther and Ruben, little Daniel? To all of them you have said good-bye forever, Rach? Are you certain?"

Rachel's eyes filled. "Last Friday morning, to everyone did I go. Even Atlee. He cried more than Esther. Levi's understanding of my decision was marred by his sadness at our going."

Jacob cleared his throat. "To everything I have said since the hearing you turned a deaf ear, Mudpie?"

"To what you did not say," Rachel said, "to the words in your heart I listened."

"I should beat you."

"All right."

He shot her a grumpy look. "You could be a little frightened."

"Never again."

"God, Rach. Do you know how badly I want to drag you from your home into a hard, brutal world?" He reached for her hand. "It would be so selfish of me if I did."

She squeezed his hand. "If you did not take us, I would make my way, babies and all, to find you. We are safer with you. Wherever we are together, Jacob, we are home. Without you, we are lost."

Datt's cranky bantam crowed.

"Till dawn we argued—"

"And chased."

He smiled. "Argued and chased till dawn. Is this what our life will be like from now on?"

"I hope so. Jacob, dawn is the beginning of a new day, a good time to begin a new life," Rachel said. "It's fitting, because I want to begin every new day with you, until there are no more days left for me here. And then I want to spend them with you in heaven."

Jacob shook his head, so torn between leaving her and taking her, he wanted to roar his frustration. "You will not be winning every discussion we ever have," he promised. "And if the world is the hell I expect it to be, I will bring you back here where you will be safe. Then you will understand it is best for all of you."

Jacob could tell by Rachel's smile that she knew she'd won this argument, if argument it were. Fate, more like.

Destiny, he thought it was called.

He shook his head again and flicked the reins. "I wish

I could believe taking you is the right thing, no matter what Atlee said."

Rachel looked curious. "What *did* Atlee say to you? I know he was upset about your decision to leave, and sad beyond belief, because he thought we should be together. But what did he tell you?"

"Wait," he kept telling me. "Just wait. God will provide. Now you know I used to believe that as much as the next man, but when you've angered Him as much as I have—"

"And I—"

He covered her hand. "No. I won't accept that. But I do worry His anger at me will splash over onto you and the little ones." He smoothed the curls at Emma's ear. She lay against him and yawned. "Pa-pop," she whispered.

"God is never angry with us," Rachel said. "You must have forgotten that. He may be saddened by our deeds, but He is never angry with *us.*"

Jacob nodded. "If for no other reason, I suppose I must keep you with me to remind me of all I have forgotten."

"There are other reasons."

Jacob all but growled. "Those reasons got us into this."

Rachel laughed, the sound pure and uplifting.

Shaking his head, Jacob flicked the reins. "Yup, Caliope. Let's go home. Wherever that is."

Reluctant or not, Jacob was taking them, and Rachel experienced an elation almost as heady as her fear had been. Dizzy relief assailed her. They left the barn, passed through the yard, then turned onto Buttermilk Hill Road. Life beckoned.

A life together, for her and Jacob and their small family.

Buggy wheels on gravel behind them got her attention, and she looked back, but she could not believe her eyes.

Jacob pulled over, and Rachel feared he'd changed his mind. "Why are you stopping?"

"There's someone behind us. It's slow going with all this—"

Levi, market buggy piled high with possessions, pulled beside them. "Nice morning to go flittin'," he said. "Do we know where we're going?"

Jacob lowered his head—in shock or thanksgiving, either or both. His shoulders tensed, relaxed. When he looked at his father finally, his wet-eyed gaze expressed hope. And disbelief. "Datt."

"You're not leaving this old man behind. I plan to watch those babies grow up."

"Ah, Datt," Jacob said, blinking.

"I'll lead," Levi said. "I need to drop off the papers for the farm at your father's, Rachel. It'll give you a chance for a last good-bye. I know you'd like that."

Like it and hate it, she thought, nodding, filled with renewed pain for leaving Pop and Esther.

Levi moved ahead and waved them on.

They passed the cemetery at a slow canter. In their hearts, Rachel knew they were all saying their last farewells.

When her pop's farm came into view, Rachel shivered. She could do this, she could. She must, because if she did not remain strong, she was afraid Jacob would turn around and take her back.

Levi stopped his buggy, but did not alight.

Rachel examined every window for a glimpse of Es or Pop. But no one looked back. The clapboards on the house were whitewashed, the garden neatly rowed and swelling with abundance, the farm buildings orderly and well kept.

The barn had been her playground. She loved it most.

As if responding to her thoughts, an unseen hand threw the barn doors wide, the yawning doorway making the barn smile. Sunlight glinting on the upper windows made it wink.

A good-bye to cherish.

Movement altered the barn's smile.

A horse. Moving. Something behind it. Pop. Driving his market buggy, two trunks and Mom's favorite painted cabinet lashed to the back.

Rachel straightened. Oh. Oh.

Ruben, Esther at his side with little Daniel, drove their buggy out next, attached trailer following.

Atlee came trotting after them, his smile so wide, Rachel imagined him as a young man. She hadn't seen such a spring in his step since he was eighty, and she laughed.

Totally bewildered, Jacob took Emma. "Go."

Rachel jumped down and ran. Her pop enveloped her in a hug, then swung her in a wide circle, his hearty laugh bringing her great gulping sobs. Did her eyes confirm what her heart desperately hoped was true?

Her father held her close. "Ach, Rachel mine, don't cry. Do you think we could let you go from us forever? A weak Bishop I am who cannot shun his own daughter, no, nor lose her either."

"A Bishop with a heart," she said against his ear.

Esther hugged them both. "We're coming with you."

"We don't even know where we're going." Rachel straightened her father's hat. "Blind faith, Pop?"

"You're going to Winesburg, Ohio," Esther said. "We all are."

"We are?" Rachel looked toward Jacob near their buggy, waiting, unsure, Emma wrapped around his leg, Anna and Mary in his arms, and Aaron leaning sleepy-eyed against him.

Rachel giggled and her heart expanded.

Love, it was called.

"What if I had not caught up to him this morning?" Rachel asked, lightheaded for their close call.

"I was prepared to stop him when he passed here,"

Ruben said. He feigned a loud yawn. "I have not slept in two days for watching."

Esther laughed.

Levi squeezed Rachel's arm. "And I was prepared to bring you here. My Jacob, you know, is too stubborn just to be told. We knew he would need to step into Hell for a while before he would see reason.

"When he didn't go before today, we knew he would leave this morning," her pop said. "So here we are. Jacob looks like he's worried we're taking you back."

"Because you made it clear he would not be welcome as your son-in-law," Rachel said.

"Guess I need to be forgiven," he said.

"Forgiveness is a good thing," Rachel said, kissing him on the cheek.

"Beginning again is too," her father said. "Let's go tell him."

As they approached, Jacob's expression, part naughty little boy, part confused little boy, made Rachel love him more.

"We're going to Winesburg, Ohio, Jacob," Rachel said, taking Anna from him and drawing Emma too.

"What are you talking about?"

Ruben slapped him on the back. "Atlee found us a new community. They call themselves the Bontranger Amish after their leader, Zeb Bontranger. They are expecting us. Seems they have broken with their strict Amish neighbors and have brought along a good share of Amish sinners who wish to begin again. Atlee says they believe in repentance more than shunning, and are committed to looking ahead, rather than back. Should take four, maybe five days to get there. They have even given us directions to friends' and relatives' homes where we will be welcomed along the way."

Jacob shook his head, as if this was too much to comprehend. "Amish," he said. "Together."

Rachel nodded, tears blurring his dear face. Then Ruben took Anna from her and gave her back to Jacob, took Rachel by the hand, and walked her to his trailer. He knocked on the oilcloth-covered mountain tied to the back and threw the cloth off. "Built it myself," he said. "Not a real Gutenberg, but—"

"Never was a Gutenberg," Atlee said.

Everybody looked at him as if he'd grown horns.

He patted it. "Just like mine, just like a Gutenberg."

Rachel was the first to laugh.

Jacob shook his head. "Those press parts would not have fit."

Ruben slapped Atlee on the back. "Old coot!" He turned to Rachel, still shaking his head. "In Winesburg, there is a farm waiting for us, with an old sawmill building for the press. They need a newspaper, Rachel."

"And a Bishop," her father said. "A Bishop with a heart."

Rachel covered her face with her hands.

Esther took her into her arms and together they shed tears of joy.

The men, Jacob's look stunned, joyful, waited indulgently.

Atlee stood by Rachel, hat in hand, like a little boy waiting for a pat on his head. He cleared his throat.

Rachel let go of Esther, took his hand, and smiled. "Oh, Atlee." This strong-willed patriarch had been there for them all their lives. He would be the greatest loss in leaving the Valley.

"For you, Mudpie, did I do this already. For your care of me last winter. And for your babies," he said, turning to Jacob. Her Jacob, standing beside her, children climbing on and hanging off him, kissing and hugging them and shouting with laughter.

"You will never have to leave them," Rachel told Jacob.

"Or you," Jacob said, pulling her close. "I will never have to leave you again."

Atlee swatted Jacob's arm. "As should be. Your hide I should paddle. Did I not say, 'Wait, God will provide, already?' But did you wait?"

Jacob took the scold he deserved quite well, Rachel thought. She hugged Atlee hard, his bony frame reminding her he would soon walk with God. She kissed his parchment cheek. God had a treat in store.

The bent, white-haired man blushed. "Sell your farms I will," he said. "And send you the money, less my fee already." He cackled and slapped his knee. "A fee for the taking care of. It makes a good bargain, ain't?"

They were still smiling as they climbed into their buggies. Memories of Atlee would accompany them, even if he could not. Their caravan set off, four buggies in a row, precious futures before them. The Sauders, Zooks, and Millers were flittin'.

Rachel was happier than she had ever been.

When they got as far as the Yoder farm, four-year-old Abby Yoder sat on a rock by the side of the road waving them down.

Jacob stopped the buggy.

The little girl came forward, offering a wrapped parcel. "Grossmommie's corncakes for your journey," Abby said with a shy smile. "Godspeed."

Jacob regarded the parcel. "Annie and Saul Yoder just said good-bye."

"I know," Rachel whispered.

Junior Adam Stoltzfus, Great-Grossdaudy Weingardt, and little Jake Yost waited at the Beaver Dam crossroads where their farms met.

Rachel squeezed Jacob's arm, and he pulled the buggy to a stop.

Adam silently gave them a cloth-wrapped sausage. Weingardt pushed a jug of tea into Jacob's hand with a mumbled blessing. Little Jake came around to Rachel's side and handed her a cloth embroidered with a likeness of the valley. "Just for pretty," he said. "And to remember."

Jacob cleared his throat as they set off again. "Our friends have sent their young ones, who don't break the ban by speaking to us, to say good-bye for them."

"Weingardt's not so young," Rachel said. "Ninety, maybe."

Jacob smiled. "Stubborn, that one. Always breaking the rules."

"Like us," Rachel said.

He squeezed her hand. "Like us."

He pulled their buggy to a stop, the heavy traffic at the Strasburg crossroads making it necessary to wait their turn.

Jacob looked toward the Valley and sighed. "Family and community are unusual gifts," he said. "I have learned, with your help, Mudpie, that it is not the place makes a home, it is the people. You were right. Wherever we are together, we are home."

Rachel leaned over and kissed his cheek, right there before God and half the village, and took his hand. "And what better home is there, than where one is welcomed with open arms, where the past is forgotten, and the future is filled with hope."

Jacob looked back at the row of buggies.

His Datt waved. So did Ruben. The Bishop nodded.

"And if the people there happen to be the ones we love, there is nothing more perfect under God's heaven than that."

Epilogue

In marriages between widows and widowers, the November wedding rule did not hold. This sun-blessed, late September day Bishop Ezra Zook's daughter, Rachel, was marrying the man she had loved since she was three, she insisted: Jacob Sauder.

As Bishop of the Winesburg, Ohio, Bontranger Amish Community, he stood proudly—sorry, Lord, make that humbly—waiting for the bride and groom to rise from their knees, so he could join two people who'd traveled to perdition and back to reach each other.

His daughter, Esther, big with child, and her husband, Ruben Miller, a good, hardworking man, stood witness.

The congregation—their new friends—shared joyously in the blessing on the couple, smiling openly at the first row of guests, Ezra's five fidgety grandchildren, four of them children of the bride and groom.

There, the Bishop saw in many eyes, was a story they would like to know. But he had lived among them for weeks and he knew no questions would be asked. They had stories aplenty of their own that would never be told.

Only their devotion to living the Plain and simple life, in accordance with God's plan, mattered to their scarred souls.

With open arms, they welcomed blemished and wounded spirits.

As should be.

This morning Ezra had helped Jacob move his things from the *daudyhaus*—which the poor man had patiently shared with him and Levi since they arrived—into Rachel's bedroom in the main house, where she and the children had settled.

In nine months' time, Ezra fully expected at least one more grandchild, if not two, to be added to their family.

Esther and Ruben occupied the house on the opposite side from him and Levi, one as large as the main house, praise be, because they were set upon filling it with Amish offspring themselves.

What did it matter if they were Beachy Amish, Bontranger Amish, or Amish Mennonites, North Dakota Amish, Pennsylvania Amish, or Ohio Amish, as long as they lived their faith?

Go out from among them and be ye separate. That was what all of them were doing . . . as a family. Together.

He placed his hands on Jacob's and Rachel's heads for their first blessing as man and wife, and looked up, far beyond blue skies and sun-splashed clouds. Well, Mary mine, we have come a long way together. Rachel and Jacob will sit at the corner table today. Esther expects a little one soon, and much to our Ruben's dismay, he is a favorite choice for Preacher come spring.

Ach, Mom, our Rachel and our Esther are happy.

ABOUT THE AUTHOR

Annette Blair is the Development Director and Journalism Advisor at a private New England secondary school. Happily married for thirty-three years, Annette considers romance a celebration of life. This, her love of history, and her fascination with the Amish made an Amish historical romance inevitable. Annette immerses herself so deeply in her research, she has even learned to drive an Amish buggy—with her husband as an intrepid passenger in the back seat. Now that's a hero!

Annette loves hearing from her readers.

ablair@edgenet.net
www.eclectics.com/annetteblair

or

PO Box 302
Manville RI 02838

Put a Little Romance in Your Life With
Fern Michaels

__Dear Emily   0-8217-5676-1 $6.99US/$8.50CAN

__Sara's Song   0-8217-5856-X $6.99US/$8.50CAN

__Wish List   0-8217-5228-6 $6.99US/$7.99CAN

__Vegas Rich   0-8217-5594-3 $6.99US/$8.50CAN

__Vegas Heat   0-8217-5758-X $6.99US/$8.50CAN

__Vegas Sunrise   1-55817-5983-3 $6.99US/$8.50CAN

__Whitefire   0-8217-5638-9 $6.99US/$8.50CAN